"Mary Balogh has masterfully woven a romantic tale of the importance of family, of compassion, and of love and forgiveness in this fifth book in her series about the Huxtable family. *A Secret Affair* will not disappoint, and you'll be pleasantly surprised by the 'secrets.' "
—Fresh Fiction

SEDUCING AN ANGEL

"With her inimitable, brilliantly nuanced sense of characterization, elegantly sensual style, and droll wit, best-seller Balogh continues to set the standard to which all other Regency historical writers aspire while delivering another addictively readable addition to her Huxtable family series." —*Booklist*

"One of [Balogh's] best books to date."
—A Romance Review

AT LAST COMES LOVE

"Sparkling with sharp wit, lively repartee, and delicious sensuality, the emotionally rewarding *At Last Comes Love* metes out both justice and compassion; totally satisfying." —*Library Journal*

"*At Last Comes Love* is the epitome of what any great romance should be. . . . This novel will leave you crying, laughing, cheering, and ready to fight for two characters that any reader will most definitely fall in love with!" —Coffee Time Romance

THEN COMES SEDUCTION

"Exquisite sexual chemistry permeates this charmingly complex story." —*Library Journal*

"Balogh delivers another smartly fashioned love story that will dazzle readers with its captivating combination of nuanced characters, exquisitely sensual romance, and elegant wit." —*Booklist*

"Mary Balogh succeeds shockingly well."
—Rock Hill *Herald*

FIRST COMES MARRIAGE

"Intriguing and romantic . . . Readers are rewarded with passages they'll be tempted to dog-ear so they can read them over and over." —McAllen *Monitor*

"Wonderful characterization [and a] riveting plot . . . I highly recommend you read *First Comes Marriage*."
—Romance Reviews Today

"Peppered with brilliant banter, laced with laughter . . . and tingling with sexual tension, this story of two seemingly mismatched people struggling to make their marriage work tugs at a few heartstrings and skillfully paves the way for the stories to come."
—*Library Journal*

"The incomparable Balogh delivers a masterful first in a new trilogy. . . . Always fresh, intelligent, emotional and sensual, Balogh's stories reach out to readers, touching heart and mind with their warmth and wit. Prepare for a joyous read." —*Romantic Times*

"A memorable cast . . . refresh[es] a classic Regency plot with humor, wit, and the sizzling romantic chemistry that one expects from Balogh. Well-written and emotionally complex." —*Library Journal*

SIMPLY LOVE

"One of the things that make Ms. Balogh's books so memorable is the emotion she pours into her stories. The writing is superb, with realistic dialogue, sexual tension, and a wonderful heart-wrenching story. *Simply Love* is a book to savor, and to read again. It is a Perfect Ten. Romance doesn't get any better than this." —Romance Reviews Today

"With more than her usual panache, Balogh returns to Regency England for a satisfying adult love story." —*Publishers Weekly*

SLIGHTLY DANGEROUS

"*Slightly Dangerous* is the culmination of Balogh's wonderfully entertaining Bedwyn series. . . . Balogh, famous for her believable characters and finely crafted Regency-era settings, forges a relationship that leaps off the page and into the hearts of her readers." —*Booklist*

"With this series, Balogh has created a wonderfully romantic world of Regency culture and society. Readers will miss the honorable Bedwyns and their mates; ending the series with Wulfric's story is icing on the cake. Highly recommended." —*Library Journal*

SLIGHTLY SINFUL

"Smart, playful, and deliciously satisfying . . . Balogh once again delivers a clean, sprightly tale rich in both plot and character. . . . With its irrepressible characters and deft plotting, this polished romance is an ideal summer read." —*Publishers Weekly* (starred review)

SLIGHTLY TEMPTED

"Once again, Balogh has penned an entrancing, unconventional yarn that should expand her following." —*Publishers Weekly*

"Balogh is a gifted writer. . . . *Slightly Tempted* invites reflection, a fine quality in romance, and Morgan and Gervase are memorable characters." —*Contra Costa Times*

SLIGHTLY SCANDALOUS

"With its impeccable plotting and memorable characters, Balogh's book raises the bar for Regency romances." —*Publishers Weekly* (starred review)

"The sexual tension fairly crackles between this pair of beautifully matched protagonists. . . . This delightful and exceptionally well-done title nicely demonstrates [Balogh's] matchless style." —*Library Journal*

"This third book in the Bedwyn series is . . . highly enjoyable as part of the series or on its own merits." —*Old Book Barn Gazette*

SLIGHTLY WICKED

"Sympathetic characters and scalding sexual tension make the second installment [in the Slightly series] a truly engrossing read. . . . Balogh's sure-footed story possesses an abundance of character and class."
—*Publishers Weekly*

SLIGHTLY MARRIED

"*Slightly Married* is a masterpiece! Mary Balogh has an unparalleled gift for creating complex, compelling characters who come alive on the pages. . . . A Perfect Ten." —*Romance Reviews Today*

The Temporary Wife

A Promise of Spring

MARY BALOGH

DELL
NEW YORK

2012 Dell Mass Market Edition

The Temporary Wife copyright © 1997 by Mary Balogh
A Promise of Spring copyright © 1990 by Mary Balogh
Excerpt from *The Proposal* by Mary Balogh copyright © 2012 by Mary Balogh

Published in the United States by Dell, an imprint of The Random House Publishing Group, a division of Random House, Inc., New York.

DELL is a registered trademark of Random House, Inc., and the colophon is a trademark of Random House, Inc.

The Temporary Wife was originally published in mass market in the United States by Signet, an imprint of Dutton Signet, a division of Penguin Books USA Inc. in 1997.

A Promise of Spring was originally published in mass market in the United States by Signet, an imprint of Dutton Signet, a division of Penguin Books USA Inc. in 1990.

This book contains an excerpt from the forthcoming title *The Proposal* by Mary Balogh. The excerpt has been set for this edition only and may not reflect the final content of the forthcoming book.

ISBN: 978-0-440-24545-2
eBook ISBN: 978-0-345-53250-3

Cover photograph: © Herman Estevez

Printed in the United States of America

www.bantamdell.com

9 8 7 6 5 4 3 2 1

Dell mass market edition: March 2012

The Temporary Wife

1

*I*T BEING NOT QUITE THE THING TO ADVERTISE IN THE London papers for a wife, Anthony Earheart, Marquess of Staunton, eldest son and heir of the Duke of Withingsby, advertised instead for a governess.

He advertised in his own name, with the omission of his title and connections, to the decided amusement of his friends and acquaintances, who rose to the occasion with marvelous wit.

"How many children do you *have*, Staunton?" Harold Price asked him at White's the morning of the advertisement's first appearance. "Would it not be more appropriate to hire a schoolteacher? One capable of managing a full schoolroom?"

"What you should do, Staunton," Cuthbert Pyne added, "is hire a full staff. For a whole *school*, I mean. One would not wish to jeopardize the education of the budding scholars by crowding too many of them into one classroom."

"Are all their mamas to come and fetch them each afternoon, Tony?" Lord Rowling asked before inhaling the pinch of snuff he had placed on the back of one hand. "Do you have a salon large enough to hold them all while they wait? And will they wait amicably in company with one another?"

"Are you sure you wish to educate them *all*, Staunton?"

Colonel Forsythe asked. "Do you have enough estates needing stewards and managers, old boy? Does *England* have enough estates?"

"You have forgotten Wales, Forsythe," Mr. Pyne said. "And Scotland."

"But it is hardly fair to everyone else's by-blows if all the positions are filled by Staunton's," the colonel said, speaking with an exaggerated whine of complaint.

"I believe Tony is not in search of a governess at all," Sir Bernard Shields said. "He is in search of a new mistress. I hear you dismissed the delectable Anna just last week, Tony—with rubies. You have decided to look elsewhere for her replacement than the green rooms of London? You have decided to search for someone who can provide conversation as a diversion while you are, ah, at work?"

"Or someone who can offer instruction," Lord Rowling said. "It is said, you know, that one is never too knowledgeable to stop learning. And who better to learn from than a governess? And in a schoolroom with all its desks and tabletops on which to practice one's lessons. The mind boggles."

"I daresay," the very young and very earnest Lord Callaghan said, "Staunton is hiring a governess for one or more of his nieces and we are slandering him by imagining otherwise."

The Marquess of Staunton did not participate in the conversation beyond the occasional lifting of an eyebrow or pursing of the lips. He looked on as if he were nothing more than a mildly interested observer. He had no children as far as he knew. He had no estates—yet. He had tired of Anna after only six weeks and was in no hurry to employ a replacement. Mistresses, he was finding, were less and less able to satisfy his jaded appetites. He knew all their tricks and skills and was bored by them—Rowling was wrong about there being more to learn. He had no dealings with any of his nieces—or nephews either, for that matter.

No, he was not in search of either a governess or a mistress. He was choosing himself a wife, as he made clear to Lord Rowling when the two of them were strolling homeward later.

"Is that not usually done at Almack's or in someone's ballroom or drawing room?" Lord Rowling asked, chuckling as if he believed the whole matter was a joke devised for his amusement. "And without the necessity of an advertisement, Tony? You are Staunton, after all, and will be Withingsby one day. You are as rich as Croesus and have the looks to turn any female head even if you were a pauper. Yet you have advertised for a wife in the guise of a governess? What am I missing, pray?" He twirled his cane and touched the brim of his hat to a lady whom they were passing.

"I cannot find what I am looking for at Almack's," the marquess said, no answering amusement in his face. He had the grace to continue when his friend merely looked at him with raised eyebrows. "She must be a gentlewoman—I'll not go lower than that, you see. She must also be impoverished, plain, demure, very ordinary, perhaps even prim. She must have all the personality of a—a quiet mouse."

"Dear me," Lord Rowling said rather faintly. "A quiet mouse, Tony? You? Do you feel such need to dominate the woman you will take to wife?"

"The Duke of Withingsby has summoned me home," the marquess said. "He claims to be ailing. He reminds me that Lady Marie Lucas, daughter of the Earl of Tillden, is now seventeen years old—old enough, in fact, for the match arranged for us by our families at her birth to be elevated to a formal betrothal. He informs me that the eight years of my absence from home have given me sufficient time in which to sow my wild oats."

Lord Rowling grimaced. "Your father is not display-ing a great deal of wisdom," he said. "You have amassed a sizable fortune during those eight years, Tony." But he grinned suddenly. "As well as acquiring a well-deserved reputation as one of London's most prolific rakes. You plan to marry your quiet mouse merely in order to em-barrass his grace, then?"

"Precisely," the marquess said without hesitation. "I did consider merely ignoring the summons, Perry, or an-swering it but refusing to wed the child who has been carefully chosen and groomed as the next Duchess of Withingsby. But this idea of mine will be infinitely bet-ter. If his grace is not already ailing in all truth, he soon will be. If he has not yet got the point of the past eight years, he soon will. Yes, I shall choose my wife very carefully indeed. I daresay there will be a number of ap-plicants."

Lord Rowling looked aghast, perhaps only now un-derstanding that his friend was in deadly earnest. "But, Tony," he said, "you cannot *marry* the dullest creature you can find merely to annoy your father."

"Why not?" Lord Staunton asked.

"Why not?" His friend made circular motions in the air with his cane. "Marriage is a life sentence, old chap. You will be stuck with the woman for the rest of your life. You would find the situation intolerable."

"I do not intend to spend the rest of my life with her," the marquess said. "Once she has served her purpose she will be pensioned off—a governess could hardly ask for a better fate, could she?"

"And she might live to the age of ninety," Lord Row-ling pointed out. "Tony, you will want *heirs*. If you get them on her, she will wish—and quite reasonably so—to be a *mother* to them. She will wish to live in your home while they grow up."

"I have an heir," the marquess said. "My brother William, Perry. And he has sons—or so Marianne informs me. One can only hope that they are sturdy."

"But a man craves heirs of his own body," Lord Rowling said.

"Does he, by Jove?" The Marquess of Staunton looked surprised. "This man certainly does not, Perry. Shall we change the subject? This particular one grows tedious. Do you go to Tattersall's tomorrow? I have my eye on a promising-looking pair of grays."

Lord Rowling would have liked to continue the original conversation until he had talked some sense into his friend, but he was soon conversing about horses. After all, he had known the Marquess of Staunton long enough to understand that he had a will of iron, that he said and did exactly what he wished to say and do, without reference to other people's preferences or to society's dictates. If he had decided to choose a wife in such an unconventional manner and for such a cynical, cold-blooded reason, then choose her he would, and marry her too.

The Marquess of Staunton, meanwhile, although he talked with enthusiasm about horses and then the races, inwardly contemplated with some satisfaction his return to Enfield Park in Wiltshire and the effect of that return on the Duke of Withingsby. It would be the final thumbing of the nose to the man who had begotten him and made his life miserable for the twenty years following his birth. For eight years, ever since he had left home after that final dreadful scene, he had lived independently of his father, refusing any financial support. He had made his own fortune, at first by gambling, then by reckless investments, and finally by more prudent investments and business ventures.

His father had clearly not got the point. But he would. He would understand that his eldest son was once and for all beyond his power and influence. Oh yes, marrying imprudently—and that would be an understatement for the marriage of the Duke of Withingsby's heir to an impoverished gentlewoman who had earned her living as a governess—would be the best possible thing he could do. He longed to see his father's face when he took his bride to Enfield.

And so he waited for replies to his advertisement, replies that began coming the very day after its first appearance in the London papers and kept coming for several days after that in even larger numbers than he had expected. He rejected several applicants, sight unseen—all those below the age of twenty or above the age of thirty, those with particularly impressive recommendations, and one young lady who so wished to impress him with her knowledge of Latin that her letter was written in it.

He interviewed five candidates before discovering his quiet mouse in the sixth. Miss Charity Duncan had been shown into a downstairs salon and had chosen to stand in the part of the room that was not bathed in sunlight. For one moment after he had opened the door and stepped inside the room, he thought she must have changed her mind and fled. But then he saw her, and it struck him that even her decision to stand just there was significant. In addition, she was dressed from head to toe in drab brown and looked totally self-effacing and quietly disciplined. She was the quintessential governess— the sort of employee even the most jealous of wives would not object to having in the same house with her husband.

"Miss Duncan?" he asked.

"Yes, sir." Her voice was quiet and low-pitched. She curtsied to him without once raising her eyes from the carpet before her feet. She was on the low side of medium height, very slender, perhaps even thin, though her cloak made it impossible to know for sure. Her face looked pale and ordinary in the shadows. The brown of her hair blended so totally with the brown of her bonnet that it was difficult to know where the one ended and the other began. Her garments were decent and drab. He was given the impression that they were not quite shabby but very soon would be. They were genteel-shabby.

She was perfect. His father would be incensed.

"Please be seated," he said, indicating a chair close to where she stood.

"Yes, sir," she said and sat down, as he expected, with a straight spine that did not touch the back of her chair. She folded her gloved hands in her lap and directed her gaze modestly at her knees.

She was the picture of prim gentility. She was quite perfect! He decided there and then that she would do, that his search was at an end. He was looking at his future wife.

CHARITY DUNCAN SAT close to the window in order to make the best of the last of the daylight. It would not do to light the candle one moment before it became absolutely necessary to do so. Candles were expensive. She was mending an underarm seam of one of her brother's shirts and noting with an inward sigh that the cotton fabric had worn thin. The seam would hold for a while, but there would be a hole more difficult to mend sooner than that.

Her task was taking longer than it ought. Her eyes—and her mind—kept straying to the newspaper that was open on the table. Buying a paper each day was her one extravagance, though it could not exactly be called that. She knew that Philip liked to read it by candlelight after he got home from work, but in the main the purchase was for her own sake. She must find employment very soon. For almost a month she had been looking and applying and—all too rarely—attending interviews. She had even applied for a few situations more menial than a governess's or a companion's position.

No one wanted her. She was either too young or too old, too plain or too pretty, too high-born or too well-educated, or . . . Or prospective employers became too pointed in their questions.

But she would not give in and abandon the search. Her family—one sister three years younger than herself at home and three children considerably younger than that—was poor. Worse than poor. They were deeply in debt and had not even known it until the death of their father a little over a year ago. And so instead of being able to live a gentleman's life, Philip was compelled to work just to support his family. And she had insisted on working too, though there was precious little money a woman could earn that was sufficient to share with others or to pay off debts.

If only there were some way of making a huge fortune quickly. She had even considered some spectacular robbery—though not seriously, of course. She ought not to complain, she thought, her task at the shirt finished at last. At least they were not quite destitute. Not quite, but close enough. And there seemed to be no real light at the end of the proverbial tunnel.

But Philip was home, and she rose to smile her greeting, to kiss his cheek, to serve his supper, to ask about his day—and to draw his attention to the one advertisement in today's paper that looked like a possibility.

"It does not say how many children there are or what ages or genders they are," she said with a frown when they had progressed to that topic. "It does not say whether they live here in London or in the Outer Hebrides or at the tip of Cornwall. But it does say that there is a position available."

"You do not have to take employment at all, Charity," Philip Duncan said. It was his constant theme. Philip believed in taking full responsibility for his womenfolk.

"Oh, yes, I do," she said firmly. "It is the only suitable position offered in today's paper, Phil. And there was nothing at all at the agency yesterday or this morning. I must try for it at least."

"You can go back home," Philip said, "and allow me to support you as I should. You can go back home where you are wanted and needed."

"You know I will not do that," she said, smiling at him. "You cannot possibly support us all, Phil, and you ought not. You ought to be able to live your own life. Agnes—"

"Agnes will wait," he said firmly. "Or she will tire of waiting and marry someone else. But it is unseemly for my sister to have to take employment."

"I need to feel that I am doing something too," she said. "It is not fair that I should sit at home working on my embroidery and cultivating a pretty garden just because I am a woman. And I *am* the eldest.

"I'll try for this one position," she said. "If I am unsuccessful, then perhaps I will go back to the country. It is beginning to look as though I am unemployable, does it not?"

"Go back home, Charity," Philip urged. "I am a mere clerk now, but I will rise to a better position and earn more money. Perhaps I will even be wealthy someday. And indeed you are not cut out to be in service. You do not have the necessary spirit of subservience. You lost the last position because you could not keep your opinions to yourself."

"No," she said, grimacing. "I was of the opinion that the children's father ought not to be molesting the prettiest chambermaid against her express wishes and I said so—to both him and the children's mother. He really was horrid, Phil. If you had known him, you would have disliked him excessively."

"I have no doubt of it," he said. "But his behavior to another servant was not your concern, Charity. The girl had a tongue of her own, I daresay."

"But she was afraid to use it," she said, "lest she lose her position."

Philip merely looked at his sister. He did not need to say anything.

Charity laughed. "I had no wish to remain there anyway," she said. "But I do wish positions were more easily come by. Six interviews in the past month and nothing to show for them. Perhaps I had better hope that Mrs. Earheart and her children *do* live in the Outer Hebrides and that no one but me will be intrepid enough to join them there." She sighed. "Perhaps I should include in my letter of application my willingness to go to the ends of the earth. Perhaps they will pay more to compensate me for the remote situation."

"Charity," Philip said, "I wish you would go home. The children miss you. Penny says so in all her letters. You have been like a mother to them ever since Mama died."

"I shall not mention my willingness," she said as if she had not heard him. "I might sound overeager or groveling. And I shall try for this one last position. I shall probably not even receive a reply and all your wishes will be granted. But I shall feel such a helpless *woman,* Phil."

He sighed again.

But Charity was proved wrong in one thing. Five days after she sent her letter of application to Mr. Earheart, she received a reply, inviting her to attend an interview the following morning. She felt her heart begin to palpitate at the very thought. It was so difficult to endure being questioned, more as if one were a commodity than a person. But it was the only way to employment. How cruel it was, though, to actually have an interview, to be this close, only perhaps to have one's hopes dashed yet again.

"This will be the seventh," she said to Philip when he came home from work late in the evening. "Will this be the lucky one, do you suppose?"

"If you really want the position, Charity," he said with a sigh, "you must behave the part. Governesses, like other servants, you know, are to be seen and not heard."

She grimaced. Not that she was ever loud or vulgar. But she was a *lady*. She was accustomed to considering herself the equal of other ladies. It was hard to accustom herself to the knowledge that there was a despised class of shabby-genteel people—of whom she was one, at least as long as she sought employment. It was something that had to be ignored or endured. "I must be demure, then?" she said. "I may not offer my opinions or observations?"

"No," he said bluntly—and she realized with a sudden wave of pain that Philip must have had to learn the same lesson for himself. "You must convince the man, and his wife if she is present, that if they employ you, you will blend very nicely into the furniture of their home."

"How demeaning," she said and then bit her lip, wishing she had not said the words aloud.

"And, Charity"—he leaned across the table that separated them and took her hand in both his own—"do not accept the position even if it is offered if he—well, if he is a young man. Not that youth has anything to say in the matter. If he is—"

"Lecherous?" she suggested.

Her brother blushed. "If you suspect he might be," he said.

"I can look after myself, Phil," she said. "When my former employer glanced at me with that certain look in his eye during the early days of my employment, I looked right back and chilled my eyes and thinned my lips." She repeated the look so that her brother grinned despite himself.

"Be careful, Charity," he said.

"I shall be," she promised. "And demure. I shall be a veritable mouse. A quiet, drab, brown little mouse. I shall be so self-effacing that he will not even realize I am in the room with him. I shall be . . . "

But her brother was laughing out loud. She went around the table to stand behind his chair and wrap both arms about his shoulders. "Oh, you do that all too rarely these days, Phil," she said. "All will work out, you will see. We will be rich somehow and you will marry Agnes and live happily ever after."

"And you?" He raised a hand to pat her arm.

"And I shall live happily ever after too," she said. "Penny will be able to marry and I shall stay with the children until they are all grown and happily wed, and then I shall settle into a contented and eccentric spinsterhood."

He chuckled again as she lightly kissed the top of his head.

But for all that she was nervous the next morning when she arrived at the house on Upper Grosvenor Street to which she had been summoned for an interview. The hall was unostentatious but elegant. So was the servant who answered her knock on the door. So was the empty salon into which she was shown. She instinctively sought out the part of the room that was out of the light from the windows. She tried to master the beating of her heart. If she did not secure this position, she would begin to lose confidence in herself. She had already half promised Phil that she would go home without trying further. She would . . . But her thoughts were interrupted by the opening of the door.

He *was* young—no more than thirty at the outside. He was also handsome in a harsh sort of way, she thought to herself. He was of somewhat above medium height, with a slender, well-proportioned figure, very dark hair and eyes, and a thin, angular, aristocratic face. The sunlight shining through the windows was full on him as he came through the door. In its harsh glare the cold cynicism of his expression made him look somehow satanic. He was expensively and elegantly dressed. Indeed, he looked very much as if he might have been poured into his well-tailored coat and pantaloons—a sure sign that he was a gentleman of high fashion.

He did not look like a kind man. He looked like the sort of man who would devour chambermaids more than he would seduce them. But she must not judge the man before he had uttered even a single word. She felt demeaned again, alone in a gentleman's house without servant or chaperon, because she herself was now a servant—an unemployed one. Her eyes dipped to focus on the carpet before his own found her in the shadows. She concentrated hard on cultivating the manner of a typical governess.

"Miss Duncan?" he said. His voice was as haughty and as bored as she had expected it to be, though it was a pleasant tenor voice. There was no pretense of charm in it. But why should there be? He was conducting an interview for a governess for his children.

"Yes, sir," she said, trying to look dignified but not over-proud. She kept her back straight. She was, after all, a lady.

"Please be seated." He indicated a chair that was close by and out of the glare of the sunlight, for which fact she was grateful. Interviews did not get easier with experience.

"Yes, sir," she said, seating herself, keeping her eyes lowered. She would answer the questions concisely and honestly. She would hope there would be no awkward questions.

Mr. Earheart seated himself on a chair opposite hers. He crossed one booted leg over the other. His hessian boots were of shining, expensive leather. His valet must have labored hard to produce such a shine. There was an air of wealth and confidence and power about the man. Charity felt distinctly uncomfortable in the pause before he spoke again.

2

*H*OW DID ONE CONDUCT AN INTERVIEW FOR A FU-
ture wife? the Marquess of Staunton wondered.

"The letter of recommendation from the rector of
your former parish is impressive, Miss Duncan," he
said.

"Thank you, sir," she said.

"However," he said, "it was written all of one year
ago. Have you had employment since then?"

She stared at her knees and appeared to consider her
reply. "Yes, sir," she said.

"And what was it, Miss Duncan?"

"I was governess for eight months to three children,
sir," she said.

"For eight months." He paused, but she did not pick
up the cue. "And why was the position terminated?"

"I was dismissed," she said after hesitating for a few
moments.

"Indeed?" he said. "Why, Miss Duncan?" Had she
been unable to control the children? He could well
imagine it. She seemed totally without character.

"My—my employer accused me of lying," she said.

Well. She was frank at least. He was surprised by her
reply and by the fact that she did not immediately proceed to justify herself. A meek mouse indeed.

"And did you?" he asked. "Lie, I mean."

"No, sir," she said.

He knew how it felt to be accused falsely. He well knew the feeling.

"Is this your first attempt to find employment since then?" he asked.

"No, sir," she said. "It is the seventh. The seventh interview, that is."

He was not surprised that she had failed to get past any of those interviews. Who would wish to employ such a drab, spiritless creature to educate his children?

"Why have you been unsuccessful?" he asked.

"I believe, sir," she said, "because everyone else has asked what you just asked."

Ah, yes. Her confession doubtless brought any normal interview to an abrupt halt. "And you have never thought to lie?" he asked her. "To pretend that you left your employment of your own free will?"

"Yes," she admitted, "I have thought about it, sir. But I have not done so."

She was also a very moral little mouse. Someone once upon a time had told her that it is wicked to lie, and so she never lied even in the service of her own interests. Even if it meant she would never again be employed. She clung to a puritanical morality. His father would be appalled.

"For which proof of your honesty you are to be commended, Miss Duncan," he said. "I may be able to offer you something."

She looked up into his face for the first time then, very briefly. Long dark lashes swept upward to reveal large, clear eyes that were as blue as the proverbial summer sky. Not the sort of gray that sometimes passes for blue, but pure, unmistakable blue itself. And then the eyes disappeared beneath the lashes and lowered eyelids again. For one disturbing moment he felt that he was about to make a ghastly mistake.

"Thank you, sir," she said. She sounded a little breathless. "How many children are there? Do they live here with you?"

"There are no children," he said.

He waited while she studied her knees, transferred her gaze to his knees, and raised her eyes to his chest—perhaps even to his chin.

"No children?" She frowned. "My pupils, then, sir, are—are . . . "

"There are no pupils," he said. "I am not in search of a governess, Miss Duncan. It is another position entirely that I have to offer."

The little mouse obviously sensed that a big bad cat was about to pounce. She jumped to her feet and turned in the direction of the door.

"I am not about to suggest anything improper, Miss Duncan," he said, remaining seated. "Actually I am in search of a wife. I am willing to offer you the position."

She half turned back to him but did not look directly at him. "A wife?" she said.

"A wife," he repeated. "I am looking for a Mrs. Earheart, Miss Duncan. Temporarily, that is. At least, the marriage would be forever, I suppose, since such things are next to impossible to dissolve by anything less drastic than the death of one of the partners. If you have any romantic notion of marrying for love and living happily ever after, then I must bid you a good morning and proceed with the next interview. But I daresay you have not, or if you have, then you must realize that such a dream is unrealistic for someone in your situation."

She raised her eyebrows but did not contradict him. Her body was still turned toward the door. Her head was still half turned toward him.

"The marriage would be permanent," he said. "But our being together as a married couple would be temporary—for no longer than a few weeks at a guess. After that you would be free again, apart from the small encumbrance of being Mrs. Earheart instead of Miss Duncan. And you would be very comfortably well-off for the rest of your life."

She was frowning down at the carpet. But she was not hastening from the room. She was clearly tempted. It would be strange if she were not.

"Will you not be seated again, Miss Duncan?" he asked.

She sat, arranged her hands neatly in her lap again, and studied her knees once more. "I do not understand," she said.

"It is really quite simple," he said. Her face was perhaps heart-shaped, he thought. But that description glamorized her too much. "I need a wife for a short period of time. It has crossed my mind that I might employ someone to act the part, but it would be far more—effective to have a real wife, one who will be bound to me for life."

She licked her lips. "And after the short period of time is over?" she asked.

"I would settle five thousand a year on you," he said, "in addition to providing you with a home and carriage and servants and covering your year-by-year household expenses."

She sat very still and said nothing for a long while. She was thinking about it, he thought. About five thousand a year, about a home and a carriage of her own. About never again having to apply for a position as a governess.

"How do I know that you speak the truth?" she asked at last.

Good Lord! He raised his eyebrows and favored her with his frostiest stare while his right hand curled about the handle of his quizzing glass. But his indignation was wasted on her lowered eyelids. Her hands, he could see, were clasping each other rather tightly in her lap. He supposed that to someone like her there must seem to be the very real possibility that this was all a cruel joke.

"There will, of course, be a written contract," he said. "I will have it here together with my man of business this afternoon, Miss Duncan—shall we say at three o'clock? You may, if you wish, spend some time alone with him and question him about my ability to fulfill my part of the agreement. Are you willing to accept my offer?"

For a long time she did not answer him. Several times her mouth opened as if she would speak but she closed it again. Once she bit into her lower lip, once into the upper. She pulled carefully at each finger of her right glove as if preparing to take it off and then pulled it firmly on again with a tug at the wrist. She spoke at last.

"Seven thousand," she said.

"I beg your pardon?" He was not sure he had heard aright, though she had spoken plainly enough.

"Seven thousand a year," she said more firmly. "In addition to the other things you mentioned."

A quiet little mouse who nevertheless had her eye to the main chance. Well, he could hardly blame her.

"We will of course settle upon six," he said, his eyes narrowing. "You accept my offer, then, Miss Duncan? I may cancel the other interviews I have scheduled to follow yours?"

"Y-yes," she said. And then, more firmly, "Yes, sir."

"Splendid." He got to his feet and reached out a hand for hers. "I will expect your return here promptly at three o'clock. We will marry tomorrow morning."

She set her hand in his and got to her feet. Her eyelashes swept up again, and he found himself being regarded keenly by those steady blue eyes. He resisted the urge to take a step back. She must be looking at the bridge of his nose, he thought. She appeared to be gazing right into the center of both his eyes at once.

"What happens," she asked, "when you meet the lady you really wish to marry and spend your life with?"

He smiled at her rather frostily. "The woman does not exist," he said, "with whom I would consider sharing even one year of my life."

She drew breath to speak again but closed her mouth without saying anything. Her eyes dropped from his.

It had all gone remarkably well, he thought a few minutes later after she had left. He had expected to be peppered with questions, most notably about what she would be expected to do during the weeks before she was set free to live out her life on what must appear to her to be a vast fortune indeed. Miss Charity Duncan had asked nothing. He had expected to be burdened with all sorts of confidences. She had offered none. He knew nothing about her except what had been in her letter of application. She was three-and-twenty years old, was the daughter of a gentleman, could read and write and figure, could speak French and draw and play the pianoforte, and had had experience in the care and education of children, whom she liked.

He also knew that she was quiet, demure, neither pretty nor ugly, and shrewd. The only thing about her that had surprised him had been her demand for more money than he had offered. No, there had been something else too—her eyes. They were quite at variance with the rest of her. But then even the plainest, dullest woman was entitled to some claim to beauty, he supposed.

And so she was to be his wife tomorrow. He raised his eyebrows and pursed his lips, considering the thought. Yes, she would do, he decided. Very nicely indeed.

SHE SAT BY the window, trying to garner the last of the daylight for her task. She was darning the heel of one of

Philip's stockings. It was only six o'clock, but the light was fading. The narrowness of the street on which they had lodgings and the height of the buildings on the opposite side did nothing to help. How she longed sometimes for the countryside again. No, it happened more often than sometimes. She sighed.

What was she going to tell Phil when he came home from work? She still could not quite believe even herself in the reality of the day's events. She had gone to Upper Grosvenor Street this morning, hoping with all the power of her will that she would be offered the governess's position. Yet even as she had approached the house her inward concentration on the interview ahead had been distracted by the foolish dream of finding a priceless jeweled necklace in the gutter or of finding some other unexpected road to a fortune.

Instead of offering her a position as governess, Mr. Earheart—handsome, elegant, cold in manner—had offered her marriage. It was like some bizarre fairy tale—except that in a fairy tale he would have offered because he had fallen instantly and desperately in love with her. Mr. Earheart merely wanted a temporary wife, but he was willing to keep her very handsomely indeed for the rest of her life. She had made sure that the written agreement stated that. She would not be cut off in the event that he predeceased her. She would have six thousand a year for the rest of her life, besides the other things he had mentioned during the morning.

She and Penny and the children could live very comfortably on six thousand a year. They could have Papa's debts paid off in no time at all. Philip would not be too happy about not being the one to save them from their impoverishment, of course, but he would come around to reality. And he would be able to marry Agnes.

She knew, of course, what she was going to tell Philip when he came home. She had had many solitary hours in which to rehearse her story. But it went much against the grain to lie. She was not sure she was going to be able to do it. But she must—she had no choice. She could not possibly tell him the truth. For one thing, he might have her carried off to Bedlam. It was difficult even for her to believe that what had happened really had happened.

Oh, dear, she thought. She was darning over a patch that had already been darned once. Poor Phil, he spent nothing on himself and everything on his brothers and sisters. She brushed impatiently at her cheek after a tear had plopped unexpectedly onto the back of her hand, startling her.

And then she felt the welling of panic that had been assaulting her at regular intervals ever since she had arrived home after signing those papers. Tomorrow she was going to marry a stranger—and a rather daunting stranger at that. She was doing it entirely for money. But after it was done there would be no going back. There would not—never ever—be a real husband or a real marriage for her. Not that there would have been anyway. But there was something rather frightening about the certain knowledge that . . .

But Philip was home, looking weary after his day's work, and she smiled warmly at him, set aside her darning, and got to her feet to ladle out his soup and cut a slice of bread.

"You look tired," she said, tilting up her cheek for his kiss.

"One is supposed to be tired in the evening," he said. "Mmm, that smells good, Charity." He plopped wearily onto his chair.

She sat at the table with him while he ate, her elbow resting on it, her chin in her hand. She did not know how to begin, and so she waited for him to start the conversation. He asked her if there had been any letter from home and then, when she shook her head, assured them both that it was too soon to expect another when they had heard as recently as the end of last week.

"Ah," he said at last, obviously just remembering, "you had an interview this morning. Forgive me for not asking about it sooner. How was it?"

She smiled at him. "I was offered the position," she said.

His spoon paused halfway to his mouth. "Ah," he said again. "Well, that is good news. Are they pleasant people, Charity? Where do they live? How many children are there?"

"Very pleasant," she said. "Wiltshire. Three." She held carefully to her smile. "And yes, it is good news."

He was trying to look pleased for her, she could tell. "It was *Mr.* Earheart who interviewed you?" he asked. "Did you meet Mrs. Earheart, Charity?"

"Oh, yes, indeed," she said, "and the children too. They are all exceedingly pleasant, Phil. You would like them. They are leaving for the country tomorrow. I will be going with them."

"Tomorrow," he said, frowning. "So soon?"

"Yes." She smiled gently. "I have made enough soup to last you for three days, and I have made some of the currant cakes you so like—a dreadful extravagance, I know, but I wanted you to have them."

"Perhaps I should ask for an hour off tomorrow," he said, "so that I can see you on your way and assure myself that your new employers are worthy of you. What time will you be leaving?"

"No, Phil." She stretched out her hand to touch the back of his. "There is no need to do that. I would hate saying good-bye to you and then having to be cheerful for the children immediately after. I would much rather you did not come."

Her brother covered her hand with his own and patted it. "As you will, then," he said. "But Wiltshire is not so very far away, Charity. And nothing is irrevocable. If you do not like the position, then you may leave it at any time and return home. Penny will be very happy and the children will be ecstatic."

"Nevertheless, it is a position to which I shall commit myself," she said. "Why should you be the one to support us all?"

"Because I am the man of the family," he said.

"Phooey!" She got to her feet, picked up his empty bowl, and refilled it without even asking if he wanted more. Philip, she thought, was going to be very angry with her. And that might be an understatement. But after tomorrow morning he would be able to do nothing about it. The loneliness of facing her own wedding quite alone washed over her for a moment, but she pushed self-pity firmly aside. What did she have to pity herself for? She was going to be a wealthy woman—a pitiable fate indeed!

They did not stay up late. Philip was tired and his days began early. The light had gone and they always used candles sparingly. Besides, partings were always difficult. There never seemed to be anything to say during the last few hours together—perhaps because there was altogether too much to say. And this time was worse than ever because in the little they did say so many lies were necessary. He asked about the children who were to be her pupils and she was forced to invent genders and ages for them.

She hated lying. But how could she tell the truth? There would be a time for the truth, when she was finally able to care for her family herself, when it would be far too late for any of them to exclaim in horror at the madness of what she was doing. Yes, there would be a time. But it was not now.

She got up early in the morning, as she had done every

day since joining her brother at his lodgings in town, to get his breakfast and to pack a couple of slices of bread and some lamentably dry cheese for his midday meal—and a currant cake as a special treat. She hugged him tightly and wordlessly when he was ready to leave.

"Take care," he said, his arms like iron bands about her. "I hate the way you feel forced into doing this, Charity, when I am the man of the family. One day you will be free again to live the life of a lady, I promise you."

"I love you," she said. *In a few hours' time, Phil, I am going to be the wife of a very wealthy man. I am going to be a very wealthy woman. Oh, Phil, Phil.* "Tears! How silly I am." She laughed and dashed at them with her hands.

And he was gone. Just like that. The room was empty and cold and still half dark. It was her wedding day. She and Penny had played weddings sometimes as children—they were always joyful, lavish affairs. But this was the reality. This was her real wedding day. She blinked impatiently at more tears.

"ARE YOU QUITE MAD, Tony?" Lord Rowling asked during the weekly evening ball at Almack's while the Marquess of Staunton languidly surveyed the female dancers through his quizzing glass. "Are you really going to go through with this insanity?"

"Oh, absolutely," the marquess said with a sigh. He gestured about him with one jewel-bedecked hand. "Behold the great marriage mart, Perry—Almack's in London during the Season. All the most marketable merchandise is here on display in this very room and all the prospective buyers are looking it over. I am a buyer. Why would I not be? I am the heir to a dukedom—and the duke is reputedly ailing. I am eight-and-twenty years old and growing no younger. I have merely chosen to shop in a slightly different market."

"You *advertised* for a governess and chose a wife," Lord Rowling said, shaking his head. "You chose a total stranger after a short interview. You know nothing about her."

"On the contrary," the marquess said, his glass pausing on one particular young lady and moving slowly down her body from face to feet. "She comes highly recommended by the rector in whose parish she grew up. She was dismissed from her last post after eight months for lying, a charge which she denies. She is a plain, quiet, moral little mouse. And she *bargained* with me, Perry, and squeezed more money out of me than I had offered. She will do admirably. March's chit has put on weight since the start of the Season. Whoever takes her will find himself with a decidedly plump wife within five years. But then some men like plump wives."

"Tony!" his friend said, exasperated. "Your cynicism outdoes anyone else's I know. But this marriage scheme goes beyond the bounds of reason."

"Why?" the marquess asked. "If I were to address myself to the papa of any young lady here present, Perry, he would snap me up in an instant, my reputation as an incurable rake not withstanding. And so would she. I am a matrimonial prize. She would know nothing of me apart from superficial details, and I would know nothing of her. We would be strangers. Is there any real difference between marrying one of these females and marrying a little mouse of a governess who almost salivated at the prospect of coming within sniffing distance of my fortune? There is only one significant difference. The mouse will be easier to shed when she has served her purpose."

Lord Rowling took his snuffbox from a pocket, but he held it unopened in one hand while he stared at his companion. "You are making a mistake, Tony," he said. "A ghastly and an irrevocable one. What if the woman refuses to be shed?"

The Marquess of Staunton merely raised one haughty and eloquent eyebrow. "Like all brides, Perry," he said, "she will promise obedience tomorrow morning. I believe I will dance with Miss Henshaw. She has been warned of my reputation and blushes most prettily and looks away in sweet confusion every time she accidentally catches my eye—which she is at pains to do quite frequently."

He strolled off to pursue his mission, but the main task of the evening had been accomplished. Rowling had agreed to attend his wedding as a witness. Staunton did not often frequent Almack's or any other fashionable ballroom for that matter. He set about amusing himself for the evening. His last evening as a single man. He examined the thought as he danced with the blushing Miss Henshaw and concentrated upon deepening her blushes. But he did not find the thought in any way alarming.

Tomorrow was his wedding day. Merely another day in his life.

3

TRUE TO HIS PROMISE, LORD ROWLING ARRIVED IN Upper Grosvenor Street in good time the following morning to accompany the groom to the church, where the marquess's man of business, as the other witness, awaited them. The Marquess of Staunton, to his friend's fascination, appeared as coolly composed—and as immaculately tailored—as if he were planning a morning stroll along Bond Street.

"You are quite sure about this?" Lord Rowling asked as they prepared to leave the house. "There is nothing I can say to persuade you to change your mind, Tony?"

"Good Lord, no," the marquess said, placing his hat just so on his head and raising his eyebrows to his servant to indicate that he was ready to proceed out of doors.

The church was not one of London's most fashionable. It looked gloomy enough to Lord Rowling, as did the street on which it was situated and as did the heavy gray sky overhead. The groom appeared quite unaffected by gloom—or by elation either. He nodded to his man of business and strode without further ado toward the church door. His two companions exchanged glances and followed him.

Inside the church, seated quietly in a shadowed pew at the back, the bride waited. She was dressed as she had been the day before, her bridegroom noticed immediately. She had made no attempt to get herself up in a bride's frippery. He had not thought to give her money to buy herself new clothes, the marquess thought belatedly—a new dress for today, bride clothes to take with her into her more affluent future. And they were to leave for the country soon after the wedding. There would be no time for shopping. Well, no matter. It would be better to take her exactly as she was.

"Miss Duncan?" He half bowed to her and held out his arm for hers.

"Yes, sir." She stood up, looked at him briefly, and then lowered her gaze to his arm. She appeared not to know whether she should lay her own along the top of it or link her own through it. He took her hand in his free one and set it on his wrist. He did not pause to present her to Lord Rowling. He was impatient.

"The rector is waiting," he said.

"Yes, sir." She glanced to the front of the church.

His mouth felt surprisingly dry and his heartbeat surprisingly unsteady. She was a total stranger. She was about to become his wife. For the rest of a lifetime. For a moment his mind touched upon the notion that he might live to regret this day. But he suppressed the thought, as he had done when he had awoken soon after dawn and again while he had breakfasted. He despised last-minute nerves. He led his bride forward.

Without all the pomp and ceremony that had accompanied every society wedding he had ever attended, the nuptial service was really quite short and unremarkable, he found. The rector spoke, he spoke, she spoke, Rowling handed him a ring, which he placed on her finger, and he found that it was too late to wonder if he would regret the day. Miss Charity Duncan no longer existed by that name. She was his wife. His first feeling was one of relief. He bent his head and briefly placed his closed lips close to the corner of her mouth. Her skin was cool.

The rector was congratulating them then with hearty good humor, his man of business was doing his best to look festive, and Rowling was smiling and being charming. There was the register still to sign.

"My very best wishes to you, Lady Staunton," Rowling said, taking one of her hands in both of his and smiling warmly at her.

"Wh-what?" she asked.

"You are unaccustomed to the sound of your own new name," he said, raising her hand to his lips. "My best wishes for your felicity, ma'am."

"You are Charity Earheart," the marquess explained to her, "Marchioness of Staunton."

"Oh," she said, looking full at him with wide and startled eyes—and this time he really did take a step back. "Are you a *marquess*?"

"Staunton, at your service, my lady," he said. He really should have given greater consideration to those eyes yesterday. But it was too late now. "May I present Lord Rowling?"

It was raining when they came out of the church—a chilling drizzle oozed downward out of a gray and dreary sky.

"A good omen," Rowling said with a laugh. "The best marriages always proceed from wet wedding days, my grandmother is fond of saying. I believe she married my grandfather during a thunderstorm and they enjoyed forty happy years together."

But no one seemed prepared to share his hearty optimism. The Marquess of Staunton hurried his silent bride toward his carriage. There was breakfast to take with their two wedding guests, his wife's trunks to collect from her lodgings, and a journey to begin. He had written to his father to expect him tomorrow. He had not mentioned that he would be bringing a wife.

He seated himself beside her in the carriage, lifted her

hand to his wrist again, and held it there with his free hand while the other two men seated themselves opposite. He felt almost sorry for her—a strange fact when he had just ensured her a future infinitely preferable to what she could have expected as a governess. Besides, he was unaccustomed to entertaining sympathetic feelings for anyone. For the first time it struck him as strange that no one had accompanied her to her wedding. Was she so totally without friends?

The leather of her glove was paper thin on the inside of the thumb, he noticed. There was going to be a hole there very soon.

He was a married man. The stranger whose gloved hand rested lightly on his wrist was his wife, his marchioness. There was a strange unreality to the moment. And a stark reality too.

SHE WAS A married lady. She had walked to that quiet, rather gloomy church this morning, gone inside as herself, as Charity Duncan, and come out again a mere half hour later as someone different, as someone with another name. Everything had changed. Nothing would ever be the same again. She was Charity Earheart, the . . .

She turned her head to look at the taciturn man beside her on the carriage seat. He had not spoken a word since his footman had carried out her small trunk from Philip's lodgings—the carriage had appeared to fill the whole street and had attracted considerable attention—and he had asked her in seeming surprise if there was nothing else.

"No, sir," she had said and had thought that probably she should have called him *my lord*.

She was . . . She felt very foolish. And he must have felt her eyes upon him. He turned his head to look at her. His eyes were very dark, she thought. They were almost black. And quite opaque. She had the peculiar feeling that a heavy curtain or perhaps even a steel door had been dropped just behind his eyes so that no one would ever be able to peep into his soul.

"I am—*who?*" she asked him. She could not for the life of her remember. "You are the Marquess of *What?*"

"Staunton," he said. He had an aquiline nose, rather thin lips. One lock of very dark hair had fallen across his brow above his right eye and curled there like an upside-down question mark. "Eldest son of the Duke of Withingsby. His heir, my lady. We travel to Enfield Park, his seat in Wiltshire, so that you may be properly presented to him."

He really was a marquess. Lord Rowling had not been teasing her. He was not after all plain Mr. Earheart. But of course his servants had called him *my lord* and had called her *my lady.* And he was the son *and heir* of a duke. The Duke of Withingsby. He would be a duke himself one day. She would be . . . No, she would not. Not really.

"Why would you marry without your father's knowledge?" she asked. "And why me? I am a gentleman's daughter, but one would expect a future duke to look for somewhat higher qualifications than that in a wife."

His smile was rather unpleasant, she thought, despite the fact that it revealed very white teeth. But the smile in no way touched his eyes. "Perhaps, my lady," he said, "that is just the point."

He had married her to spite someone? His father?

"Do you and your father have a quarrel with each other?" she asked.

He continued to smile—with his lips. "Shall we say," he said, "that the more displeased his grace proves to be, the more gratified I shall be?"

She understood immediately. She would have had to

be stupid not to. "So I am a mere pawn in a game," she said.

His smile disappeared and his eyes narrowed. "A very well-paid pawn, my lady," he said. "And one who will be titled for the rest of her life."

It was as well, she thought, that they were to remain together for only a few weeks—just until she had given the Duke of Withingsby a thorough disgust of herself, she supposed. She did not believe she could possibly like this man. What sort of man married a stranger merely to displease his father?

Not that she had any cause for moral outrage, of course. She had accepted the offer he had made yesterday—gracious, was it really only *yesterday*?—without demanding to know anything about the man beyond the fact that he had the means to keep the promises he made her. She had married him for those promises. She was the sort of woman who would marry a stranger for money. It was an uncomfortable admission to make, even—or perhaps especially—to oneself.

It would be very difficult for this man to become anything but a stranger, she thought, even though she was apparently to spend a few weeks in his company. Those eyes! They had no depth whatsoever. They proclaimed him to be a man who chose not to be known, a man who cared nothing for the good opinion of others. They almost frightened her.

"Was it not rather drastic," she asked him, "to marry beneath you merely to score a point in a game? Would not the quarrel have blown over in a short while as quarrels usually do?" She should know. She had grown up in a household with five brothers and sisters.

"Perhaps my father and I should have kissed and made up instead?" he said. "You may spare such shallow observations on life for your pupils, my lady.

Though of course there will be no more of them, will there?"

Charity was hurt. Shallow? As the eldest she had learned early to understand others, to identify with them, to be a mediator, a peacemaker. What a thoroughly unpleasant man he was, she thought, to speak with such contempt to a lady—and again she was jolted by the realization that he was her husband. She had promised him obedience. For the rest of her life, even after these few weeks were over and she was back home with the children, she would not really be free. Any time he chose he could demand anything he wished of her. But no, that was a foolish worry. He would be as glad as she to sever all but the unseverable tie that bound them.

"I would have thought," she said after a couple of minutes of silence, "that a man who expects to be a duke one day would have wished to produce some heirs of his own." Even as she spoke she wished she could simply stop and bite down hard on her tongue. She felt as if her cheeks had burst into flames. She had been trying to understand clearly his motives for marrying her—and had unfortunately thought aloud.

"Indeed, my lady?" The tenor lightness of his voice did not at all match his dark, satanic looks, she thought. At the moment it was quite soft—but deadly cold. "Are you volunteering your services?"

She found herself desperately and deliberately wondering if he had tied the intricate knot of his neckcloth himself or if his valet had done it for him. She lowered her eyes to it. She had lain awake last night wondering, among other things, if . . . His words now seemed to indicate that he had not intended *that* to be one of her duties during the coming weeks.

"You *are* my wife." His voice was still soft and pleasant—and seemingly chiseled out of the ice of the North Pole.

"Yes, sir." She knew very well that his valet must have helped him into his coat. He could never have shrugged into it himself. It fit him like a second skin and displayed admirably the breadth of his shoulders. She wondered if the famous and very expensive Weston was his tailor.

"We are going to have to stop early," he said, looking past her to the window and narrowing his eyes again. "Confound it, it is raining again and heavily too."

She found the rain a welcome relief from the direction the conversation had taken. It was something—one of about a hundred questions—she ought to have asked yesterday before agreeing to anything, certainly before signing any papers. But she had not thought of it until much later, until she was sitting at home darning Philip's stockings, in fact. But then she could hardly have asked the question anyway—"Do you intend to bed me, sir?" The very thought of asking such a thing aloud could turn her alternately hot and cold.

He was very handsome and even rather alarmingly attractive. He was also quite unpleasant. Quite undesirable as either a husband or a l—or a lover.

If it did not happen, of course—and fortunately it seemed very unlikely that it would—then she would go through life without ever knowing what it felt like to be fully a wife. She would never have children of her own. It was something she had fully expected for a long time—certainly since Papa's death and her understanding of the family's poverty. It was also something that seemed even more depressing now that there was no doubt at all, now that there was no hope . . . She would have liked to know . . . She thought she knew what happened, but knowing such a thing and experiencing it were vastly different things, she supposed. But the trend of her thoughts distressed her. They were not the thoughts of a proper lady.

The rain became first heavy and then heavier and finally torrential. The road became a light brown sea of mud, and it was impossible to see more than a few yards from the windows of the carriage. After fifteen minutes of very slow progress and some alarming slithering, the carriage turned into the cobbled yard of a wayside inn that was not at all the sort of establishment one might expect the Marquess of Staunton, heir to a dukedom, to patronize. At least, that was what his disdainful expression told Charity as they waited for the door to be opened and the steps to be set down.

She thought of what Lord Rowling had said of rainy wedding days. If he was correct, theirs should be the most blissful marriage in the history of the world. She smiled rather ruefully to herself.

She was hurried inside the dark, low-ceilinged taproom of the inn beneath a large black umbrella that the marquess held over her head. She stood shaking the water from the hem of her dress and cloak while he talked with the innkeeper, an enormous man who looked more irritated than delighted at the unexpected business the rain was bringing to his inn.

"Come," her husband said finally, turning back to her and gesturing her toward the steep wooden staircase up which the innkeeper was disappearing. "It seems that the inclement weather has made this a popular hostel. We are fortunate to have arrived in time to take the last empty room."

It was not a large room. The ceiling sloped steeply down fully half of it. One small window looked down upon the inn-yard. There was a washstand and a small table and chair. There was really no room for any other furniture, for the rest of the room was dominated by the large bed.

"You may leave us." The marquess nodded curtly to the innkeeper, who withdrew without a word. "Well, my lady, this will have to substitute for the suite of rooms I have reserved at a posting inn fully twenty miles farther along the road. We must dine in the public dining room and trust that the fare will be tolerably edible."

The bed was like an extra person in the room, unavoidably visible, embarrassingly silent.

"I am sure it will be, sir," she said, tossing her bonnet and her gloves onto the bed with what she hoped was convincing nonchalance.

"You will wish to freshen up and perhaps even to lie down for a short while before dinner," he said. "I shall leave you, my lady, and do myself the honor of returning to escort you to the dining room."

She had no idea where he would go in such a shabby little inn. To the taproom, probably, to imbibe inferior ale. Doubtless his jaded palate would object quite violently. But she did not really care. She was too busy feeling relieved that at least for the moment she was to be alone in this horribly embarrassing chamber. She had never before thought of a bed as an almost animate thing. She had always thought of beds as merely pieces of furniture upon which one slept. But then she had never before stood in a bedchamber with any gentleman other than her father or her brothers. She had never had to contemplate spending a night in a bedchamber—and in the same bed—with a gentleman.

But she was *married* to this particular gentleman, she reminded herself, lying down on the bed—it was decidedly hard and rather lumpy, though it appeared to be reasonably clean—after removing her shoes and her hairpins. Philip would be thinking about her all through the day, imagining her getting to know Mr. and Mrs. Earheart, her new employers, and their three children. He would be hoping that they continued pleasant and that the children were not taxing her energies too much during the journey. He would be looking uneasily out at the rain, worried for her safety. He would be waiting for her first letter.

What would he be thinking, she wondered, if he knew that she had been wed during the morning, that she was now Charity Earheart, Marchioness of Staunton, one day to be the Duchess of Withingsby? That during the coming weeks she was to be used as a pawn in a foolish quarrel between the marquess and the duke, his father. That after that she would be a lady of substance with six thousand a year in addition to a home and servants and a carriage. Papa had never kept his own carriage. They had only ever had Polly as a servant and she had stayed for the last ten years or so only because she considered herself one of the family and had nowhere else to go.

Oh, Phil, she thought, closing her eyes. He would be able to have their own home to himself. He would be able to take Agnes there, and they could begin their own family. Without the burden of Papa's debts and the necessity of supporting and providing for all the children, he would be able to manage very well as a country gentleman.

Oh, Penny. How was she managing at home alone, without either Phil's help or her own? Penny was just twenty. And pretty and sweet-natured. She should be thinking of beaux and of marriage. Were the children all well? Did they have enough to eat? Did they all have sufficient clothes? Were they missing her as dreadfully as she was missing them?

Soon, she told both them and herself silently. Soon she would be back with them. All would be as it used to be or as they had imagined it to be until Papa had died and they had realized the impoverishment of their situation. They would never be poor again or unsafe—or separated.

Yes, she had done the right thing. How could she have refused such a totally unexpected and irresistible offer?

It had been like a gift from heaven. How else could she possibly think of it? She closed her mind to the possibility that it might be just the opposite, especially when one considered the satanic appearance and the flat eyes of the Marquess of Staunton.

Of course she had done the right thing. It was too late now anyway to give in to doubts.

Of course she had done the right thing.

BY MIDNIGHT THE rain appeared to have stopped. The Marquess of Staunton stood in the open doorway of the inn taproom, one shoulder propped against the doorpost, gazing out across the cobbled yard and shivering slightly in the chilly air. But it was, of course, far too muddy and far too late to move on tonight.

He was the last of both the taproom's patrons and the inn's guests to linger downstairs. Behind him the innkeeper tidied up for the night with deliberately audible movements. He was clearly hinting that his last remaining customer should consider taking himself off to bed.

"The sun will be shining in the morning, m'lord," he said.

"Mmm, yes," the marquess agreed. They would have sunshine for their arrival at Enfield Park. How delightful! His lips tightened into a thin line. He should, he thought altogether too belatedly, have merely ignored his father's summons. He should have made no answer at all to it. Better yet, he should have answered curtly and courteously to the effect that he was too busy with his own affairs to avail himself of his grace's kind hospitality. What concern of his was it that the duke was ailing? Had his father taken any notice of him when he had broken his leg and very nearly his neck too during that curricle race to Brighton six years ago? None whatsoever.

All ties between him and his father had been severed for eight years. He was not bound to Withingsby even by financial ties. He was independently wealthy. He had been under no obligation to pay any attention to that letter when it had come. He wondered why he had felt somehow obligated, somehow caught up in the past again as if it had never been laid properly to rest. As if the bonds had not been fully severed.

He should have ignored the letter. He should have found some way of renouncing his birthright. Let William be duke after their father. Let Claudia be duchess. His lip curled at the thought. What an irony there would be in that. Claudia as the Duchess of Withingsby.

Claudia . . .

The innkeeper was clearing his throat. "Can I get you anything else tonight, m'lord?" he asked.

"No." The marquess straightened up, stepped back inside the room, and closed the door. "I am for bed. Good night." He turned toward the stairs.

Consummating his marriage had been no part of his plan. What possible pleasure could be derived, after all, from bedding an innocent brown mouse? From dealing with skittishness and pain and tears? And blood. Besides, he had not married for pleasure.

He still had no intention of consummating the marriage. But the sleeping arrangements the rain had forced upon him in this sad apology of an inn were a considerable annoyance to him. For one thing, he was a restless sleeper and did not like sharing a bed. He only ever shared one for sexual activity, never for sleep. For another thing the very idea of conducting that most private of all activities—sleeping—in anyone else's company offended his notions of privacy.

Tonight more than ever he felt the need for privacy. Instead of which, he was doomed to spending what remained of the night, not only in the same room as his bride, but in the same bed.

There was enough light from a lantern hung over the stable door in the yard below to allow him to undress in their room without the aid of a candle and to slide beneath the covers of the bed on the side closest to the door. She was lying quietly asleep on the far side of the bed.

His wife! He found himself wondering if she had any family. Not only had no one come to the church with her, but no one had come rushing out of her lodgings when his carriage had stopped for her trunk. Did she have no one at all of her own? No family? No friends? Well, soon enough she would have any number of the latter, he thought cynically. It was very easy to find friends when one was in possession of six thousand pounds a year. And was it possible that that small trunk held all she possessed in the world? Where were the rest of her belongings? Was it really possible to live with so few?

But he was not curious about her. He did not want to know anything about her other than what he knew already. Most certainly he did not wish to pity her. She was not in any way pitiable—he had ensured that yesterday in the contract they had both signed and this morning in the marriage service. He would quell all curiosity. She would serve a purpose in his life and then she would be well rewarded. He always rewarded well the women who were of service to him. This one was not performing the usual service, of course, but she would be adequately compensated for her time nevertheless. He need feel no other sense of responsibility toward her.

He addressed himself determinedly to sleep.

4

 $\mathcal{T}$ HE MARQUESS OF STAUNTON FOUND THAT SLEEP was eluding him. Totally. And he became aware of something gradually—two things, actually. He could feel the warmth of her along his right side, although they did not touch. He could also feel the stillness and quietness of her—she was far too still and far too quiet to be sleeping. But then it seemed reasonable to suppose that sleeping would be quite as difficult for her as it was for him.

"You should be asleep," he told her. "Tomorrow will be a busy day." He felt an unreasonable annoyance with her for being awake, for intruding even further into his privacy than her mere physical presence already made inevitable.

"I have counted all the sheep in England," she said.

He pursed his lips.

"I had just started on those of Wales when you spoke," she said. "Now I shall have to begin all over again."

He had expected a meek little "Yes, sir." He was reminded somehow of her eyes, which he had found himself unaccountably avoiding during dinner, when she had sat directly opposite him at their table. He found her eyes threatening, though he would have been hard-pressed to explain exactly what he meant by that if he had been called upon to do so or to explain why his mind had chosen that particular word to describe their effect on him. Now her words suggested a certain sense of humor. He did not want her to have a sense of humor—or those eyes. He wanted her to be nondescript, devoid of character or personality.

"And this is the lumpiest bed it has ever been my discomfort to lie upon," she said.

"My apologies," he said curtly. "This was not my choice of accommodation for the night."

She was silent. But not to be ignored. He was aware of her as a wakeful human presence in his room, in his bed. He turned restlessly onto his side, facing her. She did not have her hair decently confined beneath a cap, he could see, his eyes having accustomed themselves to the dimness of the room. It was spread all over her pillow. It looked long and slightly wavy. It looked rather attractive. Again he felt annoyed. He had conceded the fact that she had fine eyes. That was entirely enough beauty for his bride to possess. He had chosen her partly for her plain appearance.

What *did* innocence feel like? he wondered irritably. It was one thing—perhaps the only thing—that was outside his sexual experience. She was lying on her back with her eyes closed. But she turned her head on the pillow even as he watched her and opened her eyes. He could smell her hair. It smelled of soap. He had never thought of the smell of soap as being erotic. And neither was it. He frowned.

"One thousand three hundred and sixty-four," she said after the silence had stretched rather uncomfortably. Her voice sounded strained. Humor, he thought with a flash of insight, was her manner of self-defense. She was in bed with a man for the first time ever, after all. It must be a somewhat alarming feeling for her.

"There is another way," he said and listened in some

alarm to the echo of words he had uttered without any forethought. "Of inducing slumber, I mean."

"Pretending that one may sleep all day tomorrow if one wishes?" she said altogether too quickly. "It does work sometimes. I shall try it."

He raised himself on one elbow and propped the side of his head on his hand. "You are my wife," he said, realizing that he was getting into deep waters when he had intended not even to get his feet wet.

"Yes." Her conversation had finally been reduced to monosyllables. Her eyes were wide, he could see, but in the darkness they did less damage than when their color was clearly visible.

"I have no intention of asserting my conjugal rights by force," he said. "However, if sheep have not achieved their purpose and the bed has failed to lull you, I am willing to offer my services." He had bent his head closer to hers. Was he mad? But there was no way of retreating now unless she said no. He willed her to say no.

"Oh," was all she said. But the breathlessness of the word assured him that she understood very well.

"If you wish to try it," he said. He was surprised and not a little alarmed to find that his body had already rebelled against his will and hardened into arousal. Yet he did not even consider her desirable. "If you do not, we will address ourselves to sleep again and perhaps try the greater tedium of counting sheep's legs."

She stared back into his eyes only inches from her own. He could see that he had not left her with any monosyllabic answer to give. She was silent. But there was no withdrawing from the question now. And now his body was willing her to say yes.

"Do you wish to try it?" he asked her.

"Yes," she said in a whisper.

He would not have been surprised by a refusal. She had been an impoverished gentlewoman just yesterday, forced to earn her living as a governess, forced to suffer any insult or indignity her employers cared to subject her to—the last ones had accused her of lying over something. Today she had achieved the respectability of marriage with the prospect of a more than comfortable settlement for life after a mere few weeks spent in company with him. She might very easily have avoided the one aspect of marriage that he understood was generally distasteful to respectable women. He did not imagine that his bride was either a sensual or a passionate woman. Quite the opposite. But he had given her a clear choice—he wondered how many men gave such a choice to their brides on their wedding night—and she had whispered yes.

Well, then. So be it.

SHE EXPECTED HIM to kiss her. His mouth was only inches from her own. She could smell the brandy he had been drinking. If he had kissed her, she could have closed her eyes and concentrated on the sensation created by his mouth against her own—she had found his kiss at church quite shockingly intimate even though his lips had not quite touched her own. If he had kissed her, she might have hidden behind her closed eyes and her feelings while the other thing happened.

She did not understand why she had said yes, except that she was weary of trying to sleep and failing to do so, and she had been strangely disturbed by the warmth of him on the bed beside her, and she knew that this was probably her one and only chance in life to experience the deepest intimacy of all. And because the mere smell of brandy was intoxicating her.

He did not kiss her. Or move his head away. He continued to half lean over her and look into her eyes. His own appeared quite black. His hair was tousled. The hand that was not propping up his head touched her. She felt immediately as if she had been touched by a flaming torch even though it was only her shoulder he touched at first. His hand moved firmly downward to her breast, circled beneath it, lifted it. She thought she might well find it impossible to draw the next breath of air into her lungs. She felt horribly embarrassed. Her breasts were rather large—too large, she always thought.

And then her nipple was imprisoned between his thumb and the base of his forefinger and he squeezed them together almost as if he was unaware that it was there, causing her excruciating pain, though it was not like any other pain she had ever experienced. This was undoubtedly pain, but it shot off upward into her throat and across to her other breast and downward into her belly and along her inner thighs so that she ached and yearned all over. Her breath shuddered and jerked out of her, quite audibly.

She was alarmed. She wished she had said no. Was it too late now? But she was curious too. She wished he would kiss her. Was this not supposed to be romantic? Was it not supposed to be—love? She realized the absurdity of that youthful assumption even as she thought it. This was not love. But it was certainly—exciting. It was not supposed to be exciting. It was supposed to be love—a sweet and gentle thing. Somehow the buttons of her nightgown had come undone and he was repeating his actions on her other breast—her naked breast.

This time pain had her gasping for air.

But his hand had moved on downward beneath the low opening of her nightgown—and on down to the source of the ache the pain had created. She had parted her legs slightly and tilted her hips to allow his hand easier access before her brain understood just where his hand was and exactly what it was doing there. She felt engulfed by embarrassment and by unfamiliar and uncontrollable achings and yearnings. His fingers were parting, probing, stroking. She could hear sounds of wetness. She would have died of embarrassment, she was sure, if such an act had been within the power of her will.

She opened her eyes suddenly. He was still propped on one elbow. He was still looking down at her. He took his hand away and lifted her nightgown—all the way to her waist. Well, this part she knew about, she thought. She knew what to expect. She drew a deep breath and held it. She was not sorry she had said yes. He was a stranger and she did not believe she could ever like him—partly because she did not believe she could ever know him—but he *was* her husband, and he was undeniably attractive. On the whole she was glad there was to be this experience in her life—just this one time.

"Let it out," he told her. "You cannot possibly hold it long enough. Breathe normally."

It was easy enough for him to say that, she thought as he moved over her and a considerable portion of his weight settled on top of her. She could feel his hands pushing beneath her, spreading over her buttocks, holding them firm. Her inner thighs were against the outside of his legs, pushed wide. He seemed to be all hard, unyielding muscle. She felt horribly defenseless. But he had given her the choice, and she had said yes. She would say it again if the choice were given her again. Curiosity and fear and excitement were a heady blend, she found.

At first it was enormously frightening. Apart from the conviction that there could not possibly be room, either in breadth or in depth, there was all the fear of being impaled, destroyed while she was pressed wide and was helpless to defend herself. Then there was the terrified certainty that indeed there was not enough room and that she was about to tear into unbearable pain. Then he was deep, deep inside and holding hard and still there, and she knew with startled surprise that there was after all room and that she would survive—and that it felt unfamiliar and exciting and really rather good.

But she had been right to guess that knowing and experiencing were two quite different things. She could never have imagined the utter carnality of the sensation.

And then she discovered—during several minutes of shocked amazement—that in fact she had not known at all. Only about penetration. She had had no inkling of the fact that penetration was only the beginning. He pumped in and out of her with hard, smooth strokes until the ache his hands on her breasts had already created became raw pain—pain that was not really pain but for which there was no other more suitable word in her vocabulary. And certainly it was beyond bearing and growing more so with every inward stroke.

"Oh," she said suddenly, alarmed and amazed as she pressed her hands to his buttocks in an attempt to hold him still and deep and as inner muscles she had still not consciously discovered clenched convulsively. "Oh."

He answered her mute appeal instantly. He pressed hard into her tightness and held there. "My God," he murmured against the side of her head. "My God!"

Something that she thought might well be death beckoned and she followed without a struggle. Whatever it was closed darkly about her and felt wonderful beyond belief. Nothingness. Total, blissful nothingness.

She was half aware of his moving again, faster and harder than before. She was half aware of a flood of heat deep inside as he sighed and held still again and relaxed his full weight down onto her. Death was not after all to be feared, she thought foolishly and very fuzzily. Death was the fulfillment of all that was most desirable.

She slept. She grumbled only very halfheartedly when the wonderful heat and weight that bore her down into the mattress was lifted away from her and far lighter blankets covered her instead. Yes, she thought with the last thread of consciousness, there was a method vastly superior to counting sheep.

And love was not always sweet and gentle. And love was not always love.

THE ROAD HAD dried sufficiently by the following morning to make travel possible. And the landlord at the inn where they had stayed the night had proved quite correct in his prediction. The sun shone from a sky that was dotted prettily but sparsely with fluffy white clouds. Fields and hedgerows looked washed clean in the morning air.

It was the perfect day for a homecoming.

The Marquess of Staunton gazed moodily and sightlessly out through the window on his side of the carriage. *Damn and blast,* he was thinking, verbalizing the words in his head with silent venom.

She had actually been blushing when she had joined him in the inn dining room for breakfast. She had looked like the stereotypical bride the morning after her wedding night. She had even been looking almost pretty— not that he had spent a great deal of time looking into her face. He had addressed himself to his breakfast without being in any way aware of what he ate beyond the fact that it was inordinately greasy.

What the devil had possessed him last night? He had felt not one glimmering of sexual interest in her from the moment of spying her in the shadows of the salon where she had waited to be interviewed to the moment during which she had started to talk about sheep and Wales and lumpy mattresses. Not one iota of a glimmering.

And yet he had consummated their union during the very first night of their marriage—and had done so with great enthusiasm and more than usual satisfaction. He had fallen asleep almost immediately after lifting himself off her and had slept like the proverbial baby until dawn.

What if he had got her with child? It had been almost his first thought on waking up—*after* he had rejected the notion of waking her up and doing it again with her. A pregnancy would complicate matters considerably. Besides, children of his own body were the very last things he wanted. The very idea of impregnating a woman made him shudder. He had always been meticulous about choosing bedfellows who knew how to look after themselves—until last night.

He had the uneasy feeling this morning that he might have been at least partly deceived in his wife. True, she had been innocent and ignorant and awkward and virgin. She had also been a powder keg of passion just waiting to be ignited. And he had provided the spark. And had heedlessly spilled his seed in her.

She had proved him wrong in his conviction that he had nothing new to learn sexually except what it felt like to mount a virgin. Very wrong. He had known women come to sexual climax. It happened routinely with all his mistresses. But he had understood last night with humiliating clarity that women faked climax just as they faked delight in the whole process, knowing that for a conceited man it was important not only to receive pleasure in bed but also to believe that he gave it. Thus many women earned their daily bread—making their employers feel like devilishly virile and dashing and manly fellows.

Charity Earheart, Marchioness of Staunton, had taught him a lesson last night—quite unwittingly, of course. The shattering reality of her own untutored, totally spontaneous response to being bedded had exposed all the artificiality of all the other women he had ever known. His wife had made him feel stupidly proud of his performance. She had made him want more—he had wanted it as soon as he awoke.

He was furious, the more so perhaps since he did not quite know on whom to concentrate his fury. On her? She had merely reacted to what he did to her. On himself? His lips thinned. Was he incapable of being alone with a woman—even such a woman as the one he had married—without making an idiot of himself?

"It is pretty countryside," she said, breaking a lengthy silence.

"Yes, it is." She had tried several times to initiate conversation. He had quelled each attempt with a curtness bordering on the morose. He had no wish to converse, especially on such intellectually stimulating topics as the prettiness of the countryside.

It would not happen again, he decided. They would have separate bedchambers at Enfield, of course, and would be expected to keep to them except for brief, discreet, and dutiful couplings. But the door between their rooms would remain firmly and permanently closed. He would not touch her again with a ten-foot pole.

"What is Enfield Park like?" she asked him.

He shrugged. "Large," he said. But such a brief answer crossed the borderline between moroseness and downright rudeness. She had done nothing wrong, after all, except to say yes last night. But he was the one who had asked the question. "The house is Palladian in style, massive, with wide lawns and flower beds and ancient trees all about it, sloping down at one side to a lake and up on the other side to woods and planned walks and artful prospects. There is a village, there are farms, some old ruins—" He shrugged again. "There are all the usual trappings of a large estate. It is extremely prosperous. Your husband is like to be a very wealthy man, my lady—far more wealthy than he already is—and quite well able to keep you in comfort for the rest of your life."

"Is your mother alive?" she asked. "Do you have brothers and sisters?"

"My mother died," he said curtly, "soon after giving birth to her thirteenth child. There are five of us still living." He did not want to talk about his mother or about her frequent pregnancies and almost as frequent stillbirths. The number thirteen did not even include the four miscarriages. Devil take it, but he hoped he had not impregnated his wife. "I have two brothers and two sisters."

"Oh," she said. He could see that her head was turned in his direction. He kept his eyes directed beyond the window. "Are they all still at home?"

"Not all," he said. "But most, I believe." Marianne wrote to him occasionally—she was the only one. She had married the Earl of Twynham six years ago. They had three children. Charles must be twenty now. Augusta would be eight—twenty years younger than he. There had been seventeen pregnancies in twenty years for his mother. He did not want to think of his mother.

"How happy you must be, then," his wife said—he had almost forgotten that she shared the carriage with him, "to be coming home. How you must have been missing them."

She set one hand on his arm and he turned his head sharply to look pointedly down at it and up into her eyes. "It is the first time in eight years, my lady," he said, and he could hear the chill in his voice. "And my absence has been entirely voluntary. I come now only because the Duke of Withingsby is in failing health and has summoned me, doubtless so that he can assail my ears with a recounting of my shortcomings and a listing of my responsibilities. There are certain burdens attached to being the eldest of five living children and to being the heir to a dukedom and vast and prosperous estates."

Her very blue eyes had widened. They were a truly remarkable feature, lending considerable beauty to the rest of her features. He felt annoyance that she had kept them hidden through most of their initial interview. They detracted severely from the overall image she projected of a quiet brown mouse. Had she trained them on him from the start of that interview, he would not even have asked her to sit down. He would have dismissed her almost immediately. And her face was definitely heart-shaped.

"You have been without your family for eight years?" she said, her voice warm with sympathy. "Oh, it must have been a dreadful quarrel indeed."

"It was a matter with which you need not concern yourself, my lady," he said chillily, attempting to stare her down. It was something he was adept at doing. Very few people in his experience had been able to hold his gaze when he had no wish for them to do so.

She gazed right back at him. "I believe you must have been very deeply hurt," she said.

He clucked his tongue, made an impatient gesture with one hand, and turned back to the window. "Spare me your shallow analysis of what you know nothing about," he said, "and of a person you know nothing of."

"And I believe," she said, "you have protected yourself by shutting yourself up inside yourself—like a fortress. I believe you must be an unhappy man."

He sucked in his breath. He felt furious almost to the point of violence. Except that he had never been one to work out his anger or his frustrations in violence. He felt the icy coldness that the effort of control always caused in him. He turned his head once more to look at her.

"My lady," he said, his voice very quiet, "you would be very well advised to be silent."

Something flickered for a moment in her eyes—he

thought it was probably fear—and was gone again. She tipped her head to one side, frowned fleetingly—and held his gaze. But she obeyed him.

He set his head back against the comfortable cushions of the carriage and closed his eyes. He kept them closed for a long time, letting the anger flow out of him, admitting that it was ill-founded. The woman was his wife and was being taken to his childhood home to meet his family. It was to be expected that she would feel some curiosity even if the arrangement they had was more in the nature of employment than marriage. He could not expect her to behave as if she were totally inanimate, after all.

He spoke again at last, without opening his eyes.

"You do not have to concern yourself with what will happen when we arrive at Enfield Park," he said. "You need not worry about creating a good impression or any impression at all for that matter. I will speak for you. You may think of yourself as my shadow if you will. You may behave as you did when we met two days ago."

"Why?" It was not a defiant question. It sounded merely curious.

"The Duke of Withingsby is extremely high in the instep," he said. "He has an enormous sense of his own consequence and of that of his whole family. Although his heir has been busily sowing his wild oats for eight years and acquiring an unsavory reputation as a rake— did you know that about your husband, my lady?—his grace will now expect great things of him. A glittering and politic marriage, for example."

"Your marriage to me will of course be seen as a disaster," she said.

"Undoubtedly," he agreed. "I have married a governess, an impoverished gentlewoman. At least I have spared him someone from the *demimonde*."

"And you wish for a wife who is not only of inferior birth and fortune," she said, "but also lacking in charm and manners and conversation. A mere shadow."

"You need not worry," he said. "No one will openly insult you. Anyone who dares do so will have me to deal with."

"But who," she asked in her low, pleasant voice, "will protect me from your insults, sir?"

His eyes snapped open. "You, my lady," he said, "are being paid very well indeed to serve my purpose."

"Yes," she said, looking steadily back at him, "I am."

The words, even her expression, were quiet and meek. Why, then, did he have the distinct impression that war had been declared?

He closed his eyes again.

5

ENFIELD PARK IN WILTSHIRE WAS DAUNTINGLY grand. Yet even as the thought flashed into Charity's mind she realized that it was a gross understatement. She had lived most of her life in a cottage that boasted eight bedchambers abovestairs and was set amidst a few acres of pleasing parkland. She had been a frequent visitor at nearby Willowbourne, the home of Sir Humphrey Loring and his family—Cassandra Loring, a mere eight months younger than she, was her particular friend—and had always thought it imposing. Both properties would fit into one corner of Enfield Park and never be noticed.

At first, after the carriage had passed between massive stone gateposts and by a small stone lodge, she mistook the dower house off to the right of the driveway for the main house itself and then felt foolish when she realized her mistake, though she had not spoken it aloud, for she had been almost awed by its size and the classical perfection of its design. And that was just the dower house? It must be—the marquess had murmured the information and the carriage had continued on past.

The driveway wound between flowering hedgerows, beyond which stretched dense and ancient woodlands. They seemed to have passed into a quieter, more shadowed world despite the clopping of the horses' hooves and the creaking of the carriage wheels. Charity stared about her in wonder. But the woods fell away behind them as they approached a river and crossed it over a covered Palladian bridge—it was a magnificent structure, she saw, leaning closer to the window. The driveway climbed slightly on the other side of the bridge, passing between well-kept lawns and flower beds and the occasional old tree with massive and gnarled trunk. There were wooded hills over to the right, Charity could see. But almost before she could notice them, her attention was taken wholly by the house itself, which had just come into view.

It was an almost laughable misnomer to call it a house. It was a vast mansion of classical design. It was grand enough to do a king justice. It could easily be a palace. But it was the home of the Duke of Withingsby, her father-in-law. One day her husband would be duke and owner of it all. And she had thought yesterday morning that she was marrying a plain Mr. Earheart.

Charity swallowed. He was very silent—as he had been for most of the day and yesterday too. She had tried to make conversation, though admittedly she had chosen topics that did not lend themselves to a great deal of intelligent discussion. She had expected this morning—naively, as it had turned out—that it would be easier to communicate with him today. Though she had not for a moment mistaken what had happened the night before for love and had not expected it to make any difference at all to his plans for the future, she had nevertheless expected that there would be greater ease and warmth between them.

How wrong she had been. The opposite was true. The fact that they had had conjugal relations—though it was very hard to believe that it had happened with this elegant, almost morose man beside her—appeared to have meant nothing at all to him and merely made her annoyingly self-conscious. She kept remembering where and how he had touched her and tried not to stare at his hands—they were long-fingered, very masculine hands. She kept remembering that he had been deep inside her body, and moving vigorously there for what must have been several minutes. She kept remembering the amazingly intense pleasure his movements had given her.

It had happened with this immaculately tailored, stern-faced, very handsome stranger. It should have brought them closer together, even without the dimension of love. How could they continue strangers when they had shared bodies? But she had a great deal to learn, it seemed. He had told her earlier that he had earned a reputation as a rake. That meant that last night's activity was very familiar to him. She was merely one of a long string of women—and without a doubt the least expert of them all. It was a strange thought. To her the experience had been earth-shattering. She was not yet sure whether she was glad to have experienced it or whether in light of the future it might have been better if she had never known.

But the carriage was fast approaching the house—the mansion—and the discomfort she had lived with all day increased tenfold. Even if she were coming here as a governess she would be quaking with apprehension. But she was not coming as a governess. She was coming as the wife of the heir—the temporary wife. The unexpected wife. She smoothed her hands over the folds of her brown cloak and was thankful that her gloves had not worn into holes—yet.

"Ah," her husband said from beside her, "my arrival has been noted." He chuckled softly—a rather chilling sound.

The great doors at the top of the marble steps had opened and two people—a man and a woman—had stepped outside. For one foolish moment Charity forgot that the duchess was deceased. Two such grand personages, both dressed elegantly in black, could only be the duke and duchess, she thought. But of course they were not. They were merely servants—the housekeeper and the butler at a guess.

"His grace observes every occasion of any significance with the utmost formality and correctness," the marquess said. "The return of the prodigal heir is an occasion of significance." His second chuckle sounded just as mirthless as the first.

There was no time for Charity to become even more nervous than she already felt. Liveried footmen had appeared on the terrace, and they opened the door of the carriage and set down the steps almost before it had rolled to a complete halt. And then she was standing on the cobbles, feeling dwarfed by the massive pillars that flanked the steps and overwhelmed by the occasion, watching her husband receive the homage of the black-clad servants with icy courtesy. They turned to precede him up the steps while he offered her his arm.

His face was hard and cold, his eyes opaque. His face was also devoid of all color. He wore so heavy a mask, Charity realized with a sudden flash of sympathy, that there was no penetrating it to the real man behind. Not even through the eyes, usually a mask's weak point. He was coming home to his father and his family after eight years. How different from the homecoming she imagined for herself in a few weeks' time.

He dropped her arm when they reached the wide doorway and stepped inside ahead of her. This was the point at which she was to become his shadow, she thought, but rather than being offended that he did not lead her forward, she was glad of the chance to be insignificant. Her first impression of the hall was of vastness—of marble and pillars and classical busts and a towering dome. It would have been an intimidating room under any circumstances. But these were clearly not any circumstances. Two rows of silent servants, women on the left, men on the right, flanked the central path across the hall to a short flight of wide steps that led up to what might be a grand salon.

At the foot of the steps, arranged as if for a theatrical tableau, was a group of people, clearly *not* servants or even ordinary mortals. In the center, and slightly in front of all the others, a man stood alone. A man who so closely resembled the Marquess of Staunton as he might appear in twenty-five or thirty years that for a moment Charity felt somewhat disoriented.

She was, she realized then, in the presence of the Duke of Withingsby.

The marquess paused for a moment to look left and right, an ironic half-smile on his lips. Then he fixed his eyes on his father and moved forward across the hall, his boots clicking hollowly on the marble floor. Charity took one step forward to follow him. But a hand closing firmly about her upper arm stopped her progress. She turned her head to look into the disdainful face of the housekeeper.

"You will move to your left, girl," the woman said quietly, "and stand behind the line of servants until someone can attend to you."

Charity felt a welcome wave of amusement. She had been mistaken for a servant! "Oh, I think not," she said, smiling. But she stood where she was.

"Impertinent baggage," the housekeeper said coldly, her voice still low enough that it did not carry. "I will deal with you myself later. Stand where you are."

The marquess was bowing to his father, who was inclining his head in return. Everyone else in the group—the brothers and sisters?—stood watching. None broke ranks to greet the brother they had not seen for eight years. Charity felt chilled. How different her own homecoming would be, she thought again. She would have brothers and sisters hanging off every available part of her person and all would simultaneously be talking shrilly in order to be heard above everyone else. Nothing but a polite murmuring reached her ears across the expanse of this chilly hall.

And then her husband turned, looked back until his eyes found her, raised haughty eyebrows, and extended one hand. Charity could not resist one cool glance at the housekeeper, whose own eyebrows had disappeared almost beneath the frill of her cap, before moving forward. The hall seemed a mile long. But finally she was close enough to raise her hand and place it in the still-outstretched one of her husband. She kept her eyes on their hands. This was the moment during which she was to become a pawn, the moment of triumph for her husband. Well, she certainly looked the part, she was forced to admit—*that* had just been proved beyond a doubt. She would act it too. He was paying her well enough, after all. And it was not a difficult part to play given the circumstances. Heaven knew she felt tongue-tied enough. And her legs were feeling anything but rock-steady.

"Your grace," the marquess said, "allow me the honor of presenting to you the Marchioness of Staunton."

He did not call his father "Papa," Charity noticed, or even "Father." He called him "your grace." How very peculiar. It must have been a real world-stopper of a quarrel. And he had used his North Pole voice. She curtsied. And disconcerted by the utter silence that succeeded her husband's words, she raised her eyes to look at the Duke of Withingsby.

He looked even more like his son from close up. The only significant difference was the silver hair at his temples and the almost gray tinge to his complexion. He was looking back at her with a stern, set face and hard eyes—even in facial expression and manner he resembled his son. He presented, she was forced to admit, a somewhat formidable aspect.

"My lady." He broke the silence and half inclined his head to her. Even his voice—even the *tone* of it—was like his son's. Except that he had found ice even chillier than that at the Pole. "You are welcome to Enfield Park." Not by the flicker of an eyelash did his grace display shock or even surprise. He looked back at his son. "You will wish to greet the rest of your family, Staunton, and to present them to Lady Staunton."

Her husband had certainly won this round of the game, Charity thought ruefully, even if his father had not given him the satisfaction of collapsing in horror or erupting into a towering rage. He had just learned of his son's marriage and had just met his new daughter-in-law and had greeted her with about as much enthusiasm as he might be expected to show to his lordship's valet. Except that his eyes, with one cold sweep, would probably not have noted and dated and priced every garment the valet wore. She had the peculiar feeling that his grace had even detected the hole that had not yet quite been worn in her glove at the pad of her thumb.

His grace stood to one side.

"William?" Her husband's voice sounded strained and Charity realized anew that his return home was not as lacking in emotion as he would have her believe—and as perhaps he believed himself. He was bowing to a young man on the right of the silent group of relatives, a young man who was clearly his brother, though he was not as tall or as dark in coloring. They must be very close in age. "Claudia?"

The young lady who curtsied to him was extremely beautiful. She was blond and tall and dressed fashionably in a shade of green that matched her eyes.

"Anthony," they both said.

"May I present my wife?" he asked, and Charity became involved in another round of formal bows and curtsies. "My brother, Lord William Earheart, my lady. And Lady William."

Was this how an aristocratic bride could expect to be greeted by her husband's family? Charity wondered as he turned to the next couple. No hugs? No tears? No smiles or kisses? Just this stiff formality, as if they were all strangers? She felt rather as if she were suffocating. But of course most aristocratic brides would meet their husbands' families before the ceremony. And would be properly approved by that family. Oh yes, her husband had won this round of the game all right. This was a disaster.

Lady Twynham—also fashionably and tastefully dressed—was the marquess's sister. She called him Tony and accused him of never answering any of her letters and presented him to the Earl of Twynham, a portly man of middle years, who looked bored with the whole proceeding. She inclined her head to Charity and said nothing at all. Her eyes, like her father's, assessed the brown bonnet and cloak that her sister-in-law was wearing.

Lieutenant Lord Charles Earheart was a slim, fair-haired, handsome young man, who bowed with equal stiffness to both his brother and his sister-in-law. One could hardly blame him, perhaps, when the marquess had not even been quite sure of his identity.

"Charles?" he had said. "You *are* Charles? Lieutenant, is it?"

He must be younger than Philip, Charity estimated. Nineteen? Twenty? He would have been just a boy when his brother had left home, and they had not seen each other during the eight years since. How very sad it was. Perhaps, she thought suddenly, without this marriage she would not have been able to see her own brothers and sisters for eight years or longer—all the younger ones would have grown up without her. It was already a year since she had seen them last.

And then there was the youngest one, a girl. She was expensively dressed and elaborately coiffed and unnaturally quiet and still and dignified for such a young child. She was very dark in coloring, and she had the narrow, aristocratic face of her eldest brother—and of her father. She would be handsome rather than pretty when she grew up.

"Augusta?" the marquess said. For the first time there was some softening in his tone. "I am your brother Anthony. This is my wife."

"How pretty you look in blue, Augusta," Charity said kindly. "And how pleased I am to make your acquaintance."

The child executed two perfect curtsies. "My lord," she murmured. "My lady."

Well. And that was that, Charity thought. The scene had been played out and she would have to say that the Marquess of Staunton had won his point resoundingly. But perhaps the welcome home would have been just as chilly even if she had not been with him. There was no way of knowing. She knew nothing of the quarrel that had sent him from home and kept him away. And she had no way of knowing either what was to come next. She had not thought beyond this moment and she did not know if her husband had either. With a hand at the small of her back he was turning her in his father's direction again. The housekeeper stood just a few feet off. She had doubtless been summoned by some silent communication—a lifting of the ducal eyebrow, perhaps.

"Mrs. Aylward," the duke said, "you will conduct the Marchioness of Staunton to the marquess's apartments, if you please, and see to her comfort there. Tea will be served in the drawing room in precisely half an hour. You will attend me in the library, Staunton."

Did anyone ever *smile* here? Or do anything with any enthusiasm or spontaneity? Charity was supposed to be quiet, dull, and demure, and she had been all three ever since setting foot over the threshold. But she was oppressed by the atmosphere, offended by it. These people were *family*. Family members were supposed to love and support one another. And she was, however temporarily, a member of this family. This silver-haired, stern gentleman was her *father*-in-law. Some gesture was necessary—even imperative—if she was to maintain any of her own identity. She smiled warmly at him and curtsied again.

"Thank you," she said, and she hesitated for only the merest moment, "*Father*."

Nobody said anything—or rather everybody continued to say nothing. But Charity did not believe she imagined a collective stiffening in everyone around her just as if she had opened her mouth and uttered some obscenity. She turned her smile on her husband, who bowed to her.

"I shall see you shortly, *my love*," he said, throwing just a little emphasis onto the final two words.

They jolted her. He had never mentioned that part of his plan was to pretend that they had a fondness for each other. But then he had not said a great deal at all about his plans. She turned and followed the housekeeper toward a marble arch and the grand staircase beyond it.

"My lady," the housekeeper said stiffly as they began the ascent, "we were not informed of the fact that his lordship was bringing a wife to Enfield Park. I do beg your pardon."

"For calling me an impertinent baggage?" Charity said, laughing. She could just imagine the woman's embarrassment. "I was amused, Mrs. Aylward. Please forget it."

But Mrs. Aylward herself looked far from amused, especially at the open reminder of her own words. It must be a rule of the house, Charity decided, that no one was allowed to smile beneath its roof. Her laughter had echoed hollowly and disappeared without a trace. She felt that sense of oppression again. This was not going to be easy. She must hope that the first stage of her marriage would last for very few weeks. She longed for home and for the familiar, cheerful, *smiling* faces of her family.

The marquess's apartments, on the second floor, consisted of two large bedchambers, connected by adjoining dressing rooms, and of a study, and a sitting room of equal size. It was clearly an apartment designed for a married couple.

"I shall have the bed aired and made up immediately, my lady," the housekeeper said, leading her into one of the bedchambers, a square, high-ceilinged room, whose predominant colors of green and gold gave it a spring-like appearance. It was by far the least oppressive room Charity had seen in the house so far. It was also a chamber into which her room at home would fit four times over, she was convinced.

"What a lovely room," she said, crossing the soft carpet to look out of one long window. It faced across a lawn to a horseshoe-shaped lake and trees beyond. "And what a glorious view."

"I shall see that your luggage is brought up and your maid shown to your dressing room without further delay, my lady," Mrs. Aylward said. "You will wish to change and freshen up for tea."

Oh, dear.

"I have no maid," Charity said, turning to smile at her, "and only one small trunk. But a pitcher of hot water and soap and towels would be very welcome. Thank you, Mrs. Aylward."

The housekeeper was too well trained to look appalled, though like many of her breed she had perfected the look of well-bred disdain. She used the look on Charity now. But during eight months as a governess and during six interviews for another position, Charity had grown accustomed to ignoring such looks and reminding herself of her own inherent dignity.

She was, however, made aware of her somewhat embarrassing predicament—one that had not been apparent to her when she had first agreed to marry or even after she knew her husband's true identity. Only now, in this house, among these people, did she become uncomfortably aware that apart from her rather aged gray silk and her well-worn sprigged muslin, she had nothing suitable for wearing in genteel company. And this company was going to be somewhat higher on the social scale than genteel. She had a few other good clothes at home, of course, but she had not thought it appropriate to take them with her when she took employment.

She wondered if her husband realized the poverty of her wardrobe and concluded that he must—he had advertised for a governess, after all, and he had seen her trunk and had even asked if that was all she had. She wondered if he would be embarrassed by her shabby appearance, and concluded immediately that he would not. It was all part of his plan. He wanted her to be just as she was—or as she had appeared to him during that interview in Upper Grosvenor Street. He wanted her to be a drab little mouse, and probably a shabby one too. She could begin to see why. Even the housekeeper had mistaken her for a servant. The Duke of Withingsby must be totally incensed at the knowledge that she was his heir's *wife*. She looked down at her brown cloak and tried to see it through his eyes. Yet there was nothing he could do to alter the situation. Oh, yes, her husband must indeed feel that he had won this round of the game.

Charity had no right to feel bitter. She had no reason to feel anything except an eagerness that this charade be over and done with as soon as possible.

Mrs. Aylward left her alone after promising to send up her trunk and assign a maid to her care—until her own should arrive from London, she added with the certain and disdainful knowledge that there was no such person.

Charity looked about at the magnificence of her room and hugged her arms about herself. On the whole she would have preferred to be in a small attic room, about to begin a new job as a governess. Except that then she would have little hope of ever returning to her family or of ever expecting the happy settlement in life of her brothers and sisters.

She had done the right thing. Of course she had.

6

As a boy, the Marquess of Staunton had often had the fanciful feeling that the dome above the great hall settled its weight upon his shoulders as soon as he stepped inside the doors, rather like Atlas's world. Eight years after leaving home and setting himself free, he experienced exactly the same feeling as soon as he crossed the threshold again.

It was a feeling of heaviness and darkness. And the people who still haunted his dreams and his nightmares even though he had freed himself from them in all his waking moments were there, waiting to pull him in again, to drag him under until he gasped for air and sucked in water instead and knew himself doomed. He was glad indeed that he had brought a wife with him, that he had the undeniable means with which to defy their subtle influence. And they were *all* there, he saw at a glance.

None of them had ever been to London during the eight years he had spent there. That was a strange fact when one considered their social rank and the adult ages of all of them except the youngest. It was a chilling reminder of the power the Duke of Withingsby wielded over his family. His eldest son and heir had left without his permission. None of his other children would be allowed to meet him and perhaps be contaminated by his influence. Even Twynham must be under the ducal thumb. He had never brought Marianne to town or even come there alone, to the marquess's knowledge. He had never met his sister's husband.

And so in leaving his father he had been severed from his whole family—even from the baby. It was the choice he had been forced to make—the choice that had almost killed him. He had left behind the baby and twelve-year-old Charles. He noticed the young girl among the silent group behind the duke. She must be that baby. And the very young man must be Charles. He tried not to remember how many times he had tortured himself, especially during the early years, with wondering if it had been cowardly to leave them. And how many times he had felt cruelly punished with the fierceness of his longing for them.

His father looked not a day older than he had looked then, though the grayish tinge to his complexion proclaimed the fact that he had not lied about his failing health.

All these things the marquess noticed and felt during the first seconds after he had stepped through the doorway into the great hall. During those moments he was almost overwhelmed by unaccustomed emotion. He had trained himself not to feel at all. And by God, he would put that training to use now when he most needed it. He looked mockingly at the silent lines of immaculately clad servants before crossing the hall and beginning this charade of a family reunion.

Nothing surprised him. His father welcomed his son home with chill pomp just as if he had not left in bitterness and been gone and living independently for eight years. And—as he might have expected—his father greeted the news of his marriage without a flicker of public dismay—or enthusiasm. He met this daughter-in-law with chill courtesy. So did all the others. But the marquess was glad of the formality. Without it, he did not know quite how he would have looked William in the eye, or Claudia, or how he would have been able to speak to them. He had seen, almost before he was properly through the door, almost before he saw his father, that they were there, side by side, husband and wife. And that Claudia was more beautiful than she had ever been.

It was enormously satisfying to him—even more so than he had expected—to present his wife. To sense the blank shock in his father's whole being. To display to *them* that he had married from personal inclination after all, that he cared not one fig for dynastic considerations. He had not realized until this very moment that he had had more than one reason for choosing a bride as he had and for marrying her before coming home.

And then came the crowning moment. Just as she was about to be led away by the housekeeper, his wife smiled. No, she did not just smile—she lit up the hall with the warmth of her expression, and despite the terrible drabness of her clothes she looked suddenly quite startlingly lovely. And she called his grace *Father*. It was a priceless moment. No one had ever been so familiar with the Duke of Withingsby. There was nothing even remotely vulgar in either her smile or her words. They were just shockingly out of place in this household.

And so an idea was born in him and he had called her his love—a definite vulgarity in the ducal vocabulary. He knew a moment of quite exquisite triumph, far in excess even of what he had dreamed.

He followed his father into the library but did not stand just inside the door, as he had always used to do when summoned there, facing the seated duke across the wide expanse of the oak desk in a position of distinct subordination. No, he would never stand there again. He crossed the room to the window and looked out across the lake.

"How are you, sir?" he asked. His father was not languishing on his deathbed, but he was undoubtedly in poor health. And his health was the reason for this homecoming.

His grace ignored the question. "Your marriage is of recent date," he said. It was not a question. The marquess did not doubt that his father was familiar with every move he had made during the past eight years, though not a single letter had been exchanged between them—until the one that had summoned him home.

"Yesterday," he said. "A union that was consummated last night," he added, glad suddenly that it could be said in all honesty. Though he would have been just as married even without the consummation.

"Who is she?" the duke asked.

"She was Miss Charity Duncan, a gentlewoman from Hampshire," the marquess said. "She earned her living as a governess before marrying me."

"I suppose," his father said, "you were seduced by blue eyes and a seductive smile and bold impertinence."

Seductive? Bold impertinence? His quiet little mouse? His lips twitched but he said nothing. His father would soon realize how far wide of the mark his initial judgment of his daughter-in-law was, though it would not hurt at all if she smiled more often. He turned from the window and looked at the duke, who was seated, as expected, behind his desk—from which vantage point he had dispensed chill justice on servants and children alike for as far back as his son could remember. And no love at all.

"I married her," he said quietly, "because I chose to, sir. I passed the age of majority seven years ago."

"You married her," his grace said, "in defiance of me and in defiance of your upbringing. You have married a woman of shabby gentility and questionable manners. She was very carefully chosen, I daresay."

"Yes, sir," his son said, the sense of triumph building in him. "For love."

It was something he had not intended to claim, something he had never even considered claiming, since love—in any of its manifestations—was an emotion that gave him the shudders. But the idea had occurred to him when she had so shocked his family with a single word and a dazzling smile. It was a good idea. The Dukes of Withingsby and their heirs did not marry for love—especially shabby gentlewomen. The idea that his heir had been indiscreet enough to form a love match would strike his father as the ultimate vulgarity.

"Tillden will be arriving here tomorrow with his countess and his daughter," the duke said. "They are coming to celebrate the formalizing of a betrothal between Lady Marie Lucas and my eldest son. There is to be a betrothal ball the night after tomorrow. How will you explain yourself to them, Staunton?"

"I believe, sir," the marquess said, "I have no explaining to do."

"You were fully aware of the match agreed upon seventeen years ago," his grace said. "And if you had forgotten, my letter of a couple of weeks ago would have reminded you—the letter you received even before you were acquainted with the present marchioness, I daresay. Tillden may well consider you in breach of contract."

"If there is a contract in existence," his son replied coolly, "it does not bear my signature, sir. If the agreement was verbal, it was not ratified by my voice. The contract is not my concern."

"A young lady who has grown up expecting to be the Duchess of Withingsby one day," his grace said, "is about to be severely humiliated."

"I had no part in raising her hopes," the marquess said. "And I believe you must agree, sir, that this conversation is pointless. I am married. The ceremony has been performed, the register signed and witnessed, and the union consummated."

His father stared at him coldly and quite expressionlessly. It was a moment of acute triumph for his son, who held his gaze.

"It is to be hoped," his grace said at last, "that you know how to dress your wife, Staunton. The garments she wore for travel will disappear without trace after today, I trust? It was my distinct impression that my housekeeper mistook her for a maid."

So that was why she had still been standing just inside the door when he had turned to present her to his father? The marquess smiled inwardly.

"My wife pleases me as she is," he said. "I care nothing for the clothes she wears."

"A nonsensical attitude when the appearance of your wife reflects your own position in society," his grace said. "As she appeared on her arrival, she is hardly fit to occupy a place in the kitchen."

"As my father and our host," the marquess said, the stiffness and chilliness of his voice quite at variance with his secret satisfaction, "you have the right to say so, sir. I will, however, be pleased to debate the issue with anyone else who feels obliged to utter similar sentiments."

What *did* she have in that small trunk of hers? he wondered.

"You will wish to go upstairs before coming to the drawing room for tea," the duke said. "You will wish to escort Lady Staunton down. You will not wish to be late. And you will instruct her ladyship on how I am to be addressed, Staunton."

His son stood looking at him for several moments before moving to the door without another word. He could remember how as a boy he had adored his father, whom he rarely saw, how he had fed off every comment about his own likeness to the duke, how the whole of his boy-hood had seemed to be shaped about the desire to please his father, to emulate him, to be a worthy heir to him. All his efforts had gone unnoticed. And yet every failure at a lesson, every episode of boyish mischief, every reported bickering with a younger sibling had brought him to this very room for an interrogation and a lecture, while he had stood before that desk, knowing that at the end of it all there would be the command to bend over the desk for the painful and never brief caning.

He could not count the number of times he had been caned by his father. Neither could he count the number of times his father had shown him affection, since there were no such numbers to count.

He might have forgiven his father's harshness toward himself—perhaps. But the duke had shown no love to anyone—not even to his wife, who had borne him thir-teen children and had miscarried four others. And his grace had expressed only impatience and irritability when his eldest son had tried to persuade him to see his youngest daughter after her birth—and after the duch-ess's death.

It had been one of his reasons for leaving home.

He had come to hate his resemblance to his father—the outer resemblance and, more important, the inner resemblance. He had come to hate himself. Until he had freed himself. He was free now. He had come back when summoned, but he had come on his own terms. The Duke of Withingsby no longer had any power over him.

But devil take it, he thought as he took the stairs up to his apartment two at a time, that dome was pressing down on his shoulders again.

THE APARTMENTS HE had occupied from the time he left the nursery until the time he left home had been prepared for him again. They must have been kept for him all this time, he thought. His declaration that he was leaving, never to return, had been disregarded—and indeed, here he was, back again. He had rather expected that the apartments would have been given to William and Claudia. But apparently not. They must be in some lesser apartment.

He found his wife in the private sitting room. She was standing at the window, looking out, though she turned her head as soon as he opened the door. The room, which he had never used, looked strangely cozy and lived-in and feminine, he thought, though nothing had changed in it except for the fact that she was standing there. It was a woman's room, he realized, or a room that needed a woman's presence.

It seemed suddenly strange to have a woman—a wife—in these long-familiar rooms.

For the first time since he had known her she was not wearing brown. She had changed into a high-waisted dress of sprigged muslin. It looked somewhat faded from many washings. Her hair was simply styled and knotted behind. It was lighter in color than he had thought at first. She looked, he thought, like someone's poor relation—a very poor relation. She also looked surprisingly young and pretty. She had a trim figure—a rather enticing figure, as he remembered clearly from his exploration of it the night before.

"The view is magnificent," she said.

"Yes." He crossed the room to stand beside her. He had always been somewhat oppressed by the house. In the outdoors he had known freedom—or the illusion of freedom. The late-afternoon sun slanted across the lake, turning it to dull gold. The woods beyond—his boyhood playground and enchanted land—were dark and inviting.

"You are very like your father." She was looking at his profile rather than out the window.

"Yes." His jaw tightened.

"And you hate being like him," she said quietly. "I am sorry I stated the obvious."

He did not like her insights, her attempts to read his character and his mind. He shared himself with no one, ever—not even his closest male friends. She must understand that she was not to be allowed a wife's privilege of probing into every corner of his life—the very idea was nauseating. She must be reminded that theirs was purely a business arrangement.

"I married you and I brought you here, as you very well know," he said, turning to look at her—she looked very directly back with those splendid blue eyes of hers, "to prove to his grace that I live my own life my own way. No one is allowed to direct my life for me and no one is invited to intrude on my privacy. I am the Duke of Withingsby's heir—nothing but my death can change that. But beyond that basic fact, I am my own person. You are the proof I have brought with me that I will not do anything merely because it is expected of the heir to the dukedom."

"You did not have the courage merely to tell him that?" she asked.

"You, my lady," he said, "are impertinent."

She opened her mouth to speak but closed it again without saying anything. She did not look away from him, though. She stared at him with wide eyes. He had the strange feeling that if he looked deeply enough into them he would see her soul. If she kept herself that wide open, he thought in some annoyance, sooner or later life was going to hurt her very badly indeed.

"You played your part well on your arrival," he said. "You may confidently continue as you began. You need not be embarrassed by your lack of a fashionable wardrobe. And you need not be embarrassed by any lack of conversation—my family is not easy to converse with. We are expected in the drawing room immediately. You may stay close to me and leave the conversation to me. There is no necessity for you to impress anyone."

She half smiled at him. "Augusta must have been very young when you went away," she said.

"She was one week old," he told her. "I stayed for my mother's funeral." He had shed no tears for his mother. He had sobbed painfully, the child in his arms, just before he left. The last tears he had shed—the last he would ever shed.

"Ah," his wife said softly, and he could have sworn that she had slipped inside his head again and knew that he had wept over his last ever contact with love. Over his last foolishness.

He would not have her inside his head—or anywhere inside himself.

"Ours was a brief courtship," he told her briskly. "You were governess at the home of an acquaintance of mine. I met you there, we fell in love, and we threw all caution to the winds. We married yesterday, mated last night, and are embarking upon a deeply passionate relationship today."

She blushed and her eyes slipped from his for a few moments. But she looked back at him steadily enough. "Then, my lord," she said, "you must learn to smile."

He raised his eyebrows.

"You look," she said, her eyes roaming over his face, "like a man who has married a stranger with the sole purpose of angering and perhaps disgusting someone else. You look like a man who is wallowing in bitter and unhappy triumph."

His eyes narrowed. He found himself wondering if one short interview two days before had been sufficient time in which to learn about her character—or what he had thought to be lack of character. But perhaps she had a point, he had to confess.

"You will have your smiles, my lady," he said. "But below-stairs, where they will be seen by others. We have no need of them when we are alone."

"No," she said.

"Take my arm." He offered it. "We are late. His grace does not tolerate unpunctuality."

"That is why we have stood here talking instead of going down immediately?" she asked him. There was a look very like merriment in her eyes.

But he merely waited for her to take his arm.

THE DUKE OF Withingsby's family had moved directly to the drawing room from the hall. Although the fine weather might have tempted some of them out of doors to stroll until it was time for tea, they all felt an unexpressed need to remain together and to be out of the earshot of servants.

"One might have guessed," Lord William Earheart said, the first to speak after the door had been closed, "that when he so meekly agreed to return to Enfield scarcely more than a week after his grace wrote to him, Staunton would have a trick or two up his sleeve. I would have advised his grace to leave the letter unwritten if my opinion had been sought."

"Oh, William," his wife said reproachfully, releasing his arm and setting hers about Augusta's shoulders, "you would not have. You know you have longed for Anthony's return as much as anyone."

"What in thunder are you talking about?" He frowned moodily. "Have *you* been longing for his return?"

"I cannot believe it," the Countess of Twynham said, sinking gracefully onto a sofa. "I cannot believe it. How *could* he? It is one thing to run away to town for a few years—I would imagine it is many a young man's dream to do so. It is one thing to live wildly there and to gain a reputation as a—" She glanced at Augusta. "Well, it is one thing. It is another thing entirely to *marry* without his grace's permission and to bring his bride home here without a word to anyone. Did you *see* her, Claudia? I would die of humiliation if my *maid* were seen in such garments."

Claudia, Lady William, had led Augusta to the window and had sat with her in the window seat. "Perhaps, Marianne," she said, "they had a trying journey. There was all that rain yesterday, you will remember. Who would wish to wear good clothes in that weather?"

"But who the devil *is* she?" the Earl of Twynham muttered while busying himself at the sideboard, pouring a glass of brandy while there was still time. No hard liquor was permitted during tea at Enfield. "Did Staunton say? He would have if she had been anyone, you may be sure. It will be a trifle embarrassing when Lady Marie arrives tomorrow, eh?"

"Oh!" Marianne waved a handkerchief in the air as if she were about to succumb to a fit of the vapors, and then pressed it to her nose. "I shall *die*. And it is too late for his grace to stop her from coming. And Tony knew about her coming. He must have known. How could he do this to us? I cannot believe it. He has married a nobody and brought her here to humiliate us all. And she is a dreadfully vulgar creature, as was plain for all to see."

Lord William combed his fingers through his hair. "She called his grace *Father*," he said and winced. "She had not been in the house five minutes. Can you imagine Lady Marie calling him *Father*? She would know better. I would not be in his grace's shoes tomorrow for all the tea in China."

"But Lady Staunton does have a lovely smile," Claudia said. "Perhaps we should wait and make her acquaintance before making any hasty judgments. What do you think, Charles?"

Lieutenant Lord Charles Earheart was standing beside her and Augusta, looking out of the window.

"I would not have come home on leave if his grace had not summoned me," he said. "Not when I knew that Staunton had been invited too. I have no thoughts on his arrival or on the fact that he has brought a wife with him. It is nothing to me."

If he had intended to speak with cold dignity, he failed miserably. His voice shook with youthful passion. Claudia reached out and touched his hand. He did not pull away, but neither did he turn his head to acknowledge her smile of sympathy.

"And what do you think of your eldest brother, Augusta?" Claudia asked.

"I think his lordship looks very like his grace," Augusta said. "I think he looks disagreeable. And I think her ladyship is very ugly."

The Earl of Twynham sniggered while his wife waved her handkerchief before her face again. "'Out of the mouths of babes . . .'" she said. "You are quite right, Augusta. He looked very disagreeable indeed, as if he were enjoying the whole dreadful scene. And *she* has no pretense to beauty or anything else either, I daresay. It would not surprise me to learn that Tony had found her in someone's kitchen—or in someone's schoolroom more like. One wonders if she is even a gentlewoman. I will find it extremely difficult to be civil to her."

"His grace will be civil, you may be sure, Marianne," Lord William said. "And he will expect no less of us. She *is* Lady Staunton, after all, whoever or whatever she was before Staunton decided to marry her."

"And she will be the duchess in time," his sister said in deepest disgust. "She will be the head of this family and will take precedence over Claudia, over me—over all of us. It will be quite insupportable. Twynham and I will come to Enfield very rarely in the future, I daresay. Well, there are ways and ways of being civil, Will. I shall be civil."

Lord Twynham sniggered again. "One wonders how Withingsby will manage things tomorrow," he said. "Tillden will not be amused, mark my words. And she already takes precedence over you, Marianne. She is Staunton's marchioness."

"We must all be civil today and let tomorrow look after itself," Claudia said. "Anthony has come home again and he has brought a bride of whom he is fond. He called her *my love*. Did anyone else hear him? I was touched, I must say."

Her husband snorted. "The Dukes of Withingsby and their heirs do not marry for any such vulgar reason as love," he said, "as you know very well, Claudia."

She flushed and lowered her face to kiss the top of Augusta's head. Lord William had the grace to flush too, but there was no chance for any more conversation. The doors opened to admit the duke. He crossed the room in the silence that greeted his arrival and took up his stand with his back to the unlit fireplace, his hands at his back.

"Staunton is not here yet?" he asked rather unnecessarily. "He is late. We will await his pleasure." The coldness of his words did not invite any response.

His family proceeded to wait in uneasy silence. The Earl of Twynham clearly considered gulping down the last mouthful from his glass, but he regretfully and unobtrusively set the glass down on the sideboard instead. Claudia hugged Augusta, for whom the chance to take tea in the drawing room with the adults was a rare and questionable treat, and smiled reassuringly at her.

7

CHARITY WAS COMING TO EXPECT MAGNIFICENCE AT Enfield Park. Even so, she found the drawing room quite daunting when she first stepped inside it. The drawing room at home was more in the way of a cozy sitting room, a place where the family gathered when they were all together in the evenings or when they were entertaining friends and neighbors. This room was like—an audience chamber was the only description that came to mind. The high-coved ceiling was painted with a scene from mythology, though she was not at leisure to identify which. The walls were hung with huge paintings in gilded frames—landscapes mostly. The furniture, heavily gilded and ornate, spoke of wealth and taste and privilege. The doorcase was elaborately carved. The marble fireplace was a work of art.

But she had little chance to do much more than catch her breath and focus her attention on the people who occupied the room—the duke standing formally before the fireplace, everyone else arranged about the room, either standing or seated. No one moved or said a thing, though every head turned toward the door as she came through it, her hand on her husband's arm.

Her sprigged muslin felt about as appropriate to the occasion as her shift would have been.

A moment later, after the first shock of the ordeal was

over, she could have shaken every one of them. Their *brother* had come home, yet no one spoke a word to him. What, in heaven's name, was the *matter* with them? The answer was not long in coming. Most eyes turned after a few moments toward the duke, and it was clear that everyone waited for him to speak first. He took his time about doing so, though no words were necessary to convey the message that he was displeased.

A man ought not to be allowed to get away with being such a despot, Charity thought—but it was a thought she must certainly learn to keep to herself.

"Now that it has pleased Staunton to favor us with his company," his grace said at last, "we may have the tea tray brought in. Marianne? You will ring for it, if you please. Lady Staunton may be excused from her duties for this occasion."

It took Charity a fraction of a second to realize that she was the one being excused. From pouring the tea? *Her?* But of course, she realized in some shock. As the wife of the marquess she was the most senior lady present. She became even more aware of her sprigged muslin.

"Tony, do come and sit beside me and tell me why you never answer my letters," Marianne said, having got to her feet to pull the bell rope. And since she did not even look at Charity and since the sofa on which she sat could seat only two in comfort, it was clear that her invitation was not meant to include her brother's wife.

But Charity had glanced toward the window and the small group gathered there. Claudia was seated on a window seat with Augusta, one of her arms about the child's shoulders, and Charles stood beside them. Claudia caught her eye and looked on her kindly—or so Charity chose to believe as she crossed the room toward them. She would not be a shadow no matter what her husband wished. She was a lady and ladies were never merely other people's shadows, even their husbands'.

She smiled warmly. "You have been allowed to come to the drawing room for tea, Augusta?" she said. "I am so glad."

"Just for today," Claudia said. "For a special occasion. For Anthony's homecoming. The other children are not so fortunate despite long faces and even some pleading."

"The other children?" Charity asked.

"Anthony has not told you?" Claudia asked. "But then he has not even met any of them himself yet. There are Marianne and Richard's three—two girls and a boy—and William and my two boys. Perhaps after tea you would care to come up to the nursery to meet them. They would be overjoyed, I can promise you."

Charity could have hugged her as she accepted the invitation. There was at least *someone* human at Enfield Park. How had Claudia been able to find a dress fabric that so exactly matched her eyes in color? she wondered.

"Charles." Charity smiled at him. "You are on leave from your regiment?"

"My lady." He made her a stiff bow. "I was summoned by his grace."

"*My lady,*" Charity said softly. "I wonder if you would be so good as to call me by my name, since I am your sister? It is Charity. My name, I mean."

"My lady." He inclined his head to her.

Well. Charity turned to look back into the room and found herself being surveyed from head to toe by a very disdainful Marianne. The marquess was seated beside her, looking as cynical and satanic as he had looked during that morning on Upper Grosvenor Street. Lord Twynham—Claudia had called him Richard—was standing by the sideboard, looking morose. William, also standing, was in the middle of the room, staring moodily at nothing in particular. The duke had not moved from his position of command at the fireplace.

Charity wondered what everyone would do or say if she suddenly screamed as loudly as she could and flapped her arms in the air. She was alarmed when she realized that she was quite tempted to put the matter to the test. But she was saved by the opening of the door and the advent of the tea tray and a better idea.

She crossed the room with all the grace she could muster—her mother had often accused her of striding along in unladylike manner, and even Penny had sometimes hinted the same thing when they walked out together.

"Do set it down," she said to the servants, indicating the table that was obviously intended for the tray. She walked around the table to the single chair that had been set behind it. She smiled at her sister-in-law. "I shall pour, Marianne, and save you the bother." She turned the same smile on the duke. "Thank you, Father, for the kind thought, but you do not need to excuse me from any of my duties as Anthony's wife." Finally she turned the smile on him and made it ten times more dazzling. She considered blowing him a kiss, but no—she would not be vulgar.

She was convinced for one ghastly moment that the proverbial pin might have been heard to drop on the drawing-room floor if someone only thought of dropping it there—despite the fact that the floor was sumptuously carpeted. But her husband got to his feet just in time.

"You may certainly pour a cup for me, my love," he said. And then he did it, what she had told him he must do. He *smiled* at her—with his mouth and his very white teeth and with his eyes and with his whole face. He smiled and in the process transformed himself into a dazzlingly vital and handsome man, not to mention a knee-weakeningly attractive one. Charity wondered if her hands would be steady enough to lift the teapot and direct the tea into the cup without also filling the saucer.

She had to remind herself very sternly that he was merely acting a part and that in a sense so was she.

She had *never*, she thought, had to work so hard to earn her daily bread. It was true that this time she was earning vastly more than just daily bread, more than she could ever have dreamed of earning, in fact. But even so . . .

But even so, she was not sure she would have agreed to all this if she had only known what was facing her.

SHE HAD CHANGED into a gown of gray silk for dinner. It had a modest neckline, modest sleeves, modest everything else. It was not shabby. Neither was it in the first stare of fashion—or even in the second stare for that matter, her husband thought. It looked like the sort of decent, unremarkable garment a governess might wear when taking the children down to the drawing room so that their parents might display them before family guests. It was the sort of garment designed to make her invisible. She wore no jewelry with it.

He stood in the doorway of her dressing room, which her new maid had opened to his knock, surveying her with slightly narrowed eyes.

"You may leave," he told the girl, who curtsied and scurried away without even glancing at her mistress for confirmation of the command.

She had done admirable things with his wife's hair. It curled softly about her face and was coiled prettily at the back. He would have preferred the usual plain style, but he would say nothing.

"Why did you choose to preside over the tea tray this afternoon?" he asked her. She had taken him totally by surprise. He had been almost enjoying himself, feeling everyone's discomfort almost like a palpable thing, watching their fascination with his wife, who had been dressed so very simply in her shabby sprigged muslin—and in such marked contrast to the elegant, costly, fashionable attire of everyone else. He had puzzled them all, he had been thinking, thrown them all off balance—even his father, he would wager. They did not know what to make of him or of his sudden marriage. They were all perhaps a little afraid of him. And they were all doubtless fully aware of why they had been summoned to Enfield Park. Part of it assuredly was their father's health—but that was only what had instigated his decision to bring on the moment of his heir's betrothal to the lady chosen for him at birth. There was even a ball planned to celebrate the event very publicly.

"Because, as your father reminded me," his wife said in answer to his question, "it was my duty to do so as the wife of his eldest son."

"There is no necessity for you to—do your duty as you put it," he said. "You know that was not my intention in bringing you here."

"But by choice you married a lady, my lord," she reminded him. "A lady knows what is expected of her after she marries even if she cannot quite dress or act the part of a future duchess. You may rest assured that your family thoroughly despises my appearance and my recent background and my lack of connections and fortune. They are welcome to do so as there is nothing I can—or would—do to alter any of those things. But I will not have them believe also that my upbringing was defective. That would be a lie and a slur on my mother's memory."

So much for his quiet mouse. She did not really exist, he suspected. Miss Charity Duncan had, of course, acted a part during that interview. She had badly wanted the position of governess—she had already failed at six previous attempts—and had behaved as governesses were expected to behave. He had taken the act for reality and had not perceived that there was a great deal of character behind the meekness—he should, of course, have taken more note of those shrewd blue eyes. He had been deceived. But there was truth in what she said now. Everyone this afternoon had treated her with subtle, well-bred condescension. She was not of their world. It must be an appalling thought to all of them that one day she would be wife of the head of the family. His father must feel that everything he had lived for was crashing about his ears.

"No one will openly insult you," he assured her, not for the first time. But now he felt more personal commitment to seeing that it was so. "No one would dare."

She smiled and came toward him. "Insults are only really effective," she said, "when the person insulted cares for the good opinion of the insulter. I will not be insulted here, my lord." She took the arm he offered.

And that, he thought, had been a quiet, charming, very firm setdown. She cared nothing for anyone in this house, her words told him. Well, neither did he. He had not come home because he cared. He had come in order to assert himself and his independence once and for all. And perhaps to lay a few ghosts to rest—though the thought had popped into his mind only now and surprised him. There were no ghosts to lay to rest. Everything that was past was long dead and done with.

"I would know more about your family," she said as he led her from the dressing room toward the grand staircase, seeming to contradict what she had just implied. "Perhaps you will enlighten me more tomorrow."

"I have seen none of them myself for eight years," he said. "There is nothing to tell, my lady."

"But you must have boyhood memories," she said. "William must be close to you in age, and Marianne too."

"William is one year my junior and Marianne two,"

he said. Then the almost annual stillbirths and miscarriages had started.

"It must have been wonderful to have a brother and
sister so close to you in age," she said.

Yes, he had always adored and protected and envied
the smaller, weaker, but sunnier-natured Will. He would
have changed places with him at any time if it had been
possible, except that he could never have protected Will
from all the harsh burdens of being their father's heir.

"I suppose so," he said. "I do not often think of my
boyhood."

"You had not met Lord Twynham before this afternoon," she said, looking at him. "But you had met Claudia. Were she and William married before you left?"

"A month before," he said curtly. He did not want to
talk about Claudia. Or about Will. He did not want to
talk.

"She is very beautiful," she said.

"Yes." She was still looking at him. "Yes, my sister-in-law
is a lovely woman."

Fortunately there was no time for further conversation. The family was assembled in the drawing room,
and dinner was ready. Marianne and Claudia, he saw at
a glance—Augusta doubtless was not allowed to join
the family for dinner—were both splendidly gowned
and decked out in jewels. The men were all immaculately tailored, as was he. Formal dress for dinner had
always been a rule at Enfield, even when they dined
merely *en famille,* as they did tonight.

"My lady?" The duke was bowing and offering Charity his arm to lead her in to dinner. It was something he
would do, of course, because it was the correct thing to
do. He would also seat her opposite himself, at the foot
of the table. But how it must gall him to be compelled to
show such deference to a woman who looked—and had
very recently been—the quintessential governess.

She smiled warmly at him and laid her arm along his. "Thank you, Father," she said.

The marquess pursed his lips. He had not for a moment expected such warm charm as his wife was displaying, but he was not sorry for it. It was, in fact, preferable to the timid, demure behavior he had anticipated and hoped for. Life at Enfield had never been conducive to smiles—or to warmth. And none of the Duke of Withingsby's own children had ever addressed him by any more familiar name than *sir*. He wondered if his wife had noticed that, and concluded that she probably had. He almost wished that she would call his grace *Papa*. He suppressed a grin.

But he sobered instantly. Was he expected to lead in Claudia as the lady next in rank to his wife? But William, he was relieved to see, was already offering her his arm. William, who had not exchanged a word with him and scarcely a glance during tea. Once his closest friend and at the last his deadliest enemy. Well, it was all in the past. Twynham and Marianne were going in to dinner together. The marquess brought up the rear with Charles.

Charles also had had nothing to say to him during tea. He had been a twelve-year-old boy eight years ago—an active, intelligent lad who had looked on his eldest brother with open hero worship. There was no such look now. It had been impossible to explain to the boy just why he was leaving. He had not even attempted an explanation. He had left without saying good-bye. He had shed tears over the baby. He had been unwilling to risk them over his young brother.

"So you are the tallest of us after all," he said now.

"So it would seem," his brother said.

His grace, at the head of the table, bowed his head and they all followed suit. There was, of course, the solemn and lengthy prayer to be intoned before the food was served. It felt strange to be back, the marquess thought, to be among people who were strangers to him at the same time as they were almost as familiar to him as his own body. And he felt, after an interval of eight years, as if in some strange way he had carried them with him for all that time, as close as his own body. He felt all tangled up with them again, as if he were not free of them after all. It was a suffocating feeling.

He looked up as the prayer ended to see his wife at the foot of the table, smiling and turning to make conversation with William beside her. He felt such a relief that he had married her and brought her with him that for the moment it felt almost like affection.

CHARITY HAD LIED during dinner. When Marianne had asked about her family, in the supercilious way that appeared to come naturally to her, Charity had told the truth about her father—except that she had made no mention of his debts—but had claimed to be an only child. She had even been forced then to a second lie in explaining that her father's property had been entailed on a distant male relative and that as a consequence she had taken employment as a governess.

Despite what she had said to her husband earlier about her immunity to insult in this house, she had found herself unable to bear the thought of having her brothers and sisters subjected to the veiled contempt these people clearly felt for a family so low on the social scale when viewed from their superior height. She could not bear to watch the effect of poor Phil's story on them.

Her family was her own very private property. She would not even try to share them with these cold people. Part of her regretted what she had done in accepting the Marquess of Staunton's strange offer—for a number of reasons, not least of which was the lie it forced her to live. Part of her hugged to herself the knowledge that it would all ultimately be worthwhile—she would be re-united with her family and no one would ever again be able to force them apart.

The duke looked along the length of the table at her when they had finished eating and raised his eyebrows. She smiled at him—how difficult it was to continue smiling and not give in to the oppressive atmosphere of the house!—and rose to her feet to lead the other two ladies from the room.

Claudia was the only one who talked to her. She told Charity more about her two boys, whom Charity had met briefly in the nursery after tea, and said that she must come to the dower house tomorrow to see them again.

"Though of course," she added, "the houseguests are expected tomorrow afternoon. You must come in the morning, then, unless you are a late riser. I daresay you are not, though, if you are accustomed to presiding over a schoolroom." Her words were spoken without any apparent contempt.

The houseguests—yes. The duke had spoken of them at dinner. The Earl and Countess of Tillden and their daughter were coming. It surprised Charity that guests were expected when the duke was clearly ill and it had been his failing health that had caused him to summon her husband home. But perhaps the earl and his family were close friends. Somehow it was difficult to think of the Duke of Withingsby as having close friends.

Certainly the advent of guests would add to her own awkward position. She had no experience with anyone more illustrious than Sir Humphrey Loring. And she had so few clothes, and nothing at all suitable for such company. But she would not allow herself to panic. That was the whole point, after all, was it not? She had been brought here in order to be an embarrassment.

"Lady Staunton," Marianne said loudly when the gentlemen had joined them in the drawing room, "do please favor us with a rendering on the pianoforte. I will not insult you by asking if you play. Teaching the instrument must have been one of your duties as a governess."

"Yes, indeed," Charity said, getting to her feet. "And I had the best of teachers too, Marianne. My mother taught me."

The pianoforte was a magnificent instrument. Charity had been itching to play it ever since teatime. She sat and played, aware as she did so that the duke stood before the fireplace. Marianne began to converse and laugh with her brothers and sister-in-law, Lord Twynham settled low on a sofa for an after-dinner nap, and the marquess stood behind the pianoforte bench.

"Wonderful, my love," he said when she was finished, smiling into her eyes and taking her hand to raise to his lips. "Will you not play again—for me?"

"Not tonight, Anthony," she said, leaning slightly toward him and looking into his eyes with warm affection before he released her hand—she had not really expected when she had agreed to all this that she would be called upon to playact. It felt disturbingly dishonest. But something else had been bothering her. She got to her feet and crossed the room to the fireplace. She hesitated for a moment—the Duke of Withingsby was a very formidable gentleman. It would be so easy to fall into the habit of cowering before him. And it was not part of her agreement to do anything more than be her husband's shadow. But she would not cower. She slipped her arm through his and smiled as his eyes came to hers in open amazement.

"Father," she said, "will you not have a seat? You look very tired. Shall I ring for the tea tray and pour you a cup of tea?" He looked downright ill. He looked as if he held himself upright by sheer effort of will.

A strange hush fell on the room. Even breathing seemed to have been suspended.

"Thank you for your concern, my lady," his grace said

after what seemed to be an interminable silence, "but I stand by choice. And I do not drink tea in the evening."

"Oh." She seemed to be stranded now, holding on to his arm with nothing further to do or say and with nowhere to go. "Then I shall stand here with you for a short while. The paintings in this room are all landscapes. Are there any portraits elsewhere? Family portraits?"

"There is a gallery," his grace said while everyone else continued to listen with apparently bated breath. "With family portraits, yes. It will be my pleasure to escort you there tomorrow morning, ma'am."

"Thank you," she said. "I should like that. Is there one of you? And of—of Anthony?"

He pursed his lips and reminded her even more of her husband. And then he told her of the family portrait that had been painted only two years before her grace's passing. He spoke of some older family portraits, including two by Van Dyck, one by Sir Joshua Reynolds.

His hand, Charity noticed, was long-fingered and well manicured, like his son's hands. It was also parchment white, the skin thinly stretched over the blue veins. He had not lied in order to lure his son home, she thought. He was ailing. She felt sad for him. She wondered if he was capable of love. She wondered if he had loved his wife. She wondered if he loved his children, if he loved her husband.

And she reminded herself that she was not interested in this family, that she was here merely to act out a charade, merely to earn her future with her own family. She wanted as little as possible to do with this strange, cold, lonely man and with his silent, morose, troubled family. And with his son, whom she had married just the day before and with whom she had lain last night. Her husband. Her temporary husband.

It had been an odd, disturbing day. She was glad it was almost at an end.

8

THE MARQUESS OF STAUNTON HAD WOKEN AT DAWN and found himself unable to sleep again even though it had taken him a long time to get to sleep the night before. He had lain down and stared upward in the near-darkness at the familiar pattern of the canopy above his bed. He had stood at the window gazing out at moonlit darkness, his fingernails drumming on the windowsill. There had been a sheen of moonlight across the lake.

He had felt restless. His brain had teemed with jumbled memories of the day—his father's gray complexion, Charles's transformation from an awkward boy to a tall, self-assured young man, Claudia's mature beauty, William's reticence, Augusta's formality, Marianne's affectionate treatment of himself, his wife seated behind the tea tray at teatime, his wife making conversation with Twynham and Will at dinner, his wife playing the pianoforte very precisely and skillfully, his wife with her arm linked through the duke's, smiling at him and forcing him into conversation.

He had smiled himself at that last memory. His grace hated to be touched. He never smiled or was smiled at. No one ever initiated conversation with him. And of course no one ever called him Father.

She was quite perfect. She was far better than the quiet

mouse he had thought would do the trick. As a mouse she would merely have been despised. She would not have disturbed the atmosphere of the house. As she was, she was causing alarm and outrage. Doubtless the very, *very* correct Duke of Withingsby and his offspring thought her vulgar. She was not, but in their world spontaneity was synonymous with vulgarity. And she was his *wife,* the future duchess. The knowledge would gall them beyond bearing.

And he had understood, standing there at the window, one definite reason for his insomnia. She was in the next room, only their two dressing rooms separating them. She was his wife. The night before he had consummated their marriage and she had responded with flattering passion. He would not at all mind repeating the experience, he had realized in some surprise—he really did not think of her as desirable.

He had gone back to bed and lain awake for some time longer, remembering the smell of her hair. It was strange how a smell—or the absence of a smell—could keep one awake. And soap! He had never found even the most expensive of perfumes particularly alluring. He could remember breathing in the smell of her hair very deliberately as his body had pumped into hers, and enhancing his own sexual pleasure with the sense of smell.

There had been definite pleasure, not just physical release.

At dawn he was awake again and could not get back to sleep. The sky looked bright beyond the curtains at his windows. There was a chorus of birdsong in progress. It was an aspect of country living he had forgotten. He threw back the bedclothes impatiently. He would go for a ride, blow away some cobwebs, rid himself of the feeling of oppression the house brought to him.

But when he stepped through the front doors some minutes later, on his way to the stables, he stopped short at the top of the marble steps. On the terrace below him stood his little brown mouse, her head turned back over her shoulder to look up at him. She was up and dressed and outside at only a little past dawn?

"Good morning, my lady," he said, amazed that he could have lain awake last night wanting this drab creature—even her eyes were shadowed by the brim of her brown bonnet.

"I could not sleep," she said. "The birds and the sunshine were in conspiracy against me. I have been standing here undecided whether to walk to the lake or up onto the hill."

"Try the hill," he suggested. "A picturesque walk has been laid out there and will lead you to several panoramic views over the park and estate and surrounding countryside."

"Then I will go that way," she said.

He tapped his riding crop against his boots, undecided himself for a few moments. "Perhaps," he said abruptly, "you will permit me to accompany you?"

"Of course." She half smiled at him.

He walked beside her, his arms at his sides. She clasped hers behind her. She walked with rather long strides, he noticed, as if perhaps she was used to the countryside. But she walked gracefully too. What had life with her father been like? How long ago had her mother died? Was she dreadfully lonely? Had the father been quite unable to make provision for her, even knowing that his estate had been entailed on a male relative? Had the relative been unwilling to provide for her? Did she miss her home and the countryside and the life of a lady? Had there been love in her home? Had there been love *outside* it—had there been a man she had had to leave behind in order to work as a governess? He was glad when she spoke and made him aware of the direction of his thoughts. He had no wish to feel curiosity about her or to know anything about her beyond what was necessary for his purposes.

"Your father really is ill," she said. "Have you discovered what is wrong with him and how serious it is?"

He had spoken briefly with Marianne in the drawing room last evening. "It is his heart," he said. "He has had a few mild attacks during the past few months. The physician has warned him that another could be fatal. He has advised almost constant bed rest."

"I believe," she said, "that your father finds it difficult to accept advice."

"That," he said, "would probably be the understatement of the decade."

"Perhaps," she said, "he would listen to you if you spoke with him. Perhaps he invited you home with the hope that you would speak, that you would lift the burdens of his position from his shoulders."

He laughed, entirely without humor, and her head turned in his direction.

"Do you love him?" she asked quietly.

He laughed again. "That is a foolish question, my lady," he said. "I broke off all communication with him for eight years. During those years I deliberately made myself into everything he would abhor. I lived recklessly, I involved myself in business and investments, I made a fortune independently of the land, and I became—"

"A rake." She completed the sentence for him when he hesitated.

"I freed myself," he said, "from him and from all this. When I returned, I came as myself, on my own terms. No, I do not love him. There is nothing to love. And I am incapable of love even if there were. You were perfectly correct yesterday when you commented on my likeness to my father."

"Why *did* he ask you to come back here?" she asked.

"With the intention of asserting his dominance over

me once more," he said. "With the intention of making me into the person he had planned for me to be since birth so that I might be worthy of carrying on the traditions he has so meticulously upheld."

"And perhaps," she said, "so that he might see his son again before he dies."

"Tell me, my lady," he said, his voice testy, "do you read romantical novels? Sentimental drivel? Do you picture to yourself an affecting deathbed scene in which father and son, drenched in tears, the rest of the family sobbing quietly in the background, are finally reconciled? Finally declare their love for each other? Promise to meet in heaven? *Pardon and Peace*—the book might be called that. Or *The Prodigal Son,* though that title has already been spoken for, I believe?"

"But not in a sentimental novel," she said. "In the Bible, my lord."

"Ah. *Touché,*" he said.

She smiled softly at him and said no more. He was agitated. Her silence had deprived him of the opportunity to work off his irritation on her. They had reached the rhododendron grove and the graveled path began to climb. Soon it would turn and they would reach the little Greek folly, from which there was an uninterrupted view down over the house and the lake beyond it.

Perhaps it was time she knew the full truth behind their marriage. "His grace summoned me home in order to marry me to the bride he chose for me seventeen years ago," he said and felt a sense of almost vicious satisfaction when her head jerked around so that she could gaze at him. "A dynastic marriage, you will understand, ma'am. The lady is the daughter of the Earl of Tillden, a nobleman of ancient lineage and vast properties, a man as high in the instep as Withingsby himself."

Her eyes widened—he could see them clearly now

even beneath the brim of her bonnet. "They are the visitors expected here this afternoon," she said.

He smiled. "I was expected to come home and to conduct a very brief courtship of Lady Marie Lucas, to celebrate my betrothal to her at a ball planned for tomorrow evening, and to marry her before summer is out," he said. "I was expected then to do my duty by getting my heirs and my daughters on her annually for the next twenty years or so. The Duchesses of Withingsby are chosen young, you see, so that there are sufficient fertile years ahead of them. It is a pity, after all, to waste such impeccable lineage on a mere couple or so of children, is it not?"

She had stopped walking. They stood facing each other. "And so you advertised for a governess and offered your chosen candidate marriage," she said. "What a splendid joke." She did not sound amused.

"I thought so," he said, his eyes narrowing. "I still think so. The guests will arrive this afternoon, my lady, unaware that they come in vain."

Her eyes searched his and he felt the familiar urge to take a step back. He did not do so. There was something unfamiliar in her eyes—anger? Contempt? He raised one eyebrow.

"I believe, my lord," she said, "you were less than honest with me. I did not know I was to be used as an instrument of cruelty. I believe I might have rejected your offer had I known."

"Cruelty?" he said.

"How old is she?" she asked.

"Seventeen," he said.

"And she is coming here today for her betrothal," she said. "But she will find you already married—to me. To a woman who is older than herself and by far her social inferior. Oh, yes, my lord, you are to be congratulated. It was a diabolical plot and is working very nicely indeed."

Her quiet contempt goaded him. How dared she!

"It seems to me, my lady," he said, "that you were ready enough to take my money and enrich yourself for a lifetime. You asked precious few questions about what would be required of you as my wife. The only question that seemed to concern you was my ability to fulfill my financial commitment to you. You forced up my price. You insisted upon an extra clause that ensured a continuation of your annual allowance in the event that I predecease you. And are you now to preach morality to me?"

Her chin jerked upward and she continued to look at him, but she flushed deeply.

"I have never made any promise to Lady Marie Lucas," he said. "I have never had the smallest intention of marrying her."

"But it did not occur to you to write to your father explaining this," she said, "telling him firmly that it would not do and that he must inform the Earl of Tillden of your decision. Instead you married me and brought me here to embarrass and humiliate them all."

"Yes," he said curtly, thoroughly irritated with the way she was making him feel *guilty*. He had no reason for guilt. His life was his own. He had made that clear eight years ago, and if the message had not been taken, then he was making it crystal clear now.

She opened her mouth as if to speak, but she closed it again and turned to walk on. He fell into step beside her. "Perhaps," she said at last, "she has had a fortunate escape, poor girl. One would not wish an innocent child of seventeen on you."

"You, of course," he said, "are far better able to handle me."

"I do not have to," she said. "When may I leave? After today's humiliation is complete?"

"No," he said. "I will need you for a while yet." He

must stay here for a while yet. There would be no real need to do so after today. He could return to his life in town and feel assured that his family would never trouble him again. But having come back, he knew he could not go again so soon or so easily. His father was ill, probably dying. William and Charles were his brothers. Marianne and Augusta were his sisters. Having seen them again, he felt the burden of the relationships again. And one day—perhaps soon—he would be head of the family. No, something had to be settled before he left Enfield—and before he could set his wife free. He was not sure what he meant by a settlement—not at all sure.

They walked onward in silence until she noticed the folly and stopped again.

"Walk around to the front," he told her. "There is a splendid view. There is even a seat inside the pavilion if you wish to sit for a while."

She did as he suggested though she did not sit. She stood for a long while in front of the folly, looking down at the house and beyond it. The scene was at its best, bathed in early-morning sunshine. If they had heard a chorus of birdsong from the house, there were whole vast choirs of them at work here.

"It will all be yours," she said after a lengthy silence. She seemed to be speaking more to herself than to him. "Yet you do not feel the need to pass it on to a son of your own."

He turned his head sharply to look at her. She stood with a very straight back and lifted chin. Such a proud, erect posture was characteristic of her, he realized. Dressed differently, she would look like a duchess. And dressed differently, she would look beautiful. It was a jolting thought. Not that dress created beauty, of course—it merely enhanced it. But he was already familiar enough with her face to admit—reluctantly—that it possessed far more beauty than he had thought at first.

She had been wearing a careful disguise of nonentity when she came to her interview on Upper Grosvenor Street. Only the eyes had almost given her away, and she had been clever enough to keep them hidden most of the time.

"You would do well to hope," he said, his eyes sweeping over her, "that I do not change my mind."

She looked back at him—and blushed.

"I will not change my mind," he said despite the alarming surge of desire her words and the look of her had aroused. "What happened between us two nights ago, though pleasant enough, was a mistake. It might yet have consequences. We will have to hope not. But you may rest assured that I will never again put you in danger of conceiving."

She did not look away from him despite the blush, which did not recede. She tipped her head to one side and prolonged the gaze. "I believe," she said at last, "that you must have loved your mother very deeply."

For a moment he was almost blinded by fury. He clasped his hands very tightly at his back, drew a few slow breaths, and was very thankful for the iron control he had always been able to impose upon his temper.

"My mother," he said very quietly, "is not a topic for discussion between us, my lady. Not now, not ever. I trust you understand?"

It was a question that could be answered in only one way and with only one word, but nevertheless she appeared to be considering the question.

"Yes," she said. "Yes, I believe that perhaps I do."

"Shall we climb higher?" He indicated the continuing path with one hand. "There are some different and equally magnificent views from higher up." He should have gone riding, he thought. He should have kept to himself.

"I think not this morning," she said. "Your father is to

show me the portrait gallery after breakfast, though I shall try not to keep him there too long. I shall try to persuade him to rest afterward."

"You do that," he said, pursing his lips.

"And then I am to call upon Claudia at the dower house," she said.

He nodded curtly. Let her do that too. Let her make friends with Claudia and with Will and with the whole lot of them if she could. She might find it harder than she imagined. Let her make friends with Tillden and with Lady Marie this afternoon. He should be feeling more than ever triumphant this morning. But she had succeeded in making him feel thoroughly out of sorts.

"Allow me to escort you back to the house for breakfast, then," he said. Though he doubted anyone else would be up even yet.

"Perhaps," she said, "you would care to accompany me? To the dower house, I mean. You did not have much opportunity to talk with your brother yesterday. And I suppose you have not yet met your nephews."

"My heirs after William?" he said. "No, I have not. Unfortunately I have other plans for this morning."

She circled around the folly ahead of him and they set off down the slope. They walked in silence, not touching.

But he spoke again as they approached the house—reluctantly, not at all sure he wanted to do what he was about to say he would do.

"Perhaps my other business of this morning can be postponed," he said. "Perhaps I will accompany you to the dower house." That was where they lived, he had discovered last evening, William and Claudia and their two sons. "After all we have been married for only two days and are deep in love and will not wish to be separated unnecessarily." His tone sounded grudging even to his own ears.

"And William is your brother," she said, smiling at him.

Yes. And William was his brother. And there were some ghosts to lay to rest, as he had realized yesterday.

PERHAPS THE DUKE of Withingsby lacked the ability to love, Charity thought, though she was by no means convinced of it—she did not really believe that it was possible to be human and incapable of love. But certainly he was capable of a pride bordering on love.

He had been at breakfast when she and her husband had returned from their early-morning walk and had entered the breakfast parlor together. He had stood and made her a courtly bow, at the same time sweeping her brown walking dress and her simple chignon—she had not summoned her maid when she had risen early—with haughty eyes.

Immediately after breakfast he had brought her to the portrait gallery, which stretched along the whole width of the house, and had proceeded to show her the family portraits and to describe their subjects and, in certain cases, the artists who had painted them. He displayed a pride and a degree of warmth she had not seen in him before.

"The people Van Dyck painted," she said, stepping closer to one canvas displaying a family grouping, "all look alike. It is not just the pointed beards and curled mustaches and the ringlets that were fashionable at the time. It has something to do with the shape of the face and the eyes—and the sloping shoulders. His paintings are easily distinguishable anywhere."

"And yet," he said, "I believe you will agree, ma'am, that the Duke of Withingsby depicted here bears a remarkable resemblance to your husband."

He did. She smiled at the likeness. "And to you too,

Father," she said. "But then I think I have never seen a father and son who so resemble each other." *And who so love and so hate each other,* she thought. She did not believe she was wrong.

"That terrier," he said, pointing with his cane to a little dog held in the arms of a satin-clad, ringleted boy, "is reputed to have saved his young master's life when the boy fell into a stream and struck his head. The dog barked ceaselessly until help arrived."

"The boy who is holding him?" she asked, stepping closer still to examine both the child and the dog.

"The duke's heir," he said. "My ancestor."

"Oh." She turned and smiled full at him. "So you owe your life too to that little dog."

"And you owe your husband to it, ma'am," he said, raising haughty eyebrows.

"Yes." She felt herself blushing for some unknown reason. But she knew the reason even as she realized that her father-in-law was noting and misinterpreting her flushed cheeks. She blushed because she was deceiving him, because even though she really was married to his son, she was not truly his wife. She did not want to deceive. It would have been far better if her husband had come alone to Enfield Park to confront his grace, to assert his determination to live his life his way and to choose his own bride in his own time.

He moved along to the next painting and the next until they stood at last before the most recent. She gazed at it mutely, as did his grace.

He looked a good deal younger in the portrait. With his very dark hair and healthy coloring, he looked more than ever like his son. The Marquess of Staunton— proud, youthful, handsome—stood at his shoulder. The other young man must be Lord William, though he looked different in more than just age from the man she had met the day before. He looked—sunny and carefree.

Marianne had not changed a great deal. The solemn child must be Charles. No one had smiled for the painter, though William seemed to smile from within.

"She must have been beautiful," Charity said. She referred to the duchess, who sat beside her husband, looking full at the beholder. Though the least striking in looks of any of them, she seemed, strangely enough, to be the focal point of the portrait, drawing the eyes more than the child did, or than the haughty duke himself, more than her proud eldest son. The painter, Charity thought, had been fascinated by her. There was a look of faded beauty about her, though it was probable that the artist had downplayed the faded part. But he had not erased the look of sadness in her eyes.

"She was the most celebrated beauty of her time," the duke said stiffly.

Was that why he had married her? For her beauty? Had he also loved her? She had borne him thirteen children. But that fact proved neither love nor lack of love. She was Anthony's mother, Charity thought. The woman about whom he still felt so deeply that he had turned to ice this morning when she had suggested to him that he must have loved her.

"She was the eldest daughter of a duke," his grace continued. "She was raised from the cradle to be my bride. She did her duty until the day of her death."

Giving birth to Augusta. Charity felt chilled. *Had* he loved her? More to the point, perhaps—had she loved him? She had done her duty . . .

I am the daughter of a gentleman, she wanted to say. *I was raised to be a lady. I too know my duty and will perform it to the day of my death.* But it was not really true, was it? She had married just two days ago and had made all sorts of promises that would never be kept. She had made a mockery of marriage—for the sake of money. Her husband had been very right about that this morning, when she had been outraged to discover just why he had married her in such haste and brought her here. She felt a pang of guilt and was surprised that she should feel so defensive, so eager to justify herself to this stern man who never smiled and who appeared to have inspired no love in his children.

"Father," she said, taking his arm, "you have been on your feet for long enough. I am truly grateful that you have brought me here and shared your family—Anthony's family—with me. But let me take you somewhere where you may rest. Tell me where."

"I suppose," his grace said, "Staunton did not even offer to clothe you in suitable fashion for your change in station."

He had silenced her for a moment. She was horribly aware of her drab walking dress, from which she should have changed for breakfast and certainly for this visit to the gallery. But she had so little else into which to change. She did not release his arm. "We married in haste, Father," she said. "Anthony wanted to come here without delay. He was anxious about your health. There was no time for shopping. I do not mind. Clothes are unimportant."

"On the contrary," he said, "appearance is of the utmost importance—especially for a woman of your present rank. You are the Marchioness of Staunton, ma'am. And of course he married you in haste. I wonder if you know *why* he married you. Are you naive enough to imagine that you are beloved, ma'am, merely because of melting looks and kisses on the hand and the conjugal activity that doubtless occurred in your bedchamber last night? If you harbor dreams of love and happily-ever-afters, you will without a doubt be severely hurt."

She swallowed. "I believe, Father," she said as gently yet as firmly as she could, "it is for Anthony and me to work out the course of our marriage and the degree of love it will contain."

"Then you are a fool," he said. "There is no *we* in a marriage such as yours. Only Staunton. You are a wife, a possession, ma'am, of sufficiently lowly rank to enable him to demonstrate to me how much he scorns me and all I stand for. He will get children on you so that he may flaunt to me and to the world the inferiority of their mother's connections."

This, Charity thought, still clinging to his arm, almost dizzy with hurt, was how she was earning her money. For Phil. For Penny. For the children. She would not lose sight of the purpose of it all. How *glad* she was now that she had had the foresight to declare herself an only child.

"Do you *feel* scorned, Father?" she asked. "Are you hurt by Anthony's marriage to me?"

He did not answer her for several silent moments. "If I am, ma'am," he said at last, "Staunton will never have the satisfaction of knowing it. You will see that I am not without resources of my own. Most games are intended for more than one player. And most games are truly interesting only when the participants play with equal skill and enthusiasm. Yes, my dear ma'am, I am feeling fatigued. You may help me downstairs to my library and then ring for refreshments for me. You may read the morning papers to me while I rest my head and close my eyes. You are promised to Lady William for later this morning? I will spare you after an hour, then, but not before that. My son came home to me yesterday, bringing me also a daughter-in-law. It behooves me to become acquainted with her. It would not surprise me to discover that I will grow markedly fond of her."

His voice was chilly, his eyes more so. But it did not take a genius, Charity thought, to guess what game it was his grace had decided to play. She had known from the start, of course, that she was to be a pawn. She had just not known the extent of her involvement in that role. But it seemed that every hour brought her a fuller understanding of what she had got herself into.

She supposed she deserved every moment of discomfort that had already happened and that was still to come.

9

HE WAS NOT LOOKING FORWARD TO THE REST OF the day. He was not enjoying himself at all. But then he had not expected enjoyment. Only a satisfying sense of triumph. There was still that, of course, but his wife had dampened it considerably during their early-morning walk by accusing him of cruelty. Cruelty to a young lady he could remember only as a plain and gawky child playing with Charles.

If he had come alone, he thought, he probably would have ended up marrying the girl. Even after the eight years of independence and the conviction that he was free of his father. If he had come home alone, and if Tillden had come with his daughter, he would have found it extremely difficult to avoid the betrothal everyone expected. It would have seemed more cruel then to have said no.

He was not a cruel man, merely one who wished to be left alone to live his own life. But when one was the heir to a dukedom, one did not belong to oneself, not unless one went to unusual lengths to assert one's independence.

He was walking down the driveway with his wife, on the way to the dower house to call upon Claudia. He had had no chance to assess his feelings about the visit. He did not want to assess them. He wondered if William would be at home. He wondered if he would be forced to meet the children.

"You went into the village earlier?" his wife asked.

"Yes," he said. "I went to talk to his grace's physician. The man has been brought from London merely to tend to his health, but according to his own complaints, he is abused and ignored at every turn."

"Your father is sick," she said. "He tires very easily."

"He is dying," he said. "It *is* his heart. It is very weak. It could fail him any day or it could keep him going for another five years. But he refuses to rest and to turn over his responsibilities to a steward's care, as he has been advised to do."

"Then we must persuade him to do so," she said.

They had stepped onto the Palladian bridge and had stopped by unspoken assent to view the river and the lawns and trees through the framework of the pillars.

We? He looked at her sharply and raised his eyebrows. "We must?" he asked.

She was alerted by his tone and turned her head to look back at him. "He called you home," she said. "He must have found it difficult to do so, to make the first move when he is such a proud man. He wants to settle his affairs, my lord. He wanted to see you married to the lady of his choice. He wanted to see you take over from him here so that he could rest and face his end in the knowledge that the future was assured."

"He wanted the feeling of power again," he said curtly.

"Call it what you will," she said. "But you came. Oh, it was on your own terms, as you keep assuring both me and yourself. But you need not have come at all. You had made your own life and your own fortune. You had left intending never to return. But you did return. You even took the extraordinary step of marrying a stranger before you did. You came."

She had the unerring ability to arouse intense irritation in him. It must be the governess in her, he decided. "What are you trying to say, ma'am?" he asked.

"That you never did break free," she said. "That you still love your father."

"Still, my lady?" he said. "*Still*? Your powers of observation are quite defective, I do assure you. Have you not seen that there is no love whatsoever in this family—or in your husband? You see what you wish to see with your woman's sensibilities."

"And he still loves you," she said.

He made an impatient gesture with one arm and signaled her to walk on. The picturesque view was lost on them this morning anyway.

"You can make his last days peaceful," she said, "and in the process you can make some peace with yourself, I believe. There is the embarrassment of this afternoon to be faced, and of course there will never be the eligible alliance your father had hoped for. But all may yet turn out well. You can stay here—there is nothing in London that makes it imperative that you return there, I daresay. And I believe your father may come to accept and even to like me a little."

There was so much to be commented upon in her short speech that for a few moments he was rendered quite speechless.

"His grace may come to *like* you a little?" he said at last. Did this woman suffer from delusions in addition to everything else?

"He showed me the gallery," she said, "and of course thoroughly exhausted himself in the process. He allowed me to help him downstairs to the library and to set a stool for his feet and a cushion for his head. He allowed me to read the papers to him while he closed his eyes. He would spare me at the end of an hour, he said, only because I had promised to call upon Claudia."

The devil! He was speechless again.

"I know you came here for a little revenge," she said, "but you can stay for a more noble reason, my lord. We can make him happy."

"*We.*" He might have shouted with laughter at the notion of the Duke of Withingsby being happy if he had not also been pulsing with fury. "You, I believe, my lady, are forgetting one very important thing. His grace may live for five years, or conceivably even longer. *We* could make him happy for all that time? How, pray? By proving to him that it is a marriage made in heaven? By presenting him with a series of grandchildren? Are you quite sure you wish to expand our business arrangement to include so much time and so much, ah, activity?"

He had silenced her at last. And of course, as he fully expected, she was blushing rosily when he turned his head to look at her. But an idea struck him suddenly. She had no family. Apparently she had no friends. She had no one. Perhaps . . . Exactly what was she up to?

"Perhaps," he said, his eyes narrowing on her, "it is what you hope for, ma'am. Perhaps you would like to emulate my mother with seventeen pregnancies during the next twenty years. I might be persuaded to comply with your wishes. My own part in such an undertaking would, after all, be slight—and not by any means unpleasurable."

"I would be a fool," she said quietly, "to want a relationship of any extended duration with you, my lord. You are not a pleasant man. The only reason I endure you at all is that I cling to the belief that somewhere behind your very carefully shuttered eyes is a person who perhaps would be likable if he would only allow himself to be seen. And there is nothing so very horrifying about large families. They happen. The agony of losses in childbirth or infancy is often offset by the great happiness of family closeness and love."

"Something you would know a great deal about," he said. He heard the sneer in his voice at the same moment as he saw the tears spring to her eyes. She had no one. Even her parents were dead, and she was only three-and-twenty.

"I beg your pardon," he said stiffly. "Please forgive me. The words were spoken heedlessly and hurt you."

When she looked at him, her eyes were still large with tears. How could he ever have convinced himself that she was plain? he thought. But irritation saved him from feeling more discomfort. Damn it all, but she was becoming a person to him. A person with feelings. He did not want to have to cope with someone else's feelings. When, for God's sake, was the last time he had apologized to anyone? Or felt so wretchedly in the wrong?

"You have a father," she said, "and brothers and sisters and nephews and nieces. They are all here with you now. Perhaps tomorrow or next month or next year they will all be gone. Perhaps you will be separated from them and it will not be easy or even possible to be with them again. Pride and other causes I know nothing of have kept you from them for eight years. You have been given another chance. Life does not offer unlimited chances."

Lord. Good Lord! Deuce and the devil take it! He had married a preacher. One with large, soulful blue eyes that he would fall into headlong and drown in if he did not watch himself.

An avalanche of leaves cascading downward over his hat and into his face broke his train of thought. He was aware of his wife waving them away from her own face and exclaiming in surprise. There was the sound of muffled giggles. Well. He and Will had done the same thing once with gravel and had been soundly spanked for it, the two of them, by the head gardener, who had soothed their pain when he was finished by promising not to report them to his grace.

His wife was looking upward, her head tipped right back. "It must be autumn," she said with loud and exaggerated surprise in her voice and in her expression, "and all the leaves are falling off the trees. I believe if you raise your cane, my lord, and swish it through the lower branches, you will dislodge more of them."

More smothered giggles.

"It is not autumn, my lady," he said, "but elves. If I poke them with my cane, they are like to fall out of the tree and break their heads. Perhaps I should give them a chance to come down on their own."

The giggles became open laughter and one small boy dropped onto the driveway in front of them. He was dirty and untidy and rosy with glee.

"We saw you coming, Aunt Charity," he said, "and lay in ambush."

"And we walked into the trap quite unsuspecting," she said. She looked up again. "Are you stuck, Harry?"

Harry was. It seemed that he was marvelously intrepid about climbing trees but found it quite impossible to descend again—or so his brother claimed. The marquess reached up and lifted him down. He was quite as dirty as the other child. He was also blond and green-eyed and scarcely past babyhood. He was just as his own son might have looked, the marquess thought, if he had married . . .

"You may make your bows to your Uncle Anthony," his wife was saying. "These two elves are Anthony and Harry, my lord."

"I was named for you, sir," the elder boy said. "Papa told me so."

Ah. He had not known that. So these were the two children they had produced, Will and Claudia.

"I am going to tell Mama that you are coming," Anthony said, taking to his heels.

"And I am going to tell Papa. You are not to tell first,

Tony." Harry went tearing along behind. He would not catch up, of course. Younger brothers never did. Until they grew up and could use stealth and deceit.

"We must be close to the dower house." His wife smiled at him.

"We are." And Will must be at home. "Take my arm. We are supposed to be in love, after all."

"You must smile, then," she reminded him.

"I shall smile," he promised grimly.

HE NOT ONLY smiled. He slid an arm about her waist and drew her closer to his side as they approached the house through neatly laid-out parterre gardens. But his arm, she could feel, was not relaxed. Neither were the smiles on the faces of Claudia and William, who had come out of the house to meet them. The little boys came dashing out ahead of them.

But at least they were smiling. They were all smiling.

"Charity," Claudia said, "I am so glad you came. And you brought Anthony. How delightful."

"Anthony?" William inclined his head. "My la—" He looked acutely embarrassed. "Charity. Welcome to our home."

There was something, Charity thought. Something very powerful. It was not just that he had offended them by going off eight years ago. They had married one month before he left. One month before Augusta's birth, before the duchess's death. Claudia was very beautiful. William and his elder brother were very close in age. Had her husband loved Claudia too?

"Thank you," she said. "It is very splendid. In fact yesterday when we were arriving, I mistook it for Enfield Park itself and was marvelously impressed."

They all joined in her laughter—all of them. She had never heard her husband laugh before. He was looking down at her—*He should be on the stage,* she thought—with warm tenderness in his eyes.

"You neglected to tell me that yesterday, my love," he said.

"You would have laughed at me," she said, "and I cannot abide being laughed at. Besides, I could not speak at all. I had my teeth clamped together so that they would not chatter. You would not believe how nervous I was."

"With me by your side?"

Her stomach performed a strange flip-flop. On the stage he would draw a dozen curtain calls for each performance.

"You were just as nervous," she said. "Confess, Anthony." She turned her face from him and smiled sunnily at the other two adults. "But the ordeal of yesterday is over and we may relax in congenial company—until this afternoon, that is. Your Anthony and Harry mounted a very successful ambush on us out on the driveway. We were showered with leaves. We had no chance at all to take cover."

"I will not ask if they were up in a tree," William said dryly. "There is a strict rule in this family that no tree is to be climbed unless an adult is within sight."

"There was an adult within sight," the marquess said. "Two, in fact. So no rule was broken."

"Uncle Anthony had to lift Harry down," Anthony said.

"Hence the rule," his father added. "Harry would find a whole day spent in the branches of a tree somewhat tedious, I do not doubt."

And so, Charity thought, they had established an atmosphere of near-relaxation through some pleasant and meaningless chitchat. But preliminaries had clearly come to an end.

"Charity." Claudia stepped forward to take her arm.

"Do come inside. I plan to tempt you. But perhaps we should consult Anthony first. We never go to town, a fact about which I make no complaint at all. But I do like fashionable clothes and it pleases William to see me well dressed—or so he declares when I twist his arm sufficiently. And so twice a year he brings a modiste from town down here to stay for a week or so with her two seamstresses. They are here now and I am trying my very best not to cost William a fortune. It has occurred to me that since the two of you married in such a hurry that you had no time to shop for bride clothes, you might wish to make use of her services too."

"Oh." Charity flushed and was afraid to turn her head in her husband's direction. The poverty of her wardrobe was very deliberate on his part. But was there any more to be proved by it now?

"I am to be saved after all, then," he said, "from the faux pas of having been so besotted and so much in a hurry to wed that I forgot I was bringing my wife directly from the schoolroom to Enfield? It is no excuse, is it, to protest that to me Charity would look beautiful dressed in a sack. Clearly his grace would disagree. Will you have clothes made, my love? For all possible occasions? However many you wish?"

Poor Anthony. He had been given very little choice. Charity could not resist looking at him and smiling impishly. "You may be sorry for offering me carte blanche," she said.

"Never." He grinned back at her and tipped his head toward hers. For one alarming moment she thought he was going to kiss her. "You must have something very special for tomorrow evening's ball."

The ball that was to have celebrated his betrothal to the Earl of Tillden's daughter? Would it still take place? She supposed it must. All the guests would have been invited. And she was to attend it? A full-scale ball? As the Marchioness of Staunton? She was not sure if the weakness in her knees was caused more by terror or excitement.

"Oh, splendid," Claudia said. "Come along, then. We will leave William and Anthony to become reacquainted— and to look after the boys, since their nurse has been given the morning off. Have you ever seen such ragamuffins, Charity? But in *this* house, you see, I insist that children are allowed to be children. And William supports me."

The two men, Charity saw, had been left standing face-to-face in the midst of the parterre gardens, looking distinctly uncomfortable. They were brothers, one year apart in age. What had happened between them? Was it Claudia?

But her mind did not dwell upon them. She would have had to be made of stone, she thought, as Claudia took her into the house, not to be excited at the thought of new clothes. And not just one new dress, but dresses for all occasions. As many as she wanted. It was a dizzying prospect. And a ball gown!

THEY STOOD QUIETLY facing each other while their wives walked away toward the house, arm in arm. The two little boys were running about the paths dividing the parterres, their arms outstretched. They were sailing ships, blown along by the wind.

The Marquess of Staunton met his brother's eyes at last. It was an acutely uncomfortable moment, but he would not be the first to look away—or to speak.

"She seems very—amiable," his brother said at last.

"Yes," the marquess said. "She is."

"I have feared that Lady Marie would not suit you," Lord William said. "I am glad you shocked us all to the roots and married for love after all, Tony."

"Are you?" The marquess looked coldly into his brother's eyes. "You have changed your opinions, then."

"I had hoped that in eight years all that business would be behind us," Lord William said with a sigh. "It is not, is it?"

"You argued most eloquently once upon a time against my making a love match," the marquess said, "and against my marrying beneath myself in station."

"An elopement would have been disastrous," his brother said. "And it would have been the only possible way. His grace would never have forgiven you."

The marquess smiled—not pleasantly. "Well," he said, "you showed a brother's care, Will. You saved me from myself and from our father's wrath. You married my bride yourself."

"She was not your bride," Lord William said sharply.

"And when I challenged you to meet me," the marquess said, "you went running to his grace for protection. I am glad you approve of my marrying for love, Will. Your good opinion means a great deal to me."

"Your eyes were clouded, Tony," his brother said. "You were beside yourself with worry over Mother—"

"Leave our mother out of this," the marquess said curtly.

"Mother was at the center of everything," Lord William said.

"Leave her out of it."

Lord William looked away and watched his sons blow out of control in the midst of an Atlantic storm and sail through a forbidden flower bed. He did not bellow at them, as he would normally have done.

"Come and see the stables," he said. "I have some mounts I am rather proud of." He called to the boys, who went racing off ahead of them, sailing ships and Atlantic storms forgotten. "I was less than thrilled when I knew you were coming home, I must confess, Tony.

Time had only increased the awkwardness. But we had to meet again sooner or later—his grace cannot survive another attack as severe as the last, I fear. Can we not put the past behind us? There are parts of it I am not proud of, but I would not have the outcome changed. I am comfortable with Claudia—more than comfortable. You do not still have—feelings for her, do you?"

"I love my wife," the marquess said quietly.

"Yes, of course," his brother said. "Everything has turned out rather well, then, has it not?"

"Admirably," the marquess said. "The stables here did not used to be in such good repair."

"No." Lord William paused in the doorway and looked to see that no groom was within earshot. "Friends, Tony? There is no one whose good opinion I crave more than yours."

"Perhaps," his brother said, "you should have thought of that, Will, before taking his grace's part over my chosen bride merely so that you might steal her from under my nose."

"Damn it all to hell!" Lord William cried, his temper snapping. "Is Claudia a mere object? A possession to be wrangled over? She had to consent, did she not? She had to say yes. She had to say *I do* during the marriage service. She said it. No one had a pistol pointed at her head. She married me. Did it ever occur to you that she loved me? I always took second place to you, Tony. You were so damned better this and better that at everything from looks to brains to sports, and of course you were the heir. I never resented any of it. You were my elder brother, my hero. But I do not suppose it even occurred to you that in one significant matter I outdid you. She loved *me*."

The Marquess of Staunton stood very still, his nostrils flared, his hands balled at his sides, reining in his temper. "This is all pointless stuff now, Will," he said. "You and Claudia share an eight-year marriage and two sons. I have recently married the woman of my choice. We will forget the past and be brothers again if it is what you wish. I wish it too." Damn his prim wife and her harping about family affection and second chances. Here he was *forgiving* the brother who had betrayed him?

Their eyes met once more—hostile, wary, unhappy.

Lord William was the first to hold out a hand. The marquess looked at it and then placed his own in it. They clasped hands.

"Brothers," Lord William said, but before the moment could become awkward again his two sons came dashing out from some inner stalls and wanted to show their uncle their ponies. And then they wanted their uncle to see them ride their ponies. They mounted up and rode about a fenced paddock, displaying the fact that they had been given some careful and superior training despite their youth.

Will loved his boys, the marquess thought, watching his brother's face as much as he watched the two children. There were pride and amusement and affection there—as well as a thunderous frown and a loud bellow of stern command when the older boy began to show off and threw his pony into confusion. Will had not followed in their father's footsteps. But then Will had always been able to withstand the gloom of Enfield better than the rest of them. He had been superior in that way too.

Had he really felt so very inferior?

Had he really won Claudia's love?

She had not married him in bitter resignation after it became obvious that she was not going to be allowed to have the man of her choice—himself—because she was a mere baronet's daughter?

Had she married for love?

It was a thought so new to him that he could not even begin to accept the possibility—the humbling possibility—that it might be true.

10

"*Y*OU ARE PROBABLY FURIOUS WITH ME," SHE SAID, "and that is why you are striding along looking shuttered and morose."

There were too many people at Enfield Park looking that way, she had decided. She was not going to be drawn into becoming one of them. And she was no longer going to be a meek observer—though from the start she had not been quite that. She had spent a splendid hour and a half with Claudia and Madame Collette—whose elaborate French accent acquired suspicious cockney overtones from time to time. They had pored over patterns and rummaged through fabrics. They had laughed and talked and measured and planned. The modiste, it appeared, was all but finished with Claudia's new clothes and had been planning—reluctantly, she declared—to return to London within a few days. But now she had agreed with great enthusiasm to go back to work, to produce a complete and fashionable wardrobe for her ladyship in very little more time than it took to snap her fingers—thus. The ball gown, of course, would take priority over all else.

Claudia had told all about the session when they had finally rejoined the men, and had forced from the marquess the declaration that he had never been so happy about anything in his life. He had smiled that dazzling smile again—directly into Charity's eyes.

But now he was striding along the driveway, staring straight ahead of him, looking too morose even to be satanic.

"*What?*" He stopped walking and swung around to face her, causing her to jump in some alarm. "Shuttered and morose, ma'am? Am I to grin inanely at the tree-tops? Am I to wax poetic about the beauty of the morning and the wonder of life? And why would I be furious with you?"

"You like me in brown," she said. "You approve of my sprigged muslin and my gray silk. You are not sorry for the fact that they are the full extent of my smart wardrobe. Now you are about to spend a fortune clothing me in lavish style for what remains of our few weeks together. You were trapped into it. But so was I, you must confess."

"I like you in brown!" he said, his eyes sweeping her from head to toe. "They are loathsome garments, my lady. The sooner they find their proper place at the bottom of a dustbin, the happier I shall be."

"Oh," she said. "You do not mind too much, then, that I will be replacing them soon—that *you* will be replacing them?"

"It was part of our agreement, was it not," he said, turning abruptly and walking on, "that I keep you in a style appropriate to your rank?"

Except that at the time he had not told her exactly what that rank was to be. And except that the agreement had referred to what she would be given *after* their separation. But she would not argue the point. She had always had sufficient vanity to enjoy acquiring new clothes. But very rarely had she had more than one new garment at a time. Claudia had insisted on a whole array of new clothes. Even the restricted number Charity had finally agreed to was dizzying.

So it was not her new clothes that had set her husband to striding homeward, looking as if he had swallowed sour grapes. He had spent that hour and a half with William and the children. With his own brother and nephews.

She touched his arm and looked into his face as she walked beside him. "Did you *talk* to William?" she asked. "Did you settle your quarrel?"

He stopped walking again, but he continued to look ahead, his lips pursed. "Tell me," he said, "have you always been a pestilential female?"

Philip would say so, though not perhaps in those exact words. Penny would not—Penny was always loyal and had often expressed admiration for her elder sister's unwillingness to sit back and allow life merely to happen around her. The children might agree, especially when she forced them into a room together after they had quarreled, instead of separating them as any sane adult would do, and would not allow them out again until they had settled their differences.

"Yes, I have," she said. "What was the quarrel about?"

His nostrils flared.

"It was about Claudia, was it not?" she said and then wished she had not. Some things were best not known for certain. It was true that she was not his wife in any normal sense and would not be spending more than a few weeks of her life with him. But even so she *was* his wife and she was still in the process of living through these few weeks.

He took her upper arm in a firm grasp suddenly and surprised her by marching her off the driveway and among the trees of the woods beyond it. It was dark and secluded and seemed very remote from civilization. He was angry. But she was not afraid.

"In the days of my foolish youth," he said, "when I believed in love and loyalty and fidelity and happily ever afters and all those other youthful fantasies, I set my sights upon Claudia. We practically grew up together—she is the daughter of a baronet who lives a mere six miles from here. I confided in my dearest friend, my brother, who was sympathetic yet sensible at the same time. He was sensible in the sense that he advised against the elopement I planned after his grace refused to countenance the match—Claudia was merely the daughter of a baronet and in no way worthy of the Marquess of Staunton, heir to Withingsby. Besides, a match had already been arranged for me. My brother advised patience. My mother advised boldness—love, she told me, was the only sound reason for marriage. But she was increasing again and very ill and I was loath to elope and leave her. And so my brother released me from all my dilemmas. He married Claudia himself—with his grace's blessing."

They had slowed their pace. He had released his hold on her upper arm. She wondered if he realized that he was holding her hand very tightly, his fingers laced with hers.

"He was afraid to tell you of his own feelings for her," she said. "And so he said nothing, even when it became imperative that something be said. People do that all the time. People can be such cowards, especially with those closest to them. He must have tortured himself over it for the last eight years."

"He need not have done so," he said. "I had a fortunate escape. I grew up. I learned the foolishness of all emotions. I learned how self-deluded we are when we believe in love."

"What do you believe in, then?" she asked him. "Everyone must believe in something."

"I believe in myself," he said, looking at her with

bleak eyes, "and in the control I have over my own life and my own destiny."

"Why did Claudia marry William," she asked, "if she loved you? If I loved you, I could not possibly marry anyone else, least of all your own brother."

"You *are* married to me," he said, and there was a thread of humor in his voice for a moment. "But you would be well advised never to love me, Charity."

Yes, she thought, she would. It would be a painful thing to love Anthony Earheart, Marquess of Staunton, her husband. But he had not answered her question.

"Did Claudia love you?" she asked.

"I believed so," he said. "She was all smiles with me and charm and friendly warmth—and beauty. Will says that she loved *him*, that theirs was a love match. It is the only explanation that would make sense of that marriage, perhaps. I used to torture myself wondering what power they had exercised over her, the two of them—Will and his grace."

"She never *told* you that she loved you?" Charity asked. "She never told you that she wished to marry you, that she would elope with you?"

"You have to understand this family," he said. "Nothing is done here with any spontaneity. I knew the difficulty with Claudia's lineage. Lady Marie Lucas was already nine years old. She had come here several times with her parents. I could not offer for Claudia before I knew quite certainly what I was able to offer and when I would be free to offer it. I was, after all, only twenty."

"I begin to understand," she said, "why eventually you decided to break free altogether. I can even understand why you gave up everything except your trust in yourself."

She could understand it, but she could not condone it. She wondered if he realized that life had lain dormant in him for eight years and was just beginning to erupt again. She wondered if he would allow it to erupt. But the choice might no longer be his. He had spoken with William earlier—William had told him that Claudia had loved *him*. Perhaps something had already begun, something that could not be stopped.

The trees thinned before them suddenly and she could see that the lake was directly ahead of them—and the lawns and the house beyond. But whereas all was open and cultivated on the opposite bank, here the trees grew almost to the water's edge, and beyond them were tall reeds. There was a wildness and an unspoiled beauty here—and civilization beyond.

They stopped walking. He was still holding her hand, though less tightly, less painfully.

"Without these woods and this lake," he said, his eyes squinting across the sun-speckled water, "I do not know how I would have made my boyhood supportable."

She said nothing to break his train of thought. He looked as if he had become unaware of her and was immersed in memory.

"Will and I played here endlessly," he said. "These woods were tropical jungles and underground caves and Sherwood Forest. Or they were a mere solitary retreat from reality. I taught Charles to climb trees here. I taught him to swim, to ride." He drew a deep breath and let it out slowly.

Yes, she knew all the power of childhood imagination, childhood companionship. She knew all the joy and sense of worth that nurturing younger brothers and sisters brought.

"Who taught you to be such a good listener?" he asked suddenly. His voice, which had become almost warm with memory, was brisker again. And his hand, she noticed, slid unobtrusively from hers—or in a manner that he must have hoped was unobtrusive. "Was it lonely growing up without brothers and sisters?"

She regretted her lie. She hated not speaking the truth. "I had childhood playmates," she said. "I had a happy childhood."

"Ah." He turned his head to look at her. "But it did not last. Life deals cruel blows quite indiscriminately. Life is nothing but a cruel joke."

"Life is a precious possession," she said. "It is what one makes of it."

"And you have been given the chance of making something quite bearable of yours after all," he said. "You are to be commended for seizing the chance without hesitation."

The mocking tone was back in his voice, the sneer in his face.

"And you have been given the chance," she said sharply, "of putting right what was wrong with your life when you ran from it eight years ago."

"Ah," he said. "You have an incurably impertinent tongue, my lady. But you mistake the matter. I ran away from suffocation. I ran to life."

"Are we late for luncheon?" she asked.

"The devil!" he said and surprised her by grinning until his eyes danced. "I would wager we are. It will be quite like old times except that his grace will probably not refuse to allow us to eat at all this time and probably will not have me wait in the library until he has finished eating and then invite me to bend over the desk to take my punishment. Hunger was never quite punishment enough, you see."

"Sternness, even excessive sternness, does not necessarily denote lack of love," she said.

He laughed and offered his arm. "You are a prim little moralist, ma'am," he said, "and talk with seeming wisdom on matters quite beyond your experience or comprehension. But then I married you for your primness, did I not? And for the hideous garments. You lied about one thing, though."

She raised her eyes to his as he hurried her through the trees in the direction of the bridge.

"You pretended to be a plain little mouse," he said. "You hid yourself very nicely indeed and should be thoroughly ashamed of yourself. I did not even suspect at the time that you are beautiful."

It was ridiculous—despicable—that such a grudging, backhanded compliment should please her so thoroughly that her knees felt weak. He thought her beautiful? Really? Even before he had seen her in her new clothes? Not that it made any difference to anything, of course. He was still a man from whom it would be an enormous relief to free herself in a few weeks' time. She was still merely the shield he had brought home with him so that he might prevent his family from penetrating his defenses. But he thought her beautiful?

"That has silenced you at least," he said.

He sounded, she thought, almost in a good humor.

THE DUKE OF Withingsby had decided against greeting his old friend the Earl of Tillden with all of the pomp he had shown his son the day before. The family was excused from gathering in the hall and were informed instead that they would be prompt in their attendance in the drawing room for tea. He sent a message to that effect to the dower house.

"Staunton and I will meet Tillden and his countess and daughter in the hall," he said.

They were sitting at the luncheon table. The marquess had already been made to feel his grace's silent displeasure for arriving ten minutes late for the meal. But he would not fall mutely into old habits.

"My wife will accompany us," he said.

"Lady Staunton," his grace said, "will await us in the library."

And it was after all pointless to argue further, his son decided. He did not do so.

And so he stood alone with his father a few hours later after word had been brought that the earl's carriage had been seen to cross the bridge. He felt nervous and embarrassed and despised himself heartily. None of this was his concern. He had never expressed an interest in Lady Marie Lucas. He had not been consulted on the decision to invite her, with her parents, to Enfield Park on the very day following his own expected arrival. His grace had taken a great deal for granted after eight silent years. The marquess had nothing for which to blame himself.

And yet he was nervous and embarrassed—and very relieved that his wife was waiting in the library, dressed in her sprigged muslin again and looking pale and calm.

The Earl of Tillden had not changed, the marquess thought as the man stepped into the great hall ahead of his womenfolk—as he himself had done just the day before, of course. Large in both height and girth, bald head gleaming, the earl might have looked genial if it had not been for the permanent frown line of dissatisfaction between his brows and if his mouth and nose had not been so unfortunately positioned in relation to each other that he always looked as if he were sniffing in disdain.

The countess appeared behind him, small and wraithlike, a perpetual smile on her face—and yet it appeared to be a smile of apology rather than of happiness. Sweet and spiritless she had always seemed—and still seemed.

Beside her was—Lady Marie Lucas. At least the marquess assumed it must be she. She was no longer, of course, the thin and gawky child he remembered. She was small, slender, and dainty, with a face of exquisite sweetness beneath hair that had used to be an almost carroty red but was now a vibrant auburn. She was a beauty by anyone's definition. And in the few moments before the duke began the ceremony of welcoming his guests, her hazel eyes found him and widened and she blushed.

She was an innocent child despite her seventeen years and her fashionable clothes and her great beauty, the marquess thought with considerable annoyance and discomfort.

"Tillden," his grace said, inclining his head graciously. "Your coachman has made good time. Ma'am, you are welcome to Enfield Park. I trust you had a pleasant journey. Lady Marie, you are welcome too."

There was a spirited exchange of greetings and bows and curtsies.

"Ah, Staunton," the earl said at last. "You arrived before us, then? Good to see you, my boy."

The Marquess of Staunton bowed. "Sir," he murmured.

"You will be surprised and doubtless gratified to see that our little Marie has grown up while you have been away," the earl said heartily, rubbing his hands together.

"And has grown into a great beauty," his grace said.

His son bowed again.

"You will do me the honor of stepping into the library before my housekeeper shows you to your rooms," his grace said.

"And how are you, Withingsby?" the earl asked as his grace offered his arm to Lady Tillden, and the marquess, for very courtesy's sake, offered his to Lady Marie. She smiled prettily and laid a delicate little hand on his sleeve. "You are looking remarkably well."

In truth his father looked gray even to the lips, his son thought.

Charity was standing quietly by the library window. The marquess, disengaging his arm from Lady Marie's, was about to cross the room to her, but his father forestalled him by reaching out a hand toward her.

"Come here, my dear," he said.

How it must gall his father to have to call her that, the marquess thought, staying where he was beside Lady Marie as Charity crossed the room and set her hand in the duke's. She smiled at him and—*he smiled back*.

"I would present you to my guests, my dear," he said. "Tillden? Ma'am? Lady Marie? Allow me to present the Marchioness of Staunton. She and Staunton were married in London two days ago."

The marquess was aware of Lady Marie beside him drawing a sharp breath.

"I am so very pleased to make your acquaintance," Charity said, smiling warmly at all three of their guests in turn. "Will you not be seated? And you too, Father? You are overtaxing your strength."

She was behaving as if she had been born a duchess. Except that most duchesses of the marquess's acquaintance did not exude warm charm.

"Married? Two days ago?" The earl's brows almost met across his frown line.

"I am pleased to meet you, I am sure, Lady Staunton," Lady Tillden said kindly, sinking into the chair closest to her. "And I wish you every happiness. As I do you, my lord." She smiled nervously at the marquess.

"Married?" The earl, unlike his wife, was not prepared to turn the moment with empty courtesies. "Is this true, sir?"

"Indeed." The marquess smiled. "His grace informed me of his poor health and naturally it was my wish to hurry home without delay. But I found myself quite unwilling to leave behind my betrothed for an indeterminate length of time. We married by special license."

"Your mama must have been distressed not to have a proper wedding to arrange, Lady Staunton," the countess said. "But under the circumstances . . . "

"My parents are both deceased, ma'am," Charity said. "I had no one's inclination to consult but my own."

"And no guardian to become stuffy about the matter," the marquess said. "Lady Staunton was working as a governess when I met her, ma'am."

"Oh, dear me," her ladyship said faintly, one hand straying to her throat.

"I want a full explanation for this, Withingsby," the Earl of Tillden said. "And I want it *now*."

"My dear." His grace patted Charity's hand. "Mrs. Aylward will be waiting in the hall. Would you be so good as to escort Lady Tillden and Lady Marie to her? You need not return here. Tea will be served in the drawing room, ladies, precisely at four."

The marquess opened the door for them and bowed as they left. His wife smiled at him as she passed. He closed the door and stood facing it for a few moments. Then he turned. This, after all, was why he had come. To shake their influence and the illusion of power they held over him once and for all. To prove to them that the Marquess of Staunton was no one's puppet.

"I believe I must demand satisfaction for this," the Earl of Tillden said, his voice tight with bruised dignity.

Good Lord! Was he talking about a duel?

"Sit down, Tillden," his grace said, doing so himself. He looked quite ill, the marquess noticed—and the twinge of alarm he felt took him by surprise. "My son has reminded me since his arrival that he has never been a party to any contract concerning Lady Marie Lucas, either written or verbal. And I must concede that he has a point."

"He does not have to be a party to it, by thunder," the earl said, his voice raised far above the level of courteous discourse. "It was an agreement made between his father and her father. When were the parties to such a match ever consulted for their consent? Do you have no control over your offspring, Withingsby, that your eldest son—your *heir*—has had the impudence to ignore an agreement entered into seventeen years ago by his father in order to marry a woman from the gutter?"

The marquess stood close to the door, his hands at his back. He spoke very quietly. He would be drawn into no shouting match. "You will choose your words with care, sir," he said, "when you speak of my wife."

"*What?*" The earl's ample fist banged on his grace's desk with force enough to send a fountain of ink spurting upward from the inkwell. "You insolent puppy. Do you dare open your mouth without your father's permission? And to threaten me?"

"I am eight-and-twenty years old, sir," the marquess said. "I have been living independently of my father since I was twenty. I live my life according to my own principles. I have married the lady of my choice, as is my right. I am sorry indeed for any embarrassment my marriage has caused you and Lady Tillden, and more sorry than I can say for any distress I have caused Lady Marie. But I will acknowledge no misbehavior in neglecting to honor a long-standing agreement concerning me, in which I had no voice."

"I will demand recompense for this," the earl said, pointing a finger first at the marquess and then at the silent duke. "I will blacken both your names to such a degree that you will be unable to show your faces in society for the rest of your lives." He stood up. "I will have my carriage brought around again and my wife and daughter summoned. I will not remain one hour beneath this roof, where honor is not worth a farthing."

"Sit down, Tillden," his grace said, his voice wearily haughty. "Unless you wish to make yourself a laughing-stock and your daughter unmarriageable. No one outside my family knows why you have come here, though doubtless there is speculation. There was never any written contract. There was never a formal betrothal.

You are here as my friend, as you have been a number of times over the years. You are here out of concern for my health. No one has ever said that the ball arranged here for tomorrow evening was to be a betrothal ball. It has been arranged to celebrate Staunton's return home and the unexpected joy of his bringing a bride with him. It has been arranged to celebrate my family's being together again for the first time since her grace's funeral. And to celebrate the visit of my oldest friend, the Earl of Tillden. This thing can be carried off with dignity."

The earl had sat again and was clearly considering the wisdom of rethinking his initial impulse.

"I am most insulted, Withingsby," he said. "I hope to hear from you that Staunton and his—his *wife* are to be severely disciplined."

"Staunton has heard my displeasure," his grace said. "Lady Staunton is quite blameless. And in the day since I have made her acquaintance I have grown decidedly fond of her."

The marquess raised his eyebrows.

"Even though she is an upstart nobody?" the earl asked. "Even though she was nothing more than a governess on the lookout for—"

But even as the marquess took a step forward, his father spoke coolly and courteously—and quite firmly.

"I have grown decidedly fond of my daughter-in-law, the Marchioness of Staunton," he said.

The Earl of Tillden, the marquess could see, would stay at Enfield, at least until after tomorrow evening's ball. He had realized that the scandal he would dearly love to visit upon the two of them would also involve his own family in ridicule and humiliation.

"You will ring for the butler, Staunton," his father said. "He will show you to your rooms, Tillden. I trust you will find everything for your comfort there. You will escort the ladies to tea at four?"

11

SHE SAT AT HER DRESSING-TABLE MIRROR, BRUSHING her hair long after she had dismissed her new maid for the night. There was little point in going to bed. She would never sleep. Her brain teemed with activity.

It had seemed so easy at first. In return for a lifetime of security for herself and her family, all she had to do was marry a man and spend a few weeks with him, meeting his family. She had very deliberately asked no questions. She had not needed to know.

It had still seemed relatively easy even after she had discovered exactly who her new husband was and who his family was. It had been somewhat nerve-racking, of course, to come to Enfield Park and to be presented to the Duke of Withingsby and everyone else. A great deal more had been expected of her than she had at first anticipated. But even so, it had been fairly easy.

If she had just done as she had been told. If she had just been content to be quiet and demure, to be his shadow. To be a quiet mouse. If she had only not looked about her and seen people—just human people caught up in the drama of life and really not doing very well at it at all. If she had just not come to care.

She sighed and set her brush down on the dressing table. She was not even going to try to sleep yet. She would go into the sitting room and write some letters—

one to Philip, one to Penny and the children. It was time she wrote to them. She had been avoiding doing so. What, after all, could she write but lies? Not that there was any point in hiding the truth any longer, she supposed, since it was too late for any of them to stop what she had done. But she could not tell them in a letter. It must be face-to-face.

She seemed to have done nothing but lie for—for how long was it? Yesterday they had arrived at Enfield. The day before that they had married. Was it really less than three days altogether? Four days ago she had not even met the Marquess of Staunton. She had merely been feeling jittery at the prospect of being interviewed by Mr. Earheart.

She took a candle with her into the private sitting room of their apartments and lit two more when she got there. She found paper and pen and ink in the small escritoire and sat down to write.

"Dear Phil . . . "

The Earl of Tillden had acted all evening as if she did not exist, even though his grace had seated him to her right during dinner. The countess had nodded sweetly and nervously in her direction whenever their eyes had met but had avoided coming close enough to make conversation necessary. Lady Marie Lucas had been taken firmly under Marianne's wing. She was a beautiful, elegant young lady, who fit into the drawing room at Enfield and blended in with the family there as if she had been born to it all—as indeed she had.

The marquess had not wished to marry her. Hence his marriage to *her*. But he had not seen Lady Marie for eight years or longer. She would have been a child. It must have been a shock to him to see her today. She wondered if he regretted . . . But she dipped the pen firmly into the inkwell. If he did, it was his problem.

"Dear Phil, You must think I am lost. Two whole days

and I am only now writing to you. Everything has been very busy and very new. I am only just settling. There are four children, not three, but the youngest is not ready for my services yet. He is a plump, adorable baby, who crawls into everything he is not supposed to crawl into, who puts everything he finds into his mouth, and who considers everything that happens—especially the exasperation of his nurse—worthy of a chuckle."

It was hard to believe that such a happy child could have come from Marianne and Richard. He had her thinking wistfully of motherhood. But no matter. She would be the world's most attentive and indulgent aunt to Phil and Agnes's children and to Penny's.

"The oldest child, Augusta, is eight years old," she wrote. "She is a grave little girl who has never learned to be a child, and she is hostile to me and to"—Charity brushed the feather of the quill pen across her chin for a moment—"Mr. Earheart. But I did coax first a smile and then a giggle from her after tea today when I told her about the lodgekeeper's two children ambushing me this morning by hiding in the branches of a tree and showering me with leaves as I passed beneath. I believe she must be fond of those children. I will have to see if I can arrange for them to play together occasionally. I do not believe she has been allowed a great deal of time simply for play."

She had told Augusta about some of her own childhood exploits, including the time she had climbed to the topmost branches of a tree close to the house to rescue a kitten who was mewing most piteously, while Penny wept and Phil sniveled on the ground below. The kitten had tired of its perch and removed itself to the ground long before Charity had climbed laboriously to the top to find it gone. And then the inevitable had happened—just as it had this morning to a lesser degree with Harry. It had taken a gardener, their father, and a passing peddler—not to mention oceans of tears and much anxious and conflicting advice from the other two children and their mother—to get her down again. Charity had milked the story for all it was worth when telling it to Augusta.

Charity stopped writing. She frowned and brushed the feather absently across her chin again. She had invented ages and genders for the three mythical children she was to teach. What exactly had she told Phil? She must be careful not to completely contradict herself. That was the trouble with lies. A good memory was essential if one was going to start telling them.

But something happened to distract her. The sitting-room door opened. She looked over her shoulder in some surprise.

Her husband was standing there. He was wearing a wine-colored brocaded dressing gown with leather slippers. His hair was disheveled but only succeeded somehow in making him look even more handsome than usual. He stepped inside and closed the door behind him.

"Ah," he said, "it *is* you. What are you doing?"

She half covered her letter with one hand, trying not to look too secretive about it.

"I thought I would write a couple of letters before going to bed," she said. "I am sorry. Did the light disturb you?"

"Not at all," he said. "To whom do you write?"

"Oh." She laughed. "To some friends."

"At your old home?" he asked. "I was under the impression that you were alone in London."

She was thankful that his curiosity did not extend to strolling across the room to look over her shoulder.

"At my old home, yes," she said.

He stood just inside the door, his hands at his back, his lips pursed, looking almost awkward. As if he felt he did not quite belong there. As if he were embarrassed.

Yet he was in his own apartments in his own boyhood home.

"I never used this room," he said as if in answer to her thoughts. "It seems like a woman's room."

"It is cozy," she said.

"Yes. Well, good night." He turned back toward the door.

"Good night, my lord," she said.

He hesitated, his hand on the doorknob. "Would you mind if I sat here while you write?" he asked. "I will not disturb you."

This was the Marquess of Staunton—that cold, haughty, cynical man? This uncertain, almost humble man?

"I would not mind at all, my lord," she said. "Please do join me."

He sat on a cozy love seat, set his elbow on the arm, and rested his closed fist against his mouth.

"Proceed," he said when she continued to look at him.

His eyes looked darker than usual—it must be a trick of the candlelight. But no, she thought as she turned back to her letter. It was more than that. Something had been lifted behind his eyes. But she would not turn back to see if she had been correct.

It had been a difficult letter to write even when she was alone. It was next to impossible now. In the course of fully twenty minutes she limped her way through another few sentences and brought a very unsatisfactory letter to an end. She waited for the ink to dry before folding the page carefully. She would have to take it into the village tomorrow. She could not set it on the tray downstairs addressed to Mr. Philip Duncan.

"I have finished." She turned and smiled—and was jolted to find that he was sitting exactly as he had been twenty minutes before. He was still watching her.

"It is a very short letter," he said. "And it is only one. I broke your concentration."

"It does not matter," she said. "I can write another letter tomorrow."

"You are gracious, Lady Staunton," he said. "Always gracious. My father appears to have grown remarkably fond of you."

"He is kind," she said.

He laughed softly. "'My dear,'" he said in his father's voice. "'Dear daughter. My dear daughter, come and seat yourself on this stool at my feet.' And then a careless hand resting lightly and affectionately on your shoulder. A soft look in his eyes."

"He is kind," she said again. The duke had made a potentially impossible evening really rather pleasant for her.

"His grace is never kind," he said, "and never affectionate. He plays a game with you, my lady. Or rather he plays a game with me. We play cat and mouse with each other."

By each pretending to an affection for her to infuriate the other. Neither of them felt the fondness for her that they showed in public.

"Does it hurt you?" he asked.

Yes, it did. It hurt dreadfully to be seen and used as a pawn rather than as a person. But she had freely agreed to be so seen and so used and she had ignored the advice to make herself into a mere shadow. Shadows had no feelings of personal hurt or of pity for those who did the hurting.

She shook her head. "It is just a temporary arrangement," she said. "It will soon be over."

"Yes." He gazed at her and she was sure she had not been wrong about his eyes. Some of the defenses had been allowed to fall. Perhaps he felt safe with her here in his own apartments late at night.

She got to her feet. "It is late," she said. "It is time I went to bed. Good night, my lord."

"Let me come there with you," he said as she reached the door and lifted her hand to the knob.

She realized her naiveté then. She had felt the atmosphere ever since he stepped inside the room, and she had thought it to be mere self-consciousness on her part. She recognized the tension now for what it had been from the start. They both—oh, yes, *both*—wanted to lie with each other again. It was open now in his words and the tone in which they had been spoken. And it was open too in her body's response to his words. There was a heavy throbbing in that most secret inner place where he had been two nights ago—and where she wanted him again.

It would not be wise. It was not love or even affection. It was not even marriage. It was need, the need of a twenty-three-year-old woman to mate, to celebrate her womanhood. It was a need that had lain dormant and almost unfelt in her until two nights ago. Now it was a need aroused with almost frightening ease. It was a need, she suspected, that might well grow into a constant craving if she gave in to it and became more familiar with the earth-shattering delights she had discovered two nights ago.

"You may feel free to say no," he said. "I will not force you or even try to persuade you."

And yet if she was honest with herself she would admit that it was already too late to prevent the craving. It had been there last night, it had been one reason for her staying up tonight, and it would be a demon to be fought for years to come. Tonight she had a chance to experience that delight again, to savor it, to commit it to memory for the barren years ahead.

"Allow me to open the door for you, my lady." His voice came from just behind her. "It was no part of our agreement. You must not feel coerced. I will not trouble you by asking again."

"I would like to lie with you," she said.

One of his hands touched her shoulder. The other reached past her to open the door. "I will take you to my bed, then, if you have no objection," he said.

"No," she said. "No, I have none."

His bedchamber was identical in size and shape to her own, but his was a masculine room, decorated in shades of wine and cream and gold. It smelled masculine—of leather and cologne and wine and unidentifiable maleness.

Did it matter that it was not for love? Or even for conjugal duty? Did it matter that it was just for need—for craving? Did the absence of either love or duty make it immoral? He was her husband. She turned to him and looked up into his eyes. Her very temporary husband. She would think about morality when he was no longer her husband, when she was alone again. Alone with her family.

Alone.

IT HAD BEEN the day of his final triumph, the day when he had at last won his undisputed independence and had moreover forced his father publicly to accept it. He had come home and faced his demons and even made some peace with them. It would no longer be a place to be avoided and his family would no longer be people to be avoided. He could be civil to Will again.

He should be rejoicing. He should be planning his return to his own life. He should be turning over to his man of business the matter of his wife's settlement.

He was not rejoicing. He was restless. He tried lying down. He tried willing sleep. It would not come. He was going to have to stay at Enfield, he admitted to himself at last. His father was gravely ill—dying, in fact. The admission brought him momentary panic. They were going to have to talk—really talk. His father was going to have to be persuaded to let go the reins of power so that he could relax and perhaps prolong his days. That meant that he, Staunton, was going to have to take over. He was going to have to stay. Indefinitely. He could not—would not—let his father die alone.

He could not keep his wife here indefinitely. He stood at the window of his room looking out into the darkness. Clouds must have moved over—there was no moonlight. There was no need to keep her here longer than a few days more, in fact. Once Tillden and his family returned home, she might be allowed to leave too. After all, he had not deceived his father about the true nature of his marriage, and he had no real wish or need to deceive him. The point was that the marriage was real and indissoluble. His father, being a realist, had accepted that. She had served her purpose. Now, soon, she might be allowed to go.

The marquess set his hands on the windowsill and leaned on them. He drew in a slow and audible breath and admitted something to himself. He wanted her. Now—in bed. But it was not she specifically he wanted, he told himself. He wanted a woman. Probably because he knew he would not have a woman for a long time. His grace had always been particularly strict about any dalliances his sons showed signs of initiating with local wenches. And his eldest son quite agreed with him. There were places enough where one might slake unruly appetites. The place where one exercised mastery and carried out the responsibilities that came with it was not one of them. He wanted his wife because she was close by—in the next bedchamber—and because she would not be there for long and he was going to be very womanless. He laughed softly in self-derision.

He wondered how she would react if he were to walk into her bedchamber now, demanding his conjugal rights. Perhaps she would give them to him without argument. His nostrils flared. He would go into his study, he decided. He would find something to do there. Some of his favorite books were there. If he thought hard enough, he would surely think of someone to whom he owed a letter. If that failed him, then he would dress again and go tramping about outside in the darkness.

But as he approached his study, he saw the light beneath the sitting-room door. And so he went there instead and invited himself to sit with his wife as she wrote her letter—and what had kept *her* up so late? he wondered. She was wearing a very plain, very serviceable white cotton dressing gown. Her hair was loose and lay in shining waves down her back.

He still wanted her. And he would admit to himself now that it was not just a woman he wanted. He wanted *her*—her innocence, her wholesomeness. He had found them enticing qualities two nights before. She had played her part well, he thought, watching her as she wrote, her posture correct yet graceful. More than well. She had shown a warmth and a charm and a graciousness that had affected them all, with the possible exception of Marianne. Even Charles had watched her this evening as she sat on the low stool by their father, a puzzled frown on his face.

She had done well. He had caught himself feeling proud of her, pretty and dignified in the appallingly dull gray silk, before realizing that pride was not an appropriate feeling under the circumstances. Not a *warm* pride, anyway.

He wondered to whom she wrote with such difficulty. Was it someone to whom she merely felt duty-bound to write? Or was it someone of whom she was so fond that she was inhibited by his presence? But he had no right to his curiosity. And no wish to be curious. When she left him, he wanted to be able to forget about her.

But tonight he wanted her. He wanted her beneath him. He wanted his face in her hair. The sooner she was out of his life the better it would be for him.

He gave in to weakness—and thought that she was going to refuse him. It would be as well if she did, though he did not know what he would do for sleep. But she did not refuse.

"I would like to lie with you," she said after he had got to his feet to open the door for her.

His wife did not mince words. And so he gave in to another weakness. He wanted her in his own bed. He wanted the memory of her there—though the thought, which took him completely by surprise, had him frowning in incomprehension.

There was no timidity in his wife—it seemed laughable to him now that he had mistaken her for a quiet mouse only a few days ago. She turned to him when they were in his bedchamber and looked full into his eyes—her own as wide and defenseless as they had ever been. He hoped they did not denote vulnerability. He hoped no one would ever hurt her deeply.

He undid the sash of her dressing gown and pushed the garment off her shoulders. He undid the buttons of her nightgown, opened back the edges, drew it down her arms, let it fall to the floor. She stood still and unresisting—and looked into his eyes.

She was beautifully proportioned without being in any way voluptuous. He had always thought that he preferred voluptuous women—until tonight.

He removed his dressing gown and pulled his nightshirt off over his head. Her eyes roamed over his body.

"We will lie down," he told her.

"Yes," she said.

He liked a great deal of foreplay and he had many

skills. He liked to mount the bodies of his women just for the final vigorous ascent to release. He never kissed his women—not on the face at least. A kiss was too intimate a thing—too emotionally intimate, that was. A bedding was a purely physical thing with no emotional overtones whatsoever.

He did not kiss his wife. His hands went to work on her in the long-familiar ritual. But although he was aroused, he could not seem to get his mind involved in what he did. The pattern had become wearying. It would no longer satisfy. Not with her. He wanted to be lying atop her body. He wanted to be warmed by her heat, soothed by her softness. He wanted to be inside her, enclosed by her femininity. He wanted his face in her hair.

And so he let go of the pattern, the ritual, the familiar skills. He lifted himself over her and lowered his weight onto her. He nudged her legs apart. He had no idea if she was ready. It took women a long time to be ready for mounting. He slid his hands beneath her and pushed carefully inside. She was smooth with wetness.

It was strange, he thought, breathing in the erotic smell of soap, how one could be taut and pulsing with arousal without feeling any of the usual animal urges to squeeze the last ounce of pleasure out of the experience. He wanted merely to be in her, to ride her, to be close to her, to be this close, to be a part of her, of her grace and her warmth and her charm, to breathe in the essence of her. He stopped thinking.

He followed instinct. He had nothing else to guide him. He had abandoned skills and expertise and familiar moves. He followed instinct, mating with her with slow and steady rhythm, prolonging with unthinking instinct the exquisite and regrettable moment when they would become even more nearly one for the merest heartbeat before becoming two and separate once more. He did not know when she twined her legs about his but was only aware of the more comfortable unison of the rhythm they shared.

He sighed into her hair. She made low little sounds of contentment. It amazed him during one lucid moment that there was no great excitement in either of them. Only something far, far more dangerous—but he shut down the thought before it could be articulated.

She lost rhythm first. Her inner muscles began to contract convulsively. Her breathing became more labored. She untwined her legs from his and braced her feet against the mattress. She pushed upward, straining against him. He thrust hard into her and pressed his hands down on her hips.

There were several moments of rigid tautness in her before she surged about him in utter, reckless abandon. She came to him in silence. She came to him with everything she had. He felt gifted, which was a strange feeling when all that had happened was that she was having a good sexual experience. A purely physical experience.

He let her relax beneath him. He savored the warmth and softness and silence of her. He waited for her breathing to become normal. Then he drove himself to the place where he longed to be, the place where he had always longed to be. Always. All his life. Though it was not a place exactly. It was . . . He heard himself shout out. He felt her arms come about him. He felt her legs twine about his again. He heard her murmur something against his ear—something exquisitely sweet and totally incomprehensible.

He felt as if he were falling and was powerless to stop himself.

12

SHE DID NOT SLEEP A GREAT DEAL. AT FIRST SHE WAS uncomfortable—his weight was heavy on her and made breathing a conscious effort, and her legs stiffened from being pressed wide. Strangely she did nothing to lessen the discomfort. She did not try to wake him or to somehow alter her position. Quite the contrary. She lay very still and relaxed so that he would *not* move. She was very conscious of the fact that they were naked together, that part of his body was still inside part of hers, that they had been man and wife together. Discomfort seemed unimportant.

Even after he had stirred and rolled off her, grumbling incoherently and keeping his arms about her so that she stayed cuddled warmly and now comfortably against him, she did not sleep much. She dozed fitfully.

Nothing had changed. Nothing at all. It had not been love. She would be very, very foolish to imagine that it might have been. She must not even for a moment romanticize what had not contained even one element of romance. They were a man and a woman with physical needs. Conveniently they were married to each other and occupying the same apartments. And so they had fed those needs and been satisfied. She was very glad that she had learned such an invaluable lesson. New knowledge was always worth acquiring. She had learned that love and romance on the one hand and what happened between a man and a woman in bed on the other were so vastly different that one might as easily compare oranges and hackney cabs.

Nothing had changed. Except that foolishly and typically—oh, so *very* typically—she had become involved. With all of them—the whole unpleasant, morose, mixed-up lot of them. Why could she not merely have continued to see them that way and held herself aloof?

She had always been the same. She might have been married when she was one-and-twenty, to a gentleman who was personable and eligible and of whom she was fond. But her mother had been dead for only four years and everyone still needed her, she had insisted—even though Mama's widowed sister had been quite prepared to take over the care of the family. After Papa's death, when the whole world came crashing about their ears, she had insisted on becoming involved in supporting the family and paying off the debts even though everyone had tried to persuade her that she was needed more at home. And at her last employment, of course, she had caused her own dismissal by becoming involved in the distress of a pretty chambermaid who was too weak-willed to stand up for herself.

And now she had done it again. She cared. She cared for the Duke of Withingsby, who loved no one and whom no one loved—or so they all thought, foolish people. She cared about Augusta, who had a childhood to retrieve, and about Charles, who still felt betrayed by the brother who had abandoned him when he was still only a lad—oh, yes, she had worked that one out for herself. She cared about Claudia, who had caused a bitter rift between two brothers, and who must know it and be distressed by it despite all her smiling charm. She cared for William, who must be torn by guilt and by some indignation too if it was true—it probably was—

that Claudia had always loved him. The only ones she did not particularly care about were Marianne and Richard, though she loved their children.

Oh, yes, she cared all right. Stupid woman. And she cared for this man, this poor, troubled man who thought he was in such firm command of his own life. How very foolish men could be. How very like children they were—blustering and bullying and glowering and utterly vulnerable. She had been almost frightened by his vulnerability earlier when he had shouted out just at the moment when she had been realizing that the extra heat she felt inside was his seed being released. He had sounded so lost. She had wrapped herself about him, feeling an overwhelming tenderness, and murmured comfort to him just as if he were one of the children who had fallen down and scraped a knee.

"It will be all right," she had assured him. "Everything will be all right, dear."

Dear! She hoped fervently he had not heard. The Marquess of Staunton was not exactly the sort of person one called *dear*. Or about whom one felt maternal. She felt anything but maternal at this particular moment. He was awake. His hand was moving in light circles over her back and her buttocks and then moved over her hip to slide up between them to one of her breasts. He stroked it and brushed his thumb over her nipple.

"Mmm," she said.

It was all either of them said. He lifted one of her legs to fit snugly over his hip, drew her closer, and came into her. She was so very naive. She had not known where his caresses were leading. She had not realized it could be done again so soon—or while they were lying on their sides. But when she tightened those newly discovered inner muscles, she could feel him all enticingly hard and long again. And deep. He withdrew and entered again.

She did not believe there was a lovelier feeling in the world. She wished it could last forever.

She slept deeply after it was over. He had moved her leg to rest more comfortably on the other one and had drawn the blankets snugly about her ears. But he kept her close—closer. He kept their bodies joined. She must leave, she decided before she slid into sleep. There could be no real reason for her to stay longer. He had made his point and his marriage was indissoluble. He was beyond the power he had imagined they wielded over him. She must leave, put her life back together again, proceed to live happily ever after with her family and her six thousand a year.

But she would think about it tomorrow.

THERE HAD BEEN some rain during the night. Drops of moisture glistened now on the grass and there was still some early-morning fog obscuring the hills and the distant trees. But it was a fine morning for a ride. The Marquess of Staunton stood on the marble steps outside the front doors, breathing in lungfuls of the damp, cool air and tapping his riding crop against his boots.

This morning there was no little brown mouse standing on the terrace below him. He had left her in bed. At his suggestion she had settled for sleep again after he had woken her for a swift, vigorous bout of lovemaking. She had turned her face into his pillow and slid her arm beneath it. She had been sleeping before he had tucked the bedclothes warmly about her.

He strode off toward the stables. Was he insane? Totally out of his mind? Three times last night, once three nights ago. What the devil would he do if he had got her with child? *If?* Four times and he was thinking in terms of *ifs?*

But he had come outside in order to refresh his mind

and in order to renew his energies after a night of expending them. He scowled. Why the devil had she been sitting up at such a late hour writing letters? If she had not been, none of that would have happened. He had already resisted the temptation to pay a conjugal visit to her room.

But he was saved after all from such troublesome thoughts. Charles was already mounted up in the stable-yard when he arrived there, and was firmly establishing with his frisky mount which of them was in charge.

"You have not forgotten your first lessons in horsemanship, then," he called from the gateway.

His brother clearly had not seen him until that moment. He touched his whip to the brim of his hat and nodded curtly. "Staunton," he said.

"But you have learned considerably more in the years since," the marquess said. "You are a cavalry officer, of course. I suppose riding comes as naturally to you as walking."

"As it does to all gentlemen, I believe," Charles said. "Excuse me, Staunton. I will be on my way."

The marquess did not move from the gateway. "For a morning ride?" he said. "It is my purpose too. Shall we do it together?"

His brother shrugged. "As you wish," he said.

It was all the fault of that pest of a wife of his, the marquess thought as he prepared his own horse, having waved away the groom who would have done it for him. That little prude with her character analyses and her moralizing, and her insistence that they were a family merely because his grace had fathered them all. When was the last time he had forced his company on someone who wished him to the devil? On that of a young puppy who had been all but insolent to him? It was all her fault that he felt this need to talk.

"You have seen active service?" he asked as they rode

out of the stableyard and headed out to the open fields and hills behind the house.

"Not beyond these shores," Charles said. "I have been in a reserve regiment."

"Have been?" The marquess looked across at him. Dressed in scarlet regimentals his brother must be irresistible to the ladies, he thought, his lips quirking. It was still hard to believe that his younger brother was no longer a twelve-year-old boy.

"We sail for Spain within the month," Charles said. "I intend to be there."

"Does his grace dispute that?" the marquess asked.

His brother did not answer.

"I suppose," the marquess said, "that he did not even approve of your choice of career. He intended you for the church, did he not?" He remembered occasionally broaching the topic with their father. He remembered promising a rebellious Charles that he would take his part and see to it that he was not forced into a way of life that held no attraction whatsoever for him. But he had left before he could keep his promise.

Charles had clearly decided that this was a conversation in which he did not choose to participate. He had taken his mount to a brisk canter.

"But I do not remember your ever saying," the marquess said, catching up to him, "that you wished to buy a commission. Your interest in a military career is of fairly recent date?"

His brother looked at him with hard, hostile eyes. "You make conversation for the sake of being sociable, Staunton," he said. "Since when have you been interested in my career or my reasons for entering it? And do not say it is because you are my brother. You are no brother of mine except by the accident of birth."

Ah. Charles had been far more deeply hurt by his desertion than he had ever expected. He had thought that the boy would recover quickly and with the resilience of youth attach his affections to someone else—perhaps Will. It had been a naive assumption. But then he had been only twenty himself at that time—Charles's age now.

"You wanted a gentleman's life," he said. "You wanted land and farms and responsibilities—even if you did not own the land, you said. You hoped that Will would enter the church or the army and that his grace would allow you to help run these estates or one of the more distant ones. I thought I might be given one of the other estates. We used to joke about it. I would allow you to live there and run it for me while I went raking off to London."

"Which is exactly what you did," Charles said. For the first time an open bitterness crept into his voice. "With vast success from all accounts."

"Do you know why I left?" the marquess asked him.

"Yes." His brother laughed. "His grace would not allow you to rut with any female within ten miles of Enfield. And with Mother dead there was nothing and no one to keep you here."

The marquess winced. Perhaps he should have forced himself to say good-bye. Perhaps he should have tried to explain. But no—there had been no way to explain the pain, the outrage, the humiliation.

"And Will would have knocked your teeth in if you had gone near Claudia," Charles added.

Ah. Twelve-year-olds sometimes noticed and understood far more than adults realized.

"I loved Claudia," he said. "I thought she loved me. But once she was married to Will, I never would have gone near her."

"You always were insufferably arrogant," his former admirer said scornfully. "Anyone with eyes in his head could see that it was Will she wanted and that Will lived in a sort of hell because he thought you were going to have her and he dared not fight you over the matter. You are not the sort of man to appeal to Claudia, Staunton. Claudia, for all her beauty, likes safety and security and tranquillity. She likes Will."

Good God! Had he been so blind? So humiliatingly self-deluded? Apparently so.

"I left for other reasons," he said. "Life had become intolerable and Will's marriage and Mother's death pushed me very close to the edge. Not over it, though. There were still you and the baby." He drew a deep and ragged breath. He had not thought of it specifically for years. He did not know now if he could talk of it. "Something else pushed me over."

If Charles did not prompt him, he would not say it, he decided. It was all in the past. He had got over it, recovered his life and his pride, forged an independence for himself.

"Well?" Charles said impatiently and rather impertinently.

"He accused me of stealing," the marquess said. "His grace, I mean. He had searched my rooms himself and found it. He was waiting there for me with it in his hand. He hit me across the face with it in his open palm. It drew blood."

He did not even look at his brother, who said nothing in the short silence that followed.

"He ordered me downstairs to await him in the library," the marquess said. "I knew what would be at the end of the wait, of course. Any one of us would have known, would we not? I was twenty years old and innocent. I told him that I would do it, that I would wait there, that I would not fight with him or argue with him further. I told him that I would take the whipping just as if I were still a helpless child. But I told him too that I would be gone before the day was out, that I would never set foot on Enfield property again, that he would never set eyes on me again. His grace would never bow to such threats, of course. It was the severest whipping he had ever given me. I had great difficulty riding my horse afterward, but I would not spend another night under the same roof with him."

Charles still said nothing.

"When I made the threat, I did not speak in haste," the marquess said. "I knew exactly what I was saying, and I knew the choices I was making. I knew that I would have to leave the baby, whom he would not even look at, and I knew I would have to leave you. You were the most precious person left in my world. But I will not use such an argument with you in self-defense. You were a child. You needed me. And I did not even have the courage to say good-bye to you. I would not have been able to leave if I had done so and I had to leave. More than my self-respect was at stake. I felt as if my very life, my soul were at stake. When one is twenty, Charles, as perhaps you will admit, one sometimes dramatizes reality in such a way. Perhaps, in retrospect, my self-respect and my life and my soul were of less importance than a child to whom I was something of a hero."

He realized then in some horror why Charles was saying nothing.

"The devil!" he said. "This is not a tale that calls for tears, Charles. It is a foolish and sordid episode from the past. The long-forgotten past. I could not even keep my vow, you see. I am here on Enfield property again after just eight years. I am on almost civil speaking terms with his grace."

Charles spurred on ahead and the marquess let him go. Twenty-year-olds who were also cavalry lieutenants did not enjoy being seen crying.

He drew his own horse to a halt. No, he would not even ride after his brother in a few minutes' time. Charles would be devilishly embarrassed, and he might feel it necessary to comment on what he had been told. Nothing more needed to be said on the matter. Charles now knew at least that he had left not merely to take his rakish pleasure in town after their mother's death had released him from any need to stay at Enfield. It would not make a great deal of difference. Certainly his reason for leaving was no excuse for what he had done. He had broken the bonds of love and trust. And he was not the only one who had suffered as a result.

He turned his horse toward home, changed his mind, and went trotting off in a different direction. He would find some open countryside and take his horse to a gallop until they were both ready to collapse.

CHARITY SLEPT FOR only half an hour after her husband had left. Despite the fact that she had slept for only the last few hours of the night and even that sleep had been disturbed when her husband had woken and wanted her again, she found that old habits refused to be ignored. She had always been an early riser.

She breathed in the smell of him on his pillow and mentally examined the mingled feelings of soreness and well-being and languor and energy that all laid claim to her. *It must be very pleasant,* she thought, *to be married permanently, to wake every morning like this.* But hers was not a permanent marriage, nor did she wish it to be. This family had more troubles than she could list on her ten fingers. She had a family of her own with whom she was quite contented. And she would be with them soon. There was the ball tonight. Tomorrow or the next day she did not doubt the Earl of Tillden would remove his family from Enfield. Then her function would be quite at an end.

Tomorrow morning she would ask the Marquess of

Staunton when she might leave. He would probably want her to stay a few days longer, but by this time next week she could reasonably expect to be home. She threw back the bedclothes and sat on the edge of the bed. How excited they would be to see her. How excited she would be! And what wonderful news she would have to share with them. She would tease them at first. She would pretend to them that she had lost her position and was destitute. And then she would watch their faces as she told them the real story.

Penny would not approve. And Phil would be thunderous. He might even refuse to touch a penny of the money or allow her to pay off any of the debts. But then she had been fighting Phil all her life. And she was the elder, after all. Somehow she would persuade him.

A short while later—she had not summoned her maid, but there had been an embarrassing moment when she had passed through her husband's dressing room, clad only in her nightgown and with her hair all tangled and disheveled, and found his valet there clearing away his shaving things—Charity descended to the breakfast room. It was still very early. She hoped no one else would be there yet. She hoped *he* would not be there. She would not quite know how to look at him or what to say to him. But only Charles was there, looking youthful and handsome in his riding clothes.

"Oh, good morning," she said, smiling warmly. "Are you an early riser too? But I daresay you are if you are a military officer."

"I have been out riding," he said. He had risen from his place and held out a hand for hers. When she gave it to him, he raised it to his lips. It was a wonderfully courtly gesture from so young a man.

"Have you?" she said. "Did you see Anthony? He got up very early too and said he was going riding." She flushed when she realized what her words had revealed.

"I rode a short way with him," he said.

"Did you?" She seated herself and leaned a little toward him as a footman poured her coffee. "And did you two talk? I have never known a family in which the members did less talking on important matters."

His eyes looked suddenly guarded. "We talked," he said.

"Good." She helped herself to a round of toast from the toast rack. "And have you forgiven him for abandoning you when you were just a boy?"

"He has told you, then?" he asked.

"No," she said, smiling. "Even to me he has said very little about the past. I do not know what happened, only that something did and that until everyone is willing to talk about it, nothing will ever be healed. You loved him once."

"Yes," he said. "More than anyone else in the world. He could do no wrong in my eyes even though I was aware of his faults. Arrogance, for example."

"I think arrogance comes naturally from his position and upbringing and his looks," she said, sharing a conspiratorial smile with him.

"Do you love him?" he asked softly.

Her hand paused halfway to her mouth and she set down the piece of toast she had been about to bite into. How could she answer such a question? Only one way, she realized. She had committed herself to a lie when she had accepted the Marquess of Staunton's proposition.

"Yes," she said. "Faults and all. Even though I have wanted to shake him until he rattles from the moment we arrived here. He is so foolishly *reticent*."

He smiled and Charity found herself pitying any very young lady on whom he turned the power of that smile—if he did not intend offering his heart with it.

"I thought you were a fortune hunter," he said. "I hated Tony when he arrived here, but even so I found myself outraged on his behalf. I thought he had been duped. I am sorry. I have seen since that I completely misjudged both you and Tony's ability to choose a bride wisely. I like you."

"Thank you," she said. "Oh, thank you." She felt around in vain for a handkerchief—her face had crumpled quite ignominiously. "How very foolish."

"No," he said gently, and he pressed a large gentleman's handkerchief into her hand. "You have been treated abominably here, though even his grace was thawing by last evening. You have shown great courage in continuing to smile and treat us civilly when we gave you such a cold welcome."

"Well." She blew her nose. "I believe I have had enough breakfast." She had had two bites of toast and half a cup of coffee. "No, you need not get up."

She wanted nothing more than to rush from the room and find somewhere dark to hide herself. He had thought she cried because he had been kind to her and told her he liked her. That was not the reason at all. It was the other thing he had said—*I thought you were a fortune hunter.* The words had torn at her like a barbed whip.

But she was not to escape so easily. The door of the breakfast room opened and Lady Tillden stepped inside with Lady Marie Lucas. There were curtsies and bows all round and considerable embarrassment. Charity and Lady Tillden settled into a dreary and thoroughly predictable discussion of the weather, which had been rainy last night and was now a little foggy, though there were signs that the fog was lifting, and there was considerable hope that the clouds might move right off later. Perhaps the sun would even shine—as it often did by day when there were no clouds. They were in amicable agreement with each other.

Beyond their own conversation Charity was aware of Lieutenant Lord Charles Earheart bowing over the hand of Lady Marie, as he had bowed over hers a short while ago, and raising it to his lips and exchanging a smile and a few quiet words with her.

"Good morning," he said. "How pleased I am to see you again. It has been all of eighteen months."

"I did not think you would be here," she said. "I thought you would be away with your regiment."

"I am on leave," he explained.

"I hoped you would not be here," she almost whispered.

"Did you?" he said, sounding unsurprised. "But I am, you see."

"Yes," she said.

"And are you still sorry?" he asked her, looking very gravely into her eyes.

But the weather as a topic of conversation had been exhausted, and Lady Tillden, with a sweet and nervous little smile for Charity's benefit, turned her attention to the conversation between her daughter and Lord Charles. They began to discuss the weather.

Charity excused herself and left the room. She ascended the first five stairs to her room at a walk. She took the rest at a run and two at a time.

I thought you were a fortune hunter.

13

By THE TIME HE DRESSED FOR THE BALL, THE MAR-quess of Staunton was feeling better pleased with the day than might have been expected. He had suc-ceeded in keeping himself at some distance from the houseguests while being perfectly civil when he was in company with them. It helped that both Marianne and Charles had exerted themselves to see to the entertain-ment of the guests, Marianne taking the carriage into the village with the ladies in the morning, Charles taking the barouche with all three of them during the afternoon on a drive about the park and a picnic at the ruins.

The Earl of Tillden, it seemed, had decided upon the wisdom of behaving as if the idea of a betrothal between his daughter and the Duke of Withingsby's heir had never for one moment disturbed his mind. He was spending an amicable few days with an old friend.

Charles himself had been quiet. He had made no at-tempt to seek out his brother with any comment on what he had heard during their early-morning ride. On the other hand he had not deliberately avoided him ei-ther. And the hostility had gone from his eyes, to be re-placed by a blank look that was hard to read. On the only occasion he had been forced to use his brother's name, though, he had not addressed him as *Staunton*, or even as *Anthony*, but as *Tony*. The marquess almost despised himself for the warmth the sound of that name brought him.

Then there was William. He had come to Enfield during the morning to discuss some small matter of estate business with his father. His grace had summoned the marquess to the library, had directed his younger son to spend an hour with him explaining various aspects of the running of the estates, and had left them alone together. They had been awkward and businesslike at first until some trivial detail had amused them both simultaneously and they had laughed together. After that, though they had looked self-consciously at each other and there had still been some awkwardness for a while, something had changed. Something indefinable. They had become brothers again without anything having been said—they had merely continued to discuss the matter at hand.

And the marquess, thinking afterward of Claudia, had realized that all that sordid and rather humiliating business was indeed past history. He felt nothing for her beyond a very natural appreciation of her beauty. The bitterness was gone. Perhaps—probably—after all, she had not been coerced. And, after all, perhaps Will had not acted dishonorably except in a very understandable reluctance to admit to his brother that they loved the same woman. Will had been only nineteen years old at the time. One could hardly expect him to act with the firmness and maturity of a man.

Even Augusta had thawed during the day. Not so much to him, perhaps, as to Charity, but she had smiled at him and had looked like a child. He had walked as far as the bridge with Will to enjoy the sunshine that had succeeded the morning mist—and had met Charity and Augusta coming in the opposite direction. Charity had been to the dower house for more fittings, especially for the ball dress that was being prepared in great haste for the evening. She had taken Augusta with her to play with the boys. How had she managed to pry his sister from the schoolroom in the middle of the morning? By the simple expedient of asking his grace and asking Miss Pevensey, the governess.

His grace had released his daughter from the schoolroom merely because his daughter-in-law had asked it of him?

"But of course," his wife had said when he put the question to her. "He agreed that such a beautiful morning ought not to be wasted."

She had blushed rosily as soon as they met and while they talked, he had noticed. She had clearly been remembering the night before, something he would prefer to forget if he could.

And so he had tried to focus on Augusta, who was, he had noticed, both dirty and disheveled—and for once looking like an eight-year-old child.

"You bring back distinct memories, Augusta," he had said, first fingering the handle of his quizzing glass and then lifting the glass to his eye, "of tree climbing and games of chasing and hide-and-seek. Except that I believe Will and Charles and I—and even Marianne on occasion—usually sported cuts and bruises and torn clothes as well as mere dirt."

She had glanced at him with considerable fright in her eyes.

"You will, of course," he had said, "change your frock and wash your hands and face and comb your hair before his grace sets eyes on you at luncheon. And if he should invite me to the library in the meanwhile and put me to the torture, I shall grit my teeth and swear that when I met you at the bridge there was not even one speck of dirt on your person, even on the soles of your shoes."

That was when she had smiled at him—a huge, sunny child's smile, complete with wrinkled nose.

Yes, the marquess thought now as his valet finally perfected the knot in his neckcloth and picked up his dark evening coat to help him into it, the day had gone rather well. Though of course, with all the preparations for the night's festivities in progress and with the Earl of Tillden and his family still at Enfield as guests, there had been very much a sense of meaningful activity being suspended. There was more to be settled, he realized, than getting on more comfortable terms with his brothers and sisters—and that had been no part of his original plan in coming here. There was something to be arranged and settled with his father. And there was his wife to deal with.

He must send her on her way soon, he had decided during the day. For one thing, she had already fulfilled her function. He had been accepted as a married man who could not be made to fit into anyone's preconceptions about how the Marquess of Staunton should live his life. For another, it would be easier for her to leave now and cause another commotion within his family before they had quite recovered from the first. It might as well all be settled once and for all. And then too she might as well go before he could increase the already strong chance that she was with child. And before he could become too accustomed to her convenient presence in the room next to his own at night.

He had hired Miss Charity Duncan to do him a service. That service had not included warming his bed at night.

He leaned closer to the looking glass in order to place a diamond pin in the center of the folds of his neckcloth. But his hands paused in the task. He was also wearing a jeweled ring. What jewels did his wife have to deck herself out with? At least she would not have to wear the atrocious gray silk to the ball. Claudia's modiste had finished the ball gown for her. He expected that it would be pretty and fashionable and of suitably costly fabric. But she would have no jewels to wear with it.

It had been the whole point, of course—to bring to Enfield a bride who had clearly been impoverished when he married her, to flaunt before his family the fact that birth and fortune and fashion and beauty—all the usual reasons why a man of his rank chose a bride—meant nothing to him.

And yet now he felt strangely guilty. How must she have felt for the past few days, as different in appearance from his family and their guests as it was possible to be? How would she feel tonight, in her new ball gown, her throat and wrists and ears bare of jewels? And yet she was his wife, the most senior lady in rank at tonight's ball. Word had quickly spread in the neighborhood that the ball, which rumor had had it would be a betrothal ball for the Marquess of Staunton, was in fact being held in celebration of his marriage.

Why had he not thought to buy her a wedding gift—a bracelet, a necklace, a ring? Even Anna, who had served as his mistress for six weeks earlier in the spring, had been dismissed with rubies.

He closed his eyes and thought. There was the gold chain and locket that his mother had given him on his eighteenth birthday, a miniature of herself inside. He had worn it constantly for a year after her death. He had it with him. He also had with him—ah, yes—a string of pearls he had bought as an enticement for the young dancer he had intended to employ after Anna. He had changed his mind about her and about his need of a mistress from the *demimonde*. He still had the pearls. He had brought them with the vague notion of presenting them to Marianne or Augusta.

He dismissed his valet and found them. They were rather splendid—he had always lavished the best of everything on mistresses and prospective mistresses, on the cynical assumption that a generous protector could usually command the best services and exclusive services.

He did not know what her gown looked like. He did not even know the color. She had laughed when he had asked—and looked remarkably pretty and youthful doing it—and told him that it was a secret. But it did not matter. Pearls would match anything. He warmed them in his hand. Perhaps it might be argued that he owed her nothing since her payment was very well looked after indeed in the agreement they had both signed. But she had done her job well, and more than well—though the pearls would not be payment for sexual favors. He frowned down at his hand. The thought was distasteful. She was his wife.

He would give her the pearls because she was his wife. They would be a wedding present even though theirs was not a normal marriage.

He tapped on the door of her dressing room a minute later and waited for her maid to open it. But her ladyship was not there, the girl informed him, bobbing him a curtsy. She had already gone down to the drawing room, summoned there by his grace.

Well. He slipped the pearls into a pocket and followed his wife downstairs. His grace had chosen to show an affection for his daughter-in-law that he had never shown his own children. It was deliberate, of course. He was attempting to discompose his son, to convince him that he was not at all rattled to have been presented with a future duchess chosen from the lower ranks of the gentry, a future duchess who had until recently earned her living as a governess.

It did not matter. The marquess was not disconcerted. It amused him that his grace was lavishing attentions on Charity. He looked forward to seeing her in her new ball gown. He would present the pearls to her in a more public setting than he had intended. He would clasp them about her neck himself. Perhaps she would favor him with one of her warm smiles.

HER GOWN WAS of white silk covered with a tunic of white lace embroidered all over with gold rosebuds. The embroidery was slightly larger and more densely spaced at the hem and the cuffs of the short sleeves and at the neckline, which was quite fashionably low. Claudia had produced a pair of long gold evening gloves and had insisted that she wear them. Her new maid, who was very clever with her hands, had performed wonders with her hair, so that it was all curls and ringlets without looking in any way too girlish for her age or marital status.

She felt, Charity thought, gazing at her image in the glass, quite beautiful. She found herself totally enchanting, and then grinned at herself and her own self-conceit. But she did not care if she was being conceited. She was not expressing her thoughts to anyone else but herself, after all. She thought she looked quite, quite beautiful. She felt like a princess going to a grand ball—and that at least was not far off the mark. She was the Marchioness of Staunton, daughter-in-law of the Duke of Withingsby, and she was going to her very first ball—in a ballroom whose splendor had quite taken her breath away when she had peeped in at it late in the afternoon—as the guest of honor. She was even to stand in the receiving line with his grace and her husband.

Would he think her beautiful? It did not matter if he did or not, she decided. But, oh, of course it mattered. He had found her desirable last night—her cheeks had been turning hot at regular intervals all day long at the memory of last night. But she really did not know whether that had been just because she had been there and available—and willing—or whether he found her personally attractive. It did not matter if he found her attractive or not. Yes, it did—she grinned at her image again. She was going to enjoy tonight. She was going to forget that all this was only a very temporary arrangement. She was going to forget that she was only a sort of Cinderella—except that no prince would scour the countryside searching for her, slipper clutched in one hand, after she had gone. She was simply going to enjoy herself.

She waited impatiently for her husband to come to escort her to the drawing room. There was dinner to be sat through first, of course, before any of the outside guests would begin to arrive for the ball. But she would feel that the evening had started once she left this room. She wondered if they would all look on her in some shock now that she was dressed appropriately for the part she played. She wondered how *he* would look on her when he came into her dressing room. She intended to be looking right at him so that she could see his first reaction.

She *hoped* he would approve of her appearance.

She smiled brightly when his knock came at the door and nodded at her maid to open it. She cooled her smile—she must not look like an exuberant schoolgirl. But it collapsed all the way when she saw that it was a servant, not her husband. His grace requested the honor of her company in the drawing room immediately. She hesitated. Surely her husband would not be long. Should she tap on his dressing-room door? But somehow, despite her relationship to him and the intimacies they had shared, the Marquess of Staunton did not seem quite the person with whom one felt free to take such liberties.

"When his lordship comes, Winnie," she said to her maid, "please tell him that his grace has summoned me to the drawing room."

Fortunately she felt familiar enough by now with the family not to feel too awed to walk into a room alone. Of course this evening it was more difficult. She felt dreadfully self-conscious of her very different appearance. Even the footman who opened the door into the drawing room for her looked startled, she thought, until she realized the absurdity of the thought. Footmen were trained not to look startled even if a herd of elephants wearing pink skirts galloped by.

Claudia beamed at her and William pursed his lips and looked very like his brother for a moment. Marianne raised her eyebrows and Richard exerted himself enough to bow. Charles took her hand, bowed over it— he was himself looking irresistibly handsome—and told her with a roguish wink that Tony was a lucky devil. The Earl of Tillden and his family had not yet come down. His grace stood with his back to the fireplace and looked her over with keen eyes. She smiled at him and curtsied.

"You wanted me, Father?" she asked. His face looked less gray than usual. He must have been resting, as she had advised him to do and as he had promised to do.

"Yes. Come closer, my dear," he said.

She stepped closer and smiled at him. The attention of the rest of the family was on them, of course. He held something in one of his hands, she saw when he brought it from behind his back.

"I gave her grace a gift on our wedding day," he said. "On her passing it reverted to me. It is my wish to give it as a gift to the bride who will one day hold her grace's title and position. To my eldest son's bride. To you, my dear."

She looked down at his open palm. It was a large and beautiful topaz surrounded by diamonds and set into a necklet of diamonds. It was an ornate and heavy piece of jewelry that must be worth a king's ransom. Not that it was its monetary value that turned Charity's mouth and throat dry. It was the other value of the piece. It had been his gift to his wife—his wedding gift. And now he was giving it to her? It matched her gown, though it was altogether too heavy for the gown's delicacy. But that did not matter. The necklet blurred before her vision and she blinked her eyes rapidly.

"Father." She looked up into his eyes. "You must have loved her very much." Extremely silly words that had no relevance to anything. She did not know why she had said them—or whispered them, rather. She had barely spoken aloud.

She would not have been able to put into words afterward even if she had been called upon to do so what happened to his eyes then. They turned to steel. They turned to warm liquid. Neither description would have served and yet both were close, opposite as they were.

"Oh, yes," was all he said, so quietly that she doubted that even in the quiet room anyone had heard the exchange.

"Turn," he said. "I shall fasten it about your neck."

She turned—and met Marianne's eyes. They were full of disbelief, resentment, envy. Marianne was the elder daughter. She must have expected that her mother's most precious piece of jewelry would be given to her or left to her at her father's death. It felt cold and heavy and alien about Charity's throat. Her father-in-law set his hands on her shoulders and turned her when he had clasped the necklet in place.

"It is where it belongs," he said and then shocked her by lowering his head and kissing her first on one cheek and then on the other.

"Thank you, Father," she said. She was choked with gratitude, with discomfort, with—with love. She cared so very much for him, she thought. She did not know why except that there was a deep sadness in her for him and a deep tenderness. She loved him. He was her father—her husband's father.

A very dangerous thought.

She moved to one side so that she would not monopolize his attention, using the tray of drinks on the sideboard as an excuse. She picked up a glass of ratafia. She had just finished drinking it a few minutes later when the door opened and she saw that her husband had arrived. She stood very still, watching him, waiting for him to notice her. In his dark evening clothes and crisp white linen and lace he looked even more handsome than ever. And more satanic. But if she had ever been even a little afraid of him, she was so no longer. She just wished she did not have certain memories . . . But for this evening she would not try to force them from her mind. This was the evening she had set herself to enjoy.

His eyes found her almost immediately. As his father had done a short while ago, he stood still and swept her from head to foot with his eyes. She read admiration there and something a little warmer than admiration. She smiled at him.

And then his eyes came to rest on her throat.

Something in his look alerted her. She felt cold, breathless. She felt danger even though his expression did not change and he did not move for a few moments. Even when he came slowly toward her, his face was expressionless. She felt panic catch at her breath. She felt the urge to turn and run. Yet she could not understand the feeling. She continued to smile at him.

"Where did you get that?" His voice, very quiet, stabbed into her like a sharp needle. His eyes looked suddenly very black.

Her hand went to the necklet. "It was your mother's," she said foolishly.

"Where did you get it?" His nostrils flared.

"Your father gave it to me," she said. "As a bridal gift.

It is very beautiful." *I will give it back before I leave*. But she could not say those last words aloud. They had an audience—a very attentive audience.

"Take it off," he said.

"Your father—"

"Take it off." His face was white. And suddenly she was terrified of him.

She did not move her hands fast enough. He raised one of his own, curled it about the topaz, his fingers grazing over her skin none too gently, and jerked at the necklet. The catch held fast and she grimaced with pain.

"Turn around," he said.

She turned and tilted her head forward. His fingers fumbled at the catch for what seemed endless moments before she felt the weight of the necklet fall away from her neck into his hand. She did not lift her head or turn around—everyone was behind her and everyone was loudly silent. So silent that she heard the words her husband spoke to the duke after he had crossed the room to the fireplace.

"This is yours, I believe, sir," he said.

"On the contrary, Staunton," the duke said, "it is Lady Staunton's. I have made it a gift to her."

"I decline the gift," his son said. "I will provide any clothes and jewels that my wife will wear."

"It is her ladyship's," his grace said. "I will have none of it."

"Then it will lie there until someone chooses to pick it up," the marquess said. And there was the thud of something falling to the floor.

The door opened at the same moment to admit the Earl and Countess of Tillden and Lady Marie Lucas.

William was stooping unobtrusively to pick up the necklet as Charity turned. But it was all she saw. She hurried from the room with her head bowed. She was not even sure she would go up to her room to fetch her things. She was not sure she could bear to stay at Enfield even that long. But a hand closed about her arm before she had taken half a dozen steps away from the drawing-room door.

"Charity?" It was Charles's voice.

"No," she said, pulling her arm loose. "No, please."

But he would not let her go. He stepped in front of her and she ran right against his chest. She did not have the energy to push away again. She rested her face against him and breathed in noisy, shaky gasps.

"Let me take you to another room," he said, "where you may recover yourself. You did nothing wrong. You must believe that. You got caught in the middle. You did nothing wrong."

"No, she did not." The other voice was quieter and came from behind her. "I'll take her, Charles."

"Only if you promise on your honor not to harm her," Charles said, his voice hardening. "Her neck is bleeding."

"I promise," the marquess said. His voice was bleak and dull.

"I suppose it was *that*," Charles said, "to which you referred this morning."

"Yes," the marquess said. "He has come straight from hell, Charles. We have the devil himself as our sire. A noble distinction. Come with me, Charity, please?" His hands touched her shoulders.

She straightened up. "Thank you, Charles," she said. "I hope I have not damaged your neckcloth."

"It is not nearly so elaborate as Tony's anyway," he said, smiling. "I tied it myself." He strode back into the drawing room.

"Come with me," her husband said, and she felt the soft warmth of his handkerchief being pressed against the back of her neck, which she was only just beginning to realize was sore. "Please? I will not hurt you again. I promise I will not."

He took her into the small salon next to the drawing room and closed the door.

"You were, as Charles said, caught in the middle," he told her. He seated her on a chair and dabbed gently at her neck with his handkerchief. "That necklet was my mother's. She always said it was to be mine after her. She gave it to me before she died. She was very positive about her wish that I have it. I was the most precious person in her life, she always told me. My father missed it from her jewel collection right after her funeral while I was out riding, trying to clear my head after the emotions of the day. When I came home, he was in my room, the necklet in his hand. He accused me of stealing it. He would listen to no defense, no explanations. He punished me by whipping me. I could easily have avoided the whipping— I was twenty years old and at least as strong as he. I did not even try to avoid it. But I told him before he administered it what would happen if he did it."

"You left home," she said.

"Yes." He blew cool air against the graze on the back of her neck. "I swore I would never come back. But I came. On my own terms."

"With me," she said.

"Yes. My anger was not directed against you just now," he said. "I was blind with fury. It is no excuse, of course. I beg your pardon."

"He gave it to me deliberately," she said. "He knew it would hurt and infuriate you more than anything else he could possibly do."

"You were quite right," he said, "at the very beginning when you said that you would be a pawn in a game. I am sorry you have been physically hurt too. Does it hurt badly?"

"No," she said, getting to her feet. "Hardly at all. We have a dinner to attend."

"Now?" He laughed. "I am going to take you away

from here tonight. We will return to London and then you will tell me where you wish to settle and I will have the arrangements made as swiftly as possible. You have done well. You have earned your future of comfort and security."

"We have a dinner to attend," she said firmly, "and a ball. Perhaps you are lacking in courage, my lord, but I am not. You ran away once and have never been able to outrun the demons or ghosts or whatever you may care to call them. You will not run again, I think, when you have taken a moment to consider."

He gazed at her, his expression unreadable. He drew a deep breath at last. "And so to dinner, then, my little brown mouse," he said. "But will you wear these for me? Will they hurt your neck?"

A string of pearls was lying across his palm. They were delicate and perfect and made her want to cry.

"They are a gift," he said. "A thank you, if you will. A wedding gift, perhaps."

"I will wear them," she said, turning and dipping her head again so that he could clasp them about her neck. "They are beautiful."

"But not nearly as lovely," he said, "as their wearer."

14

IT WAS NOT SO VERY DIFFICULT AFTER ALL TO GET through dinner, the marquess found. His grace behaved as he always did; so did he. That is, they were both reticent, formally correct and courteous. It had become second nature to him to hide all feeling so deep that no one else would suspect that it was there at all.

Except that his wife suspected it. She sat in her place at the foot of the table, quite dizzyingly beautiful, smiling, animated, flushed, bright-eyed—and gazing straight through the defenses that had held everyone at bay for years to understand that he was deeply disturbed by what had just happened. At least it seemed to him that she saw through his defenses. Perhaps it was fanciful thinking. And fanciful too to imagine that she looked with just as penetrating an understanding at his father— only to discover, surely, that there was nothing behind his grace's facade. Only coldness and emptiness and even perhaps evil.

It was not even very difficult to stand in the receiving line just inside the ballroom later in the evening, greeting the guests as they arrived, presenting his marchioness to neighbors and acquaintances. It was not difficult, because although his father stood in the line too, she stood between them and was as animated, as charming, as beautiful as she had been in the dining room.

He found his mind counting back days as he smiled and bowed and made small talk with the arriving guests. But no matter how often he did the calculations he always arrived at the same conclusion. One week ago he had not even met Miss Charity Duncan. One week ago he had glanced through her letter of application and after some hesitation had set it on the pile of those to be given more serious consideration.

And now, just one week later, he was falling in love with her. The thought verbalized itself in his mind without any prior warning, and he pushed it impatiently away. He was no boy to be gulled by shallow emotion.

"I have never been so nervous in my life," she said, smiling at him during a lull in arrivals.

He raised his eyebrows. He never would have guessed it. She looked as if she had been standing in receiving lines for years. "Not even on your arrival here, my lady?" he asked.

"Oh." She laughed. "I was not nervous then. I was terrified." But she would not exclude his grace from her conversation even though he had used her shamefully earlier in the evening. She turned and set a hand on his arm. "Will you sit, Father? No one will remark upon it if you do. Almost everyone must have arrived by now, and Anthony and I can greet the latecomers." She spoke with a gentle concern that sounded almost affectionate.

As for himself, the marquess thought as, to his amazement, his father allowed himself to be led toward a vacant chair, he did not care what happened to the duke. He would not stay to concern himself with his father's health or with Enfield affairs. Tomorrow he would be on his way back to London with his wife. He would see her settled comfortably in a home of her choice and then he would resume his old life just as if there had not been this disruption of a few days. And really that was all it had been—a few days.

They did not remain in the receiving line much longer. It was their duty to lead off the first set of country dances, and the guests would be impatient to begin. The ballroom at Enfield looked remarkably festive, the marquess was forced to admit, and far more architecturally splendid than most of the London ballrooms he knew. It was a betrothal ball that had been rapidly converted into a wedding ball. The flowers and ribbons and bows that decked the room were predominantly white. But then, of course, his grace was adept at arranging such things.

Did his wife dance? he wondered suddenly. But she surely would have said something to him if she did not. And indeed she danced the steps flawlessly and gracefully. Will, he saw, had led Lady Marie into this opening set. He had not spoken to the girl himself beyond the exchange of a few courtesies. But it did not seem to him that she was nursing a broken heart. He hoped not. He did not doubt that, like him, she was merely a victim of two despotic men who assumed that it was their right to organize the lives of their offspring down to the last detail. Perhaps now she would be given a little more choice of husband, though he doubted it.

His father, he noticed, was observing the proceedings like a king from his throne, his expression proud and unreadable, his complexion tinged with gray. But he would take no notice of that last fact, his son decided. A serious illness did not hinder his grace in the pursuit of evil. He remembered being so blindly furious just a few hours ago that he had tried to yank his mother's necklet from his wife's neck without pausing to undo the catch first. He had drawn blood from the back of her neck.

And he remembered the day of his mother's funeral. He had returned from his vigorous ride, weary from the emotions and grief of the previous days, to find his father waiting in his rooms. For one moment—or perhaps for the mere fraction of a moment—his heart had leapt with something like gladness as he thought his father had come to share his grief. And then he had seen the topaz necklet in his father's hand.

In the pattern of the dance, he and his wife passed each other, back to back. "Smile, my lord," she said. "It is by far the best revenge."

And then they were back in their separate lines, performing other figures of the dance, unable to exchange anything more than looks. She was still smiling, an expression that involved her whole face and appeared to reach back far into her eyes. Perhaps, he thought in some surprise, she wore a mask as impenetrable as his own. Could she really be feeling as happy as she looked? She had been horribly shamed earlier, in front of his whole family. She had been given a precious gift and accepted into the family, so to speak, by the Duke of Withingsby himself. And then her husband had arrived, talked to her coldly in front of them all, torn the gift from about her neck, and abandoned her in her embarrassment and humiliation so that he might have his moment of confrontation with his grace.

It was Charles who had offered her comfort first. And for once—the only time during the days he had known her—she had lost her quiet self-possession. She had sagged against Charles, her breathing labored.

Yet now she had come to face his family again rather than run away as she had had the opportunity to do—it had been his full intent to take her away. She had faced them, not with anger or cold dignity or righteous recriminations, but with smiles and charm and grace. With a dignity worthy of a duchess—or of a marchioness maybe.

For his sake? Was she doing this for him? Because she had made a bargain with him and was determined to earn the generous settlement that would be hers for the rest of her life? Or was she doing it for herself? To show them all that she was not ashamed of who she was, that she could be more the person of true gentility than the best of them?

He really was falling in love with her. This time he allowed the thought to remain in his conscious mind. They crossed in front of each other in the middle of the set and he smiled at her.

"It is certainly something you should do more often," she said before she moved out of earshot again. "It is a deadly weapon."

She was referring to his smile, he thought after a moment of incomprehension. She was *flirting* with him. But even as his pulses quickened involuntarily, he knew that she was not. She was playing a part and she was doing it magnificently well. She was drawing admiring eyes despite the relative simplicity of her appearance—or perhaps because of it. She looked fresh and new and innocent and . . .

And the sooner he got her settled to a comfortable life of her own, the sooner he could retreat to the life that was familiar to him. The safe life. He did not want to be unsafe again. There was too much pain.

He bowed in the line of gentlemen and she curtsied in the line of ladies to signal the end of the set. He took her hand on his and led her toward Claudia.

"I will wish for the honor of your hand for the waltz after supper, my love," he said, relishing the chance to use the endearment. He bowed to her and raised her hand to his lips while Claudia looked on with a smile. "You will reserve it for me?"

"A waltz?" she said. "Oh, yes. But I cannot think my hand will be so in demand, my lord, that you need to *reserve* the set with me."

There was no chance for further conversation. Sir John Symonds, Claudia's eldest brother, had arrived to solicit the hand of the Marchioness of Staunton for the quadrille that was to follow.

She looked endearingly startled, her husband saw.

CHARITY HAD MADE a discovery during the ball—two, actually. The one was that the Marchioness of Staunton was a very important person indeed and more gentlemen wished to dance with her than there were sets in the evening. She amused herself with wondering how many of the same gentlemen would even notice her existence if she could suddenly appear at the ball as the person she had been just the week before—and clad in her gray silk.

The other discovery was of far greater significance and she longed to discuss it with someone, but Claudia, her obvious choice of confidant, was always in company with other people between sets, and so was she, Charity, for that matter.

Charles had eyes for Lady Marie Lucas. And Lady Marie Lucas had eyes for Charles. They danced the second set together and watched each other covertly during every set that followed it—all of which each of them danced with other partners. At supper they sat close enough to exchange some conversation even though they were not supper partners.

They were just perfect for each other. All of Charity's maternal and matchmaking instincts came to the fore. Penny, she thought, would recognize the gleam in her eye and begin to protest—she tried to hide the gleam in her eye. They were close in age, they were both beautiful people, and they were probably friends. Had not she heard that the Earl of Tillden had brought his family to Enfield a number of times over the years? Charles and Marie had probably been playmates. He was three years older than she. He had probably been her hero. And he had probably been protective of her. She wondered when childhood friendship had blossomed into love. And she wondered too if the Earl of Tillden would countenance a match between his only daughter and the youngest son of a duke—a mere cavalry lieutenant.

She had been woolgathering at the supper table and was not giving her partner the attention that was his due. She was brought back to the present when she met her husband's eyes across the room. He looked his usual cold, arrogant self, staring at her with pursed lips and hooded eyes. But he did not deceive her for a moment. The incident with the topaz necklet had shaken him dreadfully—far more than it had her. It had shaken him to the very roots, exposing wounds that he had covered over and hidden from sight for so long that doubtless he had thought them long healed.

And there was her father-in-law, sitting with the Earl of Tillden and two ladies whose identities she had forgotten, with the identical haughty, shuttered look on his face. How foolish human nature was sometimes. But she was back to woolgathering. She smiled and turned her attention to the conversation at her table.

The waltz she had promised to reserve for her husband came directly after supper. There had never been waltzes at any of the assemblies at home, but Philip had learned the steps elsewhere and had come home and demonstrated them, first with her and then with Penny and finally with Mary. They had all made very merry with the foolish dance. And she had dreamed ever since of waltzing in a real ballroom with a real partner—brothers did not qualify as real partners. Her husband, on the other hand, was as real as any partner could be.

"I know the steps of the waltz," she told him as they took their places on the floor, "but I have never danced it. I hope I will not disgrace you and trip all over your toes or mine."

"You will merely provide me with an excuse for holding you closer," he said.

She wished she had not developed the annoying habit of blushing hotly at the merest suggestion of a compliment. She had done it earlier when he had made that grossly flattering remark about the relative beauty of the pearl necklace and its wearer. She did it again now. There was something in his eyes—a slight drooping of the eyelids. She recognized the look, actually. She had learned something last night about sexual tension.

"I shall try not to make it necessary," she said.

His face remained immobile. But his eyes smiled. It was a wicked, knee-weakening expression. She should, she thought very much too late, have allowed him to hurry her back to London as he had wanted to do earlier.

She need not have worried about the dance. After the first few faltering steps she picked up the rhythm of the waltz without any trouble at all. How could she not do so when she had such a superb partner? He twirled her about the perimeter of the ballroom and she could almost imagine that her feet did not touch the floor. She had never in her life felt so exhilarated, she was sure. And not just exhilarated. His eyes held hers, breaking contact only occasionally to roam over her face and her shoulders. And that strange smile lingered there. Those very dark eyes of his had lost their disturbing opaque quality again.

"Has anyone reserved the next set with you?" he asked when she was beginning to feel regret at the knowledge that the set must be almost at an end.

She shook her head. She had not missed a single set, but apart from this one, none had been reserved ahead of time.

"Then you will remain with me," he said. "And since at Enfield strict rules of etiquette must be observed and

I dare not dance a third set even with my wife, we will go outside, my lady. We will stroll down to the lake. Unless you are reluctant to drag yourself from the festivities for half an hour, that is."

Her first foolish thought was that it would be quite improper to be alone with him. For she knew from long experience when a gentleman merely wanted to take a little air with the lady of his choice and when he hoped to take more than just a little air. The Marquess of Staunton intended to take liberties with her person.

Her second foolish thought was that she was afraid to let him kiss her. It was extremely foolish in light of what they had done together in the privacy of his bed the night before—three separate times—and in light of the fact that she was his wife. But somehow, strangely— she would not at all have been able to explain the feeling—there was something vastly different about lying with her husband and walking out into the moonlight with him while a ball was in progress. Walking out was infinitely more dangerous.

And every bit as tempting.

And just as impossible to resist.

"Fresh air and a stroll will be very pleasant, my lord," she said.

That smile in his eyes took on a dimension of true amusement. "You look," he said, "as if you are agreeing to attend your own execution."

"Oh," she said and felt her blush return with full heat. He knew that she knew he was taking her outside to kiss her. She glanced at his mouth. She had felt it once—at their wedding—coming to rest lightly beside her own mouth. It had shocked her to her toenails. What would it feel like directly against her own? It was very silly to feel breathless when she had received his body right inside her own four times in all.

But a kiss was different. She felt breathless. And the

music was coming to an end. Yes, there was no doubt about it. The dance had finished.

THEY WOULD STAY for dinner and for the ball, she had said. They would not run away. They would stay and show his family a thing or two about courage. Well, they had stayed, and even his grace would have to agree that all had gone smoothly enough. The ball was a grand success. It could almost compare to a London squeeze. He doubted that anyone had refused the invitation.

The point had been made. Tomorrow he would return to London and set his own life and his wife's in order—separately. Tonight was done with as far as he was concerned. Tomorrow had not yet come. Between the two times there was now, tonight. He had not yet decided if he would invite her to his bed again. He wanted her, of course. He guessed it would take some time for his sexual craving for her to die. He would have to work on it. But he would just as soon resist the temptation to have her tonight. If he had her once, he would want her again, and each time he would be in danger of impregnating her.

He wanted something different out of tonight. Something—he could not think of a word to describe what he wanted. Actually, there was a word but he was unwilling to use it even in his own mind. He wanted some warmth, some human closeness, some tenderness, some—romance. There, the word had come unbidden. He wanted a little romance. He mocked himself with both the word and the feeling it evoked in him. But it was what he wanted.

And so he invited her to walk to the lake with him after their waltz. He saw in her eyes that she understood him perfectly. He found it somewhat disturbing that within just a few days she had developed the uncanny knack of getting into his head with him as no one else had since the days when Will had been his closest crony. And even Will had not been so unerring in his understanding. He also saw in her eyes, of course, the mirror of his own feelings. She too wanted some romance tonight. It was an alarming realization. He should have run a mile from it. He should have danced with someone else and turned her over to another partner. He should have decided quite firmly to go to his bedchamber at the end of the ball and lock his door.

Instead he led her out through the French doors into the coolness of the evening, where several couples were strolling. He took her away from the terrace and the lights of the house, across the lawn toward the lake. He took her hand and linked his fingers with hers. Her hand was warm and smooth and curled firmly about his. When they were beyond the sight of anyone who might have been watching, he released her hand, twined his arm about her waist, and drew her against his side. After a moment's hesitation she set her arm about his waist. Her head came to rest against his shoulder. They had not said a word to each other since leaving the ballroom.

It could not have been a more perfect night for such a stroll. The air was cool but not at all cold. There was hardly a breeze. The sky was clear and star-studded. The moon was shining in a broad band across the water of the lake. They stopped walking when they were close to the bank.

"Have you ever seen anything more beautiful?" she asked with a sigh after a lengthy, perfectly comfortable silence.

"Yes," he said. "I have only to turn my head to see it." He turned his head and his mouth brushed against her hair.

"Where did you learn such foolish gallantries?" she asked, amusement rather than censure in her voice.

"Here at Enfield," he said. "Today and yesterday and

the day before." *Steady,* he told himself. *Say nothing you will forever regret. Steady.*

She said nothing.

"Will and I used to sneak out sometimes at night," he said. "I can remember swimming here on at least one occasion. Even now I dread to think what would have happened to us if we had been caught."

"Or if you had had cramps," she said.

"I suppose," he said, "rules like the one forbidding children to go out alone at night are made for their own good, are they not?"

"Usually," she said.

"And I suppose I will be as drearily prohibitive with my own children," he said.

She did not answer him.

He winced inwardly. "If having children of my own were in my plans," he said. "But childhood can be a golden age despite prohibitions and punishments. I am sorry you had no brothers and sisters of your own."

"I had companions," she said. "I had a happy childhood."

"I am glad of it," he said, tightening his arm a little. "I would not like to think of you being lonely."

And then he felt lonely himself. He was here with her, cocooned against present loneliness, but there was a strong awareness that tomorrow everything would be different. They would be traveling back to London. And after that their separate lives would begin. He would be married to her for the rest of his life, but he would probably never be with her like this again, just standing quietly in the moonlight, gazing across a calm lake. In harmony with another living person.

There was only tonight.

The anticipation of loneliness washed over him.

When he turned her in his arms, she tipped back her head and looked up at him with those very large blue eyes of hers—though he could not really see their color in the moonlight. He did not kiss her—not immediately. He was afraid to kiss her. He did not know what lay on the other side of a kiss. He was not sure he would be able to regain command of himself and his life once he had kissed her, though he could not quite make sense of his fear.

He held her against him with one arm and ran the knuckles of the other hand softly along her cheek and down beneath her chin to hold it up.

"Why did you not let me see on that day that you are beautiful?" he asked her.

"I have never been called beautiful before," she said. "I wanted the position."

"My quiet brown mouse," he said. He was rubbing the pad of his thumb very gently over her lips. He heard her swallow. "Have you ever been kissed, little mouse?"

"No." It was just a whisper of sound.

She had been bedded, but she had never been kissed. He had bedded, but he had rarely kissed. He moved his lips so close to hers that he could feel the warmth from them.

"Is this a lovely enough setting for the first?" he asked her. "Is the moment right? Is it the right man?"

"Yes." When she spoke the word, her lips brushed his.

He touched her with his lips—barely touched. He felt warmth and softness and sweet invitation. He felt her breath on his cheek. He moved his lips, parted them slightly, feeling her, feeling what she did to him. Not to his body. He expected his body to react predictably, but it did not do so. He felt what she did to his heart, or whatever unknown part of him was denoted by the name of a mere organ.

He wrapped his free arm about her shoulders, pushed his lips more firmly against hers, tasted her, was warmed by her, soothed by her, healed by her.

He knew all about tongue play. There had been a time when he had practiced it, enjoyed it. He did not touch her with his tongue or open his mouth. She parted her own lips only sufficiently to give him the softness and the warmth of her very essence. This was not a sexual encounter. He was right to have feared it. He raised his head and looked down at her.

"Thank you," he heard himself say.

He watched her eyes fill with tears and knew instinctively that they were not tears of grief or of anger or of disappointment. He drew her head to his shoulder and held it there for several minutes while she relaxed against him.

He was not after all in love with her, he thought, and he felt terror clutch at him. That was not it at all. He wished it were. Being in love was a youthful, essentially shallow thing. He was not in love with his wife.

He loved her.

"I had better take you back to the ballroom," he said.

"Yes." She drew away from him and looked at him speculatively. The tears were long gone. "Will you do something for me? Please?"

"Yes," he said.

"Will you come to the library with me," she said, "and wait there while I—until I come back?"

He searched her eyes but she offered no explanation. He would ask for none. He had said yes.

"Yes," he said again, "I will."

She frowned for a moment, but when he took her hand she twined her fingers about his and walked by his side toward the house and the library.

Tonight he would do anything in the world for her.

Tomorrow he would begin to set her free.

15

CHARITY WAS BEGINNING TO REALIZE THE ENORMITY of the mistake she had made. She had agreed quite cold-bloodedly to a marriage that was not really a marriage just for the sake of money and security. It was a horrible sin she had committed. *I thought you were a fortune hunter*—Charles's words had haunted her all day. She had married on the very foolish assumption that her feelings would be no more engaged during a few weeks of a temporary marriage than they would have been during a brief period of employment as a governess. But her feelings had become involved with almost everyone at Enfield.

And now she knew that she was to suffer the ultimate punishment for her sin and for her foolishness. Her feelings were very deeply engaged in a much more personal way than just concern for a family that was living in its own self-made hell.

She had experienced the ultimate embrace on her wedding night and again last night. But she had perhaps been too involved in the wonder of physical sensation on those occasions to feel the full impact of what was happening to her heart. She had understood with blinding clarity during that kiss at the lake. It had been exquisitely sweet, totally different from what she had expected. She had expected passion and had found tenderness. Tenderness was not something she would have associated with the Marquess of Staunton if she had not experienced it there in his arms and felt it in his lips. His lips had even trembled against her own.

She was not in a dream as they walked back up the lawn toward the house. She knew what was ahead for her, and the prospect was daunting to say the least. But there was tonight. And tonight all things seemed possible. It was a magical night, set apart from real time. And so she had suggested, quite impulsively, that he come to the library with her and wait there.

But there was magic elsewhere too.

She stopped walking suddenly, squeezing her husband's hand a little tighter as she did so.

"Look," she whispered. Perhaps she ought not to have drawn his attention to what she saw, but she sensed that he too was in a mellow mood.

Not far from the house, but hidden from it by the particularly massive trunk of an oak tree, a man in dark evening clothes stood face-to-face with a woman in a delicate white dress, his hands at her waist, her body arched toward his. Even as Charity watched, they drew closer together and kissed. Charles and Marie.

"They are bound only for heartache," the marquess said softly, drawing her firmly onward again. "He may be a duke's son, but he is only a younger son—hardly a worthy substitute for the heir, for whom she has been groomed. Her father will never allow it." He sounded more sad than cynical.

"Perhaps he can be persuaded," she said. "Charles is such a wonderful young man. My guess is that they have been friends all their lives and that they have loved each other for a year or more. Maybe all will turn out well for them."

"You must be a person who believes implicitly in the

happily-ever-afters at the end of fairy tales," he said, though there was no censure in his voice.

"No," she said. "Oh, no, I do not." She wished she could.

They walked the rest of the way in silence. The library was in darkness when they arrived there. He lit a branch of candles and turned to look at her, his eyebrows raised.

"I will not be long," she said. "You will wait?"

"I will wait," he said. His eyes, she saw—oh, his eyes almost frightened her. She could see right into their depths.

The Duke of Withingsby was strolling about the ballroom between sets, being graciously sociable. Charity stepped up to his side while he was speaking with a group of neighbors—there were so few names she remembered, though she had paid careful attention in the receiving line. She slipped an arm through his, smiled at him and at them, and waited for the conversation to be completed.

"Well, my dear," he said then. "Your success seems assured."

"Father," she said, "come to the library with me?"

He raised haughty eyebrows.

"Please?" she said. "It is important."

"Is it indeed?" he said. "Important enough to take me from my guests, ma'am? But very well. I shall not be sorely missed, I suppose."

Her heart thumped as they walked from the ballroom to the library. She had always had a tendency to meet problems head-on and to try to maneuver other people to do the same thing. Sometimes she had been successful, sometimes decidedly not. But she did not believe she had ever tackled anything quite as huge as this. What if she was doing entirely the wrong thing? What if she was precipitating disaster? But she did not believe things could be much more disastrous than they already were. She could hardly make them worse.

Her husband was standing by the window, his back to it. He did not move or say anything when she came in with his father. He merely pursed his lips. The duke also said nothing and showed no sign of surprise beyond coming to a halt for a moment in the doorway.

"Father," she said, "will you have a seat? This one, by the fireplace? It is more comfortable, I believe, than the one behind the desk. May I fetch you something? A drink?"

He seated himself in the chair she indicated, looked steadily at his son and then at her. "Nothing," he said. "You may proceed to explain what this matter of importance is."

She stood by his chair and rested a hand lightly on his shoulder. "Anthony," she said, "you brought me here two days ago with the sole intention of hurting your father and destroying all his hopes and plans. You deliberately married a woman far beneath you in rank and with the demeaning stigma of having worked for her living."

"I did not deceive you about my intentions," he said.

"And, Father," she said, "you have shown me affection yesterday and today with the sole purpose of annoying Anthony. Your plan culminated this evening in the gift of the topaz necklet, which you gave me to incense your son."

"The gift is still yours," he said. "I have not withdrawn it."

"You have both succeeded admirably," she said. "I have been hurt too in the process, but it is not my purpose here to complain of that fact. You have both succeeded in what you set out to do. You are both deeply hurt."

"You have judged the situation from the perspective

of your own tender heart, my love," the marquess said. "His grace and I do not have tender hearts. I doubt we have hearts at all."

"Why did you choose your particular method of revenge?" she asked him. "You had alternatives. You could have refused to return to Enfield when summoned. You could have come and refused to marry Lady Marie. Either would have effectively shown Father that he was not to be allowed to control your life. Why did you choose such a drastic method?"

He did not answer for a long time. His eyes moved from her to his father and back again. A curious little half-smile lifted the corners of his mouth.

"Because marrying the right woman has always been the single most important duty of the Dukes of Enfield and their heirs," he said. "Regardless of the personal inclinations of either the bride or the groom. If his bride has been chosen for him from birth, he marries her even if she feels the strongest aversion to him, even if her feelings are deeply engaged elsewhere. The right marriage, the right lineage for one's heirs, are everything. And so I married you, my lady, a woman who had answered my advertisement for a governess. Oh, yes, sir. That is exactly the way it happened."

Charity had felt the duke's shoulder stiffen beneath her touch even before the end of his son's speech.

"And you, Father," she said. "Why did you choose to give me the topaz necklet, of all the jewels that must be in your possession?"

Like his son, he did not answer quickly. There was a lengthy silence. "It was my wedding gift to her," he said at last. But the silence that succeeded his words was almost as long as the first. "My *love* gift to her. She spurned my love for over twenty years. She offered cold duty, and gave all her warmth, all her weakness, all her unhappiness to her children—most notably to her eldest son. She gave my gift to him before her death, and I whipped him for it, my lady, because I had never whipped her. Nor would have done so if she had lived as the ice in my veins for another twenty years. I whipped him for it again tonight by giving the gift to the wife with whom he had shown his contempt for me."

"You never knew the meaning of the word *love*," the marquess said.

"As you wish," his father said. "And so, my dear, you have contrived to bring us together here, my son and me, so that we may humbly beg each other's pardon and live in loving harmony for the few days that remain to me."

Yes, that had been her hope. It sounded silly expressed in the duke's cold, haughty voice.

"I told you we could not be expected to kiss and make up," the marquess said. "You are too tenderhearted, my love."

"The duchess is at the root of all this," she said. "You both loved her. And as a consequence you hate each other—or believe you do."

The marquess laughed. "He did not love her," he said. "All he did was keep her here when she would have enjoyed visits to London and the spas. All he did was burden her with yearly confinements, though she would cry to me in her anguish. She was nothing to him but a woman of the right rank and lineage to be bred until she could breed no more. My apologies, ma'am, for such plain speaking."

The duke's chin had lifted and his eyes had half closed. "She took your childhood and your youth away from you," he said. "She made a millstone of her own unwillingness or inability to adjust to a dynastic marriage and hung it about the neck of her eldest son. Her marriage and what happened within it were her concern—and mine. They should not have been the concern of any of her children, but she made them your concern. Your life has been shadowed by the demands she made on your love."

"It is a sad state of affairs," the marquess said, "when a woman can turn for love and understanding only to her children."

"It is sad for her children," the duke agreed. "But I have never spoken one word of criticism of her grace until tonight and will never utter another. She was my duchess, my wife—and there is no more private relationship than that, Staunton. If you ever again speak critically of your own wife—as you did tonight in your description of the way you obtained her hand—then you are not only a fool, but also a man without honor."

They gazed at each other, stiff, cold, unyielding.

"I think," Charity said, "that we must return to the ball. I can see that nothing more can be achieved here. I am sorry for it. And your lives are the poorer for it. But perhaps you will each remember the other's pain and the other's love."

"I believe, sir," the marquess said, "that you should withdraw to your bed rather than to the ballroom. My wife and I will see to the duties of host and hostess there. May I take you up myself?"

His father looked coldly at him. "You may ring for my valet," he said.

The marquess did so and they all waited in silence until the servant arrived to bear his master off to bed. The duke looked drawn and weary, leaning heavily on his man's shoulder. Charity kissed his cheek before he left.

"Sleep well, Father," she said.

Her husband did not immediately escort her back to the ballroom. When she turned to him after his father had left, he surprised her by catching her up in a fierce hug that squeezed all the air out of her. And then he found her mouth with his and kissed her with some of the passion she had expected at the lake.

"A crusading little mouse," he said, relaxing his hold on her. "With her head in the clouds and her feet in quicksand."

His face was stern and pale, but there was a certain tenderness in his voice. She had half expected a furious tirade.

"We have guests to entertain," she said.

"Yes, we do." He offered his arm and made her a courtly bow that had no discernible element of mockery in it.

Now MORE THAN ever he had to get away from Enfield. Tomorrow. Early. It was already early tomorrow. Yet he had not directed either his valet or his wife's maid to pack their things. It had just been too late after the ball to make such a cruel demand on his servants. Anyway, he supposed a very early start was out of the question. He would want to take his leave—of Charles and Marianne and Augusta, of Will. He would not run away this time without a word. He would want to take his leave of his father too.

He had been pacing the floor of his bedchamber. He stopped and closed his eyes. Perhaps they would remember each other's pain and each other's love, she had said. *My love gift to her,* his father had said of the topaz necklet. His mother had always claimed that his grace was cold through to the center of his heart. She had spoken openly of her husband thus to her son. Had she been mistaken? Had she *known* she was mistaken?

He had decided to spend the night alone. But his need for his wife gnawed at him. He did not believe he would be able to get through the night without her. Once they were back in London, once he had her settled in a new life, he would have to do without her for the rest of a lifetime. But tonight was different. After tonight, once he was away from Enfield, he would be able to cope alone again.

He could feel his resolution slip. Perhaps he would have held to it, he thought, if the need had been a sexual one. But it was not.

He tapped very gently on the door of her bedchamber and eased it open carefully. If she was asleep, he decided, he would leave her be. There was a long journey ahead. She needed to sleep.

At first he did not see her. He could see only that the bedcovers were thrown back from her bed and she was not there. She was over by the window, the shawl about her shoulders obscuring the white of her nightgown. She was looking back over her shoulder at him.

"You cannot sleep?" he asked, walking toward her.

She shook her head. "Did I do the wrong thing?" she asked him.

"No." He took her hands in his and warmed them with his own. They were like blocks of ice. "And you must not blame yourself for your lack of success. It was no simple or single quarrel, as you have discovered. Our differences have been a lifetime in the making. You tried. You had no obligation to feel gentle emotions for anyone in this family, least of all for my father and me, who have both used you ill. But you tried anyway. I thank you. I will always remember your gentleness. I believe his grace will too."

"He is so very ill," she said.

"Yes."

"You love him."

"Leave it," he said. "You are cold. Come to bed with me?"

"Yes," she said. "Yes, please." And she moved against him, turned her head to rest on his shoulder, and relaxed with a sigh. She was weary beyond the ability to sleep, he could tell.

If he had not felt her weariness, he would have made love to her when he had taken her to his bed. It would not have occurred to him not to do so even though he had admitted to himself that his need for her tonight was not sexual. But he had felt her tiredness, and suddenly he was overwhelmed by the need to give her something in return for what she had tried to do for him this evening.

He drew her into his arms and against his body, wrapped the bedclothes snugly about her, and kissed the side of her face.

"Sleep," he said. "I will have you warm in a moment. Just sleep. I forbid you to so much as think of sheep or their legs."

"Sheep," she murmured sleepily. "Who are they?"

She was asleep almost instantly—and so was he, he realized only a couple of hours later when his father's butler awoke him by appearing unannounced in his room.

He came awake with a start, and by sheer instinct pulled the covers up over his wife's shoulders. He remembered with some relief even as he did so that she was not naked.

"What is it?" he asked harshly and felt her jump in his arms.

"I did knock, my lord," the butler said. He was dressed, the marquess saw in the light of early dawn, but not with his usual immaculate precision. "It is his grace, my lord."

The marquess was out of bed without knowing how he had got out. "Ill?" he asked sharply. "He is ill?" He grabbed for his dressing gown, which he had tossed over the back of a chair before getting into bed.

"Yes, my lord," the butler said. "Brixton thought you should come, my lord." Brixton was his grace's valet.

"Has the physician been sent for?" the marquess asked, tying the sash of the dressing gown and moving purposefully toward the door as he did so. "Send for him immediately—and for Lord William. Have Lady Twynham and Lord Charles summoned. Lady Augusta may be left in her bed for now."

"Yes, my lord." The butler sounded uncharacteristically relieved to have responsibility lifted from his shoulders.

The marquess hurried from the room without a thought to his wife, who was lying awake in his bed.

His father had had a heart attack. There would be no recovery from this one. He was dying. That much was clear to his son the moment he hurried into his bedchamber. He lay on the bed, gasping for air. Every breath was labored. Brixton was flapping a large cloth in front of his face, trying to make more air available to him. The marquess chafed the duke's hands in a futile attempt to do something though he knew himself to be utterly helpless.

Time passed without his being aware of it. Marianne was in the room, closely followed by Charles. Then Twynham was there too, and Will and Claudia and Charity. Finally the physician appeared and they all stood back at the edges of the room watching while he made his examination and straightened up to give them the inevitable message simply by looking at them and slightly shaking his head.

The Duke of Withingsby was dying.

"Fetch Lady Augusta," the marquess said, looking at Mrs. Aylward, who was standing in the doorway.

"I will go," Charity said quietly. "I will bring her."

The duke was still breathing in audible gasps. But he was conscious. His eyes were open.

"It is time to say good-bye," the marquess said, the fact registering on his mind that they were all—family, servants, physician—looking to him for guidance. The duke was dying. He was already the acting head of the family. "William? Claudia?"

They stepped up to the bed, Claudia chalk white, Will scarcely less so. And then Marianne and Twynham, and after them, Charles. The butler and housekeeper were nodded forward to say their farewells. Even through the numbness of his mind, the marquess realized that this was the leave-taking his father would want—something strictly formal and correct, his death like a well-orchestrated state occasion.

Charity had returned with a pale and clearly frightened Augusta. She clung to Charity's hand and shrank against her and hid her face when Marianne would have taken her. And so it was Charity who led her to the side of the bed.

"You must say good-bye to your father," Charity said gently. "He is looking at you, you see."

"Good-bye, sir," the child whispered.

But the marquess could see, and Charity could see, that his grace's hand was pulling feebly at the bedcover.

"He would like you to kiss him," Charity said. "He would like you to know that he loves you and that he leaves you in the safe care of Anthony."

Augusta had to stand on her toes to lean far enough across the bed to kiss her father on the cheek. "I will be a good girl for Anthony, sir," she said. "And I will work harder at my lessons." She hid her face against Charity's skirt.

"Father." Charity had taken that feeble hand in her own. "You have been kind to me. I thank you for your kindness. I will always remember it and you." And she bent over him, kissed his forehead, and smiled into his eyes. "With love," she added.

And then she bent down, picked Augusta up in her arms, and moved with her out into the anteroom of the bedchamber.

The marquess stepped forward and stood, his hands clasped at his back, gazing down at his father.

"Clear the room." The words were whispered and hoarse and breathless, but they were perfectly clear.

"Perhaps you would all wait outside for a few moments," the marquess said without looking away from his father's face.

They all left uncomplaining except for Marianne, who was muttering to Twynham that she was his grace's daughter and was being treated like a servant by her own brother.

The Duke of Withingsby was not a person one touched uninvited, and the invitation was rarely given. But the Marquess of Staunton looked down at the pale, limp hand on the covers and took his hands from his back so that he could gather it up in both his own. It was cold despite all his efforts to warm it a few minutes before.

"Father," he said, remembering even as he spoke the idea of a sentimental deathbed scene with which he had mocked his wife, "I have always loved you. Far too deeply for words. If I had not loved you, I could not have hated you. And I have hated you. I love you." He raised the hand briefly to his lips.

His grace's penetrating, haughty eyes, startlingly alive, regarded him out of the gray face and from beneath heavy lids. "You are my son," he managed to say. "Always my favorite son, as you were hers. You will have children of your own, my son. Your duchess will be a good mother and a good wife. You have made a fortunate choice. There will be mutual love in your marriage. I envy you. You have not succeeded in annoying me."

He could say no more. He closed his eyes. His son watched him for a while and then went down on his knees and rested his face on the bed close to his father's hand and wept. He felt foolish weeping for a man he had hated—and loved, but he was powerless to stop the painful sobs that tore at him. And then the hand lifted and came to rest on his head. It moved once, twice, and then lay still while the rasping breathing continued.

It felt like forgiveness, absolution, a blessing, a benediction, a healing touch. A father's touch. It felt like love. The marquess despised the feelings at the same time as he allowed them to wash over him. His father had touched him with love.

The nature of the breathing changed. He got to his feet and crossed to the door. It was time to summon the family back into the room. It was their right to witness the end. And the end was no more than minutes away.

16

SHE SAT ON A CHAIR IN THE ANTEROOM WITH AUGUSTA curled up on her lap. The child was not sleeping, but Charity had not taken her with everyone else back into the duke's room. It had been necessary for her to say good-bye to her father, to understand what was happening, but it was not necessary for her to witness the death. Charity smoothed her hand over the child's head and occasionally kissed her forehead.

Her husband was the first to come back out of the room. He came to stand in front of the chair and his eyes met Charity's. He looked pale, weary. He had been crying, she thought. She was glad he had cried. He came down on his haunches and set a hand on Augusta's head.

"He is gone, dear," he said in a voice of such gentleness that tears sprang to Charity's eyes. "He was peaceful. He will be happy now. He will be—with Mother."

Augusta opened her eyes, but she did not move or say anything.

"But you will still be safe," he said. "I will be here with you—always—and Will and Claudia and the boys will be close by. We will be a family. I held you, you know, when you were a baby. I was the first to hold you after you were born. I did not know it was possible to love anyone as much as I loved you. I had to go away soon after and stay away for a long time. But I always loved you. And now I am home again. We are brother and sister, but fortunately I am old enough to look after you and keep you safe almost like a father."

She gazed mutely at him, but Charity could feel that there was less tension in her than there had been. In a few more minutes she would be sleeping.

"His grace knew he would have to leave you," the marquess continued. "He called me home so that I could look after you for him. Because he loved you, Augusta, and because he loved me. Because we were his children. Everything will be all right, dear. You may go back to sleep now. I will carry you to your bed and Charity will come with us." He looked at her and raised his eyebrows. She understood the silent communication and nodded. "She will stay with you, and when you wake she will be there to bring you to me or to Will or Marianne or Charles. You are quite safe."

But as he got to his feet, the butler came out of the bedchamber. He cleared his throat.

"Your grace—" he began.

Charity watched her husband flinch before turning his head.

"The physician wishes to consult with you, your grace," the butler said.

"He will wait for five minutes," the Duke of Withingsby said, "until I have carried Lady Augusta to the nursery."

He lifted the half-sleeping child into his arms and waited while Charity got to her feet. This morning, she realized for the first time since the sound of her husband's voice had woken her with a start from a deep sleep, they were supposed to be on their way back to London. Today was to have marked the end of the charade, the beginning of the secure and wonderful life with her own family that she had dreamed of ever since her own father's death.

But today there was still a part to play—not even really a part. Augusta was going to need her today. There could be no more momentous event in a child's life than the death of a parent. Augusta's needs were going to have to take precedence over all else for today, and perhaps for longer than today. For some reason it seemed that the child was turning to her for comfort rather than to Marianne or Claudia.

And Anthony was going to need her today and perhaps for a few days beyond today. He had lost his father under difficult circumstances. She suspected—and hoped—that he might have realized his love for his father before it was too late. She hoped that his father had been able to show some sign of his own love. How foolish they had been, holding out until the very end and perhaps even beyond the end. But there was a look in his face, even apart from the evidence of tears, that told her father and son had understood each other before they were separated by eternity. They had been alone together for all of five minutes.

He set Augusta down carefully on her bed, while both her nurse and her governess hovered in the doorway. The nurse was red-eyed from weeping—news traveled fast in a large house. Augusta was already sleeping. He covered her snugly with the blankets, and Charity was reminded of how he had covered *her* just a few hours before and held her while she slipped into an exhausted sleep. He straightened up and turned to her. The servants had disappeared.

"You will stay with her?" he asked.

"Of course," she said.

She took an impulsive step forward and brushed back the upside-down question mark of hair from his forehead. It fell back almost immediately. She framed his face with her hands.

"I am sorry," she whispered. "I am so sorry, Anthony." And she stood on her toes and kissed his lips.

He touched his hands to the backs of hers, held them against his face for a moment, and then removed them, squeezing them slightly as he did so.

"I am needed," he said and left the room.

It was only after he had left and she sat in the quiet room, watching the sleeping child, that she began to be plagued by terrible feelings of guilt.

IT WAS AN incredibly busy and wearying day. He had lived his own independent life for eight years and was accustomed to responsibilities. But finding himself suddenly the Duke of Withingsby a mere three days after returning to Enfield, with seemingly dozens of people turning to him for direction, was stressful, to say the least. There were the funeral arrangements to be made, letters to be written, arrangements for the guests who would arrive from some distance away for the funeral to be set in motion, early visits of condolence to be received, ordinary, unavoidable matters of household and estate business to be dealt with, the Earl of Tillden and his family to assure that of course they were perfectly welcome to stay on—and endless other tasks.

There was the shock of grief to be dealt with—his own grief and that of his brothers and sisters. Charles was perhaps the most inconsolable. The duke found his brother during the afternoon sitting in the conservatory, sobbing into his hands. But there was not the obligation to expend emotional energy on comforting him. Lady Marie Lucas sat beside him, patting his back with one small hand while the other clutched a lace handkerchief and dabbed at the tears on her own cheeks.

Augusta, released from both the nursery and the schoolroom, stayed close to Charity all day, though she came to sit on his lap during a brief spell of relaxation after a visit from the rector and his wife.

"Are you really going to stay with me?" she asked.

"Mmm." He wrapped his arms about her.

"And are you really going to be like a papa?" she asked. "Like William is with Anthony and Harry?"

"Do you want a papa?" he asked her. "Or would you prefer a big brother?"

She did not hesitate. "I want a papa," she said.

"Then I am he," he said. His mind flashed back briefly to the life he had been living and the attitudes he had held with great firmness just the week before. But that life was dead. He accepted the fact. This was not something he could fight against. He was not even sure that he *wanted* to fight. Some realities were too stark to be denied.

"And will Charity be like my mama?" she asked.

He closed his eyes. Ah. How did one cocoon a child against what would seem like cruelty? How could she ever understand?

"Do you want her as a mama?" he asked.

"Jane and Louisa and Martin have Marianne," she said, "and Anthony and Harry have Claudia. Now I have someone too. She is all my own."

"She will keep you safe," he said, kissing her forehead. "She loves you."

"Yes, I know," she said. "She told me. His grace loved me too. He never said so, but Charity says that some people cannot say it or even show it, though that does not mean they do not feel it. He always looked after me and he brought you home to look after me and be like a papa to me after he was gone. I could see this morning that he loved me. He wanted me to kiss him. His face was cold."

"He loved you, dear," he said. "You were his own little girl. And now you are mine."

He wondered how much time his father had spent with her, this child who had killed his wife. Not much, he guessed. She envied Will's children because they had a papa. But she would not remember their father with bitterness. Charity had seen to that.

It was a brief encounter. There were people and details to occupy every moment of his time until well after dinner. He wondered vaguely during the meal how it was that everyone except Augusta and his wife had been able to lay hands on black clothes so easily. They were all in deep mourning. Charity wore one of her brown dresses and looked endearingly shabby and pretty. Claudia's modiste, he heard as part of the dinner conversation, was busy making his wife a black dress to wear tomorrow.

He sat at the head of the table and looked about him. Oh, yes, a week had wrought enormous changes. It amazed him now that he had imagined—only a few days before—that he could return here and be untouched by it all. A part of him had known. Something deep within had known that he needed to bring Charity with him if he was to stand even a chance of retaining his own identity. But what he had not understood—or what he had not admitted—was what that identity was. He had not known who he was. He knew now. He was Anthony Earheart, an inextricable part of this family. He always had been, even during the eight years of his self-imposed exile.

He had never been free of them. Yet strangely, now, on the day when all freedom, all choices had been taken from him beyond recall, he felt freer than he had ever felt in his life. And it was not, he reflected, because his father was gone and could no longer exercise power over him. It was quite the opposite. It was because he had now become both himself and his father's son. His father, he realized, as he had realized this morning, had set him free to live with both those identities. His father had given him love at the last and had set him free.

Your duchess will be a good mother and a good wife. You have made a fortunate choice. There will be mutual love in your marriage.

He gazed down the table to his wife, his duchess, who was speaking kindly to a teary-eyed Countess of Tillden. Yes. Oh, yes. But she would have to be wooed, not commanded. If he loved her—and he did—then he must set her free, as he had agreed to do. And he must hope that she would freely choose to remain with him, to be his wife, to bear his children, to share a mutual love with him for the rest of their days.

He was not without hope. She possessed more warmth, more charm, more love than anyone else he had known—how first impressions could deceive! He could still feel the warmth of her hands framing his face and the look of deep sorrow—for him—in her eyes and the soft kiss she had placed on his lips. No, he was not without hope. But he had lost some of his arrogant self-assurance in the past few days, among other things. He was by no means certain of her. There was anxiety to temper the hope.

Finally, well after dinner, he was free. He had been sitting with his father, who had been laid out in his bed and looked as if he slept peacefully. But Will had come and clasped his shoulder firmly and warmly and told him he would keep watch for a while.

"Go and relax, Tony," he said. "You look as if you are ready to collapse."

The duke nodded and got to his feet—and impulsively hugged his brother, who returned the embrace.

Augusta was in bed, he was told, closely watched over by her nurse. But Charity was not in the drawing room with everyone else. She had gone outside for a walk, he was informed.

"She did not want company," Charles said, "though I offered to go with her, Tony. She looked exhausted. She has been very good to Augusta all day."

"But she will want your company," Claudia said with a smile. "She has been watching you anxiously all day long. And you look as tired as she. I believe she said she was going to wander down by the lake."

"Yes, she did," Marianne said. "And she has indeed been very good to Augusta, Tony. Her experience as a governess must have helped her, of course."

Marianne had thawed, he thought as he left the house. But she had been unable to resist that final little jibe.

He found his wife down by the lake. It was an evening very similar to the last, though she wore a shawl about her shoulders. She was sitting on the bank, gazing out across the moonlit water. He sat beside her after she had looked up and recognized him, and took one of her hands in his.

"Tired?" he asked.

"A little." Despite the peaceful picture she had presented, sitting there on the bank, she was not relaxed.

"This is all too much for you," he said. "I am sorry. It was not part of our bargain, was it?"

But she only stiffened further. "It was all my fault," she said, her voice flat.

"What?" He dipped his head so that he could look into her face.

"I killed him," she said. "Have you not realized that? With my crusading zeal, as you put it. I forced him to the library last night. I forced him to that scene of bitterness and futility. It was none of my business. As you just said, we have a bargain. I am not really your wife. This is not really my family. But I interfered anyway. I put him under that stress. And a few hours later he was dead."

Oh, God! "No." He squeezed her hand very tightly.

"No, Charity. No. You are in no way responsible for his death. I was summoned here because he was dying. His physician told me two days ago that he could go at any time. He had a perilously bad heart. It failed him early this morning. He died. His death had nothing whatsoever to do with you."

"He had been told to rest," she said.

"Advice he constantly ignored," he reminded her. "He knew he was dying, Charity. That is why he swallowed his pride and called me home. But he would not die in weakness. He wanted to die as he had lived, and his wish was granted. You did not precipitate his death. But you did do something very wonderful."

"I killed him," she said.

"I told him I loved him," he said, "that I always had. And of course I spoke the truth, though even I had not fully understood that until you forced me to face it. He spoke to me. He did not tell me that he loved me—not in so many words. But he called me his son, his favorite son. And he set his hand on my head, Charity. It may seem a slight thing, but I cannot describe what it meant to me, feeling his hand there. He tried to stroke my head but he was too weak. He might have shouted out that he loved me and it would not have had the effect on me that the touch of his hand had. He touched me because you had made him admit something to himself. He was so very nearly too late—we both were—but he was not. Because you forced that confrontation last evening. You did it only just in time."

She gazed out across the water and said nothing. But he could feel from the touch of her hand that some of the tension had gone.

"He was right, you know," he said after a few minutes of silence. "I loved my mother and resented her. I felt forced to love her. She leaned heavily on me—even when I was just a young lad. I was only twenty when she died.

She was very unhappy. She told me about the man she had loved and wished to marry. She told me how she was forced to marry my father. She even told me how he forced his attentions on her whenever she was not increasing. She used to cry to me and tell me that soon she would be increasing again because he was coming to her room each night."

He paused. He felt disloyal saying this aloud, even thinking it. But perhaps he owed his father something too. "He was right," he said. "She ought not to have burdened her own child with her unhappiness. She ought not to have spoken of the intimacies of her marriage with her son. Her confidences, the necessity of comforting her, of hating him, were a heavy burden to me. I did not even realize it until last night."

"Your mother demanded too much of your love," his wife said, "and your father demanded too little. Unfortunately, we find it difficult to see our parents as people. We expect perfection of them. He did love her. That was very clear last evening."

"Perhaps she was as much at fault as he in their marriage," he said. "Perhaps even more so. She punished him all her married life for having been forced into an arranged marriage. She made no effort to make a workable match of it. Do you think that is what she did?"

"Be careful not to allow your feelings to swing to the opposite extreme," she said. "She was unhappy, Anthony. And despite what she told you, you cannot know what happened in the privacy of your parents' marriage. No one can know except the two of them, and they are both gone."

"I believe," he said, "she might have kept us from him. He was reserved and he was stern and—he said it last evening—he would never retaliate by saying anything against her. He never did, you know. She taught us to fear him and hate him, to think of him as a man cold to the heart."

"Anthony," she said, "you loved her. Remember that you loved her. She had a hard life. All those children, all those losses."

"I wonder," he said, "if you have ever taken anything from life. Have you always been a giver? You have given my family extraordinary gifts."

But she pulled her hand from his and jumped to her feet. She brushed the grass from her skirt. "Of course I am a taker," she said. "I am going to take a home and a carriage and servants and six thousand pounds a year from you for the rest of my life—for doing nothing but enjoying myself and basking in an unexpected security. I can scarcely wait."

He got to his feet too. "You are my wife," he said. "You will be kept in comfort for the rest of your life by virtue of that fact. That is not taking. It is the nature of marriage."

She was tense again and quite noticeably weary. It was no time to woo her in the way he planned to woo her once these difficult days were past, once the funeral was over.

"You are tired," he said, "and so am I. Let me take you to bed."

"With you?" she said. "Like last night?"

"Yes," he said, "if you wish. Or to make love first if you wish. It would not be disrespectful to my father. Life always needs to be reaffirmed in the face of death."

"You have a comfortable shoulder," she said, half smiling, "and safe arms. I slept so peacefully last night. You did too. Just for tonight again, then, if you will."

"Come." He set an arm about her waist and she relaxed readily against him as they made their way back to the house.

But after all, when they were in bed together, they

made love by unspoken assent before they slept—he had never experienced silent communication with any other woman, but with her it seemed unerring. They loved slowly, warmly, deeply. She sighed into relaxation when she was finished, and he pressed himself deep and for the first time in his life quite consciously let his seed flow into the woman with whom he mated.

HE HAD RELIEVED what was undoubtedly her chief anxiety. It had seemed to her as clear as the nose on her face that she had killed her father-in-law. But of course she had not. Her husband had quite put her mind at rest on that issue.

The other anxiety gnawed at her less urgently. But it was not one she could share and not one she could talk herself out of. Quite the contrary. Her sense of guilt grew by the hour, it seemed, and there were constant reminders.

I thought you were a fortune hunter.

That had started it. She *was* a fortune hunter. She had committed a dreadful sin—oh, more than one. They multiplied with alarming speed. She had made a mockery of one of the most sacred institutions of civilization. She had married and had repeated all the marriage vows, knowing very well that she had no intention whatsoever of keeping most of them. She had done it all for money. Oh, she could try to rationalize what she had done by telling herself that she had done it for Phil and Penny and the children. But when it came to calling a spade simply a spade, then she must admit that she had done it for money.

And so the one great sin had led her into a whole series of deceptions. Her father-in-law had guessed much of the truth, but he had not realized that the marriage was only a temporary one. He had probably died in the belief that soon there would be a new heir to the dukedom. Perhaps too he had died in the comfort of the belief that Augusta would have both a mother figure and a father figure to watch over her as she grew to womanhood.

She hated to think of the deception she had perpetrated against Augusta. Augusta, she realized within a day of the old duke's death, *loved* her. It had happened suddenly but quite, quite thoroughly. Augusta was unwilling to leave her side. She would do so only to spend a little time with Anthony. Irreparable harm might come to Augusta when the truth came out.

And then there was Charles, who treated her with the easy affection of a brother, and Claudia and William, who were almost as affectionate. Even Marianne had begun to treat her with civility. Marianne's children and Claudia's always brightened considerably whenever she came in sight.

She felt a total fraud. She *was* a fraud. And all the servants called her *your grace* and treated her with marked respect, and all the neighbors who called on them with condolences addressed her by her title and looked upon her with almost awed respect.

She was a fraud.

She was a fortune hunter.

And since she was in the business of calling spades spades, then she might as well simply admit that she was a sinner.

There was only one thing she could do. The realization came to her gradually in the days leading up to the funeral, but finally it was firm in her mind. There was only one thing. It would not right all the wrongs—she thought in particular of Augusta. But it would show her sorrow for what she had done. It was the only honorable thing to do, the only thing that might in time give her a quiet conscience.

And so late on the afternoon of the funeral itself, when many of the guests had left and the few remaining ones sat in the drawing room, while Augusta slept in the nursery after the emotions of the morning, while the duke was riding with Charles for some relaxation, Charity walked down the driveway to the village, a small valise in her hand. There was a stagecoach leaving from the inn—she had checked the time.

She was going home—alone. She had left behind a note for her husband, but she had not named her destination. If she had, he would have sent her money—six thousand pounds a year. If she had, he would have sent his man of business to make sure that she had a suitable home and all the trappings that had been mentioned in the agreement. He would have insisted on paying for everything. And perhaps she would have found it impossible to resist. Perhaps she would have been tempted not to resist as much as she was able.

She had married and performed all the duties of her marriage while it lasted. Perhaps in time she would be able to forgive herself for marrying in the full knowledge that she would be called upon to fulfill those duties for only a short while. But she would never be able to forgive herself or live with herself if she accepted payment for what she had done.

Marriage was not employment.

Marriage was involvement and caring and loving. Marriage was—commitment.

She had thought him wrong when he had said she was a giver and not a taker. But perhaps after all he was right. She could not become a taker. She would lose her own soul.

Perhaps in time she would be able to forgive herself.

17

IT SEEMED INCREDIBLE TO THE DUKE OF WITHINGSBY when he thought about it later that his wife had left him during the afternoon of his father's funeral, yet he did not discover it until the following morning.

He returned from a long ride and a lengthy talk with Charles, feeling somewhat refreshed. But he understood that it had been a stressful few days for all his family. Charity had retired to her rooms for a rest, he was told. He hoped she would sleep and feel the better for it. He was busy with the remaining guests for the rest of the day. He did not call at his wife's dressing room to escort her down to dinner. When she had not appeared in the drawing room by the time dinner was announced, he sent a servant to inquire. Her maid had been told, he was informed, that her grace would not need her for the rest of the day, that she did not wish to be disturbed.

He did not disturb her. He made her excuses to his guests. She had given tirelessly of herself ever since her arrival at Enfield. They had all made demands on her energies, most notably Augusta and himself. She must be exhausted. He did not go up to check on her himself—he was afraid of disturbing her rest. And for the same reason he did not disturb her when he went to bed, though he did let himself quietly into her dressing room and noted that there was no light beneath the door of her bedchamber.

It was only when he went for a rather late breakfast the following morning, after attending to some other business first, and discovered that she had not yet been down that he went to investigate. And then, of course, he discovered the letter she had left on her pillow. Not that it was on her pillow when he first saw it. Her maid was coming from her rooms with it in her hand, a look of fright in her eyes. She curtsied and handed it to him after telling him where she had found it, and obeyed his nod of dismissal with alacrity.

"Your grace," his wife had written, "I will be leaving on the stagecoach from the village inn this afternoon. I hope you do not discover this soon enough to come after me. I know you will wish to because we signed an agreement and being an honorable gentleman, you will wish to honor it. But please do not come. And please do not try to find me. I release you from your part of our agreement. I do not wish to receive payment for what I have done. It would be distasteful and distressful to me."

He closed his eyes and drew a slow breath. He was still standing in the hallway outside her dressing room.

"I am taking with me as many of my own belongings as I can carry," he read when he looked back at the letter. "I cannot resist taking my ball gown too. I know you will not mind. And my pearls. They were a wedding gift, I believe, and there was a wedding. I will not feel guilty about taking them, then. They are so very beautiful. I am also taking some of the money I found in the top drawer of the desk in your study. I will need to pay for a ticket to where I am going and for food during the journey. Again, I do not believe you will mind. It is all I will ever take from you. Please tell Augusta that I love her. She will not believe you, but please, please find some way to persuade her to accept that it is true. I am, your grace, your obedient servant, Charity Duncan."

Charity *Duncan*. It was like a resounding slap across the face. He crumpled the letter in one hand and really felt for one alarmed moment that he was about to faint. She was Charity Earheart, Duchess of Withingsby. She was his wife—his to protect and support for the rest of his life and even beyond that if she survived him. Whether she chose to live with him or live separately from him, she would always be his. She had written of honor. How did she expect him to retain his honor when she had done this to him?

Where would she have gone? His mind scrambled about in confusion for her probable destination. He was alarmed when he realized that he would not know where in England to begin looking for her. There were only her old lodgings in London. She would have given them up. It was very unlikely she would go back there. No one there would know where she had gone. He doubted she had even told them about Enfield. She had left on yesterday afternoon's coach. The devil! Had no one seen her leave Enfield—on foot at a guess—and thought to comment to anyone else on that fact or on her failure to return?

His first instinct was to have a bag packed, to call out his carriage, and to set out after her. It seemed not to matter in that first panicked moment that he would not know where he was headed. He would stop at the inn. Perhaps the innkeeper would know her destination—though it might not be her final destination, of course. Somehow he would follow her trail.

But instinct, he realized, closing his eyes and drawing steadying breaths again—he was *still* standing outside her dressing room—could not always be followed. He could not rush off into the horizon. There were things to be done. A few guests were leaving after breakfast. He

must see them on their way. Tillden and his wife and
daughter were to leave later. He had promised Charles
that he would have a word with Tillden first. He had
arranged to have a conference with Will later in the day
so that they might set up a working relationship concerning the running of the estates. He had agreed to talk
with him at the dower house so that Augusta would
have a chance to play with the boys. He had been planning to invite Charity to go with him. There was—ah,
there were a thousand and one things that must be attended to today.

Besides, she did not want him to go after her. She did
not want to accept his support. She wanted to sever all
ties with him. He did not know how much money he
had slipped into that drawer in his desk. But he would
wager that she had carefully counted out only just
enough to purchase her ticket and the most meager of
meals. She had taken her pearls, but he knew beyond a
doubt that she would not have taken the topaz necklet,
which was lying, somewhat incautiously perhaps, in a
box on top of that same desk in his study. He had been
intending to give it back to her during a private moment—as a gift from both his father and himself.

She did not want him. She preferred freedom and independence and poverty and the life of a governess to
the alternative of being in some way beholden to him.
He felt blinded by hurt.

Ah, yes, he had been right in his assessment of her the
evening after his father's death. She was a giver. She gave
of herself with cheerful, warm generosity. She was not in
any way a taker. But did she not understand that there
could be a degree of selfishness in being all give and no
take? Did she not understand how he would feel at the
moment of reading her letter? Did she imagine that he
would sag with relief? That he would cheerfully forget
her and get on with the rest of his life?

He hated her suddenly.

He saw his guests on their way. He explained to them that his wife was indisposed and sent her apologies. He invited the Earl of Tillden into the library, explained to him that Lord Charles Earheart was to receive a sizable settlement according to the terms of his father's will and that he himself was preparing to gift his brother with one of his estates, considerably smaller than Enfield, but consistently prosperous. Lord Charles had just the day before expressed his intention of selling his commission and of living as a gentleman, administering his own estate. Lord Charles had asked of his eldest brother—and been granted—permission to pay his addresses to Lady Marie Lucas. He asked permission now through his brother to address himself to the lady's father.

Charles, the duke did not deem it necessary or even wise to explain to the earl, had had a fondness for Lady Marie all his life, and a deep passion for her for at least the past two years—a love that was reciprocated. His belief in the hopelessness of that love, since she had been intended for the Marquess of Staunton, had precipitated his decision to take a commission in the cavalry.

The Earl of Tillden blustered and bristled and was clearly offended at the offer of a younger son when he had expected the eldest. But Lord Charles *was* the son and brother of a duke, and he was a wealthy man and was to be a considerable landowner. The boy might talk to him, he agreed at last. He remained in the library while the duke went in personal search of his brother. He was not hard to find. He was pacing, pale-faced and stubborn-jawed and anxious-eyed within sight of the library door.

"He will listen to you," the duke told him and watched his brother draw in a deep breath and hold it. "Remember who you are, Charles. You are no man's inferior. You are our father's son. Good luck."

Charles walked purposefully toward the library, looking as grimly courageous as he might have looked if he had known for certain that an axman complete with ax and chopping block was awaiting him on the other side of the door.

Augusta could not simply be told that Charity was indisposed. She had to be told at least some of the truth. Charity had had to go away in a hurry, he told his sister while he was sitting on a low chair in the nursery holding her in the crook of his arm as she stood beside him. There was an aunt who was sick and needed her help. He was going to go too as soon as he was able, to find out for himself how long the aunt would need her. If at all possible he would bring her back with him. But sometimes sicknesses could go on for a tediously long time.

He despised himself for not telling the full truth. If he could not find Charity, if he could not persuade her to come home with him and be his wife in total defiance of their agreement, then he was going to have difficulties indeed with Augusta. There would have to be further lies or the confession that he had lied today. But he could not bring himself to tell the truth, to let Augusta know that Charity had never had any intention of staying at Enfield and being a permanent sort of mother to her. It would be unfair to Charity to tell the truth. It would make her sound heartless—and that would be an enormous lie.

Sometimes truth and falsehood were hopelessly confusing things.

Two days passed before he left Enfield in pursuit of his wife. The earl and his family had left—Tillden had come to an agreement with Charles, and the young couple had been permitted fifteen minutes alone together, during which time it had been agreed they might come to an understanding, though of course there could be no for-

mal betrothal until the year of Lord Charles's mourning
was at an end. Lord and Lady Twynham had returned
home with their children. Augusta had been granted an
extended holiday from the schoolroom in order to stay
at the dower house with Will and Claudia. He had
merely told everyone that his wife had had to go somewhere in a hurry and he was going to escort her home.
No one probed more deeply—he guessed that for those
two days he had looked about as approachable as his
father had always looked.

Finally the Duke of Withingsby set out on his journey,
following a cold trail to nowhere.

CHARITY TRUDGED THE three miles home from the coach
stop and walked unheralded through the open front
door of the house and into the parlor, where the children
were just finishing their tea and were clamoring at Penelope to be allowed back outside to play. David was
promising with loud insincerity not to get dirty again
and Howard was declaring that his breeches had been
torn quite by accident—he had been being very careful.
Mary was proclaiming the fact that *she* had not got
dirty *or* torn her breeches and so there was no reason
why Penny should insist on her staying inside. Howard
was just in the midst of pointing out the irrefutable fact
that Mary did not even wear breeches when Mary spot-
ted Charity standing in the doorway. She shrieked.

And then they were all shrieking or whooping and exclaiming and laughing and talking and hugging and yell-
ing. No one in the Duncan family had ever learned the
lesson that talking simultaneously with several other
people resulted in little or no communication taking
place.

"Well," Charity said at last, "here I am home again to
stay, and you have all grown at least one inch, and if I

may just sit down and be allowed a quiet bawl, I shall be myself again in no time at all."

She proceeded to do just that while Penelope rushed for the teapot and an empty cup and Mary dashed for the plate of scones—or what was left of them—and Howard told Charity how he had torn his breeches quite by accident and had then been falsely accused of being careless. David handed his sister his clean but much crumpled handkerchief.

It felt good beyond belief to be home. She did not tell the truth, of course. But she consoled herself with the thought that there would be no need of any more lies after today—or very few anyway. She told them she had not liked her new employment and so had left it. She told them that she had come home to stay, which would please Phil even if now he would have to bear the burden of their support all alone.

She was not quite sure yet if she really would stay. Perhaps after a while she would try again to find employment, but for a time at least she would be quite happy to stay where she was, licking her wounds, trying to persuade herself that doing the right thing was a virtue in itself and would eventually bring peace and contentment. She had undoubtedly done the right thing.

Penelope was openly relieved to see her. She loved the children and cared well for them, but she did not have quite the firm motherly touch that Charity possessed. Besides, she had a beau—the same gentleman who had offered for Charity once upon a time. Penny was clearly eager to accept his addresses. She was only anxious for assurance that Charity did not want him for herself.

"Of course I do not," Charity said quite firmly. "If I had wanted him, Penny, I would have had him when he was interested in me—before you grew up enough that he would see you are the prettier."

"Oh, I am not," Penny protested, blushing. "But perhaps you refused only because you were needed here, Charity."

It was partly the truth. But her feelings had not been deeply engaged either.

"I have no intention of marrying," she said. "I am going to stay here while the children grow up and then I am going to settle in to the congenial life of spinster aunt." She wondered if she was with child. But that was a complication that would have to be confronted if it proved to be so.

And so she settled back to life at home. She wrote to Philip, who would be happy, she knew. *She* was not happy about their situation, but miracles when they happened, she had discovered, were not really desirable things after all. Somehow they would manage. Somehow Phil would reach a point at which he would feel able to marry Agnes and begin a life of his own.

She tried not to think of Enfield or of any of the people there. In particular she tried not to think about *him*. It was impossible, of course. She felt sometimes as if he were actually a part of her, as if the physical oneness she had known with him in his bed had somehow passed into her soul. But she did succeed somehow in keeping him just below the level of conscious thought—for several minutes at a time and several times each day. The nights were a different matter, of course.

She kept herself busy. There was always plenty to do at home, and there was much to do beyond home too. There were friends and neighbors to be visited. She had been away for almost a year, after all. It felt very good to be back.

IT WAS AMAZING how many ladies in brown had traveled on the stagecoach and left it at various destinations to disappear either on foot or in dogcarts or private carriages or other public vehicles in every direction of the compass. He wasted several days pursuing the most promising of the leads only to find that they led nowhere. Finally it seemed he had only two places left to go—back to Enfield or forward to London. She would certainly not have returned to Enfield. Yet if she had gone to London, his chances of finding her were slim indeed. He did have one moment of inspiration when he remembered the letter of recommendation that had been written by the rector of her former parish. But try as he could he was unable to remember the name of the place in Hampshire. The letter with all the applications had been destroyed. Besides, she had left that place because she no longer had a home there. It was unlikely she would go back there now.

He went to London. And since he had to begin his search somewhere, no matter how hopeless he felt, he went to the place where she had had lodgings before she married him. Even doing that was not easy. He could not remember exactly where it was. Fortunately his coachman was a little more sure. He drove to the wrong street at the first try, but they both recognized the second street and the building.

No, Miss Duncan no longer lived there, the landlord informed the duke when he asked, and no, he did not know where she had gone. No, she had not come there within the last week. They were the answers the duke had fully expected, but until he heard them he did not realize how much he had been hoping that he was wrong. Where would he look now? There was a frightening emptiness before him. There was nowhere else to look except all of England, starting perhaps with Hampshire.

"But *Mr.* Duncan might know 'er whereabouts, guv," the landlord said after he had turned to leave. "Hif you cares to come back tonight when 'e's finished 'is work."

Mr. Duncan? The duke stared blankly at the man. Her father? He was dead. Her husband? Her brother? She had no brothers. *Her husband!* He felt his hands at his sides ball into fists. He felt his mouth go dry.

"I shall do that," he heard himself say. "Thank you." He handed the man a sovereign.

But, he thought as he was clambering back into his carriage, plotting murder, *she had been a virgin.*

One thing was very clear to him. Charity Earheart, Duchess of Withingsby, had been telling him a lie or two from the start. Not only was she not a quiet brown mouse, she was also not— Damn it, he thought, he knew nothing about her. Nothing at all. Except that she was his wife. Except that he loved her.

The day seemed endless. It seemed a fortnight long. But finally he was back at the rooming house and was informed that Mr. Duncan had returned from work no more than five minutes before. The duke climbed the stairs and knocked with the head of his cane on the door the landlord had indicated.

A rather tired-looking young man opened the door and looked at him inquiringly—a young man who bore an unmistakable resemblance to Charity. His eyes took in the elegant appearance of his visitor.

"Yes?" he said.

"Mr. Duncan?"

"Yes." The young man looked wary.

"You have a—sister, I believe," the duke said. "Charity."

A frown was added to the wary look. "And if I do, sir?" he said. "What business would you have with my sister?"

The duke sighed. "She happens to be my wife," he said. "May I come inside?"

He did not wait for an invitation. He stepped past the young man, who was staring blankly at him.

"I suppose," he said, turning, "there are a dozen other brothers and sisters too. It would explain a few things." The adept way in which she had managed them all and sorted out all their lives, for example.

"Who are you?" Mr. Duncan asked.

"Anthony Earheart—"

"Her former employer," the young man said, his brows snapping together again. "You are a married man, sir, with four young children. If I see before me the reason she felt constrained to leave her employment in such haste, then—"

"Yes, I am indeed a married man," the duke said. "I married your sister the day after interviewing her in Upper Grosvenor Street. We do not yet have four children or even one, but I have hopes. Much depends upon whether I can run her to earth. She appears to be under the illusion that by hiding herself away she can nullify our marriage."

Mr. Duncan was staring at him as if he had just dropped off some remote heavenly body. "You *married* her?" he said faintly. "And she has *left* you? She is *hiding* from you? What the devil—"

"I feel constrained to add," his grace said, "that I love my wife. I trust you know where she is. Managing the lives of the other dozen of you, I suppose."

"You *love* her? Yet she has run off from you after a mere few weeks?" the other man said. "I confess to total bewilderment, sir. And to a total unwillingness to give you any information that might put my sister in danger."

The duke sighed. "You have good fraternal instincts," he said. "I would have despised you heartily if you had fallen upon my neck without further ado and embraced me as a brother. I have Lord Rowling sitting in my carriage outside in the street, doubtless bored to incoherence at the lengthy wait. He was a witness at my marriage. My marriage papers are also in the carriage. I shall fetch both if you will promise not to bolt the door as soon as my back is turned. I mean to find my wife."

"*Lord* Rowling?" The young man's eyes had widened.

"Lord Rowling," his grace repeated. "I shall pull rank on you if all else fails, Duncan. In addition to being Anthony Earheart, you see, I am the Duke of Withingsby. Your sister, my dear sir, is my duchess. I shall fetch my proofs and then proceed to tell all. If you have always suspected your sister of an inclination to madness, it will be my pleasure to confirm your worst fears."

He left the room while Philip Duncan was still staring at him in fascinated shock.

18

THE CHILDREN WERE PLAYING ON THE LAWN IN front of the house—at least, the boys were playing an energetic game of war while Mary swung idly from the tree swing, fanning herself with a book she had been planning to read. It was a warm day.

They all saw the carriage at roughly the same moment. They stared in mingled awe and admiration at the grand conveyance with its crested door and its liveried coachman and footman. Their eyes widened simultaneously when they saw that it was slowing and turning in at the gates to drive up about the curved driveway to the front doors of their own home.

But they did not wait to watch it complete its journey. They dashed into the house as fast as they could scurry, each eager to be the one to tell the astounding news to their elder sisters. But only Penelope was in the parlor, stitching at her embroidery—Charity was out in the back garden cutting flowers to replace the slightly drooping ones that adorned each downstairs room. Penelope would have to do. A chorus of voices preceded the children as they dashed across the room toward her, all pointing backward in the direction of the door.

"Mercy!" Penelope said. "One at a time, please. *What* did you see? *Who* is coming? Mr. Miller?" she asked hopefully, her hands straying upward to check her golden curls.

But the noise ceased abruptly at the sound of another voice calling from the front doorway—they had left the door wide open during their inward dash, of course. It was a male voice. A familiar voice. They all stared wildly at one another—Penelope included.

"Phil?"

"Philip?"

"That's Phil."

"I don't believe it. It can't be."

They all spoke simultaneously.

But before they could all dash back in the direction of the hall and the front doors, their brother appeared in the parlor doorway, grinning at them.

"I thought the whole neighborhood at the very least must be gathered in here," he said. "What a noise!"

But before they could fill their lungs with sufficient air to enable them to launch into the only type of greeting worthy of a long-absent brother, someone else appeared behind him, and when Philip stepped inside the room, that someone else was fully visible in the doorway. He was an elegant, handsome, haughty-looking gentleman, clad austerely but extremely fashionably in black. His long fingers were playing with the handle of a quizzing glass. His eyebrows were raised and his lips pursed. He looked about the room unhurriedly, gazing at each of them in turn.

The Duncans for once in their lives stood perfectly still and perfectly mute. For all they knew it might be Satan himself who had decided to pay them a visit.

"Penny," their brother said, "David, Howard, Mary—goodness, how you have all grown!—may I present the Duke of Withingsby?"

If it were possible to be stiller than still and muter than mute, the Duncans were both for a few seconds.

Then Penelope recovered her manners and sank into a curtsy. Mary followed suit and the boys, noticing the movement, bobbed their heads to the truly awesome figure of a real, live duke.

"We have traveled down from London," Philip said. "His grace has important business here. Where is Charity?"

His grace had strolled across the room and was looking from the window, his hands clasped at his back.

"She is—"

But Penelope did not need to complete her sentence. Charity herself, arms loaded with flowers, had appeared in the doorway. She saw her brother immediately, and her eyes lit up.

"Phil!" she cried. "Oh, Phil, what a wonderful surprise. You did not let us know, you wretch! You are the last person I expected to see. What on earth are you doing here? Oh, let me set these flowers down so that I may hug you."

"I think maybe not the last person, Charity," he said, looking decidedly uncomfortable. "Maybe there is someone you expect less."

She looked at him in incomprehension for a moment until a movement close to the window alerted her. Her head jerked about and she looked across the room and became very still. He had only half turned toward the room. He looked steadily at her over his shoulder, his eyebrows raised.

"Charity," Penelope said into the tense and uncomfortable silence, "do you know the Duke of Withingsby? He has come with Phil on important—"

"He is my husband," Charity said quietly.

The Duncans might never be the same again. Marble statues might have considered them worth emulating.

"Perhaps," his grace said equally quietly, "I might be allowed a short while alone with my wife."

"We will step outside and admire the gardens," Philip suggested and mobilized his brothers and sisters into action. They filed past him meekly enough. But there was a chorus of sound the moment he closed the door behind him. The sounds receded in the direction of the back door.

"WELL, CHARITY."

Curiously, he looked like a stranger again. He looked alien in the surroundings of her own home. He looked again like the man who had interviewed her for a governess's position. He looked satanic. He looked—very male.

"As you can see, your grace," she said, setting down her armful of flowers on the nearest table and folding her hands in front of her, "I live in a perfectly comfortable home and enjoy the company of numerous brothers and sisters. We are not wealthy. Neither are we destitute. You really do not need to concern yourself with me at all." She wanted to shower him with questions—how was Augusta? Had he missed her? How were Anthony and Harry and Claudia and William? Had he missed her? Had Charles been heartbroken when Lady Marie went home? Was there hope for them? *Had he missed her?*

"I need not concern myself with you," he said quietly. "With my own wife."

"I am not really your wife," she said. "It was only a temporary arrangement. Its purpose was completed. I came home. You did not need to come after me."

"You are not really my wife?" he said. "Yet there was a wedding. There is a church register that records our marriage. There was a ring, which you are no longer wearing, I see. You lived in my home and were received by my family. You shared a marriage bed with me on numerous occasions. What is a real wife, pray, ma'am?"

"You are being unfair," she said. "It was our agreement—"

"It was our agreement," he said, "that you would perform a service for me, in return for which you would forever be my wife, supported by me in a manner appropriate to your rank."

"But I cannot accept that support," she said. "The payment is in excess of the service, your grace. And I cannot accept payment for being your wife. It seems to me perilously close to accepting payment as your wh— as your whore."

His eyes kindled then so that she was truly frightened. When he took a step toward her, she had to exercise all her willpower to stand her ground.

"My whore?" he whispered—the whisper made her lick her lips in terror. "My whore, ma'am? A whore would perform her best tricks for me in bed, ma'am, and would be paid for giving satisfaction there. A whore would not be given my name. A whore would not be taken to meet my father and my family. A whore would not find herself in my own bed in my own home. A whore would not find herself supported in a manner appropriate to a duchess for the rest of her life. You are not my whore, *your grace*. You are not skilled enough to be my whore. You are my wife."

She could feel herself blushing hotly. And feeling stupidly humiliated. She had not pleased him? She spoke before she had time to think.

"I am sorry if I did not please you, your grace," she said stiffly.

He stared at her. And then his eyes changed. She almost jumped with alarm when he threw back his head and laughed. She had never seen him laugh like that before.

"I am glad that I amuse you at least," she said, on her dignity.

"If you did not please me!" he said. "In bed, do you mean, Charity? You are still very much the innocent, my love, else you would know beyond any doubt that you pleased me there very well indeed."

And now she despised the smug feeling of gladness that she concentrated on keeping out of her face.

"I will not take payment from you," she said. "I thank you for showing enough concern to find me. But you need not worry. You must go back home. Augusta needs you."

He had been coming closer as she spoke. He stopped when he was within grabbing distance, increasing her nervousness. But she would not give him the satisfaction of stepping back.

"Augusta needs *you*, Charity," he said. "She needs you very badly."

Ah, this was unfair. This was grossly unfair. "My younger brothers and sister need me too, your grace," she said. "Besides, a house and servants and a carriage and six thousand a year will not serve Augusta's needs."

"Enfield needs you," he said. "It needs a duchess. It has been without one for too long."

Oh. The great stabbing of longing took her unawares and she feared it might have shown in her face. She frowned.

"And it needs an heir," he said. "An heir of the direct line."

She glared indignantly at him. "So *that* is it," she said. "You think to add to the original agreement. That was no part of it, your grace. You said—"

"And *I* need you, my love," he said. "I need you so much that I panic when I think that perhaps I will not be able to persuade you to come back with me to Enfield. I need you so much that I cannot quite contemplate the rest of my life if it must be lived without you. I need you so much that— Well, the words speak for themselves. I need you."

"To look after Augusta?" she said. She dared not hear what he was surely saying. She dared not hope. "To look after Enfield? To provide you with an heir?"

"Yes," he said, and her heart sank like a stone to be squashed somewhere between her slippers and the parlor carpet. "And to be my friend and my confidant and my comfort. And to be my lover."

"It was not part of our agreement." She must fight or she would go all to pieces. She watched someone's hands smoothing over the lapels of his coat as if to remove lint, though there was none to remove. They were her hands. But she could not snatch them away. His own had come up to cover them and hold them in place.

"No, it was not," he said quietly. "But you played unfair, Charity. You did not tell me you were not a quiet mouse. You did not tell me you were beautiful or charming or warm with concern for others or courageous or—wonderful in bed." She jerked at her hands, but he would not let her have them back. "You did not tell me you were a thief. I had to come after you to recover my stolen property."

"But the pearls—" She would have died of shame if she could. She had thought the pearls were a gift.

"Are yours, my love," he said. "They were a wedding gift. What you stole, Charity, was my heart. I have come to get it back if all else fails. But I would rather you kept it and brought it back to Enfield with you."

"Oh." Her sigh was almost an agony.

"And I am playing unfair too," he said. "I cannot deny the terms of our agreement. They are written down and signed by each of us. I will keep my side of the bargain if I must. But then you must allow me to keep it. I would far prefer to tear up the document. I have brought it with me—it is in the carriage. We will tear it up together, I hope. But I will agree to do so on only one condition. If you will be my wife in truth, then we will scrap the blasted thing. If you will not, then it must stand in its entirety. The choice is yours."

He held her hands flat against his chest. He held her eyes with his. What chance did she have?

"I am needed here," she said.

"No," he said, "not necessarily here. You are needed by your younger brothers and sister. They would perhaps like Enfield. They would perhaps like Augusta, who would adore them. Your older sister might like Enfield too."

"Penny likes Mr. Miller," she said.

"And if Mr. Miller likes Penelope," he said, "then I will concede that Enfield might be a far less attractive prospect than Mr. Miller's home. I assume he is eligible? But that is for your brother to decide. As for your brother, he and I have had a long talk. He is as stubborn as a mule and as proud as—what is the proudest thing you can think of? No matter. But he is no match for the Duke of Withingsby, my love. I am not my father's son for nothing. I can be marvelously toplofty when I wish to be. There are those who would say, indeed, that I never stop being toplofty. However it is, your brother will return here where he belongs and the debts which have kept him away working at menial drudgery will be paid off—he has not confessed to the debts, but I was not born yesterday. I gather that there is a certain paragon of beauty and charm? A Miss Gladstone?"

"Agnes," she said.

"I daresay she will be Mrs. Duncan before too long," he said, "so I will not bother remembering anything but her first name. I have everything taken care of, you see, my love. Are you with child?"

Her cheeks were instantly scarlet. She needed no looking glass to verify the fact. "No," she said.

"Ah." He smiled. "I must confess to some disappointment. But rectifying that situation will give us something to work on when we return to Enfield. Not that I intend to subject you to yearly confinements for the next twenty years. We will contrive a way to keep that from happening. But—" He stopped suddenly, dropped his hands from hers, took a step back, and turned to face away from her. "But I am babbling. I am so nervous I do not know what I am saying. Am I making any sense at all? Am I bullying you? Charity? Charity, will you be my wife?"

"It is not just, then," she said, "that you feel an obligation? That you have realized the distasteful nature of that agreement?"

He made a sound that was suspiciously like a moan.

"You really love me?" she asked wistfully.

"The devil!" he exclaimed, looking over his shoulder. "Did I forget to say it? The thing I came to say?"

"I love you too," she said. "I love you so much that it has felt to me since I came home that you are here all the time." She tapped her chest just above her heart.

"I told you you had stolen it," he said, and he smiled at her with such sudden warmth that she lost her knees and almost staggered. He turned and caught her in his arms.

"Anthony." She hid her face against his chest. "Oh, Anthony, what am I trying to say?"

"I have no idea," he said. "Has it not all been said? I would settle for a kiss in exchange for whatever we have missed. If you would just lift your face."

She did so and smiled at him while she slid her arms up about his neck. "You had better do it while we still have a moment to ourselves, then," she said. "I have never seen my brothers and sisters stunned into silence as they were when I came into the room. They have never been within a county's breadth of a duke before—especially one who looks so very toplofty. A few minutes ago they discovered that *their sister* is a duchess. But we are made of stern stuff, we Duncans. The shock is going to wear off any minute now and they are going to be bursting in here to ask a million questions each—of each of us. Be warned. It is no light task you have just talked yourself into undertaking."

"Dear me," the Duke of Withingsby said with a haughty lift of his brows. "We had better proceed with that kiss, then, your grace. Clearly I need something with which to bolster my fortitude."

"Exactly what I was trying to say," she said while she could. She was certainly prevented from saying anything else for a good long while.

After a good long while there was the sound of voices all talking simultaneously approaching from the direction of the back door.

A Promise of Spring

1

When the Reverend Paul Howard, rector at the village of Abbotsford in Hampshire, died at the age of two-and-thirty years, his death caused considerably more stir than his life had ever done. He had been a gentle, studious man, revered as a saint, honored as a guest, coveted as visitor to the sick, and largely ignored as a preacher. It was the least of their troubles, the older Miss Stanhope had once remarked to Mrs. Cartwright, to be forced to sit through the hour-long sermon each Sunday when one had only to look at the reverend's face to know that the Almighty had sent them one of his blessed angels in disguise.

In death the rector was lifted once and for all beyond the ordinary. Mrs. Cartwright told several of her acquaintances in some awe that Miss Stanhope's words had been prophetic. The Reverend Howard was walking home after visiting one of the cottages beyond the village, his nose in a book as usual, when the screaming of children had penetrated his consciousness and he had looked up to see one small child in a forbidden field, cornered by a bull that someone had obviously been annoying.

The rector hurled his precious book to the dust, roared with greater ferocity than anyone would have guessed him capable of, vaulted over the wooden fence with more agility than he would have thought possible, picked up the child and lowered him gently over the fence to join the other screaming youngsters, and turned to face the bull—for all the world like David about to take on Goliath, Mr. Watson, the farmer poet, said afterward, though Mr. Watson had not been present to witness the incident. Only the children had.

Unfortunately, the Reverend Howard did not possess a slingshot as David had done. He was dead probably even before the terrified children turned and ran screaming toward the village and help. He became an instant martyr, a man who had given his life for a child. The poor bull survived him by only a few hours.

But the people of Abbotsford and the surrounding countryside were not allowed to bask in the glory of such a sensational tragedy. They were faced with a very practical problem. Their rector had left behind him an unmarried sister. A destitute sister, as far as anyone knew. She had come with her brother five years before to live at the rectory as his housekeeper. Neither had ever spoken of any other family members. It was assumed that there were none. And the Reverend Howard had not been a wealthy man. He had been in the habit of giving away almost more than he possessed, so that Mrs. Courtney and Mrs. Cartwright were agreed that it was a wonder Miss Howard found anything in the rectory kitchen to cook. Perhaps like angels the two of them lived on air.

In the days following the death of her brother, Grace Howard seemed unaware of the unenviable position in which his heroism had placed her. Always quiet and dignified, she seemed now wholly turned to marble. Paul had been all she had left. Now she had nothing. No one. She could not think beyond that deadening fact to consider also that she now had nowhere to go and no means by which to live.

But the people about her were by no means so unaware or so apathetic. Miss Howard's brother had died in order to save one of their children. Miss Howard must be looked after.

"She could come to live with us," Miss Stanhope said to a small gathering of ladies in her parlor the day before the funeral. "Letitia and I are all alone here since Mama and Papa died and dear Bertie moved away. There is plenty of room for all three of us. But will she be willing to come? Or will she see our offer as charity?"

Most of the ladies nodded to indicate that, yes, indeed, Miss Howard might be too proud to accept such a generous offer.

"She is a dear lady," Miss Letitia Stanhope added in support of her older sister, "and would not at all upset our routine, I am sure."

"Mr. Courtney has said that I might ask her to be governess to our Susan," Mrs. Courtney said. "But Susan is fifteen already and not much longer for the schoolroom. And what is to happen to Miss Howard then? The other four are all boys." She added absently, "And they are all older than Susan anyway."

The poorer people of the village, those who worked as laborers for the Earl of Amberley, took up a collection of food and money, which they planned to present to Miss Howard after the funeral. But they knew that such a gift, although a sacrifice to them, would not solve her problem for longer than a week or two at most.

The Countess of Amberley broached the subject to her son the earl as he sat with her in the conservatory at Amberley Court after they had returned from a visit to the rectory.

"The poor lady," she said. "One can clearly see, Edmund, that she has not yet quite comprehended either what has happened or what her predicament now is. She is in a daze. And Doctor Hanson swears that she has not even cried yet. I am so glad, dear, that you thought to offer to send Mrs. Oats and a couple of the other servants over tomorrow to help when the bishop arrives for the funeral."

The Earl of Amberley sighed. "We are very privileged, Mama, are we not?" he said. "We know very well that no matter what disaster befalls us, materially we may live still with great comfort. I shall have to find a situation for Miss Howard. I don't suppose she will accept a pension from me, will she?"

"It is unlikely," his mother replied. "Perhaps the bishop will have the inspiration to appoint a new rector who will need a housekeeper. But perhaps she would not choose to stay at the rectory, with her brother gone. I have been thinking of offering her the position of companion. What do you think, Edmund?"

"Companion?" he said with a frown. "You mean to you, Mama? You would hate to have such an employee, would you not?"

"Oh, dear," the countess said, "I am afraid I would, Edmund. But what else is one to do? I feel very deeply for Miss Howard. I know just how it feels to lose someone who is everything to one. I ache with memories of Papa at a time like this."

The Earl of Amberley reached out and touched his mother's hand. "Let me talk to her first, Mama," he said. "Perhaps she has some idea of what she would like to do. Perhaps you will not have to make the sacrifice of burdening yourself with a companion."

"It would not be a burden, Edmund," she said. "Miss Howard is a sensible lady."

The earl smiled fleetingly. "Perry is taking this death hard," he said. "He was a very close friend of Howard's, you know. I was even somewhat jealous of the fact until I realized that being a friend of one person does not exclude one from being another's too. Perry and I have been friends for as long as I can remember."

Sir Peregrine Lampman did not consult with anyone on what should be done about his friend's sister. He paid a call on her the morning after the funeral, after the bishop had left and before his neighbors and friends could put into effect any of their less-than-satisfactory suggestions for Miss Howard's future. And he asked her to marry him.

SIR PEREGRINE LAMPMAN was the owner, since his father's demise three years before, of Reardon Park, a modest estate when compared with the lands of Amberley that adjoined it, but nevertheless large enough and prosperous enough to set him in the forefront of social life in the county. He lived in a neat eighteenth-century house of gray stone, built by his grandfather; the house was unimposing when compared to Amberley Court, which was set in a picturesque valley close to the sea, but it nevertheless contained no fewer than ten guest bedchambers.

Sir Peregrine was a man of sunny nature and considerable charm, a man who seemed always to be smiling. He was not particularly tall, but he was slender and graceful. His friends and neighbors were in the habit of thinking him handsome. Yet there was nothing in his appearance to set him above the ordinary. His hair was neither dark nor blond, neither straight nor curly, neither short nor long. His eyes were neither blue, nor gray, nor green, but a mixture of all three. His clothes were fashionable, yet there was no suggestion of the dandy about his person.

It was his charm and his friendliness that probably gave the impression of handsomeness. Women especially were wont to admire him. He always had a teasing word, and even sometimes a wink, for the older ladies. Miss Stanhope was in the habit of calling his behavior "outrageous," yet she was clearly pleased by his attention. Miss Letitia Stanhope frequently simpered when "dear Sir Perry" commented on how becoming her new cap looked on her. He always thought, or pretended to think, that her cap was new.

He liked to flirt with the younger ladies and girls, yet always in just the right way so that none of them would ever mistake his intentions and consider them serious. For Peregrine had never been in love, despite his five-and-twenty years, and had never thought to be. It was too enjoyable to be free to let one's eye rove, to set a blush to glowing in this one's cheek, a sparkle in that one's eye. And as for his real needs, he could satisfy those with no trouble at all during his not infrequent though never lengthy visits to London.

He particularly liked to flirt with Lady Madeline Raine, the sister of the Earl of Amberley, who was five years his junior. He had teased her and indulged her all through her girlhood when she had tried desperately to keep up with the energetic and frequently dangerous exploits of Lord Eden, her twin brother. For the past two years, since she had made her come-out, he had flirted with her. She knew the game and played it as skillfully as he. One could smile very directly into Madeline's dancing eyes, pay her the most outrageous compliments, kiss the tips of her fingers, and know that the next moment she would tap one sharply on the shoulder with her fan, laugh back into one's eyes, and whisk herself off to some other admirer.

With men Peregrine was more serious. He looked for more than amusement and light conversation from his male friends. He read a great deal and thought a great deal and liked nothing more than to have another mind against which to sound his own ideas.

He had been friendly with Edmund Raine, the Earl of Amberley, for as far back as he could remember. And they were still close friends, despite Amberley's increasing tendency since inheriting the title to withdraw into himself. Amberley had been loaded down with responsibility too early, his own father having died when he was but nineteen, his twin brother and sister only twelve, and his mother close to nervous collapse for a year or more. And Amberley spent several months of each year with his family in London. The friendship of the two men was still firm, but they were not nearly as inseparable as they had been as boys.

The Reverend Paul Howard had filled the gap left in Peregrine's life. Quiet, gentle, and saintly as he appeared to his parishioners, he was a man of fiery intellect when confronted by someone who could match him in knowledge and understanding. Together the two men explored the worlds of literature and art and science and religion and philosophy and politics, frequently disagreeing, often arguing with rising, excited voices, but never quarreling. They learned to respect each other's minds.

Peregrine was a frequent visitor at the rectory. Almost daily he was in Grace Howard's company for at least a few minutes. He rarely spoke with her at any length, as she was contained and always busy about some task. She seemed content to fade into the background behind her brother, never putting herself forward. Her large gray eyes looked on the world with great calm. Yet there was about her lovely face a certain tautness, most noticeable in the set of her lips, that occasionally made Peregrine wonder about her, about her life, about what went on behind the quiet, neat exterior that was Miss Howard.

Certainly she was capable of creating extraordinary beauty. He liked to watch her as she embroidered, the flowers and other designs creating themselves beneath her fingers so that one almost felt that if one held the linen close one would be able to smell their fragrance.

And the flower garden behind the rectory over which she toiled sometimes for hours rioted with color and heady perfumes from early spring to late autumn.

Peregrine was shocked and numbed by the sudden and seemingly pointless death of his brilliant friend. For a whole day he could think of nothing but his own loss and that empty ache left inside. It was only when he went to the rectory to pay his respects to Miss Howard that he became suddenly aware of her plight. There were six other visitors crowded into the little parlor, all talking in muted voices, as if afraid of wakening the rector, who lay in his coffin in the dining room next door.

Miss Howard sat in the middle of them, no different from usual, except that to the eyes of Peregrine, who had seen her almost daily for the past five years, there was perhaps a little more tautness about her mouth and a little more emptiness in her eyes than usual. She sat straight and serene in her black mourning dress, her hands, usually so busy, folded quietly in her lap, her eyes moving from speaker to speaker, her control never for one moment slipping.

What would she do? Where would she go? Strangely, despite the closeness of the friendship that had existed between Peregrine and the rector, they had never talked about personal matters. Peregrine had been very familiar indeed with the Reverend Howard's mind. He knew almost nothing about him as a person. He knew even less about his sister.

She would not be able to stay at the rectory. She would be destitute. As far as Peregrine knew, brother and sister had had no income apart from his pay as rector. And the rector had been generous, even careless, with his money. There would be no more money for Miss Howard.

He sat looking at her as the other callers talked and commiserated with her. And he saw a brave and a lonely woman, one whose face and bearing denoted dignity and depth of character. He saw the quiet, attractive woman who had made his friend's life comfortable and his home a place of some beauty. He saw a woman he had admired for years almost without realizing it. He saw a mysterious woman, one he had known for five years without knowing her at all.

He saw someone whom, belatedly, he wished to know.

Yet she would surely now disappear from Abbotsford to some unknown destination and to a life of dreariness or drudgery. Perhaps with her brother dead no one would ever again know Grace Howard.

Peregrine wanted to know her.

Even before he rose to his feet at the end of twenty minutes, took her cold hand in his and bowed over it, and left the stuffy, oppressive atmosphere of death and stunned grief, he knew what he must do. He returned to the rectory the morning after the funeral, before it was likely that there would be any other visitors, and asked Miss Grace Howard to marry him.

GRACE MOVED ACROSS the parlor to stand at the window that looked out on her flower garden. She stood very straight, her hands clasped in front of her. Her black mourning dress, with its unfashionable natural waistline and full skirt, its plain, high-necked bodice, and its straight long sleeves, accentuated her slimness. Her dark hair was dressed in its usual style, parted at the center, looped smoothly over her ears, and coiled at the back. She wore a small black lace cap.

"I cannot," she said, "though I must be sensible of the extreme kindness of your offer, sir. Paul would be pleased by your thoughtfulness. He valued your friendship more than I can say. But, then, you must know that."

"I wish you would reconsider, Miss Howard," Sir Peregrine said, standing in the middle of the parlor, his hands clasped behind him, watching her face in profile. It was, he realized for perhaps the first time, a rather handsome profile. "I believe you are in need of a home, and I am both free and willing to offer you one. But I will make it more secure than this one has been for you. I will make sure that an independence will be settled upon you in the event of my predeceasing you."

She turned her head to look fully at him with her large, calm eyes. "How very kind you are," she said in some wonder. "I have always liked you, Sir Peregrine. You have been the friend that Paul always needed and never had before we moved here. Now I can respect you for my own sake too. But my answer must remain no. There are far too many reasons for our not marrying."

Peregrine hesitated. "You refer to our age difference?" he asked.

A fleeting smile crossed her face before she turned back to the window. "I am five-and-thirty years old," she said. "Did you know that? I have never gone to any pains to make myself seem younger than I am. Paul was my younger brother."

"And yet," he said, "ten years is not seen as such an insurmountable gap when the man is the older."

"Men do not bear children," she said quietly.

"I have never considered children essential to the fulfillment of my happiness," he said. "If that is your only concern, Miss Howard, I beg you again to reconsider. I truly wish to have you as my wife."

"For Paul's sake?" she asked. "You wish to look after the sister he left behind? It is a kind gesture, sir, but hardly one that will carry you through a lifetime. I am more grateful than I can say, but no. You would quickly tire of a wife ten years your senior, and one who is no match for you in either charm or intellect."

"No," he said, "it is not just on account of my friendship with Paul that I offer you marriage. It is on your account. It is true that we have scarcely conversed together in the five years since you have been living here. But I have seen a great deal of you in that time and have absorbed impressions of you that I was largely unaware of myself until I have given them deliberate thought in the last few days. I like you, Miss Howard, and believe I could be happy married to you."

She turned fully to face him. Her face, he saw, was paler and more tense than usual, though she looked at him with eyes whose calm was undisturbed. "Oh," she said, "you know nothing about me, Sir Peregrine. Nothing whatsoever. I have lived for thirty-five years. And despite the tranquillity of the life you have seen me lead here, they have not been uneventful years. Not by any means. If you knew but half of what there is to know about me, you would be thankful for my refusal, sir, believe me."

Peregrine shifted the weight on his feet but did not move or withdraw his eyes from hers. "Tell me, then," he said, smiling slowly at her. "Tell me what is so dreadful in your past."

She looked away from him suddenly, up to one corner of the ceiling behind his head. "Do you know?" she said. "Did Paul ever tell you that our father is Lord Pawley? Baron Pawley of Leicestershire. Prosperous and well-respected. No, I can see that he did not tell you. Paul quarreled with our father, broke with him, on my account. And took me with him wherever he went after that. For four years while he was a curate and for five years here—nine years during which there has been no communication between our father and our older brother and us. I was sitting in here before you came, wrestling with the question I have pondered for the last several days. Should I inform my father of the death of his youngest child? The one I took away from him."

She was still gazing upward at the ceiling behind his head, but Peregrine could see even so that her eyes were bright with unshed tears. And her lips began to tremble. He took a couple of steps forward and stretched out a hand to her.

"Ma'am?" he said. "Has my question caused you pain? Forgive me, please."

She did not move or respond to his words. "I have not cried," she said, "since . . . I have not cried for more than nine years. I did not expect to do so ever again. I did not think any tears were left inside me."

But she was clearly crying now. Her facial muscles were working beyond her control. Two tears spilled from her eyes, rolled down her upturned face, and dripped onto her dress. "Paul," she said as Peregrine took one more step toward her and gripped her shoulder with one strong hand. "Paul. Oh, Paul."

And then she was crying with racking sobs that seemed to be tearing her in two, her forehead on Peregrine's shoulder, his two arms about her, holding her loosely and comfortingly.

"Do you believe in heaven?" she asked a few minutes later, having dried her eyes and blown her nose on Peregrine's handkerchief. "Do you believe Paul is in heaven? I used to believe in such a place. But how can I continue to do so when I cannot believe in God, or at least not in a good God? Do you think he is in heaven? Has something good come out of all this?"

Peregrine smiled and absently reached out to put a fallen lock of hair back from her face. "I know how Paul would answer your question," he said. "And on this occasion I think I agree with him, though we never could agree on very many ideas. Even if heaven is not a place that exists for eternity, it can be a moment in time. I know how Paul must have felt when he knew he was about to be gored by that bull. He had saved the life of a child. He had with his own hands robbed death of one victory. I suppose he had no time for clear thought. I suppose he might have known a moment of terror seeing what was facing him. But I believe too that he felt exultant, happy. He was in heaven."

Grace reached up and pushed the stray lock of hair more firmly into the rest. "Thank you," she said. "Yes, that is just what Paul would have said. I was often angry in those first years, often rebellious. But Paul could always calm me. His logic was always irrefutable. His sermons were dull, Sir Peregrine—yes, I know they were—because he worked so hard on them. But when he spoke from the heart—and it took him only a few moments, not a whole hour—he could convince me that perhaps there is a God after all and perhaps He is even good. Who knows?"

"Are you better now?" Peregrine asked. "Do you wish to sit down?"

"I need a cup of tea," she said. "And I owe you an explanation. I have not explained what happened to sever Paul and me from the rest of our family. Will you excuse me for a few minutes while I boil the kettle?"

"If I may," Peregrine said, "I shall come with you and watch you make the tea."

He perched on the corner of the kitchen table, his arms folded across his chest as she busied herself filling the kettle and setting it on the fire to boil, measuring tea into the teapot, taking two cups and saucers from a cupboard, and setting out milk and sugar. She talked as she worked, her eyes on what she was doing, not on him at all.

"I had a child," she said abruptly. "A son. He died. He drowned."

Peregrine had to swallow before he could find his voice. "I did not know you had been married," he said.

"I have never been married," she said quietly and deliberately. "My son was the child of my lover."

"I see." Why did the room suddenly seem very small and very quiet? Peregrine wondered.

"I am sure you do not," she said. "I will explain." She sat down on a wooden chair close to where he sat on the table, and watched the kettle as it began to hiss and hum.

"I did not mean to pry into your life," Peregrine said. "You need say no more if you would rather not."

"Paul and I never talked about it," she said. "Never once, even though he gave up our father and our brother for me. I must talk about it now, if you please. I grew up with Gareth. He was not even a year older than I. We were playmates, friends. We were going to be married. And then he decided quite suddenly that he must buy a pair of colors and go off to the wars. His country became more important to him than any of the plans for his life and ours. We would resume those plans when he came home, he said. We would marry, have children, live happily ever after. We became lovers for a few days before he left. And he left me with Jeremy. My son."

Peregrine could feel her pain, though she sat quietly at the table, her hands folded together. There was something in her voice, a certain throbbing that he had not heard there before. "He died?" he asked gently. "Your l— Gareth?"

She stared into the fire for a long time. He thought she would not answer. "Yes," she said, one corner of her mouth twisting into a parody of a smile. "Yes, he died. And I was left to face the fury of my father, the contempt of my brother and sister-in-law. After Jeremy was born, I had to accustom myself to hearing him called *bastard* more often than *Jeremy*. And always he had to take a distant third place behind his two cousins. A very distant third place."

She rose to lift the boiling kettle off the fire and pour the water into the teapot. She fitted the cosy very carefully over the pot. "So distant," she said, "that the governess who was entrusted with their care when they went swimming at the lake did not even notice when Jeremy's clothes became entangled in some undergrowth and dragged him down. She did not even distinguish his cries from the shrieks of the other children playing. He was four years old. And then I had to endure hearing people tell one another that that was the best fate for a bastard: death before he could realize fully the awkwardness of his situation."

Peregrine got to his feet and poured the tea.

"Paul came home from university," she said. "He was the only one to show me sympathy, the only one to stand up against all those who thought of Jeremy as of little worth because he was born out of wedlock. He had a dreadful row with Pap—with my father and my older brother. And then he told me he would take me away, that I need not live any longer with the insults and the daily reminders of my son. I could be at peace, he said. And I was so broken with the pain of it all that I let him take me away. I hope I did not spoil his life. But I do not believe he ever wished to marry and have his own family. I think I was able to provide his life with some comfort."

Peregrine leaned forward from the chair he had taken and covered her hand with his own. "I am sure of it," he said. "There is no doubt whatsoever in my mind."

She looked up at him suddenly out of her large eyes and down at the cup that was set before her. "Oh," she said. "Did you pour? So you see, Sir Peregrine, the skeleton in my closet is a very large and a very sordid one indeed. I am not by any means the person you must have thought me all these years. Not quiet, demure Miss Howard, the rector's housekeeper, but a fallen woman, mother of a bastard son, mercifully dead."

His hand was still over hers. "Will you marry me?" he asked.

She looked at him incredulously.

"I have always admired you as a woman of character," he said, "someone very much in command of her own emotions and her own life. Now I am sure that my impression was correct. Will you do me the honor of becoming my wife?"

"You ask me at the wrong time," she said, frowning. "At entirely the wrong time, sir. I am raw with the pain of my memories and the loss of my brother. I am very vulnerable."

He clasped her hand more firmly in his own. "Will you marry me?" he asked.

"Don't," she whispered. "For your own sake, don't."

"Marry me," he said. "Please. Give me the chance to put some joy into your life."

She shook her head. "I will take the joy from yours," she said.

Peregrine smiled. "Give me a chance to prove you wrong," he said. "Say you will marry me. Say it. One little word. Please?"

Grace drew a breath that shuddered out of her again. "Yes, then," she said. "Yes. Oh, God forgive me. Yes."

2

THE MISSES STANHOPE CALLED ON GRACE IMMEDI-
ately after luncheon, laden with fruit and vegeta-
bles, freshly baked currant cakes, and a chicken, for the
purpose of inviting her to stay with them until she got
settled elsewhere. It was better not to invite her to live
with them, Miss Stanhope had explained to Miss Letitia, as she might feel beholden to them; better to make it
seem that she was to be their guest and to let the term of
her stay drift on indefinitely until she forgot about leaving them. But when they called upon Grace, it was only
to have their invitation denied with gracious thanks.
Miss Howard had that morning accepted Sir Peregrine
Lampman's offer of marriage.

Well, Miss Stanhope declared later that afternoon to
Mrs. Cartwright and later still to both Mrs. Courtney
and Mrs. Morton while Miss Letitia nodded her agreement, she might easily have been knocked down with a
feather if anyone had cared to try. And she was very
much afraid that her mouth had dropped open and she
had gaped. No, Miss Letitia assured her sister, nothing
so ungenteel had happened, but she could vouch for the
fact that her sister had turned several shades paler, as
had she.

Miss Howard was to marry Sir Perry, that handsome,
sunny-natured young man they had known from child-

hood. And such a mischievous young boy he had been, for sure. Did anyone remember the time when old Mr. Watson—God rest his soul—had been sleeping peacefully through the old rector's sermon and young Perry in the pew behind had begun to snore gently? A good thrashing he had probably got for that prank, if his father's frown had been any indication of what was awaiting the boy when they arrived home.

And did anyone remember, Miss Letitia added, the time when young Perry and the young earl—not that he was earl at the time, of course—had climbed the steepest part of the cliff from the beach and Perry had got stuck almost at the top? Young Edmund had had to run back to Amberley for help. Both lads had probably been thrashed for that one too.

All the ladies appealed to remembered well and laughed and nodded and added their own reminiscences.

And now Sir Perry was going to marry Miss Howard when they had scarcely realized that he was old enough to marry anyone at all. And Miss Howard must be . . . Surely she must be . . . Well, she was older than he by at least ten years, surely. And so quiet and prim and correct. Had anyone ever seen her smile? No, no one had. A kind and gracious lady, of course. They had all grown to love her, though no one had really got to know her. Did anyone feel they knew Miss Howard? No, no one did. But surely she was not suitable as a bride for Sir Perry, who was so young and so handsome and so full of fun.

"But it is just like him to do something so noble," Mrs. Courtney suggested. "How very kind of him, for sure. Miss Howard must be very gratified indeed."

"But she is so old for a young man's bride," Mrs. Morton said. And forgetting her audience, "She is rather old to be only just starting to present him with children, you know."

Both the Misses Stanhope blushed scarlet and avoided

each other's eyes. They did not know, or at least they had been too refined to think about such a delicate matter.

Everyone paid a call at the rectory to congratulate Grace and wish her well. And there was no spite or hypocrisy in their wishes. They genuinely respected her, though they admitted that they did not know her, and they were happy that her future had been settled in such a fortunate way. They genuinely wished her well.

If most of them believed that the marriage could not possibly be successful and that it must bring unhappiness to Sir Peregrine at least, then they also wished they might be proved wrong. Peregrine was a definite favorite in the neighborhood, and Grace had been accepted as one of them both for her own sake and for the sake of her brother, who had died so that one of their children might live.

The men doubtless had their own opinions on the betrothal too and doubtless expressed them to one another over their port when they had a chance. Some of them probably shared those opinions with their wives. Mr. William Carrington, brother of the Countess of Amberley and uncle of the earl, certainly did.

"It's as likely to succeed as any other marriage," he said when quizzed on the matter by his wife.

"Oh, William," she said scornfully, "she is ten years or more older than he. How can it possibly work?"

"Well, my dear," he said, pinching her ample bottom so that she shrieked and slapped at his hand, "I am almost ten years older than you, but it seems to me that we get along tolerably well together. Except when you are slapping out at me, of course."

"William! Do behave yourself," she said. "What if any of the children should see?"

"They are not allowed into our bedchamber unannounced, my love," he said reasonably. "And if they saw, they would only discover that their papa still fancies their mama after eighteen years of marriage."

"William," she said. "But this betrothal is a different matter. She is older than he. That is unheard-of. And Perry such a happy-go-lucky young man."

"Who is to know what couples will suit?" he said. "Who would believe that a careless, teasing sort of fellow like me would still be pinching a scold of a wife like you after almost twenty years, Viola, and getting away with only a slapped hand? They will work things out between them, never fear. Leave it to them, my love. You come on over here. That pinch has whetted my appetite."

"I hope you are right about Miss Howard and dear Perry," his wife said, wandering toward him almost absentmindedly. "Oh, William, what are you about now? And in broad daylight too. Anyone would think I was still a spring chicken. Oh, dear, I really think I am old enough now that this should be done only in darkness. Oh, very well, then. Are you sure the door is locked?"

THE EARL OF Amberley paid a call on his friend when he heard the news.

"It is really true, then, Perry?" he said when they had walked out behind the stables and stood looking out over the fields of Reardon Park.

"I assume you refer to my betrothal," Peregrine said. "I have heard that tone of voice from several others in the last day. I did not look for it from you, Edmund. Yes, it is true. Miss Grace Howard has consented to honor me with her hand. She is going to be my wife."

Lord Amberley was silent for a while. "She needs help," he said. "She is quite destitute, as far as anyone seems to know. But she is older than you, Perry, and although I will admit that she is a handsome woman, she seems to be quite lacking in openness and charm. Is your gesture not just too noble? Are you prepared to ruin the whole of your life for the sake of doing a kindness?"

Peregrine allowed his friend to reach the end of his speech before throwing the whole of his weight behind the fist that connected painfully with the earl's nose.

"Damn you, Edmund," he said between his teeth, glaring as the other staggered on his feet and lifted a hand to the blood that was spurting from his nose. "Damn you to hell. You will apologize if you expect me ever to speak to you again."

The earl took a handkerchief from his pocket and mopped at his bleeding nose with a slightly shaking hand before looking at his friend again. "I am sorry," he said from among the folds of the linen. "I do apologize, Perry. What I said was unforgivable. The lady is your betrothed, and of course you must defend her honor." He withdrew the handkerchief, glanced down at it with a grimace, and raised a tentative hand to his reddening nose.

"I shouldn't have hit you," Peregrine said, turning sharply away to look out over the fields again.

"Yes, indeed you should," Lord Amberley said, checking the bridge of his nose to see if it were broken. "I could be happier without this pain, of course, but I am glad you did hit me, Perry. It proves something to me. Forgive me, please." He held out his right hand.

Peregrine took it and the friends smiled ruefully at each other. "It's not quite what you think, Edmund," Peregrine said. "It's not just because she is destitute, and it's not just because Paul was my friend. I care for her. I know that most people will never believe that. And I suppose it does not matter to me a great deal as long as she believes me. But I would like you to believe it. You are my oldest friend, Edmund, and probably the nicest person I know."

Lord Amberley squeezed his friend's hand. "It seems strange to think of you married, Perry," he said. "Somehow I have never thought of you settling down. I thought I would race you to the altar, though I have no thought of marrying before I am thirty. Three years to go yet! I wish you well. I really do. All the young ladies around here will be wearing the willow for you, you know."

Peregrine grinned. "Why would they miss me when they have you to angle after?" he said. "And Dominic twenty already and as tall and handsome as they come. And the Eden title and an estate in Wiltshire to boot. That nose of yours is shining like a beacon, Edmund. And still bleeding a little. We had better go back to the house and get some cold water for it."

THE BISHOP HAD told Grace before he left late on the day of the funeral that he would send a new rector in one month's time and that she might stay at the rectory until then. Peregrine arranged it that the new man should marry them on the day after his arrival. Grace spent the night before her wedding with the Misses Stanhope, who preened themselves indeed on the distinction of having a bride married from their house. Even dear Bertie had not been wed at home.

Grace spent the month cleaning the rectory from top to bottom and sorting through Paul's effects. His books, his most valued possessions, she gave to her betrothed. His other few belongings, including his vestments, his sermons, his watch, and pitifully few other items, she put together into a box inside her own trunk, which was by no means overflowing when it was finally packed.

Sir Peregrine Lampman and Grace Howard were married on a gray and chilly morning in spring with all their friends and neighbors in attendance. It was a quiet celebration. Both bride and groom wore deep mourning.

The Earl of Amberley and his mother, as well as his sister and brother, Lady Madeline Raine and Dominic, Lord Eden, had postponed their removal to London for the Season in order to provide a wedding breakfast in the state apartments at Amberley Court.

The gathering was a large and a quietly cheerful one. If the warm affection and hearty good wishes of a community could ensure the happiness of a marriage, then this one must prove to be one of the happiest. If any of those present still felt dismay at the age difference between bride and groom and at the disparity of their personalities, then they hid those feelings well and in all probability pretended even to themselves that they felt no such misgivings.

Peregrine took his bride home late in the afternoon and showed her the house and the garden and the stables. She had been to Reardon Park only once, several years ago when Peregrine's father had still been alive and his mother still at home.

Grace looked quietly at the long lawns and few trees behind the house and felt her husband smiling at her.

"I have an unimaginative gardener and am no better myself," he said. "If you wish to work your magic here, Grace, please feel free to do so. I have always been an admirer of your garden at the rectory."

"There is room for a rose garden here," she said. "I have always longed for a separate rose arbor. There was not enough space behind the rectory. And there should be daffodils and primroses among the trees. And flower beds." She gazed about her, obviously seeing in her mind far more than the bare green expanses that surrounded them. "There is room for a splendid orchard over there." She pointed to another stretch of lawn to the east of the house.

Peregrine laughed. "My gardener will be handing in his notice," he said. "I shall have to hire others. And I will learn from you, Grace. I have always wanted a beautiful garden, but I am afraid I gaze about me and cannot picture what can be done. You shall convert me into a devoted and domesticated gardener."

Grace looked at him seriously. "You must not curtail your activities on my account," she said. "I will be content just to be here. You must not change your life."

He smiled. "But my life has changed," he said. "Today. I am a married man now, my dear."

It seemed strange to Grace after nine years to have a maid again to help her change her dress for dinner and brush out and coil her hair. It seemed strange to go down to a dinner that someone else had planned and prepared and to have it served by a butler and a footman. Strange to have someone else clear away the food and the dishes, and to know that someone else would wash the dishes in the kitchen.

And it was strange and somewhat embarrassing to discover that, although she had her own dressing room and sitting room, she was to share a bedchamber with her husband. She had not been at all sure during the past month exactly what kind of a marriage it was that Peregrine planned.

"I thought that perhaps you were offering me a marriage in name only, Peregrine," she said when he came to her after she had dismissed her maid and stood in the middle of the bedroom, her nightgown covering her decently, her hair brushed out and lying smoothly down her back. Her one concession to vanity was the absence of a nightcap.

"Perry, if you please," he said, coming to stand close to her. "I love my mother dearly and loved my father, but I have always been appalled by the lack of sensibility they showed when they named me." He grinned. "Grace, I have married you. You are my wife. I would have offered you the position of housekeeper here if I had not wanted more of you. And I have always thought rather strange the frequent custom of a husband and wife occupying separate rooms. I will want to make love to you frequently. It is far more convenient for us to share the same bed. Is it not to your liking?"

She raised her large calm eyes to his. Her thin face was pale. "Yes," she said. "Yes, I will be the wife you want me to be, Perry."

"You have beautiful hair," he said, reaching up both hands and smoothing them lightly over it. "You are a beautiful woman, Grace." He bent his head and kissed her pale lips. "Come to bed. I will see to the candles."

As so often happened after a gloomy day, the clouds had moved off during the evening, and the night was brightly illuminated by an almost full moon and myriad stars.

Grace Lampman lay with her head turned to one side, watching her husband sleeping beside her. He looked absurdly young in the repose of sleep, his fair hair rumpled, his usually smiling face relaxed. She felt an ache of tenderness for him. Perhaps there was an end to punishment, after all. For her, that was. Only time would tell what her marrying him would do to Perry.

She had not expected to come alive again. She had given up life nine years before. Because she could never, even in her worst moments, contemplate suicide, she had been forced to keep on breathing and eating and sleeping and filling in the time until she could stop living indeed. And she had always been thankful for the small but infinitely precious gift of Paul's love and for his need of her time, that commodity that hung most heavily on her hands. But she had never expected more than that, had never felt the need of more.

Until Perry had tempted her and in her weakness she

had given in to that temptation. And even then she had hoped not to be forced back into life again. She had hoped that what he wanted of her would be no different from what Paul had accepted for nine years. She had hoped to be no more than his housekeeper, to share no more than his name.

She had always liked Perry, had always brightened at his knock on the rectory door, at his sunny smile, his frequent inquiries after her health, his praise of her embroidery and her garden. She had loved him for the brightness he had brought into Paul's life. Paul had always been different: small, gentle, studious, misunderstood and reviled by would-be friends as a boy, alienated by a family who would have liked him to be more aggressive, more ambitious as a clergyman. Perry had been not only a friend of the intellect to Paul; he had brought laughter and some gaiety into her brother's life for the first time ever.

She had liked to look at him, slender and graceful, handsome in his own very special, sunny-natured way. Yet she had never looked at him in the way a woman looks at a man to whom she is attracted. He was so much younger than she, a boy almost, though he was in fact well past boyhood. It amused her at church, and at the social gatherings she sometimes attended with Paul, to see the young girls look at him with admiration and some longing and to see him smile back and flirt with them. Yet never in a cruel manner. They knew perfectly well that he merely flirted. He did so even with the older ladies, though never with her.

She had always thought that perhaps he would end up marrying Lady Madeline Raine, a young lady of equally sunny nature and equal ability to flirt quite inoffensively. They would make a handsome and a glittering couple, Grace had thought. They could not fail to be happy together. Lady Madeline was twenty years old. But he had married a thirty-five-year-old woman instead.

Grace lifted her head from her husband's arm, on which it had been resting. His arm would be horribly cramped if he left it there. She eased it slowly down to his side. He grumbled slightly in his sleep, but did not wake. He turned over onto his side, facing toward her.

Her own youth seemed such a very long time ago, Grace thought. It could have been another lifetime altogether. She had always been restless and headstrong, stubborn, the spoiled daughter of a father who had only two sons besides her. Her mother had died soon after Paul's birth. And she had been the close friend of Gareth, only son of the Viscount Sandersford, for as far back as she could remember. Gareth, as headstrong and as stubborn as she, arrogant, intelligent, vibrant with life, yet with a streak of cruelty that often showed itself on weaker playmates, especially Paul.

She had played with him, defended him, argued with him, fought with him, and ultimately loved him. And she had given herself to him during those final days before he left for the wars, heedless to the consequences that she must have known were a strong possibility. She must have known. She had been one-and-twenty already. She could even remember feeling a stubborn, frightened sort of pride when she first suspected that she was with child, though Gareth had no longer been there to scorn with her the opinion of the world.

It had been a love with a cruel ending. A love and an ending that could only deaden anyone who survived it. And she had been dead to all intents and purposes for nine years since Jeremy had left her, and only painfully alive for more than four years before that, knowing when it was far too late to acquire such wisdom that her own selfish heedlessness of the moral code would ultimately bring more suffering to her innocent son than it would to her. She was half-dead anyway with Gareth gone. Jeremy was the only light in her life. Yet she had doomed Jeremy from the moment of his conception.

And was she to come alive again now? It was far more peaceful to live in the shadowed land of the half-dead. There was no pain there. She had fought off the pain of Paul's death, fought desperately, allowing it to force itself past the barriers she had built around her emotions only on the morning after his funeral when Perry had come to her, and put outside the barriers again immediately after.

But Perry had married her in good faith, with every intention of making her his wife indeed. And he had made her his wife, in the quiet ceremony that morning, with a strange rector taking Paul's place, and in this bed an hour before. And though she had not made the comparisons at the time, she could not help making them now. Gareth and Perry.

She had allowed Gareth numerous intimacies in those few days, because she knew she was losing him perhaps forever and because she did not care what her father or her stuffy brother and despised sister-in-law might say, and because she was young and very, very foolish. It had always happened outdoors, almost always on the hard ground, Gareth heavy on her so that sometimes she had almost screamed with the pain of stones or hard earth pressing into her back. She had loved what he did to her because it was forbidden and daring and dangerous. He had always done what he did quickly and lustily, intent on his own pleasure. But then she had assumed that that was what sexual relations were supposed to be like.

Perry had not been like that at all. Perry had called her beautiful and he had made her feel beautiful in what he had done to her very unhurriedly on the bed before he had fallen asleep. She had been embarrassed and tense at first because she was a woman approaching her middle age and he little more than a boy, and because it had been fourteen years since she had last been with a man, but he had made her feel like a woman again, like someone of worth, someone desirable before he had lain on her and come into her.

And the barriers had come crashing down under the gentle caress of his hands, the warm touch of his mouth, the soothing murmurings of his voice. She had come alive again. All her feelings had come slowly and painfully and achingly alive for him, so that when he had come inside her finally, she had been unable to present herself to him as a dutiful wife. She had become a woman opening to her lover. And if there had been any chance that she might have recollected herself before he finished, he had destroyed that chance by working slowly and rhythmically in her even at that culminating stage of his lovemaking. And so she had given herself openly to her husband and had received his gift of pleasure.

She had said nothing. She had held him with her arms, but she had kept her inner trembling in check. And she had closed her eyes and turned her face into his shoulder when he had moved to her side and put his arm beneath her. So, when he had kissed her cheek and pulled the blankets up around her shoulders, he had assumed she was asleep already and had fallen asleep himself. She did not know if he knew. She did not know if she wished him to know.

But she knew that he was a man with far greater depths of kindness and gentleness and love than she had ever suspected. She knew that he was a man in a thousand. A man who deserved the very best that life could give him. A man who should have love and laughter in his home. And children.

And she knew that she was alive again and so full of pain that she did not know quite how she could lie still so as not to disturb him. She must not allow it. She dared not allow it. It was too late now for her to come alive and be the wife Perry needed and deserved. If she came too much alive, she would become too terribly aware of the injustice she had done him, and she would not even be able to be a good wife to him. She would come to watch for signs of discontent in him. She would come to watch him with other, younger women, watching for signs of longing and restlessness. And she would come ultimately to hate him for having reminded her that life could be for living if only one had not misused one's youth so very badly.

But the tautness of her body must have disturbed him after all. His eyes were open when she looked across at him again. He was smiling, as he usually was.

"Still awake, Grace?" he asked, running one knuckle down the length of her nose. "Is this very strange to you, dear? It is to me too, I do assure you. I am not accustomed to waking up to find a wife on the pillow beside me."

"Yes," she said, "it is a little strange."

His smile faded. "I did not hurt you, Grace? Or outrage you? Or embarrass you?"

She shook her head. "I am your wife," she said.

"Yes, you are." He gazed at her in silence for a while. "Grace, I know you have a great many memories. I know that you have loved. And tonight especially the memories must be painful. I cannot compete against the father of your child. I do not wish to compete. I do not wish you to try to suppress those memories or put me in his place. I just want to give you some comfort, dear, some security. Some affection. Don't feel guilty if you are remembering him tonight."

Grace could only gaze mutely back into his eyes.

He smiled and closed the distance between their mouths.

"But I do like waking to find a wife here," he said before kissing her.

He should not have woken when he had, Grace thought. She had not had time to come to terms with her very live feelings. And perhaps she never would again, living with him by day as she must, sleeping beside him and with him by night. Perhaps she would never be able to die inside again for as long as they were wed. Perhaps she must step out into the world again and learn again how to live, how to love, how to enjoy, and how to suffer.

She found herself wanting more than the warm kiss. She wanted to know if it would always be as it had been the first time, if he would always be her lover as well as her husband. It was only when his mouth moved to her throat and his hands found their way beneath her nightgown and his weight bore down on her and his manhood came into her that she let go of her anxieties and allowed herself to become a woman beneath him again, made beautiful by the gentle force of his lovemaking.

3

SPRING WAS COMING FAST. THERE WAS NO TIME TO BE wasted indoors. Not when a large and barren garden cried out for an artist's touch. Grace could no more resist the call than a painter could resist a large bare canvas, or a pianist a new and priceless pianoforte, or a writer a block of blank paper.

Peregrine's old gardener and two new lads hired from the village began the heavy work under her directions, but it was Grace herself who did all of the planning and much of the planting, kneeling on the newly turned soil in an old black dress she had had since Jeremy's passing, an equally old straw hat shielding her neck and face from the early spring sunshine, a pair of gloves protecting her hands.

Much of the time she stood gazing about her, seeing with narrowed eyes her dream begin to take shape, seeing with her mind the fruit trees and blooms that would make their home beautiful later in the year and in the years to come.

And Peregrine as often as not knelt or stood at her side, planting bulbs and seedlings under her directions, laughing as she reached over to turn a bulb he had planted upside down ("Would it bloom in China, do you suppose?" he asked her), teasing her when she stood silent, with her narrow-eyed gaze, that she was just too weary to do more work and was merely pretending to concentrate on other matters.

Yet he admitted as he looked about him after a few weeks that already, even with much bare earth and only a few frail plants pushing their way toward the sun and rows of trees that looked impossibly fragile, his house and its surrounds were looking more like a home. It would all be a showpiece within a few years, he was convinced. And he glanced in some wonder at his wife, who was working the miracle.

They went about a great deal together in the afternoons and sometimes in the evenings, visiting their friends and neighbors, attending the few assemblies and social gatherings with which the families of the area entertained themselves. Grace was a little less withdrawn than she had been as the rector's housekeeper, recognizing that more was expected of Lady Lampman than had been of Miss Grace Howard. She discovered that her neighbors were quite prepared to accept her in her new status. She had been afraid that they might resent her rise to social prominence and her taking away of their favorite.

Peregrine was as charming and as sunny-natured as ever and every bit as willing as he had ever been to converse with the ladies and compliment them on a new cap or lace collar or a recovery from illness. But he no longer flirted.

The young ladies accepted reality, with perhaps a sigh of resignation, and wondered when they might expect the Earl of Amberley to return from London. Several were agreed that he was without a doubt the most handsome gentleman in the county even if his manner was a little more reserved than they might have wished and even if his title and wealth and property did set him somewhat beyond their touch. Others, especially the very young, protested that his younger brother, Lord

Eden, was by far the more handsome. And so tall. And with such open, pleasing manners. And would he come home to Amberley for the summer, or would he take himself off to his own estate in Wiltshire?

Peregrine went about very little on his own, a fact that somewhat disturbed Grace at first. Not that she minded having him near her. It was a pleasing novelty to have company in her gardening, and a constant amusement to discover the vast extent of his ignorance about plants and landscape gardening. But she had not wanted to tie him down. She had not wanted to kill the joy in his life. She relaxed more as time went on and he seemed to be quite happy to spend his days with her and to see his garden being transformed before his very eyes.

When they were not out of doors and not visiting or entertaining, Peregrine sat reading as often as not. It had always been his favorite hobby. He enjoyed it even more now after discovering that he could share interesting facts from his books with Grace without either boring or mystifying her. Indeed, he realized soon, Grace was an intelligent and well-informed woman. He thought of all the times he and Paul must have talked in her silent presence and he had never suspected that her mind was as active and as interesting as his friend's had been, even if not perhaps quite as knowledgeable.

Sometimes he read aloud to her as she stitched at her embroidery. And he never tired of watching the design grow from the blank linen beneath her long, slim fingers. On occasion he did nothing else but sit and watch her, her black-clad figure slim and shapely, her hair sleek, the black lace cap that she wore indoors hardly distinguishable from the color of her hair, her dark eyelashes fanning her pale cheeks as she bent to her work.

She would look up at him eventually with her large gray eyes and sometimes a fleeting smile, and he would resume his reading, not wishing to embarrass or to make

self-conscious the grace of her movements. If his parents
had made a disaster of naming him, Grace's parents
could not have picked a more perfect name for her.

He was never sure how happy or unhappy she was.
She went about her work with quiet energy and created
beauty wherever she went. She had taken quiet control
of his household and won the ungrudging respect of a
housekeeper and servants who had gone largely their
own way since his mother had left three years before to
live with his aunt, her sister, in Scotland. And he had
noticed that she was taking her rightful place among
their associates as his wife. She was no longer the silent
presence in company that she had always been when
Paul was alive.

He was not sure, either, how she felt about sharing his
bed each night. She never complained or showed any
sign of distaste or reluctance, even when he awoke her
in the middle of the night or in the early morning, as he
very frequently did. He could not leave her alone. He
had never consciously found her attractive when Paul
was alive, even though he could look back now and remember that his eyes had rested on her often and found
her pleasing to look at. She was not beautiful in any
universally accepted sense. And yet he had found her so
since his marriage to her.

He never tired of looking at her narrow, rather pale
face, her dark hair, her slim, graceful figure. And he
never tired of touching her with his hands and his mouth
and his body. There was a woman's maturity to her
body that excited and aroused him to loving her over
and over again. And she was not entirely indifferent, he
thought at times. She never openly participated in their
lovemaking, never by word or sound showed any emotion.

But her body betrayed some enjoyment. There was a
tautness to her breasts, which he occasionally touched

beneath her nightgown, a welcoming wetness when he came to her, a certain tightening of her inner muscles as he worked toward his unhurried climax, a tilting of her hips to allow his deeper penetration. And her arms always held him when he lay on her and in her.

He hoped he did not misread the signs. He would hate to discover that the nights of their marriage, which were becoming more and more magical to him, were something only to be endured for her. He knew that she did not love him, that he could never expect her to do so. She had done so much more living than he. Her eyes showed that she had lived and suffered and survived. And she had loved. He could not forget the look of agony on her face and the sounds of anguish in her voice as she had told him about her lover and her son. He could not fight against the past, against the dead. He had accepted both, had accepted her just as she was at the particular moment when he had found her, had decided that he would take just and only what she had to give.

But he did not want her to give out of reluctant duty. He wanted her life to be tranquil, secure, peaceful. She could never be happy again, perhaps. But he wanted to bring her contentment, as she was bringing it to him.

It was not at all clear to Peregrine why he demanded so little for himself from his marriage, when he was a young man who had always loved life and who had seen for several years past that it was possible to attract the interest of almost any female he cared to have. He might have married almost any beautiful young girl he wished to choose. He might have commanded her admiration and love. Yet he had chosen an aging woman of questionable beauty and charm, whose love had long ago been given elsewhere and from whom the most he could hope for was respect and affection.

However it was, Peregrine grew content, even if not

wildly happy, during the first year of his marriage. Perhaps he did not realize fully the extent to which he loved his wife. But he did know that she mattered to him, that he cared for her, that seeing to her contentment gave meaning and shape to his days, that her presence in his life gave pleasure to his days and joy to his nights.

And Grace was content. She had a home on which to lavish her energies and her creative talents. And she had a husband whose almost constant presence in her company took away the long loneliness and emptiness of nine years, even though she had had Paul during those years. She was very conscious of the selfishness of her feelings. It was all very well for her at her age to feel contentment with the quiet routine of their life. Perry, she felt sometimes, should have more excitement and gaiety. And yet he seemed not to be unhappy. The laughter had not gone from him. It played about his eyes almost constantly when they were in company and when he worked with her in their garden. And even in repose, when he was reading or sleeping, his lips had a good-humored curve.

She knew that she was capable of giving him actual pleasure, and she consoled herself with the knowledge. She knew that he admired the orchard and the rose arbor and the flower gardens she was creating around his home. And she knew that he liked to watch her at her embroidery, though she tried not to lift her head to reveal that she knew herself being observed. And she knew that he liked the quiet efficiency with which she ran his household. And strange as it seemed to her, she knew that he enjoyed making love to her at night.

And so there was a measure of contentment in her life. She lived for each day as it came, knowing from past experience and from the strange nature of their marriage that good times could not be expected to last. Although at unguarded moments, particularly at night if she lay awake as he slept beside her, she knew that she loved him, she kept the knowledge from her full consciousness. It would be easier to bear the pain in the future if she never admitted to herself that he was more to her than a kind and fun-loving and lovable boy.

And there would be pain in the future. For both of them. He could not continue contented forever with the kind of life they had established during their first year together. He was still only six-and-twenty at the end of it. Sooner or later, however kind his nature and sincere his intentions, he must realize how much of life and happiness and pleasure was passing him by while he was tied to an aging wife.

The knowledge, the discontent, the eventual misery would be painful to him. For Perry was a good and honorable man. And it would be painful to her. But not unbearably so. Not unless she began to listen too closely to the whisperings of her treacherous heart. Not unless she lost the daily battle to keep herself at least partly dead. She loved Perry as one friend loves another, as a mother loves her child, as any human being must love someone full of goodness and kindness and laughter. Not as a woman loves the other half of her being. No, never that. The whisperings were very rarely allowed to reach her hearing.

SOON AFTER HER marriage, Grace wrote to her father, on the advice of her husband, to inform him of the death of his son and of her marriage. It was a difficult letter to write. She had had no communication with her father for nine years. Indeed, she did not know for sure that he still lived.

But he was still alive. He answered her after a month, in a brief, stiff letter that gave almost no indication of his feelings on either of the events she had announced.

The only clue perhaps was in his request that she send to him any of Paul's effects that still remained.

Peregrine took the box from her and undertook the painful task of sending away all that remained to her of her brother except for his books, which were in their library. Afterward he brought Paul's vestments to her in her sitting room, where she sat with her embroidery, and laid them beside her on the chaise longue. And he bent and kissed her on the mouth, something he rarely did during the daytime.

"You must keep something of him, Grace, as I do," he said. "And I know that you would not have chosen his most valuable possession, his watch. That and everything else have been sent on their way."

And she wrapped her arms up around his neck—something she did very rarely—and looked earnestly into his eyes. "Thank you, Perry," she said.

It was not until well into the autumn that another letter came, from her sister-in-law this time, Grace saw with a lift of her eyebrows. It was too bad that Paul had been stubborn and had consequently never seen his father again after their quarrel, Ethel wrote. The same thing must not happen with Grace. She must come home while there was still time. The need for reconciliation was long overdue. She must come with her husband for Christmas.

It was a strange letter. Grace showed it to Peregrine at the breakfast table and read it again over his shoulder. Was she being invited now as an equal? Was she being offered forgiveness and therefore still being viewed as the lost sheep of the family? Was she being blamed for the fact that they had not seen Paul before his death? Did her father want her to go? Her brother? Was her father sick? And should they go?

Peregrine handed the letter back to her after reading it through twice, and looked searchingly into her eyes. "What do you want to do, Grace?" he asked. "That is all that matters. You cannot know their attitude toward you unless you go there, and you can always leave again if you find it intolerable, you know. Besides, I am invited too, and I would be there to protect you from insult. It will be as you wish, dear. Exactly as you wish."

She sat staring at the letter for several silent moments. "I was a different person," she said. "You would not know me if you could meet me as I was then, Perry. I think perhaps I deserved much of the treatment I received. I no longer blame them entirely, as I used to do. Perhaps it is time to forgive and forget."

"You want to go, then?" he asked.

"But there was Jeremy," she said. "He did not deserve any of it. And they would not welcome him back if he were still with me."

He touched the back of her hand with his fingertips.

"But he is there," she said. "I do not even know if anyone has tended his grave in nine years."

She made no decision that morning before going to confer with the cook on the day's menu. But her eyes were troubled, Peregrine saw, and she chose to go out walking alone when he sat down with a book after young Walter and Anna Carrington had called on them in the afternoon to invite them to an evening of charades the following evening.

"Tell me about your father and your brother, Grace," Peregrine said to her that night before he made love to her, easing his arm beneath her head on the pillow and pulling the blankets warmly up around her. "And about your childhood."

And she turned her cheek onto his arm and began to talk. She remembered her father as a tall and handsome man, strict even to the point of oppressiveness with his boys, generous and indulgent with her. She had loved him with all a child's mindless and uncritical faculties. And he had never seen any fault in her, despite the repeated complaints of a string of governesses, despite the accusations of a jealous older brother. But he had turned on her when she had told him—in his office one morning, her feet planted firmly on the Turkish carpet before his desk, her head thrown defiantly back, her color high—that she was going to have a child.

He had raged and stormed and ultimately—since there was nothing he could do about the matter at that late date—turned cold and acted almost as if she did not exist. In the four years when Jeremy had lived in his home, she did not believe he had once looked directly at his grandson or ever spoken his name.

"I suppose now I can see there was some leftover feeling, some grudging sort of love, in the fact that he did not turn us out," she said, "and in the fact that he never once questioned the bills for either my clothes or my son's. Or for his toys and books. And I did not spare the expenses. I did not want my son to have any less than his two cousins had."

And she told him about her older brother, Martin, with whom she had never enjoyed a close relationship, and about Ethel, his wife, who had resented her when she had first been brought to the house as Martin's wife, and who had not failed to make the most of her sister-in-law's disgrace afterward.

"But perhaps she had some reason to hate me," Grace said. "I was a headstrong, arrogant girl who did not want to share the position of privileged female in my father's home. You would not have liked me, Perry. I do not like myself in memory."

He kissed her. "You are harsh on yourself," he said. "I do not believe you can have changed so much. And I like you very well now."

But it was difficult to imagine another Grace, he thought, and a family and a life that were wholly unknown to him. Difficult to know what ghosts haunted her, what might be accomplished by bringing them to life again, what harm might be done. He closed his arm around her and kissed her more deeply.

He drew her arm more closely against his side the next morning when they were out walking along the leaf-strewn lane that passed Reardon Park, their feet crunching on the dried leaves. "You are very quiet this morning," he said. "No laments for the bare branches and the death of the leaves?"

"No," she said. "Spring will come again. It always does. That is one lovely certainty of the seasons. And there is a certain beauty in bare branches, Perry. Look at the clouds scudding along behind them. We would not even be able to see them so clearly if all the leaves were still there."

Peregrine laughed. "That is what I call making the most of a bad situation. What were you thinking about before I spoke, Grace? Your letter?"

She nodded.

"We will do what you wish, as I said yesterday," he said. "But if you want my opinion, I would say that I think you need to go back. I think you need to see your father again, and your brother and your sister-in-law too. And their children who were growing up with your son. I think you need to come to terms with your past."

"I believe you are right," she said, reaching up with her free hand to grasp his arm through which her other one was linked. "I dread going, Perry. I don't know how I can face the people or the memories. But I think I must. Not at Christmastime, though. Oh, not at Christmas, Perry. We are going to go caroling with the Carringtons and the Mortons. And the earl has invited everyone to Amberley for the evening. And I want us to celebrate Christmas Eve at the church here with our friends and to have our goose and our Yule log and mince pies at our own home here. And everything."

"My mother and my aunt are going to London during the spring," Peregrine said. "And I have been thinking to suggest to you, Grace, that we go for a few weeks too. I would like to show you the sights and take you to some of the theaters and assemblies and have you meet my mother again. And Edmund and the countess and the twins are always there too for the Season. Why do we not go to your father's home in the early spring for a while and then move on to London? And we can be home in time to enjoy our summer garden." He grinned. "Do you notice how I said 'our'?"

"Yes," she said. "We will do that, if you please, Perry. London? I have always wanted to see London."

"Only for a few weeks, though," he said. "I have never been very happy away from home for any great length of time. Now more than ever I find that I am content here. Are you, Grace?"

"Yes," she said, gazing up through the bare branches above her head to the blue sky and the racing clouds, "I am content."

It was with considerable misgiving that Grace leaned forward for her last glimpse of Reardon Park through the carriage window at the end of the following February. She had not been away from it for one night or even one full day since Perry had brought her there on their wedding day. They would miss the coming of spring there, though they had discovered a small clump of snowdrops and three separate crocuses in the grass among the trees just the day before.

Perry was holding her hand suddenly, she found, at the same moment as she realized that she could no longer see the house. He was smiling his usual cheerful, comforting smile when she turned to him.

"It will still be there when we come back," he said. "And much as I love my home when I am living there, Grace, I find that I love it even more when I am returning to it after an absence."

"Yes," she said, returning his smile and settling her shoulders back against the squabs. She was glad that he did not relinquish his hold of her hand, though he did lean over her to tuck the fur-lined rug more snugly around her legs.

Yes, Reardon Park would doubtless still be there when they returned. But would they be the same? Would everything be spoiled by the time they came back? Was this the end of their contentment, here and right now?

They were journeying back into her past. She did not know what her reception would be at home, what her relationship with her relatives. And she did not know how strong or painful the memories of Gareth and Jeremy would be when she was once more in the places where it had all happened a lifetime ago. She wanted to see her father. She wanted to see Martin. And she wanted to be close to Jeremy again. But she could not picture Perry in such a setting. Perry was everything in her present and perhaps a little of her future. She did not want him mixed up with her past. And yet she could not even contemplate going back there without him. She might become trapped there. She might never be free.

She had made no mention in her letter to her father or in the two letters she had written to Ethel of the age of her husband. She felt something of the old stubborn defiance when she thought of the look that might well be on all of their faces when they saw and looked at him. She would not care what they thought. They might look and think and say what they pleased. She did not care.

Ah, but she cared every bit as deeply as she ever had. They would think that she had made a selfish grab for Perry. And they would think he had pitied her. They would not know that there was a contentment, a certain tenderness in their marriage. And they would have her doubting again. They would revive the feelings of guilt and inadequacy that she had ignored for almost a year.

And then they were to go to London, and she must face the same ordeal when they met Perry's mother. What would she think when she met her daughter-in-law? They had met, of course, when Grace had been Paul's housekeeper. And what would others think, all the members of the *beau monde* to whom she would be presented? And what would it be like for Perry to be surrounded by people—women—younger and more vibrant and more lovely than she?

Grace let her hand lie in the warmth of her husband's and her shoulder rest just below the level of his as she gazed out of the window at the faded greens and browns of the fields and the bare branches of the trees. Spring would come soon to the land and clothe everything in bright beauty again. But not to her life. Her life was heading into autumn and perhaps even winter. A cold and stark winter.

It might well be winter when they came home again, even if all the fruit trees and flowers were blooming and the air was heavy with the scent of her roses and Perry's.

4

No ONE CAME OUT INTO THE COBBLED COURTYARD before the main doors of Pangam Manor when their carriage pulled up there, Grace noticed, except for a groom and two footmen. But then it was a cold and blustery February day. Both Martin and Ethel were waiting in the hall, however, both looking remarkably unchanged since she had last seen them.

Martin's fair hair was perhaps a little thinner on top, his figure a little stouter, his complexion a little more florid. But there was still that air of importance about him, and still the line between his eyes that had always denoted impatience with the slowness and lack of understanding of others and a general dissatisfaction with his life. Ethel was still thin and pale. And still unsmiling.

But they were there, Grace thought, moving forward to hug her sister-in-law and rest her cold cheek against Ethel's for a moment and turning to place her hands on her brother's shoulders and stretch up to kiss him on the cheek.

"You are looking well, Grace," Martin said, resting his hands on her waist for a brief moment in acknowledgment of her embrace.

"You must be very cold," Ethel said. "I have ordered tea to be brought up to the drawing room. Perhaps you would like some before I have you shown to your rooms."

Grace turned back to Peregrine, who stood silently behind her. She took his arm and watched her brother and sister-in-law as she presented him to them. Not one flicker on the face of either showed surprise or any other emotion. They were all civil politeness.

"Where is Pa—? Where is Father?" Grace asked.

"He keeps to his rooms a great deal through the winter," Ethel said, taking Grace's arm and leading her in the direction of the stairs. "But he will come down for tea when we send to let him know that you have arrived."

"He is unwell?" Grace asked.

Ethel shrugged. "He has slowed down," she said. "He is getting older, as we all are."

There seemed to be no double meaning in the words, Grace decided. And she would not look for snubs where perhaps none was meant. She was no longer Grace Howard, headstrong daughter of the house. She was Grace Lampman, and she recognized the necessity of being civil and expecting civility from those with whom she must associate.

"How are the children?" she asked.

"The children?" Ethel gave her a strange look as she led Grace into the drawing room. "Oswald is away at school. He is almost sixteen. Perhaps you had forgotten that so much time has passed. Priscilla will be down for tea. We will be taking her to town for the Season this spring. She is nearly eighteen, you know."

"Yes, of course," Grace said. "It is amazing to think that they are quite grown up already." Jeremy would have been fourteen.

Miss Priscilla Howard arrived in the drawing room at almost the same moment as the tea tray. She was a younger version of her mother, Grace saw as she rose to her feet. She was slender and fair-haired and wore a frilly pink dress that had obviously been donned for the occasion though the color did not quite suit her. Yet she was pretty enough, with a mass of ringlets bouncing against the sides of her head and the color high in her cheeks, her gray eyes sparkling with mingled shyness and excitement.

"Hello, Aunt Grace," the girl said, curtsying low. "I remember you. You really look very little different from the way you used to be. Do you wear mourning for Uncle Paul? Grandpapa does too, though Mama and Papa left theirs off at Christmas."

"You talk too much, child," her father said. "Make your curtsy to your Uncle Peregrine."

Priscilla turned her eyes on him and her blush deepened as she curtsied. "Sir," she said. And her eyes continued to scrutinize him curiously.

Perry's eyes were laughing at his niece-by-marriage, Grace saw. He bowed elegantly. "I have just overheard your mother say that you are to make your come-out this Season," he said. "I can warn her now that all the young bucks will be lined up at your door, Priscilla. And we will make that Uncle Perry, if you please."

Priscilla smiled. "Yes, Uncle Perry," she said. "Though I think you are too young to be my uncle. Have you been much in London? Mama and Papa have not been there since they were young. I am sure much has changed in all that time."

Peregrine grinned. "I daresay people went to parties and balls and assemblies and theaters and picnics and whatnot in those long-ago days just as they do now," he said. "And danced and flirted and otherwise amused themselves. And your mama would have been presented to the same queen as you are like to make your curtsy to. Grace and I will be going to London too, you know."

"Will you?" she said. "How splendid! Did you hear that, Mama?"

The girl plied Peregrine with eager questions about

London for the next few minutes while Martin and Ethel made polite inquiries of Grace about the journey.

But they were interrupted before they could finish their tea by the arrival of Lord Pawley. He left his valet in the doorway and proceeded into the room alone, leaning heavily on a cane. He was still tall and thin, Grace saw as she rose to her feet. Still severe and distinguished-looking. But the gray hair she remembered had turned to pure white, and the lines running from his nose to his chin had deepened. His eyes sought her out and looked into hers with quite as much bright keenness as ever. He was dressed in deep mourning.

"Well, Grace," he said, stopping a short distance from her, "you have come home."

"Yes, Father," she said. "How are you?"

"Well," he said. "I am glad to see that you appreciated your brother enough still to wear mourning for him."

"I loved Paul, Father," she said.

He nodded. "I suppose I did not," he said. "Present me to your husband."

Her father looked long and hard at Peregrine, Grace saw in some discomfort after she had made the introductions. She found she was holding her breath.

"I am grateful to you, sir, for taking care of my daughter at a difficult time for her," the baron said eventually before seating himself and turning to take a cup of tea from his daughter-in-law.

Peregrine was smiling, apparently quite unperturbed by the long and steady scrutiny he had just been subjected to. "Thank you, sir," he said. "But Grace and I did not wed merely because she was in need, you know. And may I express my belated sympathies on the passing of your son? Paul was a particular friend of mine. I wear mourning for him still on my own account as well as out of respect for my wife."

The baron nodded curtly and the conversation became general.

It had been very stiff and very difficult, Grace thought half an hour later as she and Peregrine followed Ethel upstairs to the bedrooms. And much, much easier than she had anticipated. If she looked back on the bitterness of her departure ten years before, it was amazing enough that they had all been able to behave civilly over tea in the drawing room.

Ethel showed Peregrine to his room, in which his valet was already unpacking his things and laying out his shaving gear, before taking Grace across the hallway to her old room.

"Do you want this room?" Ethel asked hesitantly. "I did not know. But it is still thought of and spoken of as yours." She flushed.

"Yes," Grace said, wandering across it and looking about her. "And it is just the same. The Chinese wallpaper, the green curtains and bed hangings. Why did I expect everything and everyone to be so different?"

"You look no older, Grace," her sister-in-law said. "Indeed, you look a great deal better than you did when . . . "

Grace had crossed to the window to see that, yes, she could still see along the elm grove to the summerhouse, where she had sat so often as a girl with a book or talking with Gareth. She turned to look back at Ethel. "Yes," she said. "I am feeling a great deal better."

"I am glad you have come," Ethel said. "Papa needs you, I believe. But he would never have asked for you, of course."

Grace turned completely from the window. "How did he take the news of Paul's death?" she asked.

Ethel's lips tightened. "He showed Martin your letter, ordered mourning for himself and the servants, straightened his shoulders, which were becoming stooped, and said no more about the matter," she said. "Does that answer your question?"

"Yes," Grace said. "He took it hard. I think I am glad, both for his sake and Paul's."

Perry was standing in the doorway, she saw suddenly, his face smiling, his very presence lightening the atmosphere.

"This is where you are," he said. "What a lovely room. And don't tell me." He held up a hand. "This was your room when you lived here, was it not, Grace? And you planned it and chose the wallpaper and the colors of the paint and the bed hangings and the carpet. I could walk into this room anywhere in the kingdom and say without any hesitation at all that it is the handiwork of Grace Lampman." He grinned and turned to Ethel. "Now, tell me that I am wrong and make me feel very foolish."

Ethel was smiling, Grace was surprised to see. "No," she said. "You are quite right."

Peregrine laughed and strolled right into the room. "An indoor garden," he said. "That is a thumb of the nose to English weather. I was going to suggest that you move your things to my room, Grace, but now I think I must beg to be allowed to bring mine here." He turned to Ethel, still smiling. "Grace and I share a room always. You will not mind?"

"DID SHE MIND?" he asked Grace a few minutes later when they had been left alone. "She certainly turned pink and left in some haste. But I would feel foolish to be observed creeping across here to you each night, Grace, as if I were up to no good. Better for everyone to know that we sleep together."

"Yes," she said, strangely pleased.

"You do not mind, Grace?" he asked. "Perhaps you

would prefer to have your room to yourself again? Perhaps you need some time alone? I am remarkably selfish, am I not, thinking only of my own comfort."

"No," she said sharply. "I would prefer to have you here, Perry."

He came closer to her and touched her cheek with the backs of his fingers. "This is all very hard for you, dear. Do you think I do not know that? But you have done the right thing to come. Your family wants you back again. Perhaps you are too involved in your own emotions to see that clearly. I can see more objectively. And it is so, Grace. You are loved here. And I can see just as clearly that you want them too. You have never stopped loving them. It will be hard for you, the next week or so, but it is right to force yourself to live through it. It is what you need to do."

She clasped his wrist and turned her head to kiss it briefly. "Yes," she said. "I am only sorry that you have to be involved in the discomfort, Perry."

He smiled at her. "I think you may need an arm or a shoulder to lean on from time to time," he said, "though of course you could do it alone if I were not with you. But since I am here, it will be my arm and my shoulder, Grace. And I must confess to some curiosity to know the people and places that figured so largely in your life before I even knew you. I must go back to my dressing room to shave. Perkins had gone for the water before I came across here, and there is nothing more terrifying to behold than the wrath of Perkins when he has just been forced to watch my shaving water grow cold." He bent and kissed her cheek.

GRACE WAS SURPRISED and somewhat gratified to find in the following days that Ethel was making an effort to be friendly. They spent some time together, sitting over their embroidery, wandering through the orangery, examining the shooting plants in the garden, which would be transformed into daffodils and tulips within a very few weeks.

"I am glad you have come, Grace," Ethel said on more than one occasion. "The cloud of your leaving has hung over Papa and Martin for a long time. They never mentioned either you or Paul in all those years, of course, but I know them both well enough to understand that that meant only that they were hurting deeply."

Grace looked at her sister-in-law curiously. She had never liked Ethel, had never tried to like her, perhaps. She had not wanted another young woman in the house when Martin had first brought his bride home. And she had been jealous when the births of her niece and nephew had diverted some of her father's attention from herself. Then, of course, for the last five years she had been at home, pregnant during the first, with Jeremy for the remaining four, Ethel had been the favored lady of the house.

And Ethel had gloated. She had made the most of her triumph, both for herself and for her very legitimate children. Grace had hated her, if the truth were known. But Ethel was a person like any other, she saw now. And she was clearly a person who knew and understood her husband and her father-in-law. And cared. And now she was holding out an olive branch to the sister-in-law who had treated her badly for several years and to whom she had finally returned the compliment.

"I did not even write about Paul's death until six weeks after it happened," Grace said. "I did not know if they would wish to know."

"You are as stubborn and as blind as they are, Grace," Ethel said. "You are all so similar, you know, the three of you. Only Paul was different."

Grace looked up again in surprise.

"Martin cried," Ethel said. "I was frightened, as you may well imagine. I had never expected to see him cry. And he talked on and on about how he had always ridiculed and mistreated Paul as a boy. And about how he had let him go and had never even tried to communicate with him after."

Grace pointed to a bunch of primroses, almost hidden in the grass. "Was it Martin's idea to invite me for Christmas?" she asked.

"It was mine," Ethel admitted. "But I know it was what Martin wanted, Grace, and Papa too, though they would never have said so in a thousand years. I know both of them rather well after almost twenty years of marriage."

With her brother Grace did not talk a great deal. They never had had a close relationship. Martin was five years her senior. He had always been a rather slow, plodding boy, who worked with dogged perseverance to be worthy of being his father's oldest child. And he had watched his younger sister, willful, heedless, frequently disobedient, engrossing all their father's love, though she made no effort whatsoever to ingratiate herself with him.

They had despised each other, even hated each other through most of their life. Or had they? Had they not always watched each other for the smallest sign that the other would be willing to be loved? Grace wondered now. It was strange to be back, to be involved again in the emotions she had thought long dead, and yet to be able to see her family more objectively than she had ever done, and her own part in it.

"I have seen the new enclosures and the land that was drained five or six years ago," she said to her brother one day after driving out with Ethel and Peregrine. "And Ethel says that the estate is prospering more than ever, Martin. You have worked hard."

He looked at her sharply as if to detect some sarcasm.

"Yes, I have," he said. "Papa has lost interest in the land these last few years, you know. And there was no one but me to see to things."

"You have done well," she said, and reached out to touch his hand lightly with her fingertips. She and Martin had never touched each other often.

He withdrew his hand uneasily but looked at her. "The news of your marriage took us by surprise," he said. "Are you happy, Grace?"

"Yes," she said. "Yes, I am."

"He is younger than you," he said rather jerkily.

"Yes," she said. "Ten years younger."

"Ten?" He looked away from her in some embarrassment. "Well, as long as you are happy."

"Yes," she said.

Lord Pawley did not come out of his rooms very often. But Grace made a point of visiting him there twice each day, alone in the mornings, with Peregrine later in the day.

"You have come home, then," he said to her almost every morning.

"Yes, Father," she said. "I have come home. For a visit."

"Did he suffer?" he asked abruptly on one occasion. "Was it instant?"

"Yes," she said. "It was instant, the doctor said." She hesitated. "His neck was broken when the bull tossed him. He is remembered as a great hero in Abbotsford, you know. He saved the life of the son of one of the Earl of Amberley's laborers."

Her father grunted. "Young fool," he said after an interval.

"He would like that description," Grace said gently. "Paul liked to be a fool. A fool for Christ, as his namesake said in the Bible."

Her father grunted again and said nothing more.

"You have changed," he said on another occasion.

"Have I, Father?" she asked. "I am ten years older."

He looked at her broodingly. "You have learned what I should have taught you when you were growing up, I daresay," he surprised her by saying. "I spoiled you. Gave you no training at all. It was all my fault. Everything that happened."

"No," she said. "That is not true. No one is ever entirely to blame for what happens to another. I was an adult. I had a mind and intelligence of my own. I made my own choices, my own mistakes. I blame no one else. And I do not even like the words *mistakes* and *blame*. Because they imply that Jeremy was all wrong. And he was not wrong. He was my son. Despite his death, I would not have my life any different from the way it has been. Perhaps that is something I have learned in ten years. Everything that happens in life happens for a purpose. I would not be the person I am if there had not been Jeremy. And I would not wish to be different even if I could be."

Her father continued to watch her broodingly, though he clearly had nothing more to say. She left him after a few minutes, hesitating a moment before deciding not to stoop down to kiss his head. She had not touched him since her return home.

HER NIECE WAS inclined to be friendly with the aunt she remembered as something of a favorite, probably, Grace thought, because she had spent more time with the children than any of the other adults during the four years of Jeremy's life. And Priscilla was clearly charmed by Peregrine's good looks and by his easy humor and teasing. She introduced her two special friends to him, and the three girls, giggling, dragged him off walking with them on more than one occasion, pretending to quarrel over how they were to divide his two arms among the three of them.

Grace found that she spent very little time alone with her husband during the daytime. She was happy to see him occupied and in his usual good humor—she had been very afraid that he would be oppressed by the atmosphere of her home and by the old, still-unresolved quarrels. And she was glad that her time was taken up so agreeably with her relatives, even if they had still not conversed on any matters that really concerned their relationships and even though there was much awkwardness still among them.

But it was strange not to have Perry's continual companionship, strange not to be alone with him for large segments of the day. She found herself, as she viewed Ethel's garden with her, looking back with a great deal of nostalgia on the previous spring when she and Perry had worked side by side in their own garden, often for long hours. And she often thought with some longing of their quiet afternoons and evenings, sometimes both of them reading, sometimes just Perry doing so while she sewed.

But there were still the nights, she consoled herself. There was something especially comforting about having Perry sharing the room that had been hers until she was six-and-twenty years old. She had always loved to leave the curtains back at night so that she might see the garden on her walls picked out by the moonlight. She liked to see it still, her head against his arm, just the two of them silent together.

She often lay awake long after he slept—and had done so even when they were at home—but she never minded, never fretted over what might have been called insomnia. She very consciously enjoyed every moment of their closeness. It could not last forever. There would come the time when he would tire of her, when he would want the greater freedom of a separate room. Kind as he was, the time would come, and she would let him slip away from her gradually so that he would not dream that she knew, that she was reluctant to accept the new arrangement.

Until that time came, she was happy to lie awake and enjoy the nights. And happier still when he woke, as he sometimes did, to turn to her with a sleepy smile and a gradually rekindled desire for her. He often apologized for troubling her when he took her for the second time in a night, and she would smile secretly to herself as she held him in her arms again.

AT THE END of the first week at Pangam Manor, there was only one thing Grace had not done that she fully intended to do. But the opportunity came finally when Martin had borne Perry off one afternoon to see something on the estate, Priscilla in tow, and Ethel had begged to be excused from any outdoor exertion as she had a headache. Grace assured her that she would leave her alone so that she would not feel obliged to make conversation. And she took herself off to the east end of the lake, where the private family burial ground was situated.

No one had objected to her having Jeremy buried there. No one had offered an opinion on the matter either way. But she had not wanted to have him put in the churchyard. The graves there were so close together, the tombs so elaborate. It was a place of death, heavy and black death. Jeremy was dead, of course. She had realized that. She had never, from the moment when Priscilla had come shrieking back from the lake with the news that Jeremy was drowned, been able to doubt the fact. But she had not wanted him in a place of death. She had wanted him in a place where he could become part of nature, part of the wild beauty of the universe.

There were no elaborate tombs in the family burial plot. Only neat headstones announcing essential information for the eyes of the living. And neatly mown grass and a neat wooden fence to keep out grazing animals.

The grass was short on Jeremy's grave, as on the others, Grace saw at a glance, kneeling down on it and touching the marble headstone with its legend: "Jeremy Howard. Beloved son of Grace Howard. 1796–1800. R.I.P."

Jeremy. She took her hand away from the cold stone and closed her eyes. Jeremy. A thin, wiry little boy. His father's dark curls and dark eyes. Bright, eager eyes. Her own rather long, thin face. Small white baby teeth. A dimpled chin, another legacy from his father. A surprisingly low-pitched chuckle that could quickly give place to a shrieking laugh after a little tickling. Warm, soft clinging arms. A wet baby kiss. Wet, muddy hair and a dead face. She closed her eyes more tightly and clung to the grass on either side of her.

She was lying facedown on the grass when Peregrine found her half an hour later. He had guessed where she had gone when he had returned to the house with Martin to find Ethel sitting alone in a darkened parlor. He had been expecting it since their arrival. He asked directions to the graveyard of Martin, and declined his company, with thanks.

He stood at the fence watching her for a few minutes before climbing over it, ignoring the gate, and approaching her. She was not crying. He did not think she was sleeping, though she had not moved since she had first come into his sight.

She seemed to sense his presence. She turned her head, though she did not look up.

"Do you want to be alone, Grace?" he asked. "Would you prefer that I went away?"

There was no response.

"I shall wait for you over by the trees, out of sight, shall I?" he asked, stooping down and laying a light hand on her head. She was not wearing a hat.

She shook her head. "Don't go." Her voice was muffled by her arms, on which her face rested.

He sat on the ground cross-legged beside her, his hand still on her head, and waited for her. She moved eventually and sat beside him. She did not look up.

"I don't know who it was who dragged me away from here after the funeral," she said. "I cannot remember if it was Martin or Paul. It was not my father, because he did not come. But someone took me away, very much against my will. And I did not come again. Not until now. It was terrible to leave him all alone here. He was only four years old."

He took her hand and held it in a firm clasp.

She laid her head on his shoulder. "I loved him, Perry," she said. "For four years he was my life. No, for five. I loved him every moment I carried him."

"I know," he said. "You must not feel guilty, dear."

"Do I?" she said. "Do I feel guilty? For letting someone else care for him when I should have been with him? But he was an independent little lad. He wanted to be with his older cousins. A mere mother was a nuisance when they were there to be played with."

"For having him," he said. "You feel guilty for having him, Grace. Don't. It is never wrong to give life, dear. And love."

"Isn't it?" she said. "That is a dangerous moral statement, Perry. It is not wrong to bear a bastard?"

"Don't use that word," he said. "Don't punish yourself with it. Children die every day, Grace. It is no judgment of God on the parents when they do. Your son was one of the fortunates of this world. He was dearly loved from the moment of his conception to the moment of his death. Not all children are so loved, not even those born in wedlock. Forgive yourself, dear. If you committed a sin, you have also atoned for it a thousandfold. And you have suffered for it. Let him rest in peace now. And let yourself live in peace."

Grace sat for many minutes with her eyes closed, her head resting on her husband's shoulder. She was letting Jeremy go again and wishing and wishing one thing. She was wishing that Perry had been his father.

Perry, who had been twelve years old when Jeremy was born! She sat up and smiled wearily at him.

"I am ready to go now," she said. "Thank you for coming, Perry. It must have been a dreary afternoon for you. And thank you for your words. I am not sure I can quite accept them. It is far easier to forgive others than oneself, you know. But thank you. Paul would have disagreed with you. Paul forgave me and never mentioned my sin to me after we left here. But his very silence told me that he thought it a very great sin, nevertheless."

"Yes." He smiled as he got to his feet and pulled her to hers. "Paul and I disagreed most noisily on the nature of sin. You were oppressed by his forgiveness, weren't you? You were so very quiet and withdrawn during those years, Grace. You need not fear my forgiveness. You gave love—to a man and to a child. I can only honor you for doing so, dear, and feel sad for the pain that those loves still cause you."

What had she ever done to deserve Perry? Grace wondered as he drew her arm through his and began to walk back with her to her father's house. But she could not forgive herself for all that. She never would, despite what she had said to her father. Jeremy would not have drowned if she had not lain with Gareth.

5

$\mathcal{A}$ FEW OF HER FORMER ACQUAINTANCES CALLED upon Grace during the first week. She returned some of those calls with Ethel and Peregrine and sometimes Priscilla. But she had not expected the invitation to attend a dinner and evening party at the home of Viscount Sandersford. Gareth's father had ignored her very existence after his son had gone away. He had never acknowledged his grandson by any sign whatsoever.

"Perhaps the invitation is really for you and Martin and Priscilla," Grace said uneasily to Ethel when the latter told her of the card that had arrived that morning. "Perhaps he does not know that I am here. Or perhaps he does not recognize my name and believes himself to be inviting two unknown guests."

"No," Ethel said, looking at her sister-in-law briefly but searchingly, "he specifically named you in the invitation. I can refuse for all of us if you would prefer it, Grace. We are not on intimate terms with him ourselves, as you may imagine."

Grace thought for a moment. "No," she said, "don't refuse. We will go."

After all, she thought, she had come home in order to confront her past. She might as well face all of it. There had been a time when she had liked the viscount, who had indulged Gareth as much as her father had her. She

told Peregrine of the invitation. She did not explain that
their host was Gareth's father. She had meant to, but did
not add the information when the time came. Perry must
be tired of hearing of her former lover and her son. It
seemed almost an insult to his good nature to be constantly referring to them.

Peregrine was in his usual good humor when he
crossed from his dressing room to join Grace in hers
before they left on the evening of the dinner.

"Perkins's chest has just swelled by a good two
inches," he said, grinning at Grace's image in the mirror.
"He has finally succeeded in tying a mathematical. You
see?" He indicated his neckcloth. "Don't you think the
folds quite magnificent, Grace? I feel I should be on my
way to St. James's or Carlton House at the very least."

"Quite splendid," she agreed.

"Ah," he said, "you are wearing a blue gown. I think
you are right that it is time to leave off our mourning
gradually. You look delightful in color again. Did you
enjoy your walk with Ethel this afternoon?"

"Yes," she said. "We called on two of the sick cot-
tagers. I remember them well. It was good to see them
again."

Peregrine grinned. "How delightfully silly young girls
can be," he said. "I swear those three did not stop giggling all the time I was with them this afternoon. One of
them had to purchase ribbons and another lace. And
they all had to try on a dozen bonnets each at the milli-
ner's, though they did not buy one between them. And
they found the eating of ices and cakes at the confec-
tioner's an enormous joke. The new curate saw us
through the window and came inside to pay his respects.
And they all blushed and giggled behind their hands.
The curate didn't giggle, by the way, but he did blush to
the tips of his ears."

Grace smiled at him in the mirror and dismissed her

maid. "Priscilla and Miss Stebbins will be going to London soon," she said. "And there they will join dozens of other giggling girls, Perry. It is the Season, the marriage mart."

He was laughing, she saw, his eyes dancing in merriment, his teeth very white and even. "Life there will certainly not be dull," he said.

Their group were not to be the only dinner guests. That was clear as soon as they approached Lord Sandersford's drawing room behind the straight back of a footman and heard the buzz of voices coming from inside the room. Grace was nervous. She drew Peregrine back behind Martin and Ethel and Priscilla—her father had declined to come—and tried to calm her thumping heart. The viscount was greeting two other guests, who stood between him and her view.

But finally he was able to turn to greet the new arrivals. He bowed to Ethel and Priscilla, shook Martin's hand, and turned to Grace and Peregrine. He was a tall man of military bearing, fit and well-muscled, extraordinarily handsome. His hair was dark and wavy, rather long, his face tanned even though March had scarcely begun. A slight cleft in his chin added to his attractive appearance. He regarded his guests with keen, rather mocking eyes.

"Ah, Lady Lampman," he said, taking her cold hand and bending over it as he raised it to his lips. "As lovely as ever, I see. Sir Peregrine Lampman, I assume?" He took Peregrine's hand in a firm clasp and stood exchanging pleasantries with him for a couple of minutes.

But Miss Stebbins and her mama attracted Peregrine's attention and beckoned him away. He must, it seemed, admire the ribbons that he had witnessed the girl purchase just that afternoon.

"Well, Grace," the viscount said when they were relatively alone, "are you going to faint, or are you going to scorn to do anything so weakly feminine?"

"Your father is dead, then, Gareth?" she asked, her voice sounding far away to her own ears.

He laughed. "Had you not heard?" he said. "Did you not know it was I you were to meet tonight? How famous! My father died six years ago."

"I did not know," she said. "I had not heard. Or that you had come home. Where is your wife?"

"Dead too," he said. "She was a poor thing, Grace. Weak. Following the drum was just too much for her constitution. She died in childbed more than nine years ago. And even the child did not survive."

"I am sorry," she said.

"You need not be." He shrugged. "It was all a long time ago. Come. My butler is summoning us to dinner, I see. I will lead you in. Take my arm, Grace. You are not going to faint, are you?"

"No." By sheer effort of will Grace dragged herself back along the dark tunnel that had been sucking her toward oblivion for the past several minutes, and lifted a hand that felt as if it were not quite part of her to rest on Lord Sandersford's arm. She looked around for Perry and saw him across the room offering his arm to Miss Stebbins and saying something that had both the girl and her mother laughing merrily.

PEREGRINE WAS RATHER enjoying himself. It had amused him since his arrival at his father-in-law's to find that he had been adopted as a favorite by three very young ladies, his wife's niece among them. It had always been so, he thought entirely without conceit, ever since he had grown past boyhood. He had never had to make any effort at all to attract the attention of young ladies or the liking of their mothers and older female relatives.

He had never been able quite to explain to himself his success with the ladies. And perhaps it was not any great success either, he thought. Very rarely, if ever, had he felt that one of his admirers was languishing with love for him. They merely seemed to enjoy his company and do a great deal of giggling and flirting when he was by.

Perhaps they sensed that he liked women a great deal. He had always found it a good foil to his more serious and introspective side to amuse the ladies and devise new ways to draw their laughter and their blushes.

And it was amusing to find that he could still surround himself with giggling girls and their smiling mamas even though he was a staid married man. It amused him even further to note that the same girls who derived great merriment from his company tended to blush and sigh over the thin and romantic figure of the young curate, who looked as if he could do with a good square meal. Doubtless they all dreamed of feeding his stomach and finding a way into his heart. None of them seemed at all smitten by the very handsome figure of the evening's host, who was apparently widowed and therefore perfectly eligible. But then they were very young ladies and Sandersford must be close to forty.

Peregrine stood patiently and good-humoredly behind the pianoforte stool turning pages of music as his regular trio of young girls each in turn tried to impress both him and the rest of the company with her musical talents. And he grinned across the room at Grace, who was seated with some of her former acquaintances. She looked so very suited to her name and so very lovely without the usual black mourning gown that he gazed rather too long at her and missed his cue to turn a page.

A few minutes later a delegation of young ladies asked the viscount if they might dance, and the servants came in to roll up the carpet, and a plump matron took the stool in order to play for those eager to exert themselves.

And Peregrine found that he had hardly a moment even to think of his wife. He laughed and danced his way through one vigorous set after another, assuring two young ladies that, yes, their dancing skills would be quite up to the standards of Almack's and a third that, yes, dancing in Lord Sandersford's drawing room was every bit as splendid as dancing in the grandest ballroom in London.

Peregrine was enjoying the whole experience of meeting his in-laws and the other people who had been a part of Grace's past. He liked the rather dull and plodding but solid and respectable Martin, and the serious, dutiful, and shrewd Ethel. And he was intrigued by his father-in-law, who spent most of his days shut up in his own rooms, rather like a volcano that one was never quite sure was dormant. There was a great deal of resentment and guilt and love and other muddled emotions locked up inside the old man, Peregrine was sure. He only hoped that Grace's father would not die before he had come to some sort of peace with himself.

And Grace. Peregrine, standing beside a panting Miss Horlick, sipping lemonade with her, looked fondly at his wife, who was not dancing at that moment, though she had accepted a few partners. This was a hard time for her. She was looking rather as she had looked at the rectory for five years: withdrawn, rather tight about the lips, only her eyes calm. It was only now that he realized that in the last year since their marriage her expression had relaxed, softened, and that she had bloomed into a mature beauty.

She was looking severe again. Perhaps a little less than beautiful, though it was hard for him to tell. He knew her so well, was so familiar with her every mood and expression, that he could not possibly say any longer if she was beautiful or not. He could only say that, to him, she always was. She was Grace, his wife. She was the only woman, perhaps, on whom he looked not with his customary indulgent amusement, but with something of an ache. He could make other women happy without any conscious effort. He wanted so very badly to make Grace happy, and he was not at all sure that he did so.

This time was hard for her. But it was also good for her. He was sure of that. Her life would never be complete if she could not be reconciled with her family. And that reconciliation was coming slowly, inch by cautious inch. And she could never be at peace until she was reconciled with herself, until she could forgive herself. She must have this time, agonizing as it might be for her now, to learn that there had been no connection whatsoever between the death of her child and her sin in conceiving him out of wedlock. She must learn to see that death as the tragic accident it had been.

She was looking particularly drawn tonight, Peregrine thought. It must be more than usually hard on her to be in a gathering such as this, surrounded by all the people who had known her when she lived through her five-year ordeal. His eyes twinkled down at Miss Horlick as he took the empty glass from her hand and assured her that she would doubtless survive even if Mr. Piper, her next partner, did choose to swirl her down the set as he liked to do. And his heart ached for his wife.

There was only so much he could do to help her. She must live alone through the torment of her memories. She must find her own peace. He could only be there to smile at her, to hold her hand during the worst moments, to leave her alone to find room for her memories, to hold her and love her with slow tenderness at night.

He caught her eye across the room and smiled warmly as he came toward her.

"Are you enjoying yourself?" he asked, knowing very well that she was not. "Will you dance this next one with me, Grace?"

"I have promised it to his lordship," she said, looking up at him with her large, calm eyes and setting her hand in his without seeming to realize that she did so.

"Grace?" Peregrine frowned and lowered his voice so as not to attract the attention of anyone else. "You are not going to faint, are you?"

"No, of course not." Her eyes appeared to grow larger. "Only it is hot in here, Perry. And I have been dancing. Of course I am not going to faint."

And of course being overheated did not turn one as pale as any ghost, Peregrine thought, squeezing her hand and turning his attention and his smile on the lady seated beside her.

GRACE HAD TOLD only one conscious lie in her relationship with her husband. She had told him on the day he had offered her marriage—or, rather, she had agreed with his assumption—that Gareth was dead. And yet at the time it had not seemed like a lie. Gareth was dead to her, had been since his final letter to her when she had already been increasing for six months, explaining that circumstances had forced him to marry a girl she had never heard of.

That was all. He had not explained what the circumstances were or what made them more important than returning home to marry the woman he had claimed to love for the past four years, the woman who was bearing his child. There were the usual protestations of undying love and a few enthusiastic details about life as an officer in the Guards.

He was dead. As far as Grace was concerned, he was dead. Except that she had not grieved or worn mourning for him. She had merely died a little inside and grown up a great deal and turned all her thoughts and her passion inward to the child she had so selfishly and so carelessly conceived.

The lie to Perry should be easy to correct. It had been a fairly innocent lie, and Perry was not a hard man to deal with. She should have been able to turn to him when he came from his dressing room later that night, put down her hairbrush, and simply tell him. Tell him that Gareth was still alive, that Gareth was the Lord Sandersford who had been their host that evening. It should have been easy. And it was certainly essential.

"Let me do that," Peregrine said, reaching for the brush. "You have such lovely hair, Grace. Did you send Effie to bed?"

"She was yawning rather loudly," Grace said. "Effie is quite an expert at dropping not so subtle hints."

"She is very young," he said.

"I know." Grace smiled at him in the mirror. "And very smitten with that blond-haired footman of Martin's. Have you noticed?"

He grinned back at her. "It was a pleasant evening, wasn't it?" he said. "We haven't danced since Christmas."

"Yes," Grace said, "it was pleasant." She closed her eyes. He was drawing the brush gently through her hair. Her heart was thumping uncomfortably.

"Was Sandersford ever a soldier?" he asked. "He certainly bears himself like a military man."

Grace kept her eyes closed. He had provided her with the perfect lead-in to what she must say. "Yes," she said. "The Guards. He sold out, I believe, when his father died six years ago. He . . . we . . . they have always been neighbors of ours."

"A pleasant man," he said. He laughed suddenly. "Who do you think is going to get the curate, Grace? Would you care to place a wager?"

"I think that to a young girl he must appear remarkably handsome," Grace said.

"With the added attraction of being far too thin and underfed," he added with a grin. "All those girls are just bursting with maternal concern. The only problem, as I see it, is that the poor man may never get up his courage to ask any of them. I think he can outdo any one of the girls in the matter of blushes."

"You ought not to laugh, Perry," she said, turning and taking the brush from his hand, "just because you find it so easy to converse with the ladies."

"Laugh?" he said. "When the man is in the enviable position of having at least five young female hearts beating for him? I am not guilty, Grace, I swear. He has nothing but my admiration. You did not enjoy yourself a great deal, dear." He set his hands on her shoulders and looked into her eyes. The smile had disappeared from his face.

"Yes, I did," she said. "Of course I did, Perry."

"Is it difficult for you to be with all these people again?" he asked. "Did they treat you badly before you left here?"

"No," she said. "They treated me with amazing courtesy. I was never made to feel like a pariah."

He framed her face with his hands. "The viscount too?" he asked. "And his father? They received you?"

Grace had never been suffocated by her husband's nearness before. She swallowed awkwardly and could not look away from his eyes. "I was never received there," she said, "after Jeremy."

"Ah," he said. "But this viscount wants to make amends. He seated you beside him at dinner, Grace. Was he a friend of your Gareth? A relative, perhaps?"

It should have been so easy. It was easy. He was making it as easy for her as it could possibly be. "A friend," she said jerkily, removing her eyes from his at last and lifting her hands to the lapels of his dressing gown.

"Ah," he said again, "I guessed as much. But the pain can be allowed to recede now, Grace. He wants to make a friend of you again. That was very clear. Forgive him, dear. Let it all go, the bitterness. People do behave badly, you know. We all do on occasion. We owe it to one another to give a second chance, and sometimes even a third and fourth."

"Yes," she said, running her palms along the smooth silk of his lapels. She looked up into his eyes, gathering resolution, gathering courage from the kindliness she saw there. "Perry . . . "

"Hush now," he said, lowering his head and kissing her lips. "Let's forget it all for tonight and go to bed. It is late."

"But, Perry . . . "

"Shh," he murmured against her lips. "Come and let me make love to you. Does it relax you to make love? Or is it a trouble to you?" He raised his head enough to smile into her eyes.

"You know it is not a trouble," she said. "You know that, Perry."

"Sometimes I need reassuring," he said with his old boyish grin. "You get into bed, Grace. I'll see to the candles."

She would tell him afterward, Grace decided as she got into bed. She would tell him later when they were lying quiet and relaxed, her head on his arm. Or tomorrow morning, perhaps . . .

But she did not tell him. The moment had passed. She had told the lie, and she had clung to it when the only thing to have done was to tell the truth simply and directly. And immediately. She would just have to see to it,

she decided the next day, that they did not cross paths
with Gareth again during the two weeks that remained
of their stay before they went to London.

"You did not tell me that Lord Sandersford died," she
said to Ethel when the two of them were alone, gazing
down at a daffodil bud that was about to brave the brisk
air of early spring. "Or that Gareth was home."

Ethel looked stricken. Her hand flew to her mouth.
"You did not know?" she said. "But he has been back
home for years. Oh, Grace, I am so sorry. But of course
you would not have known. You have been gone for ten
years. I am sorry."

Grace touched the bud gently.

"I wondered that you were willing to go last night,"
Ethel said. "I wondered that you did not beg me to refuse the invitation. It must have been a dreadful shock
for you. Does Peregrine know?"

"No," Grace said abruptly, and moved on.

But her hope of staying clear of Gareth for the remain-
der of their stay was not to be realized, as she might
have known.

"We ran into Sandersford," Peregrine said late one afternoon after he and Martin had ridden into the village
on some business. "He took us back with him to look at
his stables. He has enough horses to mount a whole
hunt, Grace, and still have enough left for the ladies'
carriages. Some impressive horseflesh too. He made
himself very agreeable."

"Did he?" Grace looked at him in some unease, but he
did not elaborate on what topics the viscount had made
himself agreeable about.

"And I bought you a length of blue ribbon," he said,
removing it from his pocket and presenting it to her
with a bow and a grin, "to replace the black one on your
straw bonnet. I wish I might have brought you a more

valuable gift, but village shops do not offer much beyond the purely practical."

"Thank you, Perry," she said. "It is a lovely shade. And quite as valuable as diamonds, you know."

And she could not avoid Gareth on her own account either, Grace was to discover. She was walking with Ethel one afternoon along the bank of the stream that flowed into the lake, looking for wild spring flowers, when he came riding along the road that ran parallel to the water. The road led directly from his house to the village. He stopped to hail them, and Grace reluctantly followed Ethel to the fence to exchange civilities.

"Well met," he called. "Are you ladies just out for a stroll?"

"Yes," Ethel said. "The weather is so lovely suddenly and the wild flowers blooming."

"I feel tempted to join you," he said while Grace examined the small bunch of primroses she held in her hand.

"Please do." Ethel's words, to do her justice, Grace thought, came rather stiffly and after a slight pause.

"I wonder," Lord Sandersford said, dismounting from his horse and looping the reins over the fence, "if I might beg the indulgence of a few minutes alone with Grace, ma'am?" He smiled at Ethel.

Ethel looked inquiringly at her sister-in-law while Grace said nothing, but smoothed a finger lightly over the petals of a primrose. "Grace?" she said.

Grace looked up tight-lipped into Gareth's face. "Yes," she said. "I shall follow you home later, Ethel." She resumed the absorbing task of smoothing the flower petals until the other woman had walked beyond earshot.

"Well, Grace . . . " Gareth said.

He had changed. He had always been handsome, attractive, confident of his power to charm. He had been tall and slim when he had left her. He still had all those qualities. But now he was a man, powerfully built, exuding a seductive and assured sexuality. He was the sort of man no woman would be able to resist if he set his mind on attracting her. Not that that was anything very new either.

"You have changed," he said, echoing her own thoughts.

"I am six-and-thirty years old," she said, looking finally into his dark eyes. "No longer a girl, Gareth. Time is not always kind."

"Oh," he said, "I would not say it has been unkind to you. You had the grace of a girl when I knew you. Now you have the mature beauty of a woman. But you have lost your proud look, your defiance."

"I grew up," she said.

He swung his long legs one at a time over the fence that divided them and offered his arm so that they could stroll along in the direction of the lake.

Grace shook her head, but fell into step beside him.

"You wear mourning?" he said. "You did not a few evenings ago."

"We wear it in the daytime here still out of respect for my father," she said. "We will leave it off altogether when we go to London."

"Ah, yes, Paul," he said. "He died in predictably heroic manner, I heard. Saving a child?"

"Yes," she said.

"And cut himself off from his family in equally heroic defense of your honor, I gather," he said.

"Yes."

"I would have thought the gesture unnecessary," he said. "I did not think you would run away, Grace. You used not to be a coward."

"Some things are too hurtful to be borne," she said,

"especially when they concern someone one has harmed irrevocably."

"The child," he said. "Did you care about him, Grace? My father once told me that he looked like me. Did he? Did you think of me when you looked at him?" He smiled.

"I loved him," she said. "He was my son. And, no, I did not see you when I looked at him. Or myself. I saw Jeremy. He was a quite separate person. He was not either you or me, I thank God. He was an innocent child."

"You are bitter," he said, "and I suppose that is understandable. The child was a nasty mistake, and unfortunately you had to bear the consequences. Are you still bitter that I did not come home to marry you?"

Grace's voice shook with fury when she finally answered. "Jeremy was not a nasty mistake," she said. "He was not a mistake at all. He was the most precious thing that has happened in my life, except perhaps . . . "

"For me?" he completed. One eyebrow was raised. His mouth was drawn into the ironic half-smile that she had always found so attractive. "Did I let you down very badly, Grace?"

"It was a long time ago," she said, looking away from him and walking on. "A lifetime ago."

"She was just too wealthy, you know," he said. "Martha, I mean. And Papa was in debt and my pockets to let and an officer's pay just too small a pittance for my needs. I could not have offered you much of a life, Grace. Or the child. But it was you I loved all the same. You never doubted that, did you?"

"Strangely, yes," she said.

"And did you stop loving me?" he asked.

"Very soon," she said. "Long before Jeremy was born."

"Well," he said, "my feelings are not so fickle, Grace. And I am not sure you tell the truth. There has always been something between you and me. We both knew it fifteen years ago and more. And you felt it when we met again a few evenings ago, did you not? And you feel it now, Grace, as I do. Fifteen years cannot erase a love like that we shared."

"And yet," she said, "you seem to have lived very well without me in all that time, Gareth."

He shrugged. "And what is this marriage you have contracted, Grace? What is he like, the beautiful boy? I would guess he is not much of a man."

Grace was smoothing the petals of her flowers again. "It depends upon your definition of manhood, Gareth," she said. "I daresay he would not be long on his feet in a mill against you. But there is more to a man than fists and muscles."

He laughed. "Well said," he said. "And don't tell me that that part is good with him, Grace. You need more of a man to give you that, my love. I know. I have had you, remember?"

Grace examined her flowers, her jaw set in a hard line.

"Why did you marry him?" he asked. "To spite me?"

She laughed. "You are not in my life, Gareth," she said, "and have not been for fifteen years. It is a long time. You have no part in my life any longer."

"Why, then?" he asked. "Tell me, Grace. I am curious to know."

She looked up at him. They had stopped walking. "My reasons for marrying Perry and my whole relationship with him are private matters between me and him," she said. "They are none of your concern, Gareth."

"Ah, but I believe they are, Grace," he said, "or soon will be. Will you not admit that your interest in me has been rekindled in the last few days? Come, Grace, I know you of old. You cannot lie to me."

"You are wrong," she said. "All connection between you and me is buried at the end of the lake with Jeremy.

All feeling between us was dead before that. Have you ever been there? Have you ever seen your son's grave?"

"Yes," he said. "Once." He lifted a hand and laid one finger beneath her chin. "The child is buried there, Grace. Not you and I. Despite your protestations to the contrary, you know that nothing is ended between us. Just dormant. This day has been coming. We have both known it."

His eyes had that intense, passionate look that had always mesmerized her. In years past she had invariably ended in his arms when he had looked at her like that. She felt a twinge of fear. "You are my past, Gareth," she said. "Not my present and not my future. My past."

"You think that boy is your future?" he said. "Poor Grace. He is a ladies' man. Have you not seen that? His head is already turned by the admiration of those silly girls. Imagine what will happen when you reach London and all the new little butterflies of the Season. Grace, my love! He is far too young to appreciate your mature attractions. You will lose him, you know. I would give your marriage perhaps another year. Then he will be lost to you."

"That is not your concern, and never will be," she said.

"Well," he said, "I am a patient man, Grace. We will see in a year's time. Do you wish me to walk all the way home with you?" They had been strolling back the way they had come.

"No," she said. "No, that is unnecessary."

"I shall leave you here, then," he said, patting the neck of his horse over the fence. "Is this all a secret from the estimable Peregrine, by the way? Does he know of the child? Of me? Does he know who I am?"

Grace buried her nose in her flowers. "He does not know who you are," she said. "The rest he does know, and has done since before our marriage."

"I see," he said, smiling down mockingly at her. "Then I am to make sure that the secret does not slip out, am I?"

"I am not asking anything of you," she said.

"You leave yourself very much in my power, do you not?" he said, crossing the fence again and disentangling the reins of his horse.

"No," she said. "I ask nothing of you, Gareth. No favor. You may tell Perry what you will."

Sandersford swung into the saddle and smiled down at her. "Ah," he said, "the old defiant Grace. All that is missing is that dark mane loose down your back as you toss your head. But the spark is back in your eyes. I will not tell your secret, Grace. I would not be so poor-spirited. *Au revoir,* my love. I shall see you again soon." He touched the brim of his hat with his riding whip and turned his horse's head to the roadway again.

"Good-bye, Gareth," she said, lifting her chin and watching him out of sight.

6

GRACE AND PEREGRINE WERE TO LEAVE FOR LONDON five days before her brother and sister-in-law. Priscilla was to go with her aunt and uncle, much to her squealing delight and the envy of Miss Stebbins, whose mama and papa were not leaving for another full fortnight.

"Aunt Grace," Priscilla said after Grace had spoken on her behalf and persuaded Martin to allow her to travel with them, "I will be ever so good, you will see. And I will keep you company in Portland Place while Uncle Perry goes out to his clubs—Papa says that is what gentlemen do with their time in town—and I will not beg at all to be taken about until Mama and Papa come and I remove with them to Cavendish Square."

Peregrine chuckled. "I belong only to White's and Watier's," he said, "and cannot imagine wanting to spend every hour of the twenty-four at one of those, Priscilla. I shall probably drag myself out of them long enough to take Grace about, anyway. She is as new to London as you are. And I will be delighted to have two ladies for whom I might demonstrate my superior knowledge."

"Hyde Park?" Priscilla said with sparkling eyes. "And Kensington Gardens? And St. James's Park?"

"And the Tower and Astley's Amphitheater and one or two other places you might enjoy," he said with a grin.

"Oh, Uncle Perry," Priscilla said, clasping her hands to her bosom and executing a pirouette on the carpet before him while her father frowned his disapproval, "I don't think I can wait. I really don't think I can."

"You will be waiting five days longer if you cannot remember to act more like a lady, miss," Martin said.

Peregrine winked at her as she sank into a chair, her manner more subdued. He smiled at Grace.

Grace spent much of the day before their departure with her father. She even persuaded him to take a short walk outside with her during the afternoon. Peregrine had gone with Martin and Priscilla to take his leave of the numerous new acquaintances he had made during the two weeks of his stay.

"So you are going away again, Grace," Lord Pawley said.

"Perry's mother and aunt are to be in London," she said. "I have not met his mother since our marriage."

"You will never come again?" he asked.

"I would like to, Father," she said. "I have missed you."

"It was a bungled affair," he said. "All my fault."

"No." Grace drew him to sit on a wrought-iron bench overlooking a bed of daffodils, most of which were now in bloom. "It is a mistake always to blame oneself for the past. And probably a mistake to brood on the past too."

"I wanted everything for you," he said. "Or was it really for you I wanted it? I wanted everything for myself, I suppose. And you were the only one with any spirit, although you were the girl. Or so it seemed at the time. Paul had more spirit than the lot of us put together when it came to the point, didn't he? And Martin is the one who has stayed loyal to all this." He gestured with one hand to the house and the gardens and the land beyond.

Grace took his arm and patted his hand.

"I wanted someone to be proud of, someone to boast of," he said. "I wanted you married to Sandersford and lording it over everyone for miles around. He was a fine figure of a man. *Is*, rather. Have you seen him, Grace? Yes, you went there for dinner, did you not? I was angry with both of you for making a mess of it. But only you were here to vent my anger on."

"It is all long in the past," she said.

"Hmm." He brooded on the flowers for a few minutes. "I should not have taken it out on the lad," he said.

"You were not cruel," Grace said. "You gave him a home. You provided for him."

"I gave him nothing," he said. "Nothing at all. I was punishing you. I did not even attend his funeral."

"No," she said.

"So." He seemed to forget her presence for a while. "I am judged. It is too late now. Too late to give anything to my grandson."

"It is not too late," she said. "It is never too late. There are always other people to whom you can give your love. Some of it might be given to yourself. It is time you came out into the light again, Father. You are not an old man."

"Seventy," he said. "How old would the boy have been, Grace? Jeremy."

"Fourteen," she said.

"Well," he said. "Well. I'm glad you came back, Grace. Can you be content with this husband of yours? Seems like a very young puppy to me. Fond of you, though."

"Yes," she said. "I have been very happy with him for the year of my marriage."

He nodded.

LORD PAWLEY CAME downstairs the next morning when
the travelers were about to be on their way. He stood
leaning on his cane on the cobbles, having rejected the
assistance of both his valet and his son. He kissed his
granddaughter and shook hands with Peregrine.

"Perhaps you will be well enough to visit us later in
the summer or next Christmas, sir," Peregrine said.
"You would be very welcome."

The baron nodded. "I would like to see my son's grave
before I die," he said.

Grace held out a hand. "Good-bye, Father," she said.
"I hope you will come."

He ignored her hand. "I like what you have become,
Grace," he said. "I am proud of you, after all."

She lowered her hand and looked into the fierce eyes
of her father. "Papa," she said. She set her hands on his
shoulders. "Oh, Papa, I never meant to disappoint you.
But I was never able to apologize for Jeremy. Maybe
what I did was wrong, but he was not wrong. How can
a living being, a child, be wrong? I can never be sorry
for having him, though I had him for such a short time.
But I never stopped loving you either. I never did,
Papa."

She kissed him on the cheek, hugged him quickly,
and turned away to where Ethel and Martin were both
simultaneously trying to remind an agitated, tearful
Priscilla of the thousand and one rules and pieces of
advice they had drummed into her head the night before and indeed for all the days since it had been decided that she would travel to London with her aunt
and uncle.

Peregrine, who had been standing close to Grace,
looked searchingly at his father-in-law to see that no
assistance was needed there, then he followed his wife

to the waiting carriage, handed her inside, and climbed in after her to sit beside her and hold her hand in a very firm clasp while final farewells were being said outside and Priscilla scrambled in to take the seat opposite, her father's large linen handkerchief pressed to her eyes.

He felt Grace's cheek touch his shoulder for a few moments after the carriage lurched into motion. She did not, as Priscilla did despite her tears, scramble toward the window for one final view of her relatives gathered before the doors of Pangam Manor. He clasped her hand even more tightly.

THE PRESENCE OF Priscilla did not leave the other travelers with a great deal of time for reflection or any time at all for private conversation. Even at the inns where they stayed for two nights, they were never alone together. Grace's maid was with them, riding in the baggage coach with Peregrine's valet, and could have slept in a room with Priscilla, but both her uncle and aunt thought it safer and more proper to have Grace stay with her.

Peregrine spent two restless and lonely nights, tossing and turning on his bed, wondering how he had ever got a good night's sleep before his marriage. The bed felt uncomfortably and coldly large. It was almost disturbing, he thought, how easily one became accustomed to married life, how quickly another person could become quite indispensable to one's comfort and peace of mind.

Accepting on the second night that he probably would not sleep a great deal and that he would merely make matters worse by turning restlessly from side to side and punching his pillows vengefully, Peregrine propped his head on his hands, his fingers laced together, and considered the state of his marriage and his own life.

He had been living now for a year in a marriage that he had contracted rather hurriedly and with little consideration. He had been fond of Paul and had liked Grace and had felt the necessity of looking after her. After hearing the story of her past, he had also felt a deep respect for the woman whose life he would have guessed to have been rather dull and uneventful. He had come to see that her quiet dignity had been won at great cost, that she was a woman of extraordinary strength of character.

Had he given her the comfort he had set out to give? A few weeks before he would have answered with a cautious yes. There had been no great passion in their marriage, and they had reached no high pinnacles of ecstasy. But there had been companionship and affection, mutual friendship with respect, a satisfying sexual relationship—for her as well as for himself, he believed, despite the fact that she never openly showed that satisfaction.

There was no question of the fact that she had brought him far more contentment than he had dreamed of. His house, in which he had always spent a good deal of his time and which he had always loved, had become a home under Grace's quiet and efficient management. And a place of great beauty. Indeed, he lived in far greater comfort than any man had a right to expect.

And his neighbors, of whom he had always been fond and whose company he had always enjoyed, had become friends during the past year. He had, he realized in some surprise, grown during the year from a young man whom other, older adults tended to treat with amused indulgence into a full-grown man whom they accepted as a peer. And he liked the change.

And he liked Grace a great deal better than he had when he married her. He found himself so totally com-

fortable with her that for much of his days he was almost unaware of her as a separate person. He could talk
with her, complain to her, laugh with her, be quiet with
her as if she were just another part of himself.

Then, of course, she had become a very important
part of his nights. He had always found her pleasing to
look at and had certainly not been repelled for even one
moment when he decided to offer for her by the knowledge that as his wife she must also be his sexual partner.
But he had not expected to find her quite as attractive as
he did find her. He made love to her probably far more
frequently than was normal after a year of marriage, he
thought, ruefully aware again of the emptiness of his
bed for the second night in a row.

But it was not just the lovemaking. Just to have her
there beside him in his bed was enough to fill him with
contentment and settle his mind for sleep. Even during
the fourth week of each month, when he could not make
love to her, he could feel happy just to lie with his arm
beneath her head, talking with her until one or both of
them fell asleep.

His marriage had been quietly successful, Peregrine
felt. *Had* been. He was not so sure that it still was. He
was not at all sure that their few weeks at Pangam
Manor had not sent Grace away from him. He did not
really want to think the matter through. He felt a little
ball of panic in his stomach when his mind touched on
the thought. But what else was there to do but think
when one was lying awake in a less-than-comfortable
inn bed, one's wife not beside one either to love or
merely to hold?

He had encouraged the visit. He knew that when Paul
had taken Grace from her home, the past had been bot-
tled up. It had not been erased. There was a great deal of
unhappiness, pain, anger, grief, misunderstanding throbbing beneath the surface of her life. He might have lived

with Grace for the rest of their lives in mild contentment. It could be a reasonably happy life. But there would always be that something. Peregrine had learned in his year with his wife that that calm in her eyes he had always admired was not really calmness at all. It was death. She had put all feelings of any intensity to death when she had gone away with Paul.

She had to live again. She needed to do so. And so he had taken the risk of encouraging the visit they had made. And he was not at all sure that his hopes had been realized. On the surface their visit would seem to have been successful. Her father, Martin, and Ethel had appeared genuinely pleased to see her again and had made an effort to be more than just civil to her. And she had responded. But he did not believe that any of them had talked openly about the painful events that had led to her leaving. The baron had begun to do so just before they left, and there seemed to have been something of a reconciliation in those last few minutes. But was it enough?

And had it been good or bad for Grace to revisit the grave of her son? It was impossible to know. She had been wretchedly unhappy for a few days after doing so, though perhaps no one but him would have known it. But neither of them had spoken of the matter since.

And Grace was still unhappy. Withdrawn. Taut as a bow. Haunted. And with that tightness about her face and about her mouth that had made one largely unaware of her beauty for the five years she had spent at the rectory. Perhaps it was necessary for her to go through that in order to eventually come to life again. And perhaps she would still be his at the end of it all. He did not know. But the panic was there inside him. She was not talking to him.

Oh, she was not silent with him. Had he not been her almost constant companion for a year, perhaps he would not have even realized that she was not talking to him. He had strolled out into the garden with her the evening before their departure for London. They had talked about trivialities for several minutes.

"Are you glad you came, Grace?" he had asked at last.

"Yes," she had said. "It has been good to see Father again. And Martin and Ethel. And Priscilla, of course. It is time that old quarrels were allowed to die."

"I am glad," he had said. "And so you have your family again."

"Yes," she had said.

"Has everything been put quite to rights, Grace?" he had asked.

"Yes." She had looked at him with her calm eyes. "Of course, Perry."

"What is it?" he had asked, stopping in order to look into her eyes. "What is it that is still troubling you?"

She had looked hunted, trapped for several unguarded moments. She had stared back into his eyes, and he had felt her tension, her need to communicate with him, her inability to do so. He had felt failure at that moment. She was unable to tell him about the torment that he clearly saw because he knew her. And he had been unable to do anything but stand there and look back at her as gently as he knew how, telling her with the whole of himself except his voice that he was her husband, her friend, that she might say anything in the world to him and not lose one ounce of his respect or affection.

"Nothing," she had said. "Nothing at all, Perry. Have we done the right thing to allow Priscilla to go with us, do you think? It is a great responsibility to have her in our care."

He had grinned and started to walk again, her arm tucked through his. "I will vouch for it that there will not be a silent or dull moment during the whole journey," he had said.

And so the torment was still there, safely tucked away behind the calmness of Grace's eyes. Perhaps she would never be able to bring it out and fling it from her. Perhaps all the visit had done for her was to open old wounds and scarcely close old ones at all. Perhaps he had made a mistake. Perhaps he should have sheltered her from the past, from life itself, as Paul had done. And perhaps he would lose her now. Perhaps she would find it increasingly impossible to share her inner self with him. And he would lose her.

Peregrine turned against his panic and punched his pillows with greater than usual venom. How could innkeepers reconcile their consciences with charging poor travelers through the nose for a bed and then providing them with mattresses and pillows that even a dog would not be able to sleep on? He turned onto his side, closed his eyes determinedly, and wanted his wife.

GRACE WAS HAPPY to have Priscilla with them, though she had worried a little about the responsibility of caring for an exuberant young girl for several days in London. But Priscilla was easy company and kept both her and Perry busy and amused. She made it possible for one to keep thought at bay and to keep one's husband's concern at a distance.

It was evening when they arrived at the house on Portland Place that Peregrine had taken for the Season. Far too late to go out to see what was to be seen. Anyway, they were all tired after a three-day journey and eager for a bath and a good meal and a comfortable bed. But for all that and despite her assurances to Grace when she had first been permitted to come with them to London, Priscilla wheedled a promise from Peregrine to take them out the next morning.

And out they went, every day until Martin and Ethel's arrival, and one evening too. They drove and walked in Hyde Park and St. James's, gazed in wonder at Buckingham House, where the king and queen held audiences when in town, at Carlton House, home of the Prince Regent, at the Houses of Parliament, Westminster Abbey, St. Paul's, the Tower. They visited and took out subscriptions at the library, and Peregrine left with an armful of books. He had been loudly lamenting his library at home ever since they had left there.

And they strolled up and down the pavements of Bond Street and Oxford Street, Priscilla exclaiming over all the bonnets and fans and shawls and other finery that she was convinced she could persuade her father into buying when he arrived in town. Peregrine bought her a new ivory fan and chip-straw bonnet over her blushing protests and bore Grace off to a fashionable modiste to be fitted for new gowns and walking dresses now that she had officially left off her mourning.

They went to the King's Theater one evening to see and listen to Signor Tramezani, Signora Collini, and Madame Calderini sing in the opera *Sidagero*. Peregrine and Grace sat enthralled by the music. Priscilla was perhaps more interested in the seven magnificent tiers of boxes, all decorated in gold and azure and hung with brocade curtains. And in the people who sat inside those boxes.

"Oh," she said in something like an agony before the performance began, "do you think that in a few weeks' time, some of these faces will become familiar? Will Mama and Papa be able to procure some invitations?"

"Of course," Grace said reassuringly. "You just need a little patience, Priscilla. You are going to be presented to the queen, you know. Of course there will be so many invitations that you will not know which to accept and which to throw away."

But Priscilla did not have to wait quite so long for some introductions. During the interval there was a knock at the door of their box, and a young lady and gentleman entered.

"Perry," the young lady said. "I was never more surprised in my life than when Mama pointed you out. I thought you were going to rusticate forever. It must be two years at least since you were here."

She was holding out both hands to him, an exquisitely beautiful young lady in an emerald green silk gown, with real emeralds at throat and wrist, and flaming red hair and slanting hazel eyes to ensure that the gown and the jewels did not overshadow her person.

"Leila," Peregrine said, surging to his feet and taking her two outstretched hands in his own. "You are here too? And looking quite as lovely as ever. Yes, it is two years. It seems like forever, does it not?"

"And here is Francis too," Leila said, indicating the young man behind her with a slight turn of the head.

Peregrine smiled and shook hands with her companion. "May I present my wife, Grace?" he said. "And Miss Priscilla Howard? Lady Leila Walsh and Mr. Francis Hartwell, Grace, old friends of mine."

"You are married, Perry?" Lady Leila asked rhetorically, turning toward Grace and Priscilla, who were seated side by side. "How perfectly horrid of you." She smiled impishly and extended a slim hand to Priscilla. "I am pleased to meet you, Lady Lampman. Ma'am." She inclined her head to Grace.

Priscilla giggled. "Oh, you have us mixed up," she said. "I am Priscilla Howard."

Lady Leila flushed with mortification and looked more closely at Grace. "I do beg your pardon," she said. "Perry, what do you think you are about, waving a vague hand in the direction of two ladies and expecting me to know which is which?"

Mr. Hartwell bowed to both ladies. "It takes a great deal to make Leila blush, Lady Lampman," he said. "May I congratulate you?"

Grace sat in some discomfort while Lady Leila allowed Peregrine to seat her, and prattled brightly for what remained of the interval.

"Oh, Perry," the girl said, "life is indescribably dull this early in the Season, is it not? Absolutely no one is here yet and not likely to be for perhaps another fortnight. You must come to the Halstons' rout tomorrow night. I shall see that an invitation is sent to you in the morning. There is no one on the guest list below the age of thirty, I would swear, except for Francis and me and Annabelle Halston, and Christina Lowe and Humphrey Dawes. And Silas Crawley, of course, but he does not signify. Say you will be there too. You always did know how to brighten up even the dullest gathering."

"I think not," Peregrine said. "Priscilla is not yet out, you know, and her parents are not due in London for another two days. It would not do for us to take her into society before they decide how they want her introduced."

"How tiresome," Leila said, her eyes resting on Priscilla for a moment. "But you could come, Perry. Your wife would not mind staying at home with Miss Howard, I am sure. Would you, Lady Lampman?"

Grace was saved from having to answer when Peregrine laughed. "Leila hasn't changed, has she?" he said, grinning at Mr. Hartwell. "Perhaps Grace would not mind, Leila, but I am afraid I certainly would. I see your mama looking very pointedly this way. The opera is about to resume, I take it."

Leila sighed and got to her feet. "You have not grown stuffy merely because you are married, have you, Perry?" she said. "Humphrey has not, I do assure you. He has not even brought his wife to town with him. I believe she is in a delicate way, if you understand my meaning. Lady Lampman, you will not allow Perry to become stuffy, will you? It would be a great shame, you know, when he was always the life and soul of any party." She smiled winningly as she got to her feet.

"I think Perry would find it quite impossible to be stuffy," Grace assured her. "It is not in his nature."

Peregrine was still grinning. He laid a hand on his wife's shoulder as the two visitors prepared to take their leave. "You had better listen, Leila," he said. "Grace knows me better than anyone."

"Isn't she just beautiful," Priscilla said, saucer-eyed, when they were alone in their box again. "Are ladies really allowed to wear gowns so low cut, Aunt Grace?" She giggled. "Was not that amusing when she thought I was you? She thought I was your wife, Uncle Perry. I told you that you were too young to be my uncle. How amusing it will be if other people think you are my beau instead of my aunt's husband."

Peregrine sat down, took Grace's hand in his, and set it on his sleeve. He kept his hand over it to warm it. He smiled down at her. "Leila never did have a brain in her head," he said. "I always thought it was fortunate for her that she is so pretty. And wealthy, into the bargain. Can you imagine my going to an evening party without you, Grace?"

Grace said nothing. She was glad to see that the performance on stage was about to resume. Of course it would be natural for Perry—and Priscilla—to be drawn into a young crowd. He had friends here, made during the years when he had regularly come to London for at least a few weeks of the Season. Friends below the age of thirty, as Lady Leila Walsh had put it. Friends who would want him to join them in their various entertainments and whom he would wish to join.

How had she not realized that London would be the very worst place to come with Perry? Both he and she could only become increasingly aware of the age difference between them there. It would drive a wedge between them and add an awkwardness to an already strained relationship. She had still not been able to bring herself to tell him about Gareth, even though seemingly perfect opportunities had presented themselves more than once. Even as recently as the night of their arrival in town he had asked her again what troubled her, as she lay nestled in his arms after an achingly slow and beautiful lovemaking. And again she had protested after a long and agonized silence that nothing did.

It did not matter now, she told herself. They were away from Gareth's neighborhood and unlikely to be back there for a long time. But it did matter. Her former lover, the father of her dead child, was still alive, and Perry thought him dead. They had both met him and accepted his hospitality. Perry had gone with him to view his stables and thought him a pleasant man. And she had walked alone with him and felt the unwelcome pull of his powerful personality. She had not touched him or spoken an encouraging word to him, and yet she felt as if she had been unfaithful to Perry. She had not even told Perry that she had walked with Lord Sandersford. And even if she had, she would have still been deceiving him. He would still not have known that she had walked with her lover.

Grace allowed her hand to remain on her husband's sleeve and felt the warmth of his body seep into the chill of hers. And there was a dullness inside her. She was going to lose him. It was all spoiled, their marriage. Partly because he was young and needed a young man's amusements. And partly because she had lied to him and could not tell the truth that might drive him away faster than he would go anyway.

7

By the time Martin and Ethel arrived in Portland Place late on the afternoon of the day they were expected, in order to take their daughter to Cavendish Square with them, Priscilla was in a state of high excitement. She hurled herself first at her mother and then at her father.

"It seems like forever," she said. "I thought you would never come."

"How lovely to see you again and to find you looking so well, dear," Ethel said, holding on to her dignity in the presence of her sister- and brother-in-law.

"You should watch your manners, miss," Martin said. "We have not even had a chance to greet your aunt and uncle yet."

But Priscilla was not to be cowed. There was too much news of their journey and their days' activities to be told, and too many favors by way of new clothes and future entertainments to be discussed, to enable her to act the part of the demure young lady just yet.

Consequently a full half-hour passed before the new arrivals could do more than greet Grace and Peregrine and ask after their health. Only after Priscilla dashed from the room, having suddenly remembered that she had a new bonnet and a new fan to show her mama, although they were packed already in her trunk, was Ethel able to give any news of home.

"Papa is well," she said, "and went out of doors each day after your leaving. We were very gratified, were we not, Martin? He stays altogether too much inside his rooms. And all the tulips were bursting into bloom. I hated to leave them."

"Yes," Grace agreed. "We have been lamenting our garden at home too."

"Spring is altogether a foolish time for the Season in London," Peregrine said with a smile. "Grace and I have been considering lobbying everyone here this year to see if we cannot have it changed to the winter, haven't we, Grace?"

She laughed. "This is the first I have heard about it," she said. "But I do think it a quite brilliant idea, Perry."

Ethel placed her teacup very carefully back in its saucer and examined the Wedgwood pattern closely. "Lord Sandersford has also decided to spend the Season here," she said. "Martin met him on the road to the village the day before we left. He was planning to leave a few days after us, I believe."

"Indeed?" Grace said, her voice sounding distant to her own ears. Martin, she noticed, appeared to be studying the tea leaves at the bottom of his cup.

"Splendid," Peregrine said. "And you were afraid that you would know no one here, Grace. Soon London will be filled with our friends and acquaintances and relatives. Edmund and his family should be here soon too. And my mother and aunt some time during April."

"And the Stebbinses will be bringing Lucinda," Ethel added. "I am pleased that she and Priscilla will be able to keep each other company."

Grace was thankful for the return to the room of Priscilla and the lively argument that developed between

Perry and Martin, who felt he should pay for the fan and the bonnet.

"We must give a dinner for our friends once they have all arrived in town," Peregrine said to Grace later. "And perhaps some music and cards afterward. Even some informal dancing, do you think? We do not boast a ballroom here, but the drawing room is large enough for a dozen couples. Do you think it a good idea?"

"Yes," she said. "Will there not be a great many other entertainments for it to conflict with, though, Perry?"

"We shall set the date now, then, and let our friends know as we see them," he said. "I am expecting every day to see Edmund at White's. It will be good to see him again and Madeline and Dominic. Sandersford must have made a spur-of-the-moment decision to come. He did not say anything while we were there, did he?"

"Not that I heard," Grace said.

"Perhaps he is thinking of taking a new wife," Peregrine said with a grin. "Did you know his first wife, Grace?"

"No," she said. "He was living from home when they were married."

He nodded. "Do you suppose Priscilla will get all the finery she has set her heart on in the last week?" he asked.

"I doubt it," Grace said. "Martin did not sound too encouraging even about the few things she mentioned this afternoon."

"And yet he dotes on her," Peregrine said with a laugh. "And I am sure she understands perfectly well that his bark is many times worse than his bite. It must be very difficult to be strict with a daughter, mustn't it? I would probably spend a fortune on one merely because I could not face her look of disappointment when I said no."

In the event, it was Lord Sandersford whom Peregrine

met at White's, not Lord Amberley. They were both there to read the morning papers, but adjourned to the dining room when they recognized each other.

"I was not even planning to come here this year," Lord Sandersford said. "But one does feel the pull of town amusements when spring comes, does one not? And female company, of course."

"Yes, although the social rounds can be trying year after year," Peregrine said. "Through one's youth it seems that there is nothing so enjoyable as the Season and that the rest of the year must be spent in dullness waiting for the next spring to arrive. But other interests begin to take priority as the years pass."

"And is Lady Lampman enjoying being here?" Lord Sandersford asked, looking his companion over with lazy, penetrating eyes. "It is her first time in town, I believe?"

"Yes," Peregrine said. "She has been suitably impressed with all one is supposed to be impressed with. And she is constantly busy. She is out shopping this morning with her sister-in-law and Priscilla. I think Grace is just as happy, though, at home in the country with her garden."

"Is she?" The viscount raised his eyebrows. "Then she must have changed. I cannot imagine Grace pottering around in a garden."

"No?" Peregrine looked at his companion with some interest. "What was she like when you knew her?"

Lord Sandersford's eyes looked somewhat mocking. "When she was a girl and a young woman?" he said. "Wild, graceful, beautiful. Her hair loose down her back as often as not. Confident, her chin always high, her eyes always flashing. It is hard to imagine, seeing her now, is it not?"

Peregrine considered. "No," he said. "I can see how

all those qualities would translate into Grace as she is now."

Lord Sandersford's eyes rested keenly on the other. "You were a friend of Paul's?" he asked. "Not often does friendship call upon one to enter a marriage as you did. You are to be commended."

Peregrine looked startled. "Is that how my marriage appears?" he said. "Because I am so much younger than Grace, perhaps? I am afraid I tend to forget about that. It becomes quite unimportant when one grows familiar with another person, you know. Our marriage seems a very normal one to me, I do assure you. You must not think I did something even remotely heroic. Heavens, no!"

The viscount smiled. "You disappoint me," he said. "I have thought, you see, that I might look around me for a bride among all the hopeful little girls who are beginning to crowd the fashionable drawing rooms and ballrooms. I would hate to think that after a year or so of marriage I would no longer be aware of her youth and vigor. How very dull a picture you present."

"Then I must be very poor at conveying meaning through the medium of words," Peregrine said with a grin. "I wish you luck. And joy, of course."

Sandersford inclined his head.

"It is," a tall sandy-haired gentleman with large side whiskers and mustache said, stopping beside their table and bending slightly to look into the viscount's face. "Heaven bless us! Haven't clapped eyes on you for five years or more."

"Six," Lord Sandersford said, pushing back his chair and rising to his feet in order to shake hands with the new arrival. "I sold out six years ago, Maurice. And how have the Guards managed to survive without me?"

"Oh, tolerably well, you know," the other said with a

bellowing laugh. "And they have had to do without me for the last three as well. Invalided out. My leg, you know. The knee never did heal properly. Should have had it sawn off, I daresay. Keeps giving out on me at the most awkward moments. I was kneeling at the altar for my own wedding—no one you would know, Gareth—and couldn't get up again." He guffawed with laughter once more.

"It must have been a priceless moment," Lord Sandersford said. "Would you care to join us, Maurice?"

He turned to Peregrine and introduced the two men. But his former army friend was in a rush. He excused himself after making plans to meet Sandersford the next day.

"Pleased to make your acquaintance, Lampman," he said. "And I look forward to hearing what you have been up to for the last six years, Gareth. No good, at a guess. Unless you have reformed. Female hearts and female virtue still strewn around in tatters at your feet, I suppose?" He left them, laughing.

Lord Sandersford resumed his seat. "That is what the Guards can do for you, Lampman," he said. "Some of us find afterward that we never can talk in anything lower than a quiet bellow. One wonders if he is capable of lowering his voice in his wife's boudoir, does one not?"

Peregrine excused himself a few minutes later.

THE SPACIOUS HOUSES and mansions of London's fashionable Mayfair filled up with the coming of April, and soon their wealthy and prominent residents were being offered a dizzying array of entertainments with which to amuse themselves for every moment of their days until summer should draw them home again or to one of the spas.

Ethel and Martin Howard decided that a ball given by Ethel's second cousin in honor of his own daughter's come-out would be a suitable occasion for Priscilla's first official appearance in society. Grace and Peregrine were invited, but then so was almost everyone who was someone in the social world. It was early in the Season. Many a hostess wished to establish the reputation of having attracted the biggest squeeze to her particular assembly.

Grace was looking forward to the occasion, her first grand ball at the age of thirty-six! She had not planned to dance until Peregrine laughed at her and asked if the rheumatics pained her enough that he should stop taking her walking during the daytime. And she had not planned to dress in just such a way. But Perry had gone with her to the modiste he himself had recommended and firmly forbidden all her early choices of both designs and fabrics for her evening gowns.

Was she afraid that a fashionable gown falling in elegant folds from a high waist might occasionally reveal the outline of her legs? he asked. Shocking! And—with a roguish grin for the dressmaker, who was spreading out a new set of plates for them to consider—was she afraid to reveal a little more of her bosom than a high neckline would allow? And, no, he would absolutely not hear of a turban to hide her lovely hair. Not until she was seventy years old at the very least. And if they were fortunate, perhaps those particular horrors would have gone out of fashion by then. Plumes, yes, if she really wanted, but a turban, no.

And he laughed at her again when she tried to pick out sober colors for her gowns. "Has all the black you have been wearing made you color-blind, Grace?" he asked. "Choose a different color from that gray. I insist.

You cannot really want that, can you? What would you really like to wear if you did not have to consider at all what you think you ought to wear?"

She looked around at all the bolts of cloth spread around them. "That red," she said daringly and half-jokingly, expecting another storm of protest.

"Then we are finally agreed," Peregrine said. "The red it will be for your first ball gown, Grace. And for the design, this, I think. Do you like it?"

She looked at the plate to which he pointed. "Oh, Perry," she said, "it is gorgeous. But I do not know if I dare."

"This one," he said, looking up to the dressmaker, his eyes twinkling. "And now for all the others. And you have my strict orders, madam wife, to think and see as a woman for the next hour or so, not as the sober dowager you are pretending to be."

So, almost two weeks later, she was wearing the red gown and staring at her image in the pier glass in her dressing room, wondering if she had stepped back in time. She had not expected to see herself so ever again, looking vivid and alive and, yes, feminine. Surely when Perry saw her, he would be startled at just how much bosom was showing and at just how much the fine silk did reveal of the outline of her body and legs. Only the heavy flounces at the hem kept it from clinging, she was sure.

And Effie had done wonders with her hair and the silver and red plumes that nodded above it. There was color in her cheeks, though none of it was artificial, and there was a brightness in her eyes that was unfamiliar to her gaze. She felt almost like Grace Howard again, the young Grace, the Grace before Jeremy.

She turned as the door opened behind her and Peregrine stepped into the room. She was suddenly self-conscious, convinced that she was making a foolish spectacle of herself, masquerading as a girl.

He closed the door behind his back and stood against it. And his eyes traveled down her body from the plumes to the toes of her silver dancing slippers and back up to her face again. "I am going to have to keep you at home, you know, Grace," he said. "This ball is supposed to be in honor of some poor young girl, and yet, if I take you there, no one will have eyes for anyone else but you."

"Perry," she said, pleased. "What a silly joke. But do I look all right? The color is not too vivid?"

"Blinding," he said.

"Is the bodice not cut too low?"

"Decidedly," he said. "I am not at all sure that it will please me to have other men see what a magnificent bosom you have, Grace. In fact, I am sorry now that I did not encourage the gray silk and the high neckline and the turban. I might have hidden you in a dark corner, then, and not have had above three-quarters of the men present realize that you were heavily disguised."

"How silly you are tonight," she said. "Oh, and Perkins has perfected another waterfall with your neckcloth, Perry. You do look splendid."

"Well," he said, "I cannot be quite outclassed by my wife, now, can I?"

Grace felt more lighthearted than she had felt in a long while as they drove the distance to Fitzroy Square, where the ball was to take place, and joined a line of carriages waiting to deposit their passengers before the double doors of the house. She was looking and feeling her best, she was on her way to the first grand ball she had ever attended, her niece was about to make her first appearance in society, and she had Perry at her side. She was going to enjoy herself and forget anything that might cloud her joy.

She was going to forget that Gareth was in town and had called on them two days before and stayed for almost a whole hour, making himself charming to Perry, looking at her frequently with those eyes that established ownership and that she knew from long experience meant mischief.

And she was going to forget that Perry was already going away from her. Oh, he still spent most of each day in her company and all of every evening and night. And she was not so unrealistic as to expect him to be with her for every moment. She had expected him to want to spend some time at his clubs and with former acquaintances.

She had no complaint whatsoever against him. But he was going away from her for all that. He had been unnaturally quiet for the last week, unnaturally serious. Not unkind, not in a bad mood, not silent, not even humorless. It was hard to explain in words. Perhaps she would not have even known that he was going from her if she had not lived long enough with him to know him very well indeed. But she did know him well, and so she did know that she was losing him.

It was inevitable, of course. It must have started at the opera, when that very lovely Lady Leila Walsh had reminded him that there were young people whose company and activities were waiting to be enjoyed. Yet he was married to a lady quite indisputably beyond the age of thirty. And it would have continued when Priscilla left them and took the sparkle and frenzied restlessness of her youth with her. And all their walks and rides together, all his outings alone, would have brought to his notice the young and the beautiful and the exuberant who seemed to have a monopoly on the springtime and the Season.

And Perry, because he was good and kind and honorable, was still spending most of his time with her and still treating her with deference, still entertaining her and buying her gifts by day and loving her by night. Perhaps he did not even know himself yet that their marriage was dying. Or perhaps he did know and was fighting the inevitable. Poor Perry!

But she did know and accepted the reality, though with a dull and hopeless pain inside. She had always known it would come to this and had protected herself from unbearable agony by refusing to allow herself to come fully alive under Perry's affection. But it had not happened yet. It was happening, but it was not finished. There was some time left yet. There was this evening and this ball. And she had Perry beside her, in the sort of teasing mood that she had not seen in the past week. She was going to enjoy herself.

LADY MADELINE RAINE had just rapped Peregrine on the knuckles with her fan and told him not to be impertinent. Her green eyes were dancing with merriment.

"If you are suggesting by talking so pointedly about this being my fourth Season that I have been unable to find a husband in all that time," she said, "then I shall direct Dominic to call you out. He is considerably taller than you, sir. The very idea! Have you considered that perhaps I have not wanted to find a husband?"

Peregrine grinned. "If you will recall my exact words, Madeline," he said, "you will be forced to admit that I neither said nor hinted at anything so unmannerly. I would have to say that you protest rather too much. I suspect that you have been touched on the raw."

"Ah, sir," she said, "you are unkind. Now that you are respectably married, you think you may look in scorn at everyone over the age of twenty who is not. I shall best you yet, you know, by marrying a duke."

They were dancing, and the flow of their conversation was considerably hampered by the steps of the dance, which frequently separated them. Grace, Peregrine saw, was still standing at the side of the ballroom, talking to Lady Amberley. But he did not worry about her. It was the first of four sets that she had not danced.

He still could not keep his eyes away from her for more than a couple of minutes at a time. He knew her to be beautiful, of course. And that gown could reveal nothing of her body that he did not know already. He knew her with far more than his eyes only: he knew her with his own body and with a long and intimate familiarity. But he still could not stop himself from looking at her in wonder. There was a beauty in her tonight that he had not seen before, a certain glow from within that had forced itself past the calm of her eyes and gave her vibrancy. He was not sure that he had been entirely teasing when he had said that he did not want other men to see her in all her beauty.

And yet he was proud of her and delighted at every male head that turned for a second look at her. The room was filled, of course, with young girls in their delicate whites and pastels, and it was undoubtedly on them that most of the male attention and admiration was focused. But there was a mature beauty and attractiveness about Grace that drew the eye almost like a magnet. Even Lady Sally Jersey, surrounded by her usual court, did not outshine her.

"Even Edmund is here tonight," Lady Madeline was saying. "I would dare swear that he will not attend half a dozen more balls in the whole Season. He would prefer to attend a salon and spend an evening in conversation on literary or political topics. Can you imagine?"

"It is very poor-spirited of him to be so dull," Peregrine said. "A whole earldom going to waste! It is enough to make the most sanguine of young ladies cross beyond bearing."

"Oh," she said, "I might have known I would have no sense out of you, Perry. I forget that you are rather like Edmund when you are not tormenting the ladies."

"Tormenting the ladies?" he said. "When I have been rehearsing my charms for the whole of the past week?"

Peregrine had caught Grace's eye across the room. Lord Sandersford had joined her and Lady Amberley.

Gareth.

And all the joy went out of Peregrine's evening as it had been doing out of his life for the past week, whenever he could not keep that name at bay.

He had not wanted to believe it at first. And he still did not know for sure. He had not asked anyone. But the coincidence would have been just too great. It could not but be true. Sandersford must be of an age with Grace. He had been a soldier. He had grown up with Grace, knew a great deal about her, lived at no great distance from her father. And his name was Gareth.

He had been Grace's lover. And fathered her child. And abandoned her. She had loved him. And perhaps still did. And now, having seen her again, he had followed her to London.

And Grace's unhappiness over the last weeks, that something that was troubling her, was finally explained. She had met again the man she had loved. The man she still loved? And he wanted her again. Yet she was trapped in a marriage she had made for comfort and convenience. Marriage with a younger man, who could not hope to compete with the very handsome and charismatic figure of Gareth, Viscount Sandersford.

He did not know what to do, had not known what to do for a week. His first instinct had been to go home and confront Grace. She had lied to him before their marriage, when he had admired her for being so open with him and frank about her past. And she had deceived him during their visit to her home. He had felt a hurt anger against her, an anger that had bewildered him because it was an unaccustomed emotion for him, especially directed against his wife. Their relationship had been a remarkably tranquil one over more than a year of marriage.

But he had not confronted her. He knew, without having to think very deeply on the matter, that Grace had never lied to him or withheld any truth maliciously. And he knew that she must be troubled as much by the deception she had perpetrated against him as by the renewal of her acquaintance with Sandersford. Would he solve anything by telling her that he knew? Or would he make matters many times worse?

He did not know, and he did not know what to do. He did not know if he should try to prevent meetings between his wife and her former lover—should he take her home to Reardon Park, perhaps?—or whether he should allow her to work out the problem in her own way. And he did not know if he should confront the viscount with his knowledge or stand back and let Grace make her own decisions.

He knew what he would do if he were a man, according to all the codes of manhood with which the people of his generation had been indoctrinated. He would probably challenge Sandersford to a duel and beat his wife and take her into the country. Or else he would turn her out, having discovered that her lover was still alive and still a part of her life, and send her back into the arms of the man who had taken her honor.

But he had always considered such codes silly and immature. Why should he think only of his own image, his own reputation, when there was another human being to be considered? He would prefer to think of what was best for Grace—and himself too—rather than of some inanimate code of behavior. He trusted her, when all was said and done, to do what was right. And if he must lose her, if that was what she would decide was right, then so be it. To hell with what the world might say.

Only one thing he did not consider, because he knew it was not in Grace's nature to put him in such a dilemma. He did not ask himself what he would do if she should decide to take Sandersford as her lover again while continuing with her marriage. That question he did not ask himself. He knew that he would never have to provide himself with an answer.

He smiled at Lady Madeline as the music ended and led her back to her mother.

"Sandersford?" he said pleasantly. "Ah, Edmund, where have you been hiding? Your sister tells me that you have been in town for four days already."

"And occupied by business ever since," his friend said, extending a hand to him. "But intent on enjoying myself tonight. Now let me see. The Courtneys and the Carringtons and the Cartwrights—the three C's, in fact—and the Misses Stanhope all send their regards to you and Lady Lampman, as do the Mortons and the rector and his wife. Have I forgotten anyone, Mama?"

"I think it would be safer just to say 'everyone,' dear," his mother said.

Lord Amberley smiled. "Now, why did I not think of that?"

"My dance, I believe," Lord Sandersford said, extending a hand for Grace's. "With your permission, Lampman."

Peregrine bowed.

"They make a handsome picture," Lord Amberley

said, looking after them. "Lady Lampman is in good looks, Perry. You must be treating her well." He grinned.

"I must be on my way to claim Lady Leila Walsh's hand for the next dance," Peregrine said, "before someone else steps in and takes my place. She does not lose any popularity over the years, does she?"

His eyes were twinkling as he approached the lady in question and stood politely to one side while she explained to a disappointed youth that she had no space left on her card where she might write his name. He must enjoy the evening, Peregrine told himself, or appear to do so anyway. He must not appear to mope over Grace.

"Perry, there you are," Lady Leila said, turning her slanting hazel eyes on him. "I do not know why I did not grant that dance to poor Mr. Daniels, you know. I am still quite out of sorts with you for marrying without giving me a sporting chance of taking you away from her. And I will never forgive you for the trick you played at the theater. Can you imagine my mortification at letting my eyes stray past your wife and dismissing her as far too old for you, and greeting effusively a girl who was not even out at that time? Really, Perry, your jokes get worse and worse."

"If you are going to scold," he said, "I will find the card room, Leila, and see if I cannot separate a few duchesses from their fortunes. You have that hair to live up to, I know, but you need not turn into a shrew."

He grinned at her indignant rejoinder.

Strange, he was thinking. Since his marriage, he really had grown unaware of the difference in age between himself and Grace. She was just Grace to him, a person who had become very dear to him. He could not look at her even now and see a woman of thirty-six in comparison with his twenty-six. He could see only Grace, his friend and his lover. Did she look older than he? He supposed she must. Common sense said that she must. And London society appeared to be saying that she did.

His eyes strayed to where Grace was dancing with Sandersford, his handsome face smiling down into her upturned one.

Damnation. Oh, damnation!

8

GARETH HAD TURNED ON THE FULL FORCE OF HIS charm. Grace recognized all the signs. There was his smile, of course, which had always been more attractive than almost any other man's smile because of the whiteness of his teeth. And there was the very intense and appreciative look in his dark eyes and the way he had of crinkling his eyes at the corners when he laughed. And those eyes, though very direct, knew how to flutter down to one's mouth for the merest moment, or up to one's hair.

They had laughed about that deliberate charm when they were much younger. He had never used it on her then because she would immediately have accused him of being false. But he had used it on other girls, entirely for his own amusement and hers.

He was using it on her now, Grace saw as she danced with him. Except that now it was not a boy's charm any longer, but a man's seductive power. And he was a man now who knew the irresistibility of his attractiveness even more than the young Gareth had done.

"Well, Grace," he said, "I came to town to look about me for a young wife. I came here tonight for that purpose. And it could be a successful evening. We are surrounded by young ladies, a dozen or more of them pretty, I would imagine. Yet I find I have eyes for no one but you."

"Nonsense, Gareth," she said. "You forget that I know this approach of yours from long ago. Are you trying to make a conquest of me? Did you think it would be easy? And would it amuse you to know that it was still possible?"

They were dancing close to the edge of the dancing floor, close to the windows. He drew her away from the other dancers and stood with her in the relative shelter of the long velvet curtains.

"You are right," he said. "I was being less than sincere in my manner. And I have been lying, both to you and to others I have spoken to since arriving in town. I am not here to look over this new crop of beauties, Grace. What interest would I have in young girls who know nothing about satisfying a man's needs and appetites? I came here because of you. You know that, do you not? You must have expected me to come. But if I am to be honest, then so must you. Don't talk of my conquering you. There is no conquest to be made. Is there?"

He was Gareth, she told herself, looking up at him. He was that boy she had loved dearly for years as she grew to womanhood, the young man with whom she had been intimate for the span of a few days. He was Jeremy's father. He had started her son in her. She had always expected that he would be her husband. She had always expected that there would be several children. And now he was powerfully handsome. He frightened her, suffocated her.

"No, there is not, Gareth," she said, answering only his last question. "It is an impossibility. I am married to Perry."

He made a dismissive gesture with his hand. "A mere boy," he said. "A pleasant-enough boy, I will admit. And it was decent enough of him to rescue you from an awkward situation after Paul died. But a boy nonetheless. And one who favors young ladies, as is perfectly understandable, Grace. Look at him now laughing with his partner. Do you believe he does not fancy her?"

Grace looked obediently. Perry's fair head was bent to Lady Leila's flaming red one, and they were clearly teasing each other or flirting. There was nothing unusual about the scene. But Lady Leila was indeed very youthful and dashing. And extremely pretty.

"You do not need to cling to him and be constantly humiliated by his roving eye, Grace," Lord Sandersford said fiercely. "You have more beauty and more passion in your little finger than that young lovely will ever have in her whole person. But you need a man to appreciate both and bring them alive in you. Not a boy."

"You speak as if you think me undecided, wavering," Grace said, turning determinedly from the charming picture made by Perry and Lady Leila. "I am not, Gareth. My relationship with Perry, as I told you before, is entirely a private matter between him and me. And as for you, you are a part of my distant past. There is no question of resurrecting what there once was between us."

"Oh, liar, Grace," he said, his dark eyes gazing down intently into hers. "Are you trying to convince yourself? Ours was not a love that could easily die. I put the child in you, whom you claim to have loved so dearly because he was mine, Grace. That is a bond that cannot be shrugged off even in a lifetime."

"And yet," she said, "it was of so little importance to you that you married a wealthier woman even while that child was still inside me. Don't talk to me of lifelong bonds."

"I was a boy," he said. "A headstrong, conceited boy. Let us not judge each other now from this distance of time, Grace. You were not blameless yourself. You knew the risks and the moral implications when you decided to give me a husband's privilege."

"I was foolish," she said. "Foolish and irresponsible."

He took one of her wrists in his hand. "Let us not quarrel," he said. "We have both made mistakes, Grace—me in dishonoring you, you in allowing yourself to be taken, me in marrying Martha, you in marrying Lampman. Are we going to let those mistakes ruin what is left of our lives?"

"You have been widowed for many years, Gareth," she said. "I have been married for one. What happened to the years between? If you had made such a mistake, if you wanted so badly to be reunited with me, where were you during those years?"

"I did not know where you were," he said. He shrugged. "And I did not see you. It was seeing you again a few weeks ago that brought everything back to me and made me realize what a fool I have been."

"I am sorry, Gareth," she said. "You are too late. Fifteen years too late."

"No," he said, his hand gripping her wrist almost painfully, shaking it even. "No, I will not believe that, Grace. You are bitter. I can understand that. I did a dastardly thing to leave you alone with the child and the scandal. And it was remiss of me not to come for you after Martha died. But must you punish yourself as well as me? If you turn from me now, we will waste not only those years, but the rest of a lifetime."

"Those years have not been wasted for me," Grace said. "I spent four of them with Jeremy. I have spent one of them with Perry. It is too late for us, I tell you, Gareth. Our love has long been dead. It is a thing of the past."

"You lie, Grace," he said. She knew from old experiences that his temper was rising. His jaw was set and his eyes even more intense than they had been. "Are you convinced by your own words? Are you content to go through life with the beautiful boy, watching him flirt with every pretty young girl he sees, knowing that he will be amusing himself in private with more than a few of them? Can you tell me that you love him, Grace? That you think him worth fighting for? Humiliating yourself for? Tell me that you love him, that he is everything in the world to you as I once was. And still am, I firmly believe. Tell me and I will leave you alone."

"No." Grace was glaring back into his eyes. He was as overbearing as he had ever been. They had had not a few fights in their younger days, sometimes very physical fights. "I will tell you no such thing merely because you demand it of me. And I will tell you nothing that concerns Perry. Nothing. My feelings for him and his for me are none of your concern. None, do you understand me?"

"You cannot say it, can you?" he taunted. His eyes strayed to her lips. "You cannot tell me that you love him. Because it is not true, Grace. And cannot be true. He is a boy and you are a woman."

"Shh! Oh, please hush. People are beginning to notice." Grace, angry and dazed, was aware suddenly that Ethel was standing directly in front of them, a look of deep mortification on her face. "Please," she said again, opening her fan, waving it slowly before her face, and attempting to smile, "you must not quarrel here."

Lord Sandersford released Grace's wrist and smiled with practiced charm. "Ah, a timely reminder, ma'am," he said, inclining his head. "Grace and I were merely having a friendly difference of opinion. Just like old times."

Grace noticed for the first time that the dancing had stopped. All the occupants of the room were not looking at them, she found, glancing about her in some trepidation. But Perry was making his way toward them, his face rather pale. He was smiling.

"This dancing is warm work," he said. "Would you care to come with me in search of some lemonade, Grace?"

"Yes, I would," she said, reaching for his arm, for a haven of kindliness and safety. Reaching for home. "It is hot in here. Are you enjoying yourself, Perry?"

"My feet might be worn down to stumps by the end of it," he said, his eyes twinkling down at her, "but it is all in the cause of enjoyment, so I will not complain."

"We will go riding in the carriage tomorrow, then, instead of walking, and you may have a soft pillow beneath your feet," she said, patting his hand and letting her fingers linger there, absorbing his warmth.

PEREGRINE FOLLOWED GRACE into her dressing room later that night and stood leaning against the door, watching her remove first the plumes and then the pins from her hair. She had refused to have her maid sent for at such a late hour—or such an early hour, she had amended. He strolled across to the dressing table and picked up her brush as she shook out her hair.

"I think Priscilla did remarkably well for her first appearance," she said. "Ethel succeeded in finding her a partner for every set. And it was kind of Lady Madeline to take such an interest in her, was it not, Perry?"

"Her friendship can do nothing but good for our little niece," he agreed. "Madeline has been a very popular young lady since she first came here. She could have married—and well too—twenty times over in the last three years, I daresay. Sit down, Grace. I'll brush your hair for you."

She sat obediently and closed her eyes as he drew the brush through her tousled hair and continued with the conversation about the ball and the fortunes of their various friends. And he watched her face in the mirror. It was flushed with tiredness.

He did not want to remember it as it had looked earlier that evening when he had finished dancing with Leila and glanced over to where she was standing against the windows with Sandersford. He did not at all want to remember how animated and wildly beautiful she had looked and how very handsome her companion. They had been very deep in passionate conversation, clearly oblivious to everything around them.

He did not want to remember, or how distressed Ethel had looked when he had met her eyes. Or how she had hurried across to them and said something that had perhaps saved them just in time from drawing public attention. Or how Grace had looked at him as he came up to them, her expression bewildered and remorseful. Or how she had gripped his arm afterward and touched his hand and chattered on about trivialities for all of ten minutes, quite unlike the Grace he knew.

He did not want to remember. He gazed at her reflection and tried to see her as a woman ten years his senior, a woman too old for him. A woman more suited to a man of her own age. Like Sandersford. But he could not see that older woman. He could see only Grace, his wife, looking tired and rather lovely with her red gown and her dark hair silky and straight down over her shoulders.

He set the brush down quietly, and she opened her eyes and smiled in the glass. She looked at him questioningly. The obvious next step at such a late hour was to undress and go to bed. But he had never been in her dressing room before when she was disrobing. He had never seen her without either her clothes or her nightgown.

"You will need help with all those buttons," he said. "Let me undo them for you, Grace."

She stood up a little uncertainly and turned her back to him. She bent her head, shaking her hair forward over her shoulders.

"I think someone must have thought up the idea of so many buttons down a lady's back to ensure high employment among female servants," he said. "You could not possibly manage without a lady's maid, could you?"

"And what about gentlemen and their tight coats and elaborate neckcloths?" she said.

"*Touché,*" he said with a laugh, opening the lowest button.

The silk gown was lined so that there was no need of a shift worn beneath it. Peregrine put his hands lightly against her shoulder blades and moved them up to her shoulders. He slid them down to her waist and up under her arms to cup her full and naked breasts. He bent his head to kiss her shoulder.

Grace brought her head back to rest against his shoulder. She held her gown with both hands beneath her breasts. He continued to kiss her one shoulder, to fondle her breasts, to tease her nipples with his fingers until he knew her aroused, though she made no sign.

He wanted her as he had wanted her increasingly since their marriage. He could never have enough of her, of her shapely body, the special fragrance of her, that special something beyond each individual attraction or even the sum of those attractions that made her Grace. And he needed her, as he had come to do more and more each day since he had first taken her as his bride to his home and she had become its quiet mistress and his companion and lover. The thought of life without her was terrifying. Those two nights at inns on the journey to London had been bleak experiences indeed, even though he had known that he would have her again at the end of them.

And now was he to lose her altogether? Was she going to leave him for Sandersford? Was she going to overcome that temptation and stay with him and die a little and be gone from him anyway? Peregrine quelled his panic, felt the desire in his wife's breasts, and turned her in his arms.

And he kissed her hungrily: her eyes, her temples, her ears, her throat, her mouth. He reached out to her with his tongue, something he did not normally do. His love-making usually concentrated on making what he did pleasing to her. But he was losing her, and he was pro-testing his loss, and he was too agonized to be gentle.

"Let's go to bed," he said against her mouth, and stooped down to lift her into his arms, the gown still clutched to her waist. But when he set her down beside the bed, he stripped it from her and sent the rest of her flimsy undergarments to join it on the floor. She closed her eyes as he laid her down. Her color was high. He had never unclothed her before, even between the bed-sheets. He had touched every part of her with his hands and his own body, but he had never removed her night-gown entirely.

Grace lay on the bed, her eyes closed, resisting the urge to reach out for the blankets to pull over her. She waited for Perry to undress himself and come to her. Her desire for him was more of a pain than a pleasure. There was an ache and a throbbing in her throat that could easily have her wailing and clinging to him if he did not come soon.

The evening had been an agony: Gareth and all the turmoil of her encounter with him, all the anger and the uncertainty. Her outrage that he should suggest a re-newal of their love. Her conviction that he was in her past and that her feelings for him could never be rekin-dled. Her fear that perhaps after all he would exert his power over her, that perhaps a man one had once loved, a man one had given oneself to, a man whose child one had borne, could not after all be shrugged off. Her guilt at not having told Perry the truth and the nightmare of seeing that lie grow greater in magnitude with every passing day. Her fear that somehow Gareth would have his own way, as he always had, and force her into loving him again and not loving Perry any longer.

And her terrible fear of losing Perry, of seeing an end to the most peaceful and the loveliest year of her life. If her love for him did not fade, then surely his for her would. There was her memory of watching him at the ball, gay and smiling, dancing and talking with ladies of his own age and younger, teasing them, enjoying himself. And Gareth's words about him, blocked from her memory, large and loud in her memory.

She wanted to be at home. She wanted to be at Reardon Park with Perry in the dull routine of the quiet days that had given her more happiness than she had known in her life. She wanted to be there now and forever. And she probably never would be there again. Even if they went there physically at the end of the Season, it would probably never be home again. They would never be happy there again.

She was glad of the unaccustomed fierceness of Perry's lovemaking. She was glad that when he joined her on the bed he did not spend many minutes caressing her gently with his hands and his mouth, as he usually did. She was glad that he came down directly on top of her, that he came between her thighs and thrust up into her without any prelude. And she was glad that he lay heavy on her, not easing his weight onto his arms as he often did, moving deeply and ungently in her.

She relaxed and lay still for him, as she always did, and kept her eyes closed, and waited for that ache to be quieted. He would take it away for her, she knew. Perry had never failed her. The pain would go away, the throbbing, and her fears would be put at bay again—for a while, anyway.

And he came to her deeply, as he always did, and she held her intense satisfaction private to herself, as she always did, and turned in his arms as he lifted himself to lie beside her and pulled the blankets warmly around her naked body. And she raised her mouth for his drowsy kiss and moved her head to a position of comfort on his arm and closed her eyes.

And she discovered that the ache she had been feeling was not after all a physical thing and had not therefore been eased at all by the beauty of what he had done to her body. The magic was going away faster than she could learn to cope with. Perry could no longer blot out the pain for her.

And why was there pain? When had she allowed herself to come back to life again?

DESPERATION COULD NOT restore anything, Peregrine was thinking, holding his wife to his side, his head resting on the pillow, his eyes closed. His taking of her tonight had been an utterly selfish thing. He had not made love to her. He had used her for pleasure, for reassurance, for forgetfulness. He had wanted her naked beneath him, and he had wanted to bury himself deep in her to assure himself—and her, perhaps—that he owned her, that she was his, that no other man could possibly have any claim on her. Sandersford had possessed her for a few days in the distant past. He had had her for more than a year, and he had married her.

But it was no good. There was no reassurance to be gained from taking his wife as if she were no better than his whore. And there would be no holding her by closing the grip of his possession on her. The point was that she was not a valuable property to be hoarded and hidden away. She was a person whose strength of character he had come to respect even before he had married her. And he could not keep her merely because he owned her according to the law and the church.

Peregrine lay, silent and unhappy and apparently asleep beside his equally quiet and wakeful wife until long after dawn had rendered the candles on the mantelpiece pale and redundant.

GRACE WENT WALKING in St. James's Park after luncheon the next day with Ethel and an exuberant Priscilla. Peregrine had gone to Tattersall's with the Earl of Amberley to look over some horses that the latter was thinking of buying.

"I cannot tell you what a wonderful time I had at the ball last night, Aunt Grace," the girl said, and proceeded to do just that.

Grace and Ethel smiled indulgently and seemed quite satisfied to listen to a monologue that needed no participation on their part except an occasional murmur of assent or appreciation. There was something of an awkwardness between them that the girl's presence helped to mask.

"I danced every set," Priscilla said, "and with some very handsome and amiable gentlemen. Did you see me dance with Lord Eden, Aunt Grace? He is your neighbor, is he not? He is very handsome and very tall. I think I liked Mr. Johnson best, though. He promised that he would call at Cavendish Square and take me walking in the park one afternoon. And did you know that Miss Darnford whispered to me that Uncle Perry was very charming? She looked quite mortified when I told her that he was married to my aunt." She laughed gaily.

"I was gratified to find that Priscilla made friends with several young ladies," Ethel said. "One's first appearance in society is such an important and anxious occasion."

"I do admire Lady Madeline Raine," Priscilla said. "Her manners are so easy, and all the men like her. She was obliging enough to offer to pick me up later this afternoon when she goes driving with Lord Harris. She says that her brother will come too. Lord Eden, that is, not Lord Amberley. I was not presented to him, though he is very handsome too. And very grand. He is a friend of Uncle Perry's, is he not?"

They strolled on, admiring the freshness of the leaves on the trees and the grass around them, gazing in admiration at the flowers.

"Lucinda Stebbins is supposed to arrive today or tomorrow," Priscilla said. "I can scarcely wait. And so many entertainments already engaged for, Aunt Grace. Three balls already in the next month and two soirees, one concert, and one breakfast." She counted them off on her fingers. "And your dinner party. And the invitations have not finished coming in yet. Papa says that we may expect more now that I have been seen in public and after I am presented next week."

"I am even hoping that before the Season is out we will procure vouchers for Almack's," Ethel said. "Though I have cautioned Priscilla not to set her heart on it. If Martin had the title already, of course, things might be different. Though I am not sorry he does not."

"And Lord Sandersford is to invite everyone out to his home outside London some time," Priscilla said. "It is less than a two-hour drive, he says, and the property very lovely. But I do hope he invites some other young people, or it might prove very dull."

"I did not know he owned property in this part of the country," Grace said.

"It belonged to his late wife, I believe," Ethel said hesitantly.

"I have so much to tell Lucinda," Priscilla said, twirling her parasol and performing a few skipping steps that drew an appreciative smile from a passing gentleman and a frown of disapproval from her mother.

And they would be invited, of course, Grace thought. And should she allow Perry to accept? Or should she beg him to make some excuse? Did she wish to avoid all future risk of private conversation with Gareth? Or did she acknowledge the need to face up to her past and settle once and for all her present and her future?

She did not want any change in her life. She wanted everything to remain as it had been for the more than a year since she married Perry. She had been happy in that year, or at least more contented than she had been at any other time in her life. And she loved her cheerful, smiling, gentle husband, with his private depths of learning and intelligence and insight. It was a cautious love, one that she had not expected to last. It was not the consuming passion that she had known with Gareth. But it had brought her undreamed-of contentment. She did not want it to change.

Yet she had the feeling that she must face up to Gareth, that she must find out what had happened to that passion, which had died such a sudden and bitter death. Was it dead forever? Or would it never die? as Gareth himself said. She did not want to find out. She did not want to love Gareth again. She did not want all the turmoil of that kind of passion, and she did not want any emotion that might destroy her love for Perry. But she had the feeling that she must take the risk.

It was useless, anyway, to try to cling to things as they were. Things as they had been, rather. Her relationship with Perry was already changing. She had felt it when they were at Pangam Manor. She had felt it since they had been in London. And she had known it the evening before, when they had been almost like strangers, watching each other cautiously, neither of them quite sure what was happening. But something was happening to them. It was not her imagination.

There was the way he had made love to her the night

before. She had loved it at the time. It had suited her mood and her needs exactly. But since waking and finding Perry already gone from her side, she had felt upset to remember the fierceness of his passion. There had seemed to be none of the awareness of her as a person that had always characterized his lovemaking. In retrospect, he had reminded her somewhat of Gareth, though she had never entered into Gareth's passion quite as she had into Perry's the night before.

Grace shuddered.

"Lady Leila Walsh said last night that she has heard a rumor that the Prince Regent will be at the Duchess of Newcastle's ball next week," Priscilla said. "Do you think it could possibly be true, Mama? Aunt Grace? I should positively die of excitement if it is."

9

$\mathcal{T}$HE NEXT FEW WEEKS WERE SURPRISINGLY TRAN-
quil ones. They were filled with activities, ones
that were largely shared by Peregrine and Grace. They
had both sensed that the honeymoon period of their
marriage was over and that a more difficult period, even
possibly a disastrous one, was ahead for them. And both
resisted the change and clung desperately to the quiet
and affectionate closeness they had shared for more
than a year.

They attended the opera together and heard the famous Madame Catalani in *Atalida*. They attended the
Hanover Square Rooms one evening and listened to the
concert there in company with a large gathering that
included four of the royal dukes and Princess Alexandra, mother of the Princess of Wales. They watched a
splendid and colorful military review in the park one
afternoon and attended St. Paul's together for the Easter
services. They visited an exhibition of paintings at Som-
erset House and another of paintings of famous cities at
the Panorama. They visited the Tower again and spent a
full afternoon in the armory there.

They attended some of the quieter evening entertainments as well as the balls and routs that attracted large
squeezes. They spent a few evenings at Mrs. Eunice Borden's salon, meeting and conversing with the writers and

poets and political figures with whom she liked to surround herself. She was a small, rather heavyset, curly-haired widow, somewhat younger than Grace, a particular friend of the Earl of Amberley. Indeed, Grace began to wonder with some curiosity if perhaps she was his mistress. His lordship was always there when they were, and he never left before them, however late they lingered.

Somehow, although they attended several of the more glittering entertainments of the *ton*, they avoided any more uncomfortable evenings like that of the first ball. And yet they both knew that they were living through an interval that could not last. And they both knew that they could not prolong it indefinitely. Although they never spoke to each other of their deepest desires, each wanted to go home, away from London, away from all those forces that seemed to be conspiring against their happiness. And yet each silently consented to stay.

And even in the midst of the tranquillity, there were still signs of strain. They met Lord Sandersford on more than one occasion, though Grace contrived never to be alone with him. At the opera one evening she declined his offer to take her into the corridor for some fresh air between acts, although he had looked to Peregrine for permission and had received a nod in return. And she sat next to Perry for the rest of the performance, their arms not quite touching, conversation between them dead, both of them taut with stress, while Martin and Ethel, Priscilla and Mr. Johnson laughed and exchanged comments on either side of them.

And there was the morning when they called at Cavendish Square to find Priscilla in mingled elation and despair. Four young ladies and three young gentlemen had arranged an expedition to Kew Gardens for the afternoon.

"But Lucinda declares that she will not go as she has no particular beau," Priscilla said, "though I have assured her that Mr. Johnson will be quite delighted to offer his free arm to her. It really does not signify that the numbers are not quite even."

"And yet," her mother said, "you must imagine how you would feel, Priscilla, if it were you without an escort."

"I would die," Priscilla assured the room at large.

Peregrine laughed. "If you think that Miss Stebbins would not die an equally horrid death to be escorted by an old married uncle of yours, Priscilla," he said, "perhaps I could make up the numbers. Would you mind, Grace? We have no other plans for this afternoon, have we?"

Grace encouraged the outing. It was just like Perry to step in with such cheerful kindness to save a poor girl from embarrassment. She did not even mind when he arrived home late in the afternoon and came directly to her sitting room to throw himself rather inelegantly into a comfortable chair so that he might tell her all about the expedition. It seemed that he had undoubtedly made a mortal enemy of Mr. Francis Hartwell, who had been forced to escort Miss Stebbins during the whole afternoon because Lady Leila Walsh had laid claim to Peregrine's arm. He was laughing by the time he finished.

"Do you think I might get called out onto a frosty heath at dawn, Grace?" he asked. "It sounds a deuced uncomfortable prospect to me."

"I don't think there are any frosty heaths left at this time of year, Perry," she answered, "even at dawn. I would say you are safe."

"Thank heaven for a wife's common sense," he said, laughing again. "Ah, you have finished embroidering that sprig of flowers, Grace, and I looked forward to watching you do it. What a shame. Kew had nothing to compare with it in beauty, you know."

"Silly," she said, holding the cloth up nevertheless so that he might see better the work she had done during the afternoon.

And there was that uneasiness in her again. It was not jealousy. She was not jealous of the young and vital Lady Leila, not suspicious of her husband, not accusing in any way. Only left with a feeling that there was perhaps more rightness in Perry's being with her and with those other young people than there was in his being with his own wife. And did he realize it too? Or would he come to do so soon?

Their own dinner and evening party were set for a day one week ahead of Lord Sandersford's two-day house party in the country. They had invited him—how could they not without admitting to each other an awareness of a potentially explosive situation they had never referred to? And they had invited all their acquaintances from both their homes as well as Peregrine's mother and aunt and cousin, who had arrived from Scotland a couple of days before, and a few other young people to make the gathering merrier.

Grace had been apprehensive about meeting her mother-in-law, but when they called upon her in Charles Street the day before their party, they received a gracious welcome. Peregrine's mother offered a cheek for his kiss and then hugged him. She stretched out both hands to Grace, looked her up and down, declared that she was in good looks, and then hugged her too. Perry winked at her over his mother's head.

Mrs. Campbell, too, Peregrine's aunt, greeted her with affectionate courtesy and proceeded to tell her that of course she had still not forgiven young Perry for imitating her late husband's Scottish accent so mercilessly during their last visit into England that a footman had burst into laughter and slopped a soup tureen over the table-cloth and almost got himself dismissed.

"I protest, Aunt," Peregrine said, laughing. "I could not have been above fourteen at the time. Ah cuid nae be sae ill-mannered noo, ye ken." He dodged her flying hand and caught her around the waist in order to plant a smacking kiss on her cheek.

"Grace, my dear," Mrs. Campbell said, "how do you endure it? You must be a saint, for sure."

They all laughed, and Grace felt accepted as one of the family.

And throughout the five-course dinner at which she presided the next evening, she continued to hug to herself that warm feeling of belonging. She looked down the length of the table to where Peregrine sat, entertaining his mother on his right and Ethel on his left, and felt again how wonderful it was to be a married lady with a definite place in society. And she marveled anew at how she could have lived for so many years at the rectory in a type of suspended animation. Then she caught the rather mocking eye of Gareth, seated halfway down the table.

And she knew she would not be able to avoid him for the whole evening. A chill of something like fear set her to refusing her favorite dessert and stumbling in her conversation with Mr. Stebbins beside her.

They had thought that perhaps the younger people would wish to dance. But no one suggested it. They seemed content for a while to entertain themselves at one end of the long drawing room by playing the pianoforte and singing. And then they formed two teams for charades and played with a great deal of shrieking and laughter. Some of the older people wandered over to watch while others stayed closer to the fire and talked.

Peregrine had been drawn into the game in order to make up even numbers and was having so much success that he was being loudly accused of cheating by the opposing team. Grace sat behind the teapot, talking to Lady Amberley and her mother-in-law until both ladies smiled at an unusually merry burst of laughter from the opposite end of the room and strolled across to see what was happening. Grace was not at all surprised when Lord Sandersford took their place almost immediately.

"There is something quite strange about this situation, Grace," he said. "The bulk of your guests amusing themselves with great energy at the other end of the room while you sit here behind the teapot in demure domesticity. The Grace I knew would have been in the very center of that activity."

"The Grace you knew was considerably younger, Gareth," she said. "Would it not look extremely peculiar for a matron of my age to be romping with the very young?"

"And yet your husband does," he said quietly.

Grace said nothing. She stacked the cups more neatly on the tray beside her.

"I could do violence, Grace," he said. "I want to shake you out of your torpor."

"You are quite unrealistic," she said. "You expect me to be as I was fifteen years ago. I was only a little past twenty then. I am close to forty now. I cannot stay a girl forever."

"Nonsense," he said. "Age has nothing to do with the question. You were alive then. You are half-dead now. You have been avoiding me, Grace. Are you afraid of me?"

"Of course I am not," she said, her eyes dropping from his momentarily. "But you cannot expect me to seek you out either, Gareth. I am married to Perry."

His lips tightened. "I might end up doing murder, you know," he said. "Look at him, Grace. Look at the man to whom you insist on remaining loyal. He is a boy. A thoughtless, laughing, undoubtedly empty-headed boy. Though I will grant you, a tolerably pretty one. And you call him husband? I will not accept it. I give you due warning that my patience is running out. You cannot tell me that you feel any attachment to him beyond some gratitude, perhaps. He did rescue you, I grant, after Paul died, though you might have come to me if only you had known that I was widowed and back home."

Grace's silence was stony.

"He was at Kew with Lady Leila Walsh last week," he said. "Did you know? Did he remember to tell you? Oh, with a few other young people as well to add some respectability. But very much with her, nonetheless. Do you not know that she means to have him, Grace, and that he has every intention of being had? If it is not already an accomplished fact, that is. Are you blind, or do you refuse to see?"

"And do you mean to have me, Gareth?" she said in some anger. "And do you believe that I have every intention of being had?"

"No," he said, "to the second half of what you said. You are a coward, Grace. You are afraid to examine the state of your own heart and act on what you find there. Are you afraid of the scandal? Are you afraid your Peregrine will divorce you? It is very unlikely, I do assure you. He will be happy to let you go your way while he goes his. And I do not care that much"—he snapped his fingers—"whether we can be legally wed or not when you come to me. We belong together. We will be married in all ways that matter."

"Yes," she said, "I know that you do not set much store by marriage, Gareth."

He laughed and tried to take her hand, but she moved

it away in order to adjust the angle of the teapot. She was finding his presence suffocating again. She was very aware of him, as she always had been—of his broad shoulders and his long-fingered hands, his dark hair and handsome face. She was aware and she was frightened. She could feel the pull of his power over her, but did not know the nature of that power. Did she still love him? Or did she hate him? Was she afraid of him? Or was it herself she feared?

"Sometimes," he said, "and with great relief, I see flashes of the old Grace. There was pure spite in those last words, my dear. You are still angry over my desertion, are you not?"

"My son lived the whole of his life without a father," she said.

"Well," he said, "I was not responsible for his early death, Grace."

"And the whole of his life as a bastard."

"I am sure your family was far too well-bred ever to use that word in his hearing," he said.

"But it was used in my hearing," she said. "And it was used by a few to comfort me after he died. I must be relieved, it seemed, to know that my son would not grow up to know himself a bastard."

"Come on," he said, his voice grim at last, "tell me more. This has to all come out before we can get anywhere, you and I. I think we may even come to blows before it is all over. But, yes, Grace, I mean to have you. And you will have me. Because at the bottom of your anger is your love for me. So come on. Keep talking."

"They put the label on the wrong person," Grace said. "It was his father who was the bastard. And who *is* a bastard. You are trying to destroy my life all over again, Gareth. I have been happy for more than a year. Happy!

But you must kill that happiness. I hate you now as I have hated you for years."

He smiled. But his eyes were burning down into hers. "This is better," he said. "Now we are approaching the truth. We are not there yet, but we are on the way. Keep talking."

"No!" Grace picked up the teapot with hands that were not quite steady and poured some into her empty cup. "Not again, Gareth. I am not going to forget my surroundings again as I did in that ballroom. No." She drew a few steadying breaths. "Do tell me about your late wife's property, the one you have invited us to next week. Is it large?"

"It is large enough," he said, "for us to find some privacy, Grace. We will continue this, ah, discussion there, perhaps even conclude it. We will have everything out in the open that has been festering in you for years. You will have the chance to strike at me with your fists or your fingernails if you wish. But the moment cannot be avoided. I promise you that. Now, Lady Lampman, was there anything else you wished to know about my property?"

"No, I thank you, my lord," she said. "You have been most specific."

She met Peregrine's eyes across the room and did not even try to quell the ache inside her. She knew now that it would not go away and that she could no longer expect Perry to take it away for her.

LORD SANDERSFORD'S HOUSE at Hammersmith overlooked the river and was so beautiful, Ethel declared, that it was amazing that his lordship had not made it his principal seat. But the viscount merely smiled and explained that home is something one feels in one's blood and heart and has nothing necessarily to do with obvious beauty.

His town guests had been invited to stay overnight. Ethel, Martin, and Priscilla were among this number, as were the Stebbinses and two male cousins of his late wife's. And, of course, Grace and Peregrine.

Peregrine knew as well as Grace did why they were there, that these two days in the country somehow represented a crisis in their marriage. He had known it from the moment their invitation had arrived, and even before that probably. And he had seen it very clearly at his own home the week before. He had expected Sandersford to contrive to have a private word with his wife there. And he had expected that same look of intensity in their faces he had seen at the ball.

He had expected too that Grace would not be happy afterward, that she would be feeling guilt and uncertainty. The crisis was coming, something far more powerful than had yet happened, and something that could not be averted. Oh, yes, it probably could be prevented, Peregrine granted. If he chose to assert his masculinity, his rights as a husband, there were probably several courses he could take to protect what was his own. He could take his wife home and keep her there. A very simple solution. Or he could confront her with his knowledge, forbid her to speak alone with Sandersford ever again. And he had no doubt that Grace would obey him. Perhaps she would even be relieved to have all the stress of the situation lifted from her own shoulders.

But he could not take either of those courses. He could only take the apparently unmanly course of staying quiet, of leaving his wife free to find out and to live her own destiny. Perhaps it was only in that week of his intense unhappiness that Peregrine realized fully what his feelings for his wife really were. And it was only in the same time period that he realized fully the nature of love. The terrifying nature. For love cannot take anything for itself. It can only give and leave itself wide open and defenseless against emptiness and pain and rejection.

And so Peregrine took his wife to Hammersmith with no comment upon the white, set face that had been hers for all of the previous week or on her eyes, which held desperately to their calmness during the carriage ride, in which they were accompanied by Priscilla and Lucinda Stebbins.

And in Hammersmith he allowed Grace to stay close to him without in any way following her around. He let her take his arm and hold to it throughout the tour of the house given by their host, knowing that that same host was far too skilled a man to allow her to stay there at his side for the whole of the rest of the day and the morning of the next.

They stopped in the gallery that overlooked the river and became so absorbed in examining the rare collection of Chinese porcelain there that they were scarcely aware of the glorious view from the window that had the other guests exclaiming in delight. And in the music room they admired all the various musical instruments collected by Lord Sandersford's mother-in-law.

"It is as well that we do not own these things, Perry," Grace said, "or I would spend half your fortune on music lessons so that I could play them all."

"And I would spend the other half so that I could play them too," he said. "Then, with no fortune left, Grace, we could wander the countryside, like the minstrels of old, earning our daily bread with our music."

"That sounds good," she said. "I will carry the flute, Perry, and you can load the pianoforte on your back."

They both laughed. "Perhaps it is as well we do not own them," he said.

And they walked in the gardens and down by the river and agreed with the other guests that they were fortunate indeed to have been granted such a gloriously warm and sunny day for their visit after more than a week of indifferent weather. They stood and watched as two of the cousins rowed Priscilla and Miss Stebbins out on the water, and agreed that they were quite content to keep their feet on firm—and dry—ground.

They sat side by side on the terrace to take tea and listened as Lord Sandersford, at his most charming, entertained his guests with amusing anecdotes of military life. And Peregrine felt Grace's arm brush his during a gust of laughter over one of the stories, and smiled down at her. Soon after, all the guests retired to their rooms to rest for a while and to get ready for dinner and the evening party, to which several of the neighboring families had been invited.

It would be that evening, Peregrine thought as he stood in his dressing room that opened off one side of the bedchamber he was to share with Grace. He buttoned up his shirt slowly and smoothed out the lace at the cuffs so that it covered his hands to the knuckles. There was to be dancing in the lower drawing room, Sandersford had announced, to accommodate the young people who had been invited. And doubtless the doors onto the terrace would be kept open on such a warm evening.

It would be that evening. He was powerless to prevent it, or rather, he had chosen to be powerless. He must only watch to see that the confrontation when it came was not entirely against Grace's will. He knew that she did not want it, that she resisted the moment. He knew also that she did want it, that she recognized its inevitability. But even so, the moment must not be forced on her against her will. Against that at least he could and would protect her.

LUCINDA STEBBINS HAD not taken well during the first weeks of the Season. A little overplump for most tastes and with hair that tended to be more yellow than blond and that she wore in an unbecoming style with masses of tight ringlets, she could not lay claim to any great prettiness. And her tendency to become tongue-tied or giggly in company and to blush in uneven patches of red did not add to her attractions.

Yet she was an innocent and sweet-natured girl, Grace knew, and one whom Perry had very kindly taken under his wing. He sat next to the girl at dinner and had her giggling with amusement rather than embarrassment before the end of the first course. And he danced the first country dance with her in Gareth's large lower drawing room.

Grace was happy to see that one of the cousins led her into the second dance and lingered to converse with her afterward. He was a particularly small and thin young man. It was rather unfortunate perhaps that he tried to overcome these deficiencies by padding out the shoulders of his coat and the calves of his legs and by wearing a lavender and yellow striped waistcoat and extremely high shirt points, and by putting a quizzing glass to frequent and absurdly languid use. Grace had sat next to him at dinner and had found him to be a perfectly sensible young man once she had penetrated beyond the bored superficiality of his opening remarks.

Priscilla, of course, was preening herself before the obvious admiration of the other cousin and two tolerably handsome and eligible neighbors. She had taken well with the *ton* and was clearly enjoying every moment of her triumph.

"Of course," Ethel was saying to Grace and Mrs. Stebbins, "Priscilla will not even be eighteen for another five weeks. We have no great wish for her to fix her choice this year. She is far too young to marry. We merely wish for her to gain experience."

"Lucinda will doubtless be considering some of her offers this year," Mrs. Stebbins said, "since it is doubtful that Mr. Stebbins will consent to bringing us here for another Season. He is so hopelessly rustic, Lady Lampman. Of course, we wish to choose an eligible husband for her. We do not have to accept the first offer she receives."

It was strange, Grace thought, that she had never been brought to London for a Season. She could not now remember if there had even been any question of her coming. She certainly could not recall craving any such thing. If she had, doubtless she would have had her way. In those days her father had been quite unable to deny her anything she had set her heart on.

But she had been in love with Gareth by the time she reached the age to make her come-out. And planning to marry him and live happily ever after with him. They were to travel together, visit all the fashionable cities of Europe together. There had been no need of a come-out Season.

She had thought herself very strong-willed and independent, Grace thought now, watching the dancers perform a quadrille and smiling at her husband, who was with a flushed little girl who could not be a day older than sixteen. And yet she must have been extraordinarily like a puppet on a string. Gareth's puppet. She had been twenty-one years old when he went away. They had been talking of marriage for four years. Had he ever really intended to marry her? The idea that perhaps he had not was a novel one. But not by any means an impossible one.

Gareth had always had his way. They had quarreled and fought, sometimes quite physically, but she could not now recall any important matter on which she had won. Most notably, he had refused to marry her before going away, after giving her any number of very good reasons for not doing so. At the same time he had overcome her objections to their lying together before he went. And she had lain with him with a stubborn and foolish disregard of the consequences and conceived his child.

Far from being the strong and determined girl that she had always thought herself, she had in fact been a weakling. And very, very foolish.

"It was at just such a party that I first met Martin," Ethel was saying. "I did not like him at first because he rarely smiled. I thought him haughty. But it is amazing how different a person can seem once one makes the effort to get to know him well. Martin is really a man of great sensibility, and he is frequently unsure of himself."

Mrs. Stebbins tittered. "Papa chose Mr. Stebbins for me," she said, "because he had a modest fortune and we had an ancient name to uphold. Papa's great-grandfather was Baron March, Lady Lampman. Unfortunately, his grandfather was a seventh son. I do think it important for fortune and good family to mingle. Provided that the fortune has not been made in vulgar trade, of course."

Her father should have brought her to town, Grace thought. He should have insisted that she make her come-out, be presented at court, mingle with the *ton,* meet other young ladies of her own age and other eligible young gentlemen. Perhaps she would have grown up, acquired a degree of common sense long before she had. Perhaps she would have seen Gareth more clearly if she could have compared him to others. Perhaps she would have understood his selfishness sooner.

But would it have made any difference? she wondered. She had been a headstrong girl. Doubtless she would have fought her father every step of the way and closed her eyes and her mind to any experiences that might have saved her from her own future. She had been in love and hopelessly blind. Jeremy, or his older brother or sister, might well have been born a few years earlier if her father had tried to separate her from Gareth.

But had she ever completely shaken off the power Gareth had over her, even though her eyes were now opened? Would she ever do so? She watched him conclude a conversation with a small group of men at the other side of the drawing room and begin to make her way toward her. She knew that it was toward her he came. She knew that this whole party had been planned with her in mind, and especially this evening's entertainment. Gareth was bound on getting her alone, and he would do so. Partly because Gareth always got what he wanted. And partly because she would not be able to resist finding out what the end of their association was to be. If it was the end that was now coming and not a new beginning. One never knew when it was Gareth with whom one dealt.

Ethel leaned toward her suddenly and whispered for Grace's ears only. "It is a warm night, Grace," she said, "and will doubtless be very pleasant outside. You may say that you and I have just agreed to stroll on the terrace if you wish."

Grace looked at her, startled. But she had not misunderstood. Ethel was flushed and embarrassed, not quite meeting her sister-in-law's eyes.

"Only if you wish," Ethel said. "I do not know how you feel. I never did know. But I have liked you this time. And Perry. I like Perry." She turned back to reply to a remark made by Mrs. Stebbins.

"Not dancing, Lady Lampman?" Lord Sandersford said, bowing in front of her chair and including the other two ladies in his smile. "I grant you that my drawing room is nothing in comparison with the ballrooms you have danced in during the last weeks, but you are used to country living."

"I have danced once with Perry," Grace said.

"And you must dance the next with me," he said, stretching out a hand for hers. "As your host, ma'am, I must insist on it." His dark eyes looked mockingly down into hers.

"Such a distinguished company, my lord," Mrs. Stebbins said.

He bowed his acknowledgment of the compliment while Grace could feel Ethel looking at her. She put her hand in Lord Sandersford's and rose to her feet.

"Thank you, my lord," she said.

"And now, Grace," he said, having maneuvered her with consummate skill across the room to the opened French doors, stopping on the way to smile and exchange a few words with several of his other guests, "it is time for you and me to disappear for a while. Is it not?"

"Yes, Gareth," she said, looking steadily at him, "I think it is."

He looked at her appreciatively. "You always had the courage to meet a challenge face-to-face," he said. "I am glad you do not feel it necessary to simper and protest." He offered her his arm. "Shall we take a turn on the terrace, ma'am? It is, as you just remarked, a warm evening."

Grace took his arm and walked with him into the darkness of the night.

Peregrine, withdrawing his eyes from the doors, in-

formed Miss Keating with a grin that if she expected
him to stop stumbling in his steps, she must find somewhere else to fix her very blue eyes than on his face.

Miss Keating giggled, blushed, asked if Sir Peregrine
really thought her eyes blue, not merely a nondescript
gray, and proceeded to gaze at him with even wider
eyes.

10

I DO NOT WISH TO GO OFF THE TERRACE," GRACE SAID as Lord Sandersford led her across it, ignoring the two older gentlemen who were in conversation farther along. "It would not be right."

"We will walk down by the river," he said. "We have a great deal to say to each other, Grace, and if your mood of last week prevails, we may well wish to raise our voices and even our fists. The terrace is altogether too public."

Grace said no more but allowed herself to be led in silence down over the darkened lawn, past shrubberies and flower beds, to the water's edge. Yet again he was having his way, she reflected bitterly. But there was sense in what he said.

"Now," he said finally, releasing her arm and turning to face her, "we are alone, Grace. No one is watching or listening. Neither of us has any need of a mask. Let us speak plainly, then. I want you. And I do not speak of a clandestine affair behind the esteemed Peregrine's back, though I have no doubt it would be an easy matter to cuckold him. I want you to leave him, provoke a divorce if you will so that we may marry. But if we cannot do so, then to hell with marriage. We will live openly as man and wife and dare the world to censure us."

"You have not changed at all, Gareth," she said. "You

are as selfish now as you were as a boy. You want! That is all that matters, is it not? You do not know or care what I want."

"Tell me, then," he said. "But you must be honest, Grace. You will not get away with saying what you think you ought. The truth! What is it you want?"

"I want things to remain as they are," she said. "As they were before I met you again, Gareth. I don't want change. I was happy."

"Things cannot remain as they were," he said. "'Were' is past tense, Grace. You have met me again. And you 'were' happy. You are not now. Are you?"

"No," she said.

"Then something has to change," he said. "But you cannot go back, Grace. We can never go back. Only forward. You are unhappy because you know yourself married to the wrong man. You are unhappy because you have come alive again after fifteen years. And you know that you still love me. And always will. Tell the truth now."

"How can I love you?" she said. "How can I love you, Gareth? I stopped loving you a lifetime ago. I hate you. No, not that. I am indifferent to you."

His face was angry, she saw in the moonlight. "Liar!" he said. "We will have the truth spoken, Grace. The truth at last. You hate me, perhaps. I will accept that. You are not indifferent to me."

"How could you do it," she cried suddenly, her eyes kindling. "How could you do it, Gareth? You knew you were my whole world. You knew you had ruined me, that I could hope for no other husband. And you knew I was with child. You knew. And you had said that you loved me. Many times. And you expect me now not to hate you?"

"No," he said. His eyes were burning into hers. "No, I expect your hatred, Grace. Tell me more."

"I carried him alone," she said. "I bore him alone. I had a hard time giving birth to him, and there was no one at the end of it all to rejoice with me. You were not there, Gareth, when my son was born. You were married to your heiress."

"Yes," he said.

"He was a bastard," she said. "Jeremy was a bastard. My father never looked at him, yours never acknowledged him. He was a nonperson. A beautiful, innocent child. He was your son, Gareth. Your son! You never cared about his existence. Or his death. Or about me. I hate you. I hate you!" She raised both fists and pummeled at his chest.

He did not defend himself. She was surprised to see him looking exultant when she glanced up, distraught, into his face.

"Now we are getting somewhere," he said when she finally stopped punching, the sides of her fists resting against his chest. And he took her by the upper arms and lowered his head and kissed her.

She could have pulled back. It was several moments before he moved his hands from her arms and encircled her with his own. But she did not pull back. He was so very unmistakably Gareth, though she had not been in his embrace for fifteen years, though he had been little more than a boy then and was now a powerful man. His embrace was all confident demand, his mouth pressed to hers with a fierce urgency, his hands boldly exploring her body. There was the familiar taste of him, and smell of him, that could only be Gareth.

She felt her knees weaken as she sagged against him. She felt fear at the evidence of his arousal, dread at the seeming inevitability of her own response. She fought to think of something else. Someone else. Perry.

"Grace," he whispered against her mouth, "my

sweet love, I want you. God, how I want you! Lie with me here. Now. Follow your heart. Give me your answer here with your body. You will never be sorry. I swear it."

She pushed against him and felt as if her heart would pound through her ribs and burst from her body. "Gareth," she said, "I do not love you. I do not want you. I hate you."

"Yes," he said fiercely, "I did a dastardly thing to you, Grace. I have no defense. I knowingly deserted you for wealth. And our child. And I was too ashamed to seek you out afterward. But I never stopped loving you. I cannot go back and amend the past. I wish I could, but I cannot. I can offer you only the future and my devotion for the rest of our lives."

"And yet," she said, "you would destroy me again. You know that I am married. You know that I have been happy. And you know that I want none of you. And yet you persist in forcing yourself on me."

"That is unfair," he said quietly. "You know why you were invited out to Hammersmith, Grace. Yet you did not refuse the invitation. You know why you were brought out here tonight. Yet you came freely. And you did not fight my kiss a moment ago. You are afraid to admit the truth."

"No," she said. "The truth is that you are evil, Gareth, that you cannot resist the urge to try to seduce me again. I want none of you. I want you to leave me alone."

He laughed softly. "Grace," he said, "you are such a coward. You used not to be. Is your marriage worth fighting for?"

"Yes, it is!" she cried.

"Why?" he asked. "What is good about it?"

"We are friends," she said. "We do things together. We are content together."

"Friends! Content," he said mockingly. "What a yawn, Grace. Is he good in bed?"

"What!" Her eyes snapped to his, shocked.

"Is he good?" he asked. "Does he satisfy you? Does he have you often? Ever? Or is this just a very maternal sort of relationship for you, Grace?" His eyes were mocking. "I cannot imagine the laughing boy being particularly skilled in sexual passion. And you need passion, Grace. I know. I have had you, remember?"

"You know nothing of my marriage," she said. "Nothing. It is the most valuable thing in my life. Yes, it is worth fighting for."

"And yet," he said, "you are out here arguing the matter with me. Happily married ladies are not tempted by former lovers, Grace. Why did you come?"

"I don't know," she said after a pause. She swallowed. "I don't know."

"I do," he said. "You love me, Grace. You don't love the boy. You merely feel sorry for him. You need not, you know. He will be quite happy to be released to the company of the sweet young creatures he favors."

"I love Perry!" she protested.

"So!" He laughed gently. "Perhaps I should kill him, Grace. Would you like me to play jealous lover? I notice that he does not do so. And I would be very surprised to have a glove slapped in my face by Sir Peregrine Lampman. I doubt that his knees would keep from knocking together as he did so."

"I hate you, Gareth," she said. "I hate you. I only wish I could be indifferent. You were right to say that I am not. I find that old wounds have not healed, after all. They are raw and festering again. But there is no love in me for you. None! We have talked. It is what you wished and what I felt necessary. Well, it has been done. And it is finished now. I want you to leave me alone."

"Never," he said. "Not until you can tell me that you have no feelings for me whatsoever. And I know that day will never come, Grace. I love you, and I mean to have you."

"No," she said, "you do not love me, Gareth. If you loved me, you would wish for my happiness. You would leave me alone with Perry."

"Ah," he said, "but you said you are content with him, Grace. Or *were*, rather. Contentment is not happiness, or the past tense the present. You will be happy with me one day. I promise you that."

"So," she said unhappily, "nothing has been settled. I have wasted my time coming out here with you. I am still not free of you, am I?"

"Grace," he said, passing a hand beneath her chin, "you never will be, my love. The sooner you realize that, the sooner your past contentment can give place to present and future happiness. No, nothing has been settled. You will be seeing more of me."

She gazed at him in despair. "I thought my punishment was at an end," she said. "Now I see that even in this life I cannot escape it for long."

He laughed. "A strange punishment," he said, "to give in to your own love and to come to the arms of the man who loves you."

Grace turned without another word and began to stride back toward the house.

Lord Sandersford followed silently some distance behind.

PEREGRINE BECAME AWARE that Lord Sandersford had returned to the house as he stood drinking lemonade with Priscilla and a small group of the younger people. But several minutes of anxious watching and much smiling and teasing did not bring Grace into his view. At last, when the dancing had resumed after a break, he left the drawing room as unobtrusively as he could and went upstairs to their room.

At first he thought she was not there. The candles that were burning on the mantelpiece showed him an empty bedchamber and a darkened dressing room at either side. But he looked into Grace's dressing room anyway. She was sitting in the darkness, facing away from him.

"Grace?" he said softly, and moved across the room to stand behind her and lay a gentle hand against the back of her neck.

Apart from dropping her head forward, she made no response.

"Do you need to be alone?" he asked. "Shall I go away?"

"Perry," she said. Her voice had the weariness of years in it. "Lord Sandersford is Gareth. Jeremy's father. He did not die, and I knew it all the time. I lied to you."

"Yes," he said.

"You knew?" Her hands were twisting in her lap, he could see. "And you have not confronted me? You have not thrown me out?"

"Thrown you out?" he said. "You are my wife, Grace."

"My former lover is still alive," she said. "You would not have married me if you had known that, would you?"

"What difference would it have made?" he asked.

She put up her hands to cover her face. "I have been outside with him tonight," she said. "You must have seen us go. He did not force me to go, Perry. I went freely right down beside the river with him. I think we must have been gone for half an hour. He wants me to go away with him."

He lifted his hand away from her neck. "Yes," he said. "And are you going, Grace?"

She shuddered. "Perhaps you will wish me to," she said. "I have dishonored you, Perry. I have not been unfaithful to you, but I have done what I have just said. And I listened to him."

"Grace." He moved around to stand in front of her and squatted down on his haunches. "I can understand that seeing him again after all these years has put a severe strain on your emotions. I can understand that perhaps your feelings for him have been revived. I know that perhaps now you feel trapped in a marriage that was made largely for convenience. But I know you better than you seem to think. I know that you have not been unfaithful to me without your telling me so. And I know that if you leave me, you will not do so lightly and you will tell me quite openly what you must do. You have not dishonored me. I will not have you feeling the burden of that guilt."

She was rocking back and forth, her hands still spread over her face.

"Do you love him still?" he asked, his voice tense despite his efforts to remain calm. "Do you wish to go with him, Grace?"

"I want to stay with you," she said, her voice so full of misery that his sense of relief was short-lived. "I want to stay married to you, Perry."

"Then you shall do so," he said, reaching out a hand to cover one of hers.

But she drew back from him. "Perry," she cried, "he kissed me. He held me and he kissed me, and I did not fight him off, though I would not lie with him as he wished me to do. I let him kiss me."

Peregrine swallowed awkwardly. "Are you quite sure you wish to stay with me?" he asked.

"Yes!" Her voice was fierce, though she still did not take her hands from her face. "I want to stay. But you surely cannot wish me to, Perry."

"You are my wife, Grace," he said. "You will stay with me if you wish to do so."

"Perry." She dropped her hands and looked up at him finally, though their faces were mere shadows in the darkness. "I hate him. I did not think I would after so long. I would have expected to feel nothing at all. But I hate him as if it all happened yesterday."

He nodded sadly and got to his feet. He held out a hand for hers. "Come on," he said, "let's go out of this darkness."

But she shrank from his hand. "No," she said, "don't touch me, Perry. Not yet."

Because she was feeling guilty and soiled. Soiled by Gareth's touch. Soiled more by her own moral weakness in going down to the river with him quite freely and in allowing him to plead with her to go away with him, and in allowing herself to remember and to feel a fearful sort of attraction to him again, and in allowing him to kiss her and hold her intimately and explore her with his hands as if he were still her lover. Because she had not washed herself and scrubbed herself and made herself clean for Perry. And because she knew again, seeing him stand there before her, that he was the very best thing that had ever happened in her life past or present, excepting only Jeremy. And she had nothing good to offer him in return. Not youth or beauty or vivacity. Not honor. And not even total fidelity since their marriage.

She could not put her hand in his. Not yet.

His hand closed on itself and dropped to his side. He stood before her for several moments as if he would say something. Then he strode from the dressing room and from the bedchamber.

"You forgot that Sandersford was to show us the stables this morning?" Martin asked Peregrine when he joined him in the morning room the next day.

"No." Peregrine looked over the top of the morning paper and smiled. "No, I did not forget."

"Well," Martin said, lowering himself into the chair next to Peregrine's, "you did not miss much. The stables themselves are impressive, but not many horses are kept here since it is not Sandersford's principal seat."

Peregrine closed the paper and set it down on the table at his elbow.

"Grace is well?" Martin asked. "I have not seen her this morning."

"Yes, she is well," Peregrine said. "Just tired after a busy day, I imagine."

Martin looked at his brother-in-law, looked away, coughed, and picked up the discarded paper. He looked uneasily to the door to see if anyone else was about to enter. "I can't understand why you will allow it," he said at last. "It's none of my business, of course."

"No," Peregrine said, not deeming it necessary to ask his brother-in-law to clarify what he was talking about, "but you are her brother. I understand your concern."

"You know who he is, of course?" Martin said. He did not wait for an answer. "He was always a scoundrel, with too many good looks and too much charm for his own good. One of the takers of this world. And Grace could never see it. She was besotted."

"She is not an impressionable girl any longer," Peregrine said.

"Well," Martin said, "you will be fortunate if he doesn't take her from you as he took her from her family when she was a girl. I would look to it if I were you. Not that it is my business how you choose to deal with your own wife, of course. This is deuced awkward. I should have kept my mouth shut."

"No," Peregrine said, "I am not offended. You love Grace, I see, and I can only honor you for that. Perhaps I do not handle matters as other men would. Perhaps my methods are entirely wrong. But I will tell you this, Martin: I love Grace, too, and if you will pardon my saying so, I will add that I love her many times more than any brother possibly could. She is my wife, you see. And together she and I will work out this situation."

Martin coughed again. "Sorry to have mentioned it," he said. "I thought it just possible that you did not know who he is or that you hadn't noticed what has been going on."

Peregrine smiled. "You must be pleased with Priscilla's success," he said. "And what about your son? Because I have never met him, I sometimes forget that I even have a nephew as well as a niece."

"Young fool," Martin said fondly. "He is just like we all were at his age, I suppose. Pursuing pleasure and getting into scrapes are of far more importance than studying and making an educated man of himself."

ETHEL HAD LINKED her arm through Grace's and drawn her out from the breakfast room onto the terrace. "The sky is awfully heavy," she said. "I do hope it is not going to rain again. Yesterday it seemed that the weather was going to change for the better."

"Yes," Grace said. "But I always console myself for bad weather with the thought that we would not have such very green grass and such lovely flowers if we did not also have so much rain."

"Well," Ethel said, "I hope at least that it will hold off until we have returned to town this afternoon."

"Yes," Grace agreed.

"Grace," Ethel said on a rush, "I am very concerned about you. It is none of my business, of course."

"That is what you used to say," Grace said with the shadow of a smile, "and I used to agree with you whole-heartedly. I was a horrid girl, was I not? I can scarce believe that that person I remember was me."

"He was a very attractive man," Ethel said. "I used to think secretly that it was quite understandable that you would not listen to reason. And now, of course, he is even more attractive. But, oh, Grace, he has not changed."

"No," Grace said, "he has not. But I have, Ethel. And you need not worry about me. Or about Perry. You like Perry, don't you?"

"I was shocked when I first saw him, I must confess," Ethel said. "He looked so very young and was so very youthful in his manner. But I think you have made a fortunate match, Grace. Both Martin and I are very fond of him. And Priscilla, of course. And Papa." She laughed suddenly. "Papa said, 'That young puppy is more than my Grace deserves.' I think those were his exact words."

"Did he say 'my Grace'?" Grace asked, looking at her sister-in-law with some interest. "That is how he always used to refer to me."

"Yes," Ethel said, "he definitely said that."

"Well," Grace said, "you are not to worry about me. I am not about to run off with Gareth. I hope never to see him again once we have left London."

"I am glad," Ethel said. "And Martin will be too."

"Tell me what plans you have for Priscilla in the coming weeks," Grace said with a smile. "You must be very pleased with her."

"I am," Ethel said. "And very glad that she has not settled her affections on any one particular beau. I was rather afraid that she might. We really do not want her to do that this year when she is so young. I don't think I could face losing my girl for another year or two yet."

11

IT WAS FORTUNATE, BOTH GRACE AND PEREGRINE thought, that Priscilla and Lucinda Stebbins were so talkative on the way back to London that their own silence seemed quite unremarkable. Priscilla, of course, was always in high spirits. This occasion was no exception. She had two days' worth of new people and new experiences to exclaim upon, and weeks more of the Season in town to look forward to and speculate upon.

But even Miss Stebbins was unusually voluble. Did Priscilla and Lady Lampman not think Mr. Paisley handsome? Not precisely handsome, perhaps, but in his own way really quite well-looking? Gentlemen did not have to be tall in order to be handsome, did they? Besides, character was far more important than looks. And amiability. Amiability was important, did not Sir Peregrine agree? Mr. Paisley did not go into London very often, but he was planning to attend Lord Sandersford's theater party next week. And she was going to ask Papa if they might attend too, since she was ever so eager to see Mr. Kean act. She had heard so much about him.

Peregrine recalled that Mr. Paisley was the thin, padded cousin of Sandersford's late wife. He smiled indulgently at the eager, flushed face of Lucinda Stebbins, remarked that her presence at the theater might distract Mr. Paisley's mind from Kean's performance and that therefore she might be doing him a marked disservice by attending herself, and he winked at her.

Lucinda giggled and blushed and was content for her friend to dominate the conversation for the rest of the journey home.

Peregrine himself was very aware of his wife seated beside him, her arm brushing against his occasionally when the carriage swayed unexpectedly before she had the chance to grab the strap with which to steady herself and keep away from him. And try as he would, he could think of nothing to say to her. And he could not bring himself to look at her because there would be nothing natural in his expression and he would be acutely uncomfortable.

They had not spoken, beyond the merest commonplace, awkwardly delivered and with no direct eye contact, since he had left her dressing room the night before. And they had not touched beyond the accidental contact of their arms in the carriage. He had slept in his dressing room. Or at least he had spent the latter portion of the night in his dressing room, slumped in a chair that was definitely not designed to be slept in, trying to empty his teeming and racing mind, trying to remind himself that it was good news he had heard in her dressing room. He had dozed fitfully, his head cradled uncomfortably on his arms, which he had spread on the high marble top of the washstand.

It had been good news. She had been alone with Sandersford for half an hour. She had talked with him, even allowed him to kiss her. And she had decided that she wanted to stay with *him*, that she wanted to continue with their marriage. It was what he wanted, what he had scarcely allowed himself to hope for in the past week.

And yet she had not wanted him to touch her. She had shrunk from his touch. She had decided to stay with him but would not let him touch her. And so there was no triumph at all, no joy in her decision. She had not been able to break her marriage vows, but her heart was with the man she had rejected that night.

And what could he do about it? He could not encourage her to leave him, to walk away from her marriage and plunge herself into the middle of a scandal. He could not do that. He must respect her decision as he had sworn to himself that he would do, no matter what that decision was. And so he must keep her with him as his wife, knowing her unhappy, knowing that she must force herself to remain close to him, to remain his wife in every way.

He loved her. He had been prepared to let her go if she found that Sandersford was essential to her happiness. He had been prepared to keep her if she decided otherwise. But he had not even considered that matters might be this way. He was not at all sure that he was prepared to have her person only, knowing that her heart was elsewhere. She had never been wholly his, of course. He had always known that a large part of her was in the grave with her dead son and her dead lover. Or at least, that was what he had always believed. He had not known until recently that that lover was alive. But he had always believed that at least he could bring her comfort, perhaps contentment.

And what was he to do now? Was he to live with her in silence for the rest of their lives? Without touching her? He could not do so. He loved her and wished more than anything for her happiness. But he was no saint. He was very human. If she had left him, he would have taught himself somehow to cope with her absence. But she had not left him. And so she must remain his wife. He must somehow carry on with his life as if these two days had not happened. Unless she cringed from him openly as she had done the night before. He would not be able to bear that. He would not be able to touch her if that happened again.

Peregrine reached out as Priscilla chattered on and touched the back of Grace's hand with his fingertips. She looked down at his hand and then rather jerkily across to look somewhat below the level of his eyes. She said nothing and looked away again almost immediately. But she did not remove her hand.

She had been sleeping, or pretending to sleep, when he had gone into their bedchamber the night before. It had been very late. He had wandered outside long after all the other guests had either taken their leave or gone to bed. And he had gone into the library on his return indoors, knowing by the sliver of light beneath the door that his host was there.

Sandersford had not looked surprised when Peregrine had walked in without knocking. And he had not risen. He had been sitting slouched down in a leather chair beside the fireplace, an empty glass dangling from the hand that was draped over the arm. He had not been foxed exactly, but Peregrine had guessed that he had had more than the one drink. He had regarded his guest with mocking eyes.

"Ah, the outraged husband," he had said. "Where is your glove, Lampman? You need a glove to slap in my face if the thing is to be done properly, you know."

Peregrine had walked right into the room and taken the chair opposite Sandersford's. "I have no wish to fight you," he had said. "I only want to ask that you leave Grace in peace now that she has made her decision."

Sandersford had laughed. "You find you can be generous in your triumph, do you?" he had said. "You fool! Do you think that Grace has chosen you? Do you think that she does not love me? Do you think that I could not take her away from you? Do you believe that I will not do it one day? You are a mere boy, Lampman, trying to understand the emotions of a woman."

"She is my wife," Peregrine had said. "Both duty and

inclination dictate that I protect her from harm and from harassment. I have stepped back to allow her to make her own decision about you because I know that in the past she loved you and bore your child. Now she has decided, I hope the matter is final in your mind too."

"Do I detect a threat?" Lord Sandersford had asked.

"No," Peregrine had said, "only a plea for decency. Did you once love her, Sandersford? Do you love her now? Leave her in peace then. You brought ruin and pain enough into her life once. Make some atonement now."

Lord Sandersford had leapt to his feet, his hands in white fists at his side. "By God," he had said, "if it were not shameful to whip a puppy, Lampman, I would whip you now. What do you know of Grace and me and what was between us? By what right do you judge me and lecture me, you sanctimonious fool? She was mine once. I had her body and soul, do you understand? And you think that she is yours now because she accepted your legal protection after the death of her brother? Do you think you have ever possessed her? Do you think she is yours? She is mine. She always has been and always will be."

Peregrine had kept his seat. But his face had paled. "I will not engage in such an argument," he had said. "As if Grace were a possession to be wrangled over. Did you ever see her as a person, Sandersford? Did you ever consider her feelings? Did you ever wonder when you left her with child what she felt, what she suffered? Do you have any idea now of the torment you are putting her through? Leave her alone now. Do something decent in your life."

Lord Sandersford had brought himself under control. He had refilled his glass with brandy, not offering any drink to his guest, and resumed his seat. "You are the torment in Grace's life, not me," he had said. "Do you not realize that she sees you as a boy, that you have become the child she lost? She will not harm your good name by leaving you. She will not risk hurting you. She has chosen rather to renounce the great passion of her life. But it will not be forever, Lampman. She will see soon enough that you are indeed like her child, a growing man who has to be given up to a younger woman. Do you think I have not seen your preference? And Grace will see it too. You have not seen the last of me. I will come for her when the time is right."

"I had hoped," Peregrine had said, "that you were not quite the scoundrel you seemed, Sandersford. I had hoped that perhaps there was some explanation for your treatment of Grace in the past, or at least that you would have outgrown your total selfishness. I had hoped that if she rejected you tonight, you would accept her decision and decide to put your love for her before your own selfish desires. But I see it is not so. I am sorry. Good night." He had got to his feet and made for the door.

"What?" Lord Sandersford had said, sneering. "No threats to kill me if I ever come near your wife again, Lampman?"

"No." Peregrine had turned back to him. "No threats, Sandersford. I can see no good coming from violence. And I feel no compulsion to prove my masculinity to you or anyone else. Only if you harass her, if you force yourself on her against her wishes, will I be forced to take action against you. Not otherwise. Good night."

"You are a coward," Lord Sandersford had said with a laugh. "A lily-livered boy beneath my contempt, as I suspected when I first set eyes on you."

"Strangely," Peregrine had said before letting himself quietly out of the library, "I find myself incapable of being wounded by your opinion of me, Sandersford."

GRACE'S HAND HAD turned beneath his, Peregrine noticed as he smiled ruefully at Priscilla and admitted that he could not answer her question because his mind had wandered shockingly over trying to list mentally all the young gentlemen who had been slain by her and Miss Stebbins in the past few weeks.

"A long list," he said. "Twenty-four already when your question jolted me back to reality. And I cannot now remember if I had included Mr. Paisley on that list. I think not. Twenty-five, then."

Both girls laughed.

Grace's hand was lying palm-up beneath his finger-tips.

IT WAS NOT easy, they both found, to pick up a marriage after such an emotional crisis, to piece it together again, and to continue with it. The events of the past weeks inevitably left their scars. And their uncertainties. Neither was quite sure how the other felt. Each wondered if the other was reluctant to continue with the marriage at all. But those same events had left a shyness, an awkwardness, that made it difficult, if not impossible, for them to talk openly about their feelings.

But the marriage did continue. After an almost silent journey from Hammersmith, they endured a dinner at home during which they made labored conversation, and an evening at Mrs. Borden's, when Peregrine turned in relief to his friend the Earl of Amberley for conversation and Grace almost forgot her woes in her fascination at a conversation with a portrait painter. And later that night Grace, lying cold and rigid with tension in the bed she had shared with her husband since their arrival in London, discovered that they were still to share it.

She knew that he had misconstrued her shrinking from him the night before. She knew that he had been deeply hurt. But she had been unable all day to explain to him that it was from herself she had shrunk, not from him. How could she explain when doing so would mean referring again to all those matters that she wished to put behind her? And how could she simply tell him that she loved him? Perhaps he would not wish to hear it.

They had married for convenience, he had said the night before. The words had stung. She had not been able to shake them from her mind all day. And they were true, of course. Simply true. They had not been spoken out of any desire to hurt or to set her down. They were true. She had known all along. She had not loved Perry any more than he loved her when she had agreed to marry him. It was only since—and so gradually that she could not say when it had happened exactly—that he had come to mean all the world to her.

There was no reason whatsoever to expect that the same thing had been happening to Perry. And she had no complaints. He had always treated her with the utmost gentleness and affection. He had shown understanding and respect for her feelings and her personhood in the events of the past few weeks. There was nothing to complain of. But, oh, it hurt to hear him say the bald truth with no conception whatsoever that their marriage had become for her far more than a thing of convenience.

She did not believe Gareth. She did not believe that Perry craved younger women and that sooner or later it was inevitable that he take a mistress. She did not believe that. She knew Perry a great deal better than Gareth did, and she knew that he was faithful to her, and would remain so. But was there some unhappiness in him, some longing to be able to look at a younger woman with desire, perhaps? Was he bound by a marriage that could never bring him real happiness even though he would never be unfaithful to it?

She could not ask him. There was no way of knowing the answer. But she was terrified that her behavior of the night before would drive a wedge between them so that their marriage would never bring them anything else but misery and entrapment.

It was with some relief, then, that she watched him come from his dressing room into their bedchamber on their first night back in town. She watched him with large and wary eyes as he crossed the room, sat on the edge of the bed, and touched her cheek with his finger-tips. His face was more serious than she had ever seen it.

"You said that you wish to remain married to me, Grace," he said. "It is what I wish too. But I cannot contemplate half a marriage. If my touch is abhorrent to you, you must tell me now and I will have to make some arrangement whereby we can live separately. I will not touch you against your will."

"Your touch is not abhorrent, Perry," she said, and she reached up to take his hand and bring the palm against her cheek. "And I do not want half a marriage either."

He searched her eyes before rising to put out the candles.

But Grace was not sure half an hour later, as she lay awake beside her husband, not quite touching him, that their lovemaking had brought them any closer together. She had been unable to relax, unable for a long time to respond to his hands and his lips, which had slowly and patiently tried to gentle her. Memories of Gareth's demanding, searching hands and mouth the night before kept intruding and making her feel unclean again. She had had to keep herself tense in order not to shudder.

And Perry had come to her eventually before she was ready and had hurt her, though she had shown her pain only by tensing yet again. It was only toward the end, when he had buried his face against her hair and she had known that he knew, that she had felt herself come finally to meet him, so that she had held him to her and leaned her head against his and swallowed a lump in her

throat. He had moved away from her after a few minutes and not put an arm beneath her head as he usually
did.

She did not think he was sleeping. He was too still to
be asleep.

"Perry," she whispered. She touched him lightly on
the arm.

He turned his face toward her.

"Perry," she said, "do you really want to stay here any
longer? Are you enjoying the Season?"

"You want to go home?" he asked.

"Yes." She could not read his tone. "But only if you
do. We have accepted several invitations for the next
few weeks."

"Then we will spend tomorrow morning penning our
regrets," he said. "Will the day after tomorrow be soon
enough, Grace?"

"Yes," she said. "Oh, Perry, it seems so very long since
we were at home."

"Too long," he said. He leaned forward to kiss her on
the lips and then turned over to face away from her.

And so their marriage had resumed, Grace thought as
she lay awake and knew only much later by his deep
breathing that Perry slept. It was better than she deserved, better than she could have hoped for the night
before. But there was an emptiness that was remarkably
like pain lodged somewhere in the region of her stomach. And even the fact that they were together and had
just made love and that they were planning to return
home together in two days' time had not taken away
that emptiness.

She was frightened.

"OH, PERRY, DO look. Oh, the flowers!" Grace sat forward on the carriage seat, her face close to the window

as it had been for the last two miles, though there had been no possible way that she could see Reardon Park for all of that distance. But she had seen it now: the square classical house, the trees, and the late-spring flowers that he and she had planted together the year before, all in full and glorious bloom.

Peregrine moved closer to her and looked over her shoulder. "Home," he said. "One glimpse of it is worth more than a thousand days spent anywhere else in the world. I am afraid I will never be an adventurer, Grace."

"Me neither," she said. "Oh, Perry, I could cry."

"That would be remarkably foolish," he said. "You would not then be able to see the orchard, which is about to come into view. And the servants would take one look at your face and think you were sorry to be back. The flowers do look splendid, Grace. There are so many of them that I am afraid we did not leave any to grow downward to bloom in China."

"Well," she said, "I say, let the Chinese plant their own flowers if they want them."

It was as if they had stepped out of one world that morning when they had left the inn at which they had spent the night and been transported in a matter of five hours into another world. Peregrine vaulted out of the carriage when it drew to a halt before his front doors, and turned to lift his wife down. He totally ignored the steps that the footman had lowered for their convenience. They were home and they were together and they had smiled at each other in genuine delight before the carriage had stopped completely.

Almost, he thought as he held to her waist for a few moments after her feet touched the ground, and he smiled down at her again as if all the awkwardness and stiffness and unhappiness and all the efforts to pretend that everything was normal between them had vanished during the final stage of their journey. Almost as if they could revert immediately to the quiet contentment they had enjoyed here together during the first year of their marriage.

"Happy?" he asked before releasing her.

She nodded, though her lips were trembling. He might have folded her to him and kissed her and told her that he loved her and would keep her safe and at peace for the rest of her life if the coachman and the footman had not been bustling about with two of the servants from the house and his valet and Grace's maid, all intent on emptying the baggage coach, and if their housekeeper had not been standing in the doorway, bobbing curtsies, her face wreathed in a smile of welcome.

"That surprised we were, my lady, to hear just this morning that you were on your way home already," she said when Grace moved forward to greet her. "And that glad. You go upstairs and wash yourself now. I have had hot water sent up already. And there will be warm scones and good strong tea in the parlor before you know it."

"Thank you," Grace said. "It is so very good to be home."

And it was good, Peregrine agreed. He had never been a great lover of London and the fashionable world. Now the very thought of both was enough to make him shudder. He did not believe that he would ever want to go back there again or ever leave Reardon Park again.

It was good to settle once more into the routine of their quiet life. It was good to wander in the garden and in the orchard and to see the beauty and the color with which his wife's skill and imagination had surrounded them. And to see the promise of roses in the arbor. It was good to be back among his own books and to be able to relax in his own worn chair in the library and read to his heart's content and watch again his wife quietly embroidering in the chair opposite his. Good to read to her again and to discover again that if he shared his thoughts and ideas with her, she would show interest and be perfectly capable of matching her intelligence to his.

And it was good to be back among their friends again. News of their return spread quickly, and not an afternoon passed for several days without bringing with it at least one visitor. The rector apologized for his good wife's absence, but he was delighted to announce that the latest addition to their family had arrived but three weeks before. Mrs. Cartwright lamented the fact that with both them and the earl's family gone, life had been very dull but that perhaps now there would be a little more company again. Mr. Watson came to return a book of poetry he had borrowed before Christmas.

Mr. and Mrs. Carrington were so much their usual selves that Peregrine could have laughed aloud at them, and did after they were gone and he was alone with Grace again.

"Such a fine new gown, to be sure," Mr. Carrington said with a shake of the head as he looked at Grace's muslin dress. "I daresay you will not be talking to such rustics as us any longer, Lady Lampman, and we will be as dull as we have been since you all went away, you and Amberley and the rest of them."

"William," his wife scolded. "The very idea! Lady Lampman will be thinking you are serious. Take no notice of him, my dear. William does like to tease."

"Well, I have a new coat," Peregrine said, smoothing his hands down the lapels, "made by Weston, no less. And I have been seriously wondering whether everyone in this part of the world is not now beneath my notice. Of course, if I turn my back on all my neighbors, there will be no one to admire my superior appearance, will there?"

"Exactly," Mr. Carrington said. "So you need us, after all, you see, Lampman. And we need not be dull, you will be relieved to know, Viola."

"Well, really," Mrs. Carrington said indignantly. "Your husband is every bit as bad as mine, Lady Lampman. You have my sympathy. But then he always was a dreadful tease."

"Viola gets awfully violent when she once loses her temper," Mr. Carrington said. "We had better take our leave, my dear."

"Since we have been here an hour already, I agree we should," Mrs. Carrington said. "But what he says is quite untrue, Lady Lampman. Me violent? The very idea!"

Grace joined Peregrine in his laughter after they had left.

The Misses Stanhope too were quite their usual selves. Miss Stanhope described for Grace exactly how they had decorated the altar at church for Easter, using the lace cloth she had made the year before expressly for that purpose, and how they had missed Lady Lampman when it came time to arrange the flowers. And Miss Letitia tittered at Peregrine's compliments and declared that if she had a new cap every time dear Sir Perry thought she did, she would have a whole dresser stuffed full of them.

Yes, it was good to be home again. Almost as if they had never been away. Almost. But not quite.

There was something between them. It was hard to explain it, impossible to put it into words, hard even to grasp it in coherent thought. They spoke frequently and freely on all topics. And yet there was a constraint in their conversation, something that they avoided with such care that they could not even name that something to themselves. They could sit in comfortable silence with each other. And yet sometimes that silence became loud with that unspoken something. They went about together and enjoyed the friendship of their neighbors. And yet they watched each other, not out of jealousy or suspicion, but out of some emotion or fear they could not name.

They lived together as man and wife, and yet their lovemaking was somewhat less frequent than it had been before. And though they were both satisfied by each encounter and knew the other at least not repelled, they both wondered sometimes, entirely against their will. Grace wondered if he did not dream sometimes of a younger woman. Peregrine wondered if she pined for the man she had loved since she was a girl.

And both remembered that they had made a marriage of convenience and that for the other it was still so. Each believed that love had grown on one side only.

12

AS THE SECOND YEAR OF THEIR MARRIAGE DREW TO its close, both Grace and Peregrine could reflect that it had been restored to the relative contentment they had known at the end of the first. Perhaps the only real difference was that now each of them knew what both had felt but not acknowledged the year before. And so there was a somewhat lesser contentment. It was not easy, each found, to love deeply when one believes that that love is not reciprocated. And yet each was thankful for the companionship, the loyalty, and the affection of the other.

They invited Grace's family to visit them for Christmas. The invitation was refused—the weather and therefore the roads were likely to be bad, and Oswald would be coming home from school for a few weeks. But they did promise to come later, perhaps in February if the winter turned out to be not too long and hard. Even Lord Pawley said he would come. He wished to see the grave of his younger son, Ethel added in a postscript to the letter she wrote Grace.

Grace was pleased. The reconciliation with her father that had begun the spring before had not been completed, she felt. They had been very close at one time. The gap between them after their estrangement had been correspondingly wide. She looked forward to entertaining him in her own home, and she certainly could not visit him at Pangam Manor so soon after her last visit. There was still a bewilderment, a fear about her feelings for Gareth. Not fear of him and what he might do to her, but fear of herself and a return of that weakness that had blinded her to his faults when she was younger and drawn her into a passion that had deprived her of all reason and morality.

In the meantime there was Christmas to look forward to again. Decorating the church with the Nativity scene; caroling with the Mortons and the Carringtons outside all the village homes and some of the outlying cottages too; taking baskets of food to the sick and the poor; helping the Countess of Amberley organize a party for the children at Amberley Court; buying and making gifts for servants and friends and for each other; conferring with the housekeeper and the cook on the foods to be prepared; bringing inside armfuls of holly to decorate doors and mantels; commiserating with each other over scratched hands and pricked fingers. There seemed to be a hundred and one tasks to be done, all equally delightful.

There was the usual party at Amberley Court on Christmas Day, beginning late in the afternoon so that each family would have plenty of time in which to enjoy its own company and open gifts and eat the Christmas goose before bundling up warmly for the carriage ride to Amberley.

But they were not to enjoy the warmth of the blazing log fire in the Amberley drawing room for long, it seemed. Lord Eden and Lady Madeline, who had not had a chilly journey to endure a half-hour before, were all impatience to persuade the younger guests that a brisk walk to the beach, two miles away along the valley in which the house was situated, was just the thing to settle their Christmas dinners and make room for all the good things still to come at tea and dinner.

Young people are ever resilient, Peregrine thought, settling more comfortably into his chair and feeling with some complacence that the heat of the flames was almost too hot on his feet. Walter Carrington and his younger sister, Anna, immediately leapt to their feet, eager to be on the way. And the four Courtney boys were no more reluctant. Miss Morton and her younger sister agreed to join the party when they saw how many young gentlemen there would be to escort them. And the rector's two older children, bouncing before their mother as if they thought that such motion might mesmerize her brain and induce her consent, begged to be allowed to go along too.

The Earl of Amberley grinned. "Sometimes," he said, "being a host has distinct advantages. Especially when it is a chilly Christmas and a crowd of mad youngsters suggests a walk of a mere four miles. I must stay to entertain my wiser guests, of course. But don't let me hinder you, Perry, my lad. Perhaps these young people will need the steadying influence of an older man."

"Oh, very steady," Lord Eden said with a shout of laughter. "I am only five years younger than you, Perry, and I can remember some of the scrapes you and Edmund used to get into. You were quite my idol at one time."

"At one time?" Peregrine said, delighting the Misses Stanhope and Mrs. Cartwright with his look of mock horror. "You mean I have lost my reputation for daring and recklessness? This will never do. My coat and my hat immediately, if you please."

"Oh, splendid," Lady Madeline said. "I was terrified that Dom and I were going to be the seniors of this expedition." She smiled impudently at Peregrine.

"May I come too, Perry?" Grace asked. "I like the thought of the exercise. I certainly feel the need for it."

"You mean you will do this quite voluntarily?" he

asked. "Without being tricked into it, as I have been? You are quite heroic, Grace."

"Dear Lady Lampman," Mrs. Morton remarked to Miss Letitia. "She does keep herself young for Sir Perry, does she not? I would not welcome such an expedition even if I could be taken in a carriage with a hot brick for my feet."

"It would keep a lady young to be married so late in life to such a handsome, cheerful gentleman as Sir Perry, though," Miss Letitia replied with a sigh that might well have been one of envy. Peregrine had not failed to remark on the handsomeness of her new cap—and it really was new this time, a Christmas gift from her sister.

The young people, together with Grace and Peregrine, were soon on their way, striding energetically and noisily along the valley through which a stream flowed to the sea. Anna Carrington, who had decided five years before, at the age of ten, that she was going to marry her first cousin, Dominic, when she grew up, linked her arm through his and tripped along at his side, and reminded him of the birthday she had celebrated less than two weeks before and of the fact that in another year she would be finished with the horrid schoolroom for good and would be almost grown up.

"And will dazzle not a few gentlemen when you are finally let loose on society, Anna," he said good-naturedly.

"Oh, do you think so, Dominic?" she said eagerly. And she added ingenuously, "And you too?"

"You are already dazzling me," he said, "with those rosy cheeks. No, don't frown and look offended, you goose. They look very becoming."

Madeline walked with Howard Courtney and chattered determinedly about any topic that came to mind. Howard had had a painful *tendre* for her for years, and though she had told him almost four years before that she could never look on him as more than a friend, he seemed unable to meet her without flushing and becoming tongue-tied. If only he were not such a throroughly nice person, she thought with an inward sigh, she could perhaps despise him and feel no sympathy for him at all.

Walter Carrington took Miss Hetty Morton on his arm, reflecting glumly on the fact that she was not even quite as old as his sister and no foil whatsoever for his advanced eighteen years. It was a great shame that Miss Susan Courtney had been away at her aunt's since the summer. She was growing up fast, and she was such a very pretty and timid little thing.

The older Miss Morton was proud to have the others see that she walked with two gentlemen, both her arms occupied. It was true that they were only two of the younger Courtney boys. And it was true that she had been privately annoyed to see that child Anna monopolize the attention of Lord Eden again. But even so, it was gratifying to know that there were two gentlemen eager to accompany her. It was something to tell Mama later.

Peregrine held Grace's arm snug against his side. They both wore woolen scarves wrapped twice about their necks. "You are a marvel," he said. "There are not many married ladies who would prefer a brisk walk in the December air to a cozy chat by the fire."

"The sea and the beach are at their loveliest in the winter," she said. "And you know I love the outdoors, Perry. I just hope these very young persons will not feel inhibited by my very elderly presence."

He grinned. "I would wager you could outwalk and outwork all of them put together, Grace," he said. "Your nose distinctly resembles a cherry, by the way."

"No, no," she said. "This is the Christmas season, Perry. A holly berry would be a more appropriate comparison, surely. Not that I can see my own nose to judge, of course. But I can see yours."

"*Touché,*" he said with a laugh. "Ah, look, there is the

sea already. The tide must be almost full. What a pity. I like to see the wide beach when it is out."

"But this sky looks splendid reflected in the water," she said. "Look, Perry. Lots of heavy gray clouds scudding across the sky with the sunshine behind them. And the sea looks like silver. Molten silver."

Peregrine laughed. "Most people would say it is a nasty dull day and cold into the bargain," he said. "You have a lovely creative mind, Grace. A poet's mind."

The valley opened out onto a flat golden beach with steep cliffs either side. But now, almost at full tide, not a great deal of the sand could be seen. They all walked out until they were almost at the edge of the incoming water. Anna squealed as Lord Eden threatened to pick her up and hurl her into the closest breaker.

"Shall we stroll along at the edge for a while?" Peregrine asked. "I don't think we are likely to be trapped against the cliffs yet. And if we were, we would merely have to climb up."

"Gracious," Grace said. "Is it possible?" She gazed up the almost sheer height of the cliff. "I suppose it is something you did during your boyhood, Perry. And something that was strictly forbidden, I presume."

"Right on both counts," he said meekly. "It looks as if we were both rather reckless and disobedient young people, Grace. We deserve each other, don't you think? And we dare to stroll sedately along the beach here, avoiding all those noisy, frolicking youngsters, for all the world as if we never dreamed of behaving in such a riotous manner when we were their age. We are frauds, my dear. Should we turn back, do you suppose, and confess to them?"

"Oh, Perry," she said, "you speak as if you are an old man already. Do you not long to join in with their high spirits."

"Join in?" he said. "Good Lord, no, Grace. I am no

boy, my dear. I have been a sober married gentleman for almost two years."

"Is that what I have done to you?" she said.

He looked down at her, eyebrows raised. "Made a married gentleman out of me?" he said. "Yes, certainly."

"I meant the sober part," she said.

"Not at all," he said. "I distinctly remember laughing at least three times only today. But not frolicking, Grace. That would be somewhat undignified at my age, would it not?"

"I am sometimes afraid that perhaps you crave young company," she said.

"And you do not think of yourself as young, I presume," he said. "Do you think that way, Grace? Because I like to tease young girls, perhaps? But I like to tease the older ladies too, dear. Miss Letitia Stanhope would be severely disappointed if I did not pretend each time I see her that I think her cap to be new and most charming. I like women. It is so easy to please them, to make them happy. In a quite superficial manner, of course. But I like to make people happy. You do not think I flirt, do you?"

"No!" she said. "No, I was not being in any way critical, Perry. I was not, believe me."

He took her gloved hand in his and squeezed it. "I am not sorry I married you, Grace," he said. "If that is what you meant." There was a small silence. "Are you ever sorry you married me?"

"No," she said.

He waited for her to say more. She seemed about to do so. But she did not.

"That is good," he said. "I suppose all married people sometimes wonder. But it is difficult to ask, is it not?"

"Yes," she said. "I am not sorry, Perry. Truly I am not."

He squeezed her hand. "We should turn around and walk back," he said. "But it is relatively comfortable walking with the wind almost behind us, is it not? I am not sure I have the courage to turn around."

"I think the only alternative is to go up over the cliff, then," she said. "The tide is coming in fast."

"And so it is," he said. "I am sure you would have the energy to climb up, Grace, but you might find it a little too much to haul me up with you. Let's turn back, then. Ugh! I knew it."

"Oh," Grace said. "I feel as if my breath is being blown back down my throat."

"I almost wish we had chosen to spend Christmas Day alone," Peregrine said. "I always feel most contented strolling with you. However, I suppose we must be thankful for so many congenial neighbors and friends."

"Very much so," Grace said. "And you cannot pretend that you are not going to enjoy the evening, Perry. Music in the drawing room and games and probably dancing. And plenty of conversation and food."

He grinned. "Trust my wife to know me rather well," he said. "Grace, you have holly berries for nose and cheeks. And brightly shining ones too."

"I know," she said. "I assumed that the wind was having the same effect on my face as it is having on yours."

As the evening progressed at the house, it seemed that Grace was perfectly right. Peregrine turned pages of music for Miss Hetty Morton and Anna Carrington, whose extreme youth caused the other young gentlemen to ignore them much of the time. He played a hand of cards with the rector's wife, Miss Stanhope, and Mr. Courtney, and a game of spillikins with the rector's young children. He danced with his wife and any other lady who happened not to have a partner when the music began. And in a robust game of blindman's buff, he was roundly accused of cheating when twice in a row he caught a tittering Miss Letitia despite his blindfold.

Grace was standing to one side of the pianoforte late

in the evening when there was a general lull in the festivities following supper, browsing through some music. Peregrine was at the opposite end of the room laughing with a group of others at Mr. Courtney's protestations that he would not be able to squeeze one more morsel of food inside himself until at least New Year's Day.

"At least you know that you will not waste quite away," Mr. Carrington said. "You could lose two stone without anyone noticing."

"William!" his wife said. "Oh, take no notice of him, Mr. Courtney."

"Perhaps I should hire myself out to Arabs for desert crossings," Mr. Courtney said good-naturedly. "Is there a shortage of camels, do you think?"

"Oh, do look," Mrs. Cartwright said with a titter. "Look where Lady Lampman is standing."

"The pianoforte must have been moved," Lord Amberley said with a laugh. "The mistletoe was meant to be directly above the stool. No one seems to have noticed it just where it is."

"I would wager Lady Lampman does not know it is there, the poor dear," Mrs. Carrington said.

"Well, Perry," Lord Amberley said, "what are you going to do about it?"

Peregrine got to his feet while most of the ladies smirked, Miss Stanhope blushed, and Miss Letitia clasped her hands to her bosom.

"Grace," Peregrine said a moment later, "do you realize the great danger you are in?"

She looked at him, startled out of her concentration on the music. "I beg your pardon?" she said.

"Do you not see what is threatening right above you?" he asked.

She looked up in some alarm only to have the ceiling blocked from her view by his face.

"You are standing directly below the mistletoe," he

said. "You cannot expect me to resist such invitation, can you?"

And then he kissed her on the lips, quite lingeringly enough to satisfy their audience at the other end of the room. Peregrine heard a smattering of applause, a few giggles, and a "Bravo!" as he lifted his head and grinned down at his wife.

"Perry," she said. "Everyone will have seen."

"I'm afraid so," he said. "And you had better move from there, or I will be forced to kiss you again."

Grace moved with some haste, and yet there was a warmth of feeling in her as he laid her hand on his arm and took her across the room to join their laughing neighbors. It was a warmth that had begun with their morning of gift opening and entertaining of the servants and had continued with the evening spent with congenial friends. *If it could only be like this always,* Grace thought, seating herself beside her husband and not removing her arm from his sleeve.

The carriage ride back home was a cold one, though they had a hot brick at their feet and a heavy blanket to wrap around their knees. Peregrine put an arm around Grace's shoulders as soon as they were on the way, and she snuggled her head against him.

"Tired?" he asked.

"Mmm." She closed her eyes. "I wish every day could be Christmas. There is something so very special about it, isn't there, Perry?"

"Yes," he said. And he moved one hand up beneath her chin to raise it, and kissed her.

It was rather absurd, Grace thought somewhere behind the fog of contentment and rising desire she felt over the next half-hour, to be sitting in the chill interior of a carriage with one's husband of almost two years, both dressed in heavy winter garments, kissing for almost every moment of the journey, softly and slowly exploring each other's mouth with lips and tongues, touching each other's face with gloved fingers, murmuring to each other in words that had no meaning to the ear, but only to the heart.

Equally absurd, and enchanting too, to be taken directly to her bedchamber when she arrived home and to have her husband dismiss her maid and his valet for the night and proceed to undress her himself as he had done on one other occasion and to have him kiss her all the while and worship her with his hands and take her to the bed to make love to her over and over again until finally they clung together damply and drifted toward sleep from pure exhaustion.

And absurd perhaps to imagine that he loved her, loved her with all his being and for all time and not just because it was Christmas and everyone feels love and good will at that season.

"Perry," she murmured against his warm and naked chest.

"Mmm," he said, kissing the top of her head.

And they both slept.

PERHAPS CHRISTMAS WOULD have stayed with them even beyond the New Year if Grace had not received a letter from Ethel. Certainly the magic of that day and night did not fade in the days following Christmas, but bound them together in the warmth of a deeper affection than they had known before. But the letter did arrive, and it came to drive a wedge between them again.

Not that there was anything upsetting about Ethel's letter. It was filled with news of the family, in which both Grace and Peregrine were interested, and hopes that the planned visit could be made in February or March at the latest, even though they were all suffering from colds at the moment of writing.

What was upsetting were the two enclosures. One was a separate note from Ethel, for Grace alone. The other was a sealed letter also addressed to her. It was from Viscount Sandersford, Ethel explained. She had not wanted to take it from him or send it in such clandestine manner to Grace. She was sure that Martin would blame her for doing so if he ever found out the truth. But Lord Sandersford had been very insistent. He had told her that Grace would want the letter. He had told her that if she did not send it secretly, he must do so openly and doubtless upset Grace's husband. Ethel did not know at all if she did the right thing.

Grace felt sick. She sat in her sitting room, Gareth's unopened letter clasped in one hand. She did not want to open it. She wanted to pretend to herself that Gareth was dead. She did not love him. She wondered how she could ever have done so. She wanted to forget about him. But of course he was not dead and she could not forget. Whether she liked it or not, he was a very real part of her life. She had loved him; she had shared the intimacy, even if not the reality, of marriage with him; he was Jeremy's father.

She sat for a long time with the letter in her hand. Then she got to her feet, strode from the room, and almost ran down the stairs. She opened the door to Peregrine's study in a rush, not waiting to knock first, and drew to a sharp halt when she saw that he was with his estate manager.

"I am sorry," she said. "Excuse me, please."

Both men jumped to their feet.

Peregrine came toward her, his eyes steady on her face. "What is it?" he asked. "Do you need me?"

"It can wait," she said. "Please excuse me."

But he held up a staying hand and turned to the manager. "Will you excuse us?" he said. "I shall come and see you later."

The man bowed and left the room.

"What is it, Grace?" Peregrine turned back to her, concern in his face. "Something has happened to upset you. Was there bad news in Ethel's letter? Your father?"

She did not answer but put Gareth's letter in his hand almost as if it were about to scald her.

He looked down at it and turned it over in his hand. "It is sealed," he said, "and addressed to you, Grace."

"It is from Gareth," she said. "Lord Sandersford."

"I see." He stared down at the letter for a long and silent moment before handing it back. "It is for you, Grace. Not for me."

She swallowed and took it into her own hands again. "Yes," she said. And she knew that whether she opened it or not, he was there again. Gareth. Her past. The things that would always come between her and Perry. And she knew that Perry would never make her life easier by telling her what to do. And it was that very fact that made her love him so dearly. Perry respected her as a person. He would never dominate her as her husband, even to make her life easier and their marriage more enduring.

She turned, left the room without a word, and climbed the stairs to her sitting room again. And opened the letter.

He could not live without her, Gareth wrote. A lifetime punishment for a youthful thoughtlessness was too much to bear. She must come to him. Or he would come to her. He had struck up enough of an acquaintance with the Earl of Amberley the previous spring to impose on his hospitality for a few weeks. He loved her and he would not believe that she did not love him, though he understood she was trying hard to remain loyal to her husband. He had visited Jeremy's grave almost daily since his return from London and wept there for the son he had never known and the love he had so carelessly thrown away.

The words blurred before Grace's eyes. Could he not have spared her that? And was it true? Had he finally recognized that they had had a son together and that Jeremy had been a real person, quite distinct from either of them? But she did not want to know if it was true. And she doubted that it was. Had he written that only because he knew that that of all details would weaken her? Gareth crying at Jeremy's grave! At their son's grave. She shuddered.

And what was she to do? Write to tell him that she would not come and did not wish to see him again? He would ignore her denials, she was sure. Gareth would just not believe that her love for him was dead. Gareth had always got what he wanted.

And the dread grew in her that somehow, totally against her will, he would get his way again. He would exert his power over her once more, a power she had welcomed as a girl and willingly acquiesced in. She could never make a willing surrender to him again. She hated him. But hate is very akin to love. And he knew that. He had been quite undismayed by her hatred. She was terrified that her very hatred would draw her to him.

And away from Perry. She loved Perry. His gentleness and his laughter and his quiet affection represented all the goodness and peace that had been missing from her life until she was already in her mid-thirties. And she had begun to think that perhaps she could enjoy those things for the rest of her life. But always thoughts of Gareth aroused memories of her guilt and doubts of her own worth.

She did not deserve goodness and peace. She did not deserve Perry.

She was going to lose him. And in the worst possible way. He was not going to cast her off. She knew he would never do that even if perhaps he did sometimes regret being married to a woman ten years his senior. And Gareth would not force her to go. Even Gareth would not resort to abduction. No, she would end up going quite freely to her own destruction. And she would do so in order to punish herself for a past she could never quite forgive herself for. It was inevitable. The prospect terrified her.

She was going to fight it. She was too strong a person to do anything as weak as destroy herself.

But she was very much afraid.

13

PEREGRINE WAS DOODLING ON A SHEET OF PAPER with a quill pen that badly needed mending. It scratched over the surface, setting his teeth on edge, and sent out occasional little sprays of ink to dot the page.

To be a man and a gentleman had always seemed to be an easy thing to accomplish. To have the courage to face life and live it according to one's own moral principles. To stay within the bounds of law and religion. To treat other people with dignity and respect. To protect the weak and the innocent. It all sounded easy. He had never thought himself lacking in courage or principle.

But courage was not the question with him now. The question was what was right and what was wrong. What exactly was involved in treating another person with respect? In what way exactly was one to protect the weak? It was so easy to be a gentleman in the abstract, so easy to act the gentleman with the masses of people one met in the course of months and years. But it was not easy at all to know the right course of action to take with his own wife, with the person who mattered more to him than anyone else.

It had all started up again, this business with Sandersford. Just at a time when he had been hoping that perhaps she had finally put the past behind her. Just at a time when everything seemed to be going so marvelously right with their marriage. Since Christmas Day and its wonderful, magical ending he had dared to hope that perhaps she loved him now with an undivided love, notwithstanding all the emotions and passions of her past. And it was so difficult to persuade himself to settle for less than love. Respect, loyalty, affection even, just did not seem enough to satisfy him any longer.

But his hopes had been dashed again. That damned letter! Peregrine set down his pen and leaned back in his chair, one hand over his eyes.

Had he acted in the right way? He had found himself quite unable to break the seal of that letter. It was addressed to his wife. It was from the man who had once been her husband in all but name. The man she had loved. And still had powerful feelings for, even though he did not know the true nature of those feelings. He had not been able to open that letter and read it, even though she had brought it to him herself.

And so he had given it back to her. Was he mad? Was he a man? His wife's former lover had sent her a letter in secret, undoubtedly a love letter, and he had permitted her to read it, encouraged her almost. He had refused to interfere. Should he not have torn it to shreds and gone after Sandersford to ensure that he was never again inclined to interfere in the sanctity of his marriage?

But he could not. He could not play the high-handed husband. He could not keep a wife with him by force. He could not present a veneer of respectability to the world and have a festering sore of a marriage in private. He would rather lose her than keep her against her will.

But she had brought the letter to him, unopened. Why? Was she pleading for his help? Did she want him to take the burden of the problem on his own shoulders?

Had he let her down? Was he forcing her into a course of action she did not want to take?

Why could they not talk about it? A huge silence seemed to surround the topic of Sandersford and everything he had been to her, and was. Why could they not speak of it, know each other's mind and heart? There are some things too deep and too painful for words, he concluded. He could face the prospect of losing Grace if she should ever decide that she must return to the lover of her past. But he could not face bringing on the moment, hearing the brutal truth from her lips in response to a question of his. He was a coward, then?

Peregrine reached the door of his office just as it opened and Grace came in. She held out a written sheet of paper to him.

"I have read the letter," she said. Her voice was quite toneless. "And I have written a reply." She held his eyes with her own.

He took the letter from her hand and folded it into the creases she had already made. He did not look down at all while he did so. "Then you must send it," he said. "Grace, why did you bring me his letter? And your reply? Do you need my help?" He bit his lip when tears sprang to her eyes.

"I did not want to do anything behind your back, Perry," she said.

He lifted one hand, changed his mind about laying it against her cheek, and set it on her shoulder. "May I help, Grace?" he asked.

She shook her head. "I wanted you to read the letter or tear it to shreds and forbid me ever to be in communication with Gareth again," she said. "That was foolish. You would never do anything like that, would you, Perry? For it would not solve anything but would certainly ruin our respect for each other."

"I want to stop your pain," he said. "I want to take it

on myself. But I can't. That is one thing we can never take away from another person."

"He wants me to go to him," she said. "Or he will come here for me. I have written back to say that I will not go and that I will not see him if he comes here." She had her eyes tightly closed.

Peregrine's hand squeezed her shoulder unconsciously. "Do you love him, Grace?" he asked. Every blood vessel in his body seemed to be throbbing.

"No," she said. "No, I don't love him. I hate him." There was a pause. "But there is something. I think perhaps I belong with him. I think perhaps I don't belong with you, Perry. I have wanted to do so, but I am afraid that I don't."

He could feel the pain of her first sob tearing at her as she put her hands over her face. He could feel it because he shared it. He gripped both her shoulders bruisingly, not even realizing that he did so, and bent his head forward. He could not even pull her against him to comfort her and himself. She did not belong in his arms any longer.

It had happened then, his mind told him quite dispassionately. It had happened at last. It was too late now to unask the question. He had asked it, and she had replied. It had happened.

He whirled around suddenly, grasped a porcelain figurine that happened to be within his reach, and hurled it toward the fireplace. It smashed satisfyingly against the mantel, and the pieces tinkled noisily into the hearth.

"Damn it!" he said between his teeth. "Damn Sandersford. And damn you, Grace."

He stood facing away from her, his hands in fists at his sides, appalled by the echo of his own words. There was perfect silence behind her. She had stopped sobbing.

He was surprised by the calmness of his own voice a few moments later as he moved forward to nudge together the pieces of porcelain in the hearth with the toe of his boot. "You will be wishing to leave, then?" he asked, and turned to her.

She looked at him with reddened, frightened eyes. "Leave?" she said. "Leave here? You are asking me to, Perry? Oh, God, has it come to this, then? But I don't want to go. I don't want to be with Gareth again. I want to be here with you. I want to be safe with you. But I have told you that I do not belong with you any longer. And you hate me now. How could you not? Oh, God, what is happening?"

"Perhaps we are both being hysterical," he said, turning and walking back to the desk, rearranging the objects lying on its surface, putting some distance between them. "I don't want you to leave, Grace. And you do not want to go. Not yet, anyway. You seem unsure of your feelings. Stay then until you are."

"That is unfair to you," she said.

He laughed rather grimly as he crumpled the sheet of paper on which he had been doodling earlier. "What, then?" he said. "I don't want you leaving me, Grace, when you are not even sure that you wish to do so and when I do not wish you to go. And I suppose I must be thankful that you have been honest with me. You might have hidden that letter." He turned to look at her. "Stay with me. Stay at least until you know you can no longer do so. I know you will tell me when the time comes." Was his voice as cold and abrupt as it sounded to his own ears? he wondered.

"When?" she whispered. "Are you so sure, then, of my final decision? Is it inevitable, Perry? And could you bear to have me stay permanently after all this?"

He smiled suddenly, unexpectedly, and just a little

grimly. "Let us not be morbid," he said. "I think my head is going to explode into a thousand pieces if I don't get it into the outdoors immediately. Come for a walk with me, Grace. Look, it is trying to snow out there."

"I can't, Perry," she said.

"Yes, you can." His smile had taken a firmer hold of his face. "We will take a brisk walk along the lane. I must have you with me to make beauty and poetry out of those heavy gray clouds and all the bare branches. No, you are not to cry again. I forbid it. Absolutely. Shall I send someone up for your outdoor things, or will you go yourself?"

"I'll go," she said.

So, Peregrine thought, completing the unnecessary task of tidying his desk after Grace had left, life continued on, did it? Tears dried, wounds were bound up, and life continued. Only in grand tragedy did a catastrophe happen in one sweep. In real life it came in a series of small agonies. And perhaps in the end it never came at all. Or perhaps it did. But regardless of the outcome, life continued. Life had to continue.

He glanced uneasily at the porcelain pieces on the hearth and pulled the bell rope to summon a servant.

THE NEWS THAT Grace's father and brother were coming to stay at Reardon Park with the latter's wife and daughter created stir of pleased anticipation in the village of Abbotsford and the surrounding areas. These people had discovered the year before, of course, that Lady Lampman was not as alone in the world as they had once thought but that she did have family members whom she had visited with her husband. But to know that those people were coming was a great salve to their curiosity and a boost to their social expectations, which tended to lag during the winter, once Christmas was over.

The added news that Lord Amberley was to entertain Viscount Sandersford at about the same time added an extra buzz of excitement. Was he an eligible gentleman? Mrs. Morton asked Mrs. Carrington. Mrs. Courtney, present when the question was asked, privately lamented the fact that her Susan was still away at her Aunt Henshaw's and not like to be home again until April.

The Earl of Amberley himself was surprised by the news of the imminent arrival of an uninvited guest. His acquaintance with Lord Sandersford was of short duration and was not by any means an intimate one. But his sister reminded him that the viscount was a neighbor of Lady Lampman's brother and had known Lady Lampman herself all his life.

"To be sure," he said. "I had forgotten. And he had them all out to Hammersmith for a few days, did he not, just before Perry and Lady Lampman came home? I daresay he wants to be a part of this gathering at Reardon Park."

"He is very handsome," Madeline said. "Should I fall in love with him, do you suppose, Edmund? Or is he a little old for me?"

"Heaven help us," her brother said. "You fall in love often enough when we are in London, Madeline. Can you not wait until we return there before doing so again?"

"Oh, I suppose, so," she said with a laugh. "Besides, I don't believe I could bring myself to fall in love with a gentleman beyond the age of thirty. And Lord Sandersford must be closer to forty. What a strange man he must be, though, to invite himself to the home of a virtual stranger."

"I am quite sure he knows of my friendship with

Perry," Lord Amberley said. "And I am very pleased to be able to oblige Perry."

The Countess of Amberley began to organize a dinner party in honor of her son's guest and Sir Peregrine's, and Mrs. Morton had to pay a call on both Mrs. Cartwright and Mrs. Carrington before she could decide whether to give a card party or a charades party. She finally decided on a combination of both.

Everyone agreed that the end of February was the very best time to be expecting visitors in the neighborhood. The winter had made everyone dreary, and spring had only just begun to show a few tantalizing signs that it was on the way. Lady Lampman and Sir Peregrine had told them after church that there were a few brave snowdrops blooming already at Reardon Park. But then everyone knew that the Lady Lampman had only to look at a patch of bare soil to persuade a flower to grow there. It hardly seemed fair, Mrs. Courtney commented cheerfully to her spouse during the carriage ride home.

IT WAS STRANGE, Grace thought, how life went on. No matter how bad things became, provided one survived at all, one somehow picked up the pieces of the disaster and went on living. She had proved it in the past. Gareth's leaving. The scandal of her pregnancy. Gareth's letter announcing his marriage. Her son's death. The dreadful quarrel between Paul and their father. Her leaving with him. Life had continued. She had felt dead for nine years, had even welcomed the land of the half-dead. But she had lived on, and she had eventually come back to full life.

And now she was surviving again. Barely surviving, she sometimes felt, but living on nonetheless. She was still with Perry. Somehow she was still with him. And not just living in the same house with him. They talked to each other, read together, walked together, watched together for signs of spring. They treated each other with a wary sort of courtesy. No, perhaps with more than just courtesy.

It was true that they no longer lived as man and wife. She had waited in their bedchamber the night after Gareth's letter came, the night after Perry's terrible outburst, shivering, to tell him that she could no longer share the room with him, not at least until she could offer him her undivided loyalty. But she had waited all night. He had not come then or any night since.

She missed him dreadfully. And she wanted him. But she could make no move toward him until she was quite sure of herself beyond any doubt at all. She was quite sure that she loved him and always would. But then, she had known that for a long time. It was herself she was unsure of. She was not quite sure that she belonged with him, that she deserved him, that she had anything of value to offer their marriage. She was almost sure, but not quite.

And was their reconciliation entirely up to her, anyway? Would Perry take her back even if she asked? She had been terribly disloyal to their marriage. And he had been furiously angry during that one short outburst when he had thrown the figurine. Could she expect that he would willingly forgive her to the extent of returning to their bed again?

She was glad that her family was coming. Their presence would be a distraction for both Perry and herself. And she had a feeling too that if ever she was going to straighten out her life finally, it was not only Perry with whom she had to deal but them too. And she missed her father. Having seen him again the year before, she realized how much of both their lives they had wasted apart from each other.

She felt sick on the afternoon when Lord Amberley paid a call on them and announced with a smile that Lord Sandersford was to be his guest for a few days at the end of the month. She did not dare look at Perry.

"Sandersford is your father's neighbor, Lady Lampman?" the earl asked politely.

"Yes," she said. "We grew up together."

"You will be happy to have both your family and a neighbor close to you again, then," he said.

"Yes." She called on the calmness of manner that had seen her through nine years with Paul.

"I thought you were on your way back to London soon, Edmund," Peregrine said. His voice sounded quite normal.

"Yes," Lord Amberley said. "Mama and Madeline are eager to be on the way. Dominic left two weeks ago. But we can wait until our guest leaves. I will be quite happy to have him, I do assure you."

Grace felt sick. And yet almost relieved at the same time. There had been a sense of waiting for the past two months. Nothing was over. Nothing had been settled. Now something would happen once and for all. And the confidence was growing in her that this time she was going to free herself from the power Gareth had exerted over her in one form or another for much of her life. This time she was going to take the initiative. And this time she would win.

Her only hope was to fight now, years and years too late. But, no, it was not too late. She was thirty-seven years old, but she was not dead yet or anywhere close to death, she hoped. She had a great deal of living yet to do and a great deal to live for. Oh, a very great deal.

On the whole, she was glad that Gareth was coming

to Amberley Court. Even though Perry looked white and tense in the days between Lord Amberley's visit and the arrival of her family. Even though he looked at her with haunted eyes. Yes, she was glad. Soon she would be able to offer him her undivided loyalty, if he was willing to accept it. Her love too, if he wanted it. The look on his face made her hope. But she would not think of that yet.

Not until she was quite, quite sure of herself.

ALL THE EXPECTED visitors arrived before the end of February. Grace's family, who came first, were all in the best of health. Lord Pawley was even walking without his cane and seemed quite content to sit most of the time in a room with his family rather than keep to his own room. Priscilla was her usual exuberant self and had almost eight months' worth of news to divulge to her uncle and aunt.

It was several days later before word reached Reardon Park that Lord Sandersford had arrived at Amberley Court. But Ethel clearly knew that he was coming. She took the first opportunity of their being alone together to raise the matter with Grace.

"I should not have accepted that letter to send to you," she said. "It was quite against my better judgment to do so, and I have never been able to summon the courage to confess to Martin. I sent it eventually only in the hope of saving you from just such an encounter as this, Grace. Or maybe you have invited him. Maybe you welcome his coming. I don't know. I just wish I had not got involved."

"You must not blame yourself," Grace said. "And you must not be afraid for me or for Perry."

Ethel looked both dubious and troubled, but Grace

would say no more. She followed Peregrine to his dressing room after the rector brought them the news that Lord Amberley's visitor had arrived. She stood inside the door while he looked at her in some surprise and dismissed his valet.

"Perry," she said as soon as they were alone, "I wish you to invite Lord Sandersford to tea one afternoon. Preferably tomorrow. Will you?"

He looked at her cold, set face and did not smile. "Yes, if you wish, Grace," he said. "I shall invite Edmund and the countess too. I will suggest tomorrow."

"Thank you," she said.

They looked at each other for a few moments longer, and then she turned to leave because there really was nothing more to say.

And they did not see each other alone again until late the following afternoon. In the morning Grace went into Abbotsford with Ethel while Peregrine took Martin and Priscilla to call on the Mortons.

The arrival in the afternoon of Lord Amberley, his mother, and their guest, and the added presence of Mr. Courtney and his daughter, Susan, who had returned early from her aunt's, made the whole situation somewhat more comfortable, Grace found after curtsying to Gareth and motioning him to a chair close to her own. She could better ignore the tense look on her husband's face, a look that she knew was mirrored on her own, the disapproving frowns of her father and Martin, and the anxious, guilt-ridden glances of Ethel.

She waited until Susan and Priscilla were in the midst of an excited exchange of views on fashion and everyone else seemed to be fully engaged in conversation before rising to her feet.

"May I show you our garden, Lord Sandersford?" she asked politely. "I am afraid there is not a great deal of color yet, but the daffodils are in bud."

He rose to his feet, a smile on his handsome face.

Grace was fully aware of his great height, the breadth of his shoulders, the aura of masculinity that had always surrounded Gareth from as far back as she could remember.

"I would be delighted, ma'am," he said.

She did not look at Peregrine. She held her shawl tightly about her as they went outside and walked past the flower beds and down into the orchard.

"I thought you might make it difficult for me," he said. "I thought you might refuse to see me at first."

"No," she said. "I have been looking forward to your coming, Gareth." She looked up into his handsome, smiling face. "I have a number of things that I wish to say to you."

"There is only one that I wish to hear," he said. "When will you come away with me, Grace? Immediately? There is no point in further delay, you know."

"I will not be going with you," she said, "ever. And for one simple reason, Gareth. I have no wish to do so. No, perhaps there is another reason even more important. I have no need to go away with you. You see, I have finally forgiven myself for the past and I have no further need to punish myself with you."

He laughed. "What is this?" he said. "You have been feeling guilty, Grace? You have been punishing yourself with me? Whatever do you mean?"

"I sinned against all the moral laws of our society and church when I gave myself to you," she said. "My father's faith in me was broken when he knew I was with child. I brought great shame and embarrassment to him and Martin. I caused a dreadful rift between Papa and Paul. And Paul died without any reconciliation between them. I gave birth to an illegitimate child and he died at a time when I was not taking care of him. I was sleeping that afternoon, having persuaded myself that I had a headache as a result of a fancied insult from Ethel. And after Paul's death I took an easy route to securing my future by marrying a man ten years my junior, who offered out of the kindness of his heart. That is a great deal of guilt for one human being to carry around, Gareth."

"Nonsense," he said. "We were in love; what we did was not wrong. And everyone else on your list made a free decision, Grace. You are not responsible for other people's actions."

"We were not in love," she said quietly. "You used the wrong pronoun, Gareth. *I* was in love. *You* have never loved. You do not know the meaning of the word. I fed your self-love when we were young by worshipping you and allowing you to dominate me. I satisfied your appetite for the last few weeks you were at home until you could get away and meet more desirable females. And wealthier ladies. You did not love me. And you never had the least intention of marrying me."

"That is not true," he said. "You know it is not true, Grace. Ours is the love of a lifetime. It is still more powerful than any other emotion in our lives. You are afraid to admit the truth."

"No," she said. "At last I am not afraid to admit it, Gareth. It has always been easier to believe that we shared a great love. But I was a fool and a dupe, and I can only feel enormous relief that you were not just a little more honorable than you were. I would have married you and now I would either be living a life of great misery or be so thoroughly convinced that your selfish, amoral attitude to life was right that I would have lost all sense of right and wrong."

"I will prove to you that you still love me," he said, grasping her arm in a painful grip.

"I have done a great deal of wrong in my life," Grace

said, "but I have atoned and will atone. It is hardest to forgive oneself for the dead, but I have done it. I took Papa to see Paul's grave yesterday, and he told me that he admired Paul more after their quarrel than ever before in his life. So maybe there was some small good in their quarrel, after all. And I have forgiven myself—finally—for Jeremy. I was wrong to lie with you, Gareth, but Jeremy was not wrong. And I have looked back and seen that what Perry once told me was right: it is never wrong to give life. I devoted myself to my son utterly while he lived. And I was not neglecting him at the end. It was perfectly acceptable to send him off with a governess. Ethel had done so with Oswald and Priscilla. I was not to blame. He lived as happy a life as I could give him. I have forgiven myself."

"The child was part of me," he said. "You can have me to love instead, Grace. For the rest of our lives."

"No," she said. "I do not quite understand why you pursue me now, Gareth. You never did love me, and I am no longer young. I think it must be the challenge. Had I returned home destitute and broken after Paul's death, I think you would not have afforded me a second glance. But I was married when you met me again, and happily married, to a man whose youth must have challenged your masculinity. I think that must be it. But I do not really care. Whatever your motive, you have failed. I have no feelings for you at all, not even hatred."

"You are not happily married," he said fiercely. "To that boy, Grace? Nonsense! You feel a mother's concern for him. You are afraid he will be hurt by your leaving. He will survive, never fear."

"One wrong which I have been longest in forgiving myself for," she said, "was marrying Perry. Guilt over that has haunted me for almost two years. And I allowed you to fan it. Only recently have I realized that in fact I did no wrong and that there need be no guilt. I love Perry with all of my being, and though I have made him suffer because my guilt drove me back into your power for a long time, I will spend the rest of my life trying to make him happy. Perry married me freely and has not failed in his affection for me and his kindness toward me even during this past difficult year. Perhaps he should be married to a younger woman. But the fact is that he is married to me and has shown no sign of being sorry it is so. You cannot destroy my marriage, Gareth, or even spoil it any longer. You have no more power over me."

"Liar, Grace," he said. "Oh, liar."

"Yes," she said, "you will have to convince yourself that I am being untruthful. I am not sure that you are able to cope with failure, Gareth. But then I have not really known you for sixteen years. Perhaps I do you an injustice. Perhaps you have a stronger character than I think."

"I love you," he said. "That is the strongest fact of my life, Grace."

"Then you must prove it by leaving me to my happiness," she said.

He still held to her arm. His eyes smoldered into hers. "I could win you if I wanted," he said. "I could make you admit that you love me, Grace. And I will do so one day, I do assure you."

She shook her head. "Tea will be ready," she said. "We must go inside. I am not going to ask you to cut short your visit to Lord Amberley, Gareth, or to stay away from me in future. I know I would waste my breath to do so. But I will tell you this: it will not matter to me in the future how often you put yourself in my way. It simply will not matter."

He looked searchingly into her eyes for a few moments

before releasing her arm. "Do you know, Grace?" he said. "If you had been like this at the age of one-and-twenty, I think I might have married you, after all, and be hanged to all the money that Martha brought me."

They walked side by side and in silence back to the house.

14

$\mathcal{P}$EREGRINE WENT OUTSIDE TO SEE THE COURTNEYS on their way. They were taking Priscilla with them, on the request of Susan, who appeared perfectly delighted to have a fashionable young lady to befriend. Mr. Courtney assured Ethel and Martin that Miss Howard would be returned to them safe and sound before bedtime.

Lord Amberley and his mother did not stay much longer. They rose to leave as soon as their guest came back indoors with Grace.

"You have a lovely garden," Lord Sandersford said.

"I can bear to look at it now," Lady Amberley said with a smile for Grace. "But don't expect me to come anywhere near here when all the daffodils are in bloom. Or later, during the summer. I shall be just too envious. Lady Lampman will have at least twice as many flowers as anyone else within five miles, I do assure you, Lord Sandersford."

Lord Amberley shook hands with Peregrine and bowed to Grace. "We may expect you all to dinner, then, the day after tomorrow?" he asked.

"Yes." Grace smiled. "That will be very pleasant, my lord."

She went outside with her husband again to wave the Amberley carriage on its way. But there was no chance to talk. Martin had come out behind them.

"You are fortunate to have such pleasant neighbors," he said. "Do you feel like a game of billiards, Perry?"

IT WAS GOOD to have visitors, Peregrine thought hours later. One was forced to live and function, to carry on talking and eating and doing. Even when one felt like curling up in a corner somewhere and ceasing to live, or like lashing out with one's tongue and one's fists at everyone who had the misfortune to cross one's path.

She had asked him to invite Sandersford to his own home, and he had meekly complied. And she had asked Sandersford to step out into the garden alone with her, and they had been out there for almost half an hour. While her own husband sat inside conversing pleasantly with their other visitors. Was he an utter fool? Was she making a fool of him?

But, no, he would not believe that. *Could* not believe that. She would tell him. When the time came for her to leave, she would come and tell him first. He stood at the window of the bedchamber that had been his for the past two months and leaned his forehead against the windowpane. And he gave himself up to a rare moment of self-pity. And loneliness. He saw her every day, lived with her, talked with her, and was probably more lonely than he would be if she had left him already. Then he would be able to allow the healing to begin. Now he waited in anticipation of a wound that would tear him apart.

He turned at the light tap on the door and tied the belt of his dressing gown around him. "Come in," he called without moving.

He watched Grace in silence as she stepped inside the room and closed the door behind her. She was not beautiful, was she? He could not remember ever thinking her quite so when she had lived at the rectory with Paul. Her face was too narrow, her eyes too large in comparison with the rest of her features. And she was not young. There was no youthful bloom in her face, only the character that seven-and-thirty years of living had carved there. Perhaps no one else in the world would look at her and call her beautiful. But everyone else would look at her with the eyes only. To him she was more beautiful than the loveliest rose in her garden.

She watched him from her large eyes. She wore a white silk robe over her nightgown. Her dark hair was loose down her back.

"Perry," she said, "are you willing to take me back?"

"Take you back?" He looked at her in incomprehension. "I have never sent you away, Grace."

"We have not been a married couple since Christmas," she said. "Will you have me back again? Will you forgive me?"

"Have you back?" He frowned. "I have not put you from me. You told me that you did not think you belonged with me. I would not force myself on you, Grace."

"I have broken his power over me," she said. "I do not love him, Perry. I have not done so since months before Jeremy was born. But I have been afraid of him."

"Afraid?" He took one step toward her. "Had he threatened you? Hurt you? Why did you not tell me, Grace?"

She shook her head. "I was afraid that he was my punishment," she said. "My destiny, I suppose. I had been happy for a year when I met him again, and then I thought that perhaps I did not deserve happiness. I had done a great deal of wrong in my life."

"We all have," he said.

"I know." She clasped her hands before her and looked earnestly at him. "I have come to realize that.

And I cannot do anything to change the past. I can influence only the present and the future. And I do not wish Gareth to have a part in either. I have told him that. And I have told him that he may put himself in my way as much as he wishes in the future without in any way upsetting me. I have no feeling for him at all except indifference. I do not even hate him any longer."

"You want to continue with our marriage?" Peregrine realized suddenly that he was holding his breath.

"Yes." She moved her hands to clasp behind her. "If you wish it, Perry. I fully realize that perhaps you will not. I will return home with Papa and Martin if you would prefer it."

"Grace." He spoke her name softly, reproachfully. "You are my wife. And will remain so while we both live. I would not have divorced you, you know. You would have been free to go, but you would have remained my wife."

She tried to smile. She grimaced instead.

"I have missed you," he said softly.

"Have you? And I you." But she held up her hands sharply in front of her as he moved toward her. "Perry," she said, "I am with child."

He stopped in his tracks and stared at her.

"It is true," she said. "I called on Doctor Hanson this morning when Ethel came into Abbotsford with me. I thought that for some reason I could not conceive, Perry, but it is not so. I am able to give you a child. I think it must have happened at Christmastime."

"Grace." Peregrine felt as if he were looking at her down a long tunnel. "Is it safe?"

"At my age?" she said. "Doctor Hanson says that I seem perfectly healthy and that I should not have any great problems. You are pleased, Perry?"

He moved toward her at last and took her hands in a

firm grip. "I will not forgive myself if you . . . if anything happens to you," he said.

"Having a child is always a risk," she said. "But women older than I am are giving birth every day, Perry. And it is not my first." She flushed. "There is no need to be especially frightened for me. I am not afraid. This is something I want to do. I want to give you a child."

"Oh, Grace." He lifted one of her hands to lay against his cheek and turned his head to kiss the palm. "We men are selfish brutes. For the first few months of our marriage I confess I did worry a little. I thought perhaps you would not want all the burdens of motherhood again. But then I forgot the danger to you and concerned myself only with my own pleasure."

"You are not happy, are you?" she said. "I thought it might please you to have a son. Or a daughter."

"A son," he repeated, "or a daughter." He felt a buzzing in his head as though he were going to faint. "We are going to have a child, Grace. A baby." He laughed rather shakily. "Of course I want a child. Oh, of course I am happy."

He caught her to him then and held her, his eyes tightly closed, terror for his wife's health and very life warring for control of his mind with elation at the knowledge that his child was growing in her.

"Perry?" She lifted her head for his kiss.

And, oh, it had been so long. His arms had been so empty without her, his bed so lonely. He had spent two months trying to condition himself to the probability that she would never occupy either again. But he had missed her. God, he had missed her. He wanted Christmas back again. He wanted it to be like that with her again. When they had started a new life in her.

He put her from him and swallowed. "You are with child," he said.

"It does not matter." She flushed. "Doctor Hanson

talked about it. He said it does not matter until the last months."

He touched his fingers to her face. "In our bedchamber, then," he said. "Not here. I heartily dislike this room, Grace."

She smiled and turned back to the door.

Peregrine settled his wife's head on his arm almost an hour later and made sure that the blankets were close about her. She was warm and naked against him. And relaxed. It had been as good as at Christmastime. She had made love with him, and he had felt her come to him at the end. He rested his cheek against the top of her head. And she was his. She did not love Sandersford, had not loved him for years. She wanted to continue with their marriage. And she was with child by him. They would have a nursery in their home. A son or daughter. Their child, his and Grace's.

If the child survived. And if Grace survived. But he would not think such morbid thoughts. Childbirth was always dangerous, though it was also the most natural process in the world. He would not expect the worst. He would not feel guilt at having so carelessly impregnated a woman of close to forty years. As she had said, this child would not be her first, and women older than she were giving birth every day. Seven-and-thirty was not so very old. She was his wife. He had loved her. The child had sprung from his love.

And he would not allow the thought to poison his happiness that perhaps he had trapped her, after all, despite his wish to leave her free to decide her own future. She must have suspected the truth for the past month. She had found out beyond all doubt only that morning, a few hours before her confrontation with Sandersford. But she did not love him, she had said. She had been afraid of him, afraid that he was her destiny, and not wanting it to be so. She would not have wanted to go with him even if she were not with child.

It was so. She was his. Perhaps she even loved him, though she had never said those words and he had never asked her. He tightened his arm about her and pressed his cheek to her head. She lifted one hand to his chest and murmured something in her sleep.

ETHEL HAD BEEN shocked. "You are quite sure, Grace?" she had asked in the carriage on the way into Abbotsford.

"No," Grace had said. "I am going to Doctor Hanson so that I may be sure. But I cannot think what else it can be. I am far too young for the change of life. And I believe it is true. There is a certain feeling in the mornings— not a biliousness exactly, not a dizziness exactly—that I remember from when I was carrying Jeremy."

"Is it wise?" Ethel had asked. "I mean . . . "

"You mean that I am far too old to be giving birth," Grace said. She flushed. "But, yes, it is wise. Perry deserves children just like any other man. And I want to give him a child. Just this one. There probably will be no more. It has taken two years this time. I love him, you see. And I want his child for me too, for purely selfish reasons."

"I did not mean . . . " Ethel leaned forward and touched Grace's hand. "I did not mean to insult you, Grace, truly I did not. I just never thought of such a thing, which is very foolish because you have been married only a short while and you are still quite young, so it is only natural that you would both wish for a family. I am happy for you."

And during the carriage ride home, after they had paid a call upon the Misses Stanhope and the call on the doctor, Ethel took Grace's hand in hers and squeezed it.

"I am so very happy for you, Grace," she said. "I have

been thinking of it all morning, and I have been growing as excited for you as if it were myself. Everything is all right between you and Perry, then? I have been terribly afraid . . . And Gareth at Amberley Court."

Grace shook her head. "Gareth is my past," she said, "my foolish past. Perry is my present, and he and our child are my future."

"And yet Gareth has been invited for tea?" Ethel said uneasily.

"Yes." Grace smiled at her. "I suppose there must be a definite ending to something that has figured so large in my life. My love for Gareth was a very powerful force, Ethel. And without Gareth there would not have been Jeremy. And Jeremy is still as important to me as Perry and this new child are to me now. This afternoon will be the end with Gareth. Then I can start living my present and looking forward to my future."

"Oh, be careful." Ethel looked troubled. "Do be careful, Grace. That man frightens me."

Grace merely smiled.

"Grace." Ethel sat back in her seat and looked uncomfortable. "I have wanted to say this to you since last year. In my mind I have said it a dozen times, but it is so hard to do so when I am face-to-face with you."

Grace looked inquiringly at her.

"I feel such guilt," Ethel said. "I used to hate you, you know." Her face was blotched with uneven patches of color. "You were so beautiful and so self-assured. And even when you had Jeremy, you bore yourself so proudly that I was furious with you and quite determined to hate him too. I couldn't, of course. He was such a handsome child and so good-natured. But I was jealous. And I hated you for the time you devoted to him and Priscilla and Oswald too, when I was so frequently tired with those headaches I have always suffered from. And your papa always used to watch Jeremy so hungrily when he thought no one was looking."

"It is all best forgotten," Grace said, twisting the rings on her finger.

"Yes," Ethel said, "but it must be spoken of first. Because I like you now, Grace, and I think we can become friends if there is no barrier between us. I was so wretched with guilt after you left. I thought of you with Jeremy gone when I still had my children, and with Gareth gone and Papa and Martin estranged from you. And I never had the courage to write. I wanted to, but I never could. And when you wrote and I knew you were married, and after you had accepted my invitation to visit, I wanted nothing more than to write again and tell you not to come, after all. I was too embarrassed to face you."

"We do terrible things to our own lives and those of the people around us, don't we?" Grace said. "So many years wasted, Ethel. But we must put them behind us. If we are to make amends, we must do so. For I have been at least equally to blame for the coldness there has been between us. How I hated you for having the respectability of marriage when I had been deserted and left with an illegitimate child. And we might have been sisters all these years."

"Well," Ethel said, "we will have to make up for lost time. How is Perry going to react, Grace? I do wish I could see his face when you tell him. He will make a wonderful father, you know. And I know from experience that you will be a wonderful mother."

They smiled at each other, a little embarrassed, and both turned to observe the scenery passing the carriage windows. There would be an awkwardness for perhaps a day or two. But there would be a friendship after that. And they both felt a warmth in the knowledge, though they could not yet quite share their thoughts.

SOMEHOW, NO ONE quite knew how, everyone in the neighborhood knew of the impending event long before it became evident to the eye. No one doubted the integrity of Doctor Hanson. He would certainly not have violated a patient's trust. And Grace and Peregrine told no one apart from Grace's family and Peregrine's mother by letter.

Of course, Mrs. Hanson had been at home to entertain Ethel while Grace had consulted with the doctor. And she had been known on occasion to whisper confidences to her close friends, the Misses Stanhope, on the strict understanding that the secret stop with them. And the Misses Stanhope were known to have the greatest trust in the silence of their friend Mrs. Morton. And Mrs. Morton was known fondly to the rest of her neighbors as a bit of a gossip. It was never malicious gossip, of course, and could therefore be readily forgiven. There was nothing malicious about spreading the glad tidings that dear Lady Lampman was in a delicate condition.

She was a little old to be having her first child, to be sure, Mrs. Courtney confided to Mrs. Cartwright, but she herself had been somewhat past her thirtieth year when she had had Susan, and Susan's birth had been the easiest of the six she had been through, counting the stillborn one—her second. And there was certainly nothing wrong with Susan. She was quite as pretty as any other girl in the neighborhood, Miss Morton and Lady Madeline Raine included, for all they were in a class a little above Susan's.

Dear, dear Sir Perry, Miss Letitia said to her sister with a sigh and a sentimental tear, would be so pleased. Imagine him a father and it seemed but yesterday he was a rogue of a boy up to no end of tricks. How delightful it would be if the child turned out to be a son and they could have another little mischief to look forward to.

And to think that Lady Lampman had been married from their very own home, Miss Stanhope reminded every one of their neighbors, some of them on two separate occasions. Such a dear, dignified lady.

"Well, Viola," Mr. William Carrington said when his wife had hurried into his library with the news after the departure of Mrs. Morton, "so Perry and his good lady have been doing their duty to the human race, have they? And decidedly tardy they have been too. How long have they been married?"

"Two years," she said. "I just hope that it will be safe at her age, William, considering that it is her first. Poor dear lady, I do hope so."

"She cannot be very much younger than you, Viola," her husband said. "And we completed our family fifteen years ago. They put us to shame, do they not? I feel a distinct gleam developing in my eye. Look closely now. Can you see it?"

His wife threw up her hands and shrieked. "William," she said. "What an idea. At our age? It makes me blush just to think of doing—you know. But to have another child!"

"Well, then," he said, "you should know better than to regale me with such disturbing news, Viola. I am afraid I am just going to have to make you blush, my dear. I feel quite like doing—you know."

"William," she said, blushing quite sufficiently to draw a roguish gleam to his eye. "Not here. Someone might walk in at any moment. Oh, do pray remove your hand and behave yourself."

"In our room, then," he said. "You may precede me there, Viola, since you would clearly die of mortification to have me lead you there in full view of the servants."

"William," she said. "Sometimes I think you will never grow old gracefully." She withdrew from the room without further argument.

Her husband closed his book and replaced it on the shelf unhurriedly before going in pursuit.

THE EARL OF Amberley, his mother, and his sister were preparing to leave for London and the Season when Mr. Courtney broke the news to them during a visit with his daughter.

"I am so very glad for Perry," Lady Amberley said to her son when they were alone. "He is a man who needs to be surrounded by children. I have been very much afraid that they were unable to have a family of their own."

"I think the marriage has been quite successful," Lord Amberley said. "They seem fond of each other, would you not say, Mama?"

She nodded. "He seems so devoted to her that I wonder sometimes if perhaps she is a domestic tyrant," she said, and frowned. "But that is unkind. I do hope I am wrong. And I am glad that she is to have a child. Every woman should have that experience."

It seemed that Mrs. Hanson was not privy to all her husband's secrets. Word certainly did not get past the doctor that Lady Lampman's baby was in fact not her first. He had completely hidden his shock behind the cool professional manner that he presented to all his patients under all circumstances. But the fact might certainly make the birth a little easier for her, he had explained, though there was no knowing when the pregnancies were fifteen years apart. There were, however, dangers to both the mother and the child when the mother was well past her thirtieth year.

Lady Lampman was, of course, in good health and had looked after herself well and kept herself fit, he said. Her chances were good. But he would not lie to her and assure her that there was no danger.

Grace lied to Peregrine in that one detail only. She assured him on that first night and during the months to come that there was no danger at all beyond the ordinary. And she refused utterly to give in to fear. It was there, and sometimes she awoke in a cold sweat in the middle of the night. But she was not going to give in to it. She would curl into Peregrine's sleeping form for warmth and comfort and concentrate on her happiness.

And she was very, very happy. Happier than she had been at any time in her life. Happier than she had ever dreamed of being. If only she could live through this pregnancy. If only the child would live and be healthy. If only it could be a son. A son for her to give her husband.

But she would not think of the ifs. She was going to give Perry an heir. She was not going to give him a chance ever to regret marrying a woman so much older than he. She was going to make sure that never again would the laughter be in danger of dying out of his life. And the future was hers. Theirs. He had taken her back. He had wanted her, said that he had missed her, said that she would always have remained his wife even if she had gone off with Gareth.

And she had his child in her, making her tired, making her feel nauseated in the mornings, growing in her, very much there in her even though he did not show for several months or move in her enough for her to feel. She had all the bulk and weight and ungainliness of advanced pregnancy to look forward to and all the agony of childbirth. She was entirely, utterly, deliriously happy.

* * *

Lord Sandersford had left Amberley Court the day after the dinner given there in his honor. He sent his regrets to Mrs. Morton, with the explanation that urgent and unexpected business made his immediate return home imperative.

Everyone at Reardon Park had attended the dinner, though Priscilla had confided to Grace with a giggle that it was a great shame that Lord Eden was not still there. But Lady Madeline would be there, and Walter Carrington, who was very young, to be sure—only one year her senior—but of pleasing appearance and easy manners.

Lord Sandersford, dressed with London elegance, looked extremely handsome and had clearly set out to behave with the most engaging of manners. But Grace was not to be intimidated. She did nothing during the evening to seek him out and nothing to avoid him. When he suggested after dinner that she partner him for a hand of cards with Lady Amberley and Mr. Carrington, she complied with a smile for all three and a remark to Mr. Carrington that he would not find her so easy to defeat as he had at Christmas. And she briefly touched Peregrine's hand with her fingertips when he rested it on her shoulder as he came to stand behind her.

Lord Sandersford gave her an enigmatic smile when she took her leave of him later in the evening. "I will be leaving here in the morning, Grace," he said.

"Will you?" she said. "I will wish you a safe journey, then."

"No regrets?" he asked. "No last-minute panic? If you are to change your mind, it must be done now, Grace. I have decided that I will not be coming back."

"I am happy here, Gareth," she said. "Very happy."

"Damn him," he said, taking her hand and lifting it to

his lips. "I never thought to lose a lady I fancied to a damned milksop. It is a humbling experience, my love."

"Good-bye, Gareth." Grace smiled.

"WHAT A VERY strange man," Lady Amberley said to her son after luncheon the next day, their guest having taken his departure. "Why did he come, do you suppose, Edmund?"

"I don't know, Mama," he said. "But I was watching him last evening. I had the strangest feeling that perhaps he is sweet on Lady Lampman."

"On Lady Lampman?" she said. "Oh, surely not. He is such a very handsome and charming man."

"Lady Lampman is not without beauty," he said. "I think she was probably extraordinarily handsome as a girl. I sometimes wonder about her past. There was never a mention of a family while her brother was alive, was there? Yet last spring she and Perry took themselves off to visit that family. And now a mysterious suitor from the past perhaps?" He grinned.

"Nonsense, Edmund," she said with a laugh. "You cannot possibly make a romantic figure out of Lady Lampman for all that I like and respect her."

"I think she probably jilted Sandersford at the altar twenty years ago," Lord Amberley said, "and ran away with her brother to hide from his wrath. And now he has found her again and is trying to convince her to run from Perry. Grand romance triumphant at last."

"Edmund!" She laughed merrily. "Now I know what you must do during all the hours you like to spend alone. You are writing novels. Your secret is out. My son the novelist."

"She, in the meantime, has grown passionately fond of Perry," Lord Amberley said. "And the lover has been sent on his way disconsolate. He will doubtless expire from a broken heart."

"I have not been better entertained in years," she said, getting to her feet. "I would love to stay to hear more, dear, but I have promised to go with Madeline to visit Viola. It is time to return to ordinary, mundane life. How sad!" She bent to kiss her son's cheek as she left the room.

15

$\mathcal{S}$PRING ALWAYS BROUGHT MIXED BLESSINGS TO THOSE who lived most of their days in the countryside or in a small village remote from any large urban center. There was the splendor of new life all around—new leaves on the trees, new flowers to cover the earth with color and fill the air with fragrance, new calves and colts to frisk about on spindly legs, new lambs with fresh white coats to frolic among the more staid, dirtier numbers of their elders, new warmth from a kindlier sun. And there was greater freedom and comfort of travel. One could bear to sit in a carriage for half an hour without piled blankets and heated bricks. And there was relief from winter chilblains.

But spring also took away to London or other large centers whole families, whose presence was sorely missed. Always the Earl of Amberley and his family. Last year Sir Peregrine and Lady Grace Lampman. This year the Carringtons. And Lady Lampman's family, whom everyone agreed were most genteel and amiable, returned home at the end of March. All were missed. And it would be summer before everyone could be expected to return and the round of social events be well enough attended to make them worth organizing again.

It was already quite evident to the eye that the rumors concerning Lady Lampman's delicate condition were quite correct when unexpected and very welcome news reached the village from Amberley. The earl was returning early from London with the countess and the twins and Sir Cedric Harvey, close friend of the former earl's and a regular summer visitor at the court. And if that were not enough to raise everyone's spirits, there was the added detail that Mrs. Oats, the housekeeper, had been instructed to prepare for the arrival of three or four other visitors a week later. And then, as a final touch of pleasure, the Carringtons too returned home.

In the event, the return of the Carringtons was by no means the least of the events. Mrs. Carrington visited Mrs. Morton the day after her return home and left that poor lady in a perfect dither, since by the time her visitor had left, there were not enough hours left in the afternoon in which to call upon all her acquaintances with the news. She decided upon the Misses Stanhope, since at least she would have the satisfaction of observing the effects of the startling announcement on two separate faces.

The expected guests at Amberley Court were the earl's new fiancée and her mother and brother, no less. And it seemed that the betrothal had been contracted in great haste and under somewhat scandalous circumstances, Miss Purnell—that was the lady's name—having been hopelessly compromised by one of Lord Eden's pranks, which had been intended for Lady Madeline.

"Then why is it that Lord Eden is not marrying the lady?" Miss Stanhope asked with great good sense.

"No one seems to know," Mrs. Morton said, nodding sagely as if to indicate that she knew very well but felt it indelicate to gossip about such matters. "But the earl gave a grand garden party for his betrothed in London. The Carringtons were there."

"I daresay his lordship considered dear Lord Eden just too young to take a bride," Miss Letitia suggested. "But is she pretty, Mrs. Morton?"

"Quite handsome, according to Mrs. Carrington," Mrs. Morton replied. "Very dark in coloring."

"And do you suppose the nuptials will take place here?" Miss Stanhope asked. "It would be entirely fitting. And before the summer is out, do you think?"

The ladies had a comfortable coze about all the possibilities surrounding the news. And Mrs. Morton went home with the satisfaction of knowing that she had created a stir in one household and that she would be sure to call upon Lady Lampman and the rector's wife and Mrs. Courtney and Mrs. Cartwright the next morning before the Misses Stanhope, whose morning it was to decorate the church with flowers, were abroad.

GRACE WAS GLAD of the diversion presented by the new arrivals. Her pregnancy had made her restless. Nine months seemed altogether too long to wait for an event whose outcome was so very uncertain. And once the increased tiredness of the first months was behind her, she found herself full of energy and compelled to be busy every moment of the day. Even her embroidery, always one of her favorite pastimes, seemed far too passive an activity. She wanted to be out digging in her garden, striding along lanes and roadways, cleaning the books in the library from ceiling to floor.

Dr. Hanson had told her that she must rest, that physical activity must be cut to the minimum, that she must remain indoors except when she had a carriage to take her somewhere. And even then she must be sure not to travel on the rougher roads—and that command excluded almost every road in their neighborhood. Unfortunately, he had given this professional advice in Peregrine's hearing, though he had not mentioned the dangers that he had told Grace of during her first consultation with him.

And Perry was being very protective, fetching pillows for her back and a stool for her feet whenever she sat down, forbidding all work in the garden, and allowing sedate walks that were all too slow and all too short only under the severest of protests. It was very irksome.

And quite gloriously delightful. She had been so very alone for years and years. And now she had a man fussing over her, worrying over her health, giving her commands, and being quite insistent that she obey most of them. She saw a new side to Peregrine during those months. He had never been a man to give orders. He commanded respect entirely through the kindliness and integrity of his character. But he had been very angry the morning he had caught her on her hands and knees at the edge of a flower bed, picking out some weeds with her fingers, and had taken her quite ungently by the arm and conveyed her to the privacy of the library.

There he had told her, without the merest glint of humor in his eyes, that if he caught her doing any such thing again until after her confinement, he would forbid her to leave the house without his escort. She had not asked how he would enforce such a rule. She had had no doubt as she had listened to him in silence that somehow he would. It was only the second time she had ever seen him angry.

Memory of that incident could make her smile secretly for weeks afterward. And she would sit, restless and impatient, quietly sewing, her feet resting on a stool, for many hours when Perry was with her, his nose inevitably buried behind a book, glancing down with satisfaction and hidden excitement at the swelling that was her child, feeling him move in her and kick at her, knowing that when she got to her feet again she would feel the extra weight of him. And she would think that it was quite impossible to be any happier in this life. And she would shift in her chair, often drawing Peregrine's eyes and the offer to bring her another cushion, and wonder if the nine months would ever, ever be at an end.

The arrival of Lord Amberley's betrothed and her family necessarily brought more activity and more excitement into their lives. The earl had always been Peregrine's close friend. And she liked him too. He was rather like Peregrine in some ways. He was gentle and kindly. But he was far more reserved than Perry. One felt that one liked the man but that one really did not know him at all. But both felt that he deserved a good wife, one who would know him and understand him and make him happy.

Peregrine would not be able to forbid her to attend all the social activities that must follow upon such an event, Grace thought with satisfaction. She would be able to forget her restlessness for a while.

And she was right. The only matter on which he was quite inflexible was that they not host any grand entertainment themselves. Nothing more grand than an invitation to tea.

"They will take one look at you and understand perfectly, Grace," he said with a grin. "And it is quite obvious that you have not been merely overindulging in food, or you would be fat all over."

And so they went to the Courtneys' dance and card party, where they met Miss Purnell for the first time. Grace liked her. She was darkly beautiful and quiet, though she was not shy. There was a poise and a charm about the girl that was somewhat at variance with her age. She must be about the age Grace had been when she had had Jeremy. And Grace thought that there was a fondness between the girl and her betrothed, though they danced together only once during the evening.

Grace was forbidden to dance, but she had accepted the command with a smile. "Very well, Perry," she had said. "I will be good, as you will see. But on one condition: you must not feel obliged to hover over me all evening. You must enjoy yourself."

"And I cannot enjoy myself by staying with you?" he had asked.

"No," she had said. "You know what I mean, Perry. You must promise."

"I promise," he had said solemnly, holding his right hand in the air.

But it was a mixed blessing, she found, this renewed spate of social activity. It curbed her restlessness, filled her days and her thoughts with activities that helped a long nine months to their end. But it reminded her again of how old she was to be bearing what everyone around her believed to be her first child. Much as she delighted in her growing bulk when she was at home, much as she liked to look at herself privately in a mirror, standing in profile, her hands over the rounded shape of her womb, which held Perry's child, in public she sometimes felt ungainly and unattractive. And embarrassed.

And she found herself again, as she had used to do, watching Perry when they were in company together, watching his gaiety, his smile, and his dancing eyes, listening to his laughter, and feeling that she was too old for him, too serious, too unattractive. There was no jealousy in her, only an unwilling and an unreasonable sadness.

Unreasonable because Perry had shown her nothing but affection since their marriage. And because since she had sent Gareth away and since she had told her husband that she was with child, his every look and action had shown concern for her as well as affection. She was the most fortunate of women. She was the happiest of women, she told herself over and over again.

There was only one thing lacking in her happiness. Only one very small detail. Perry had never said that he loved her, that she was all the world to him. It was a very small detail. His looks said those things. His actions said those things. And even if he did not feel that ultimate commitment to her, he was the kindest and most considerate of husbands. And he had given her a child and filled the one remaining emptiness in her life.

It must be her pregnancy, she decided, that was making her temperamental: delirious with happiness one moment, stirred by doubts and fears the next.

Peregrine, for his part, felt a similar mixture of emotions. On the one hand he was happier than he had been at any time in his life. Finally he felt that he could relax in the knowledge that his marriage would continue. And continue not just because it was too difficult and too troublesome to end, but because they both wished it to do so.

Grace had sent Sandersford on his way and claimed to feel nothing but indifference for him any longer. And her behavior during that dinner at Amberley had seemed to bear out her claim. She had shown no preference for her former lover or even any shrinking from him and no sign of distress after their final leave-taking.

The only apparent sadness she had shown since had been at the churchyard where he had taken her and her father the day before the latter returned home. The two of them had cried in each other's arms at Paul's graveside while he had stood quietly by. And of course she had been quiet and dejected for two days after the departure of her family. But that mood had paradoxically delighted him, showing as it did that her reconciliation with them was complete. Even the stern Martin had hugged Grace as if he had wanted to break every bone in her body before following Ethel and Priscilla inside their carriage.

It was very good, Peregrine found, to be able to relax again, to know that his wife was his. It was good to talk with her again on any topic that interested him, read to her, watch her about the tasks he was willing to allow. It was good to be free to love her again. And it was very good indeed to watch her growing larger with their child, growing more beautiful to his eyes with every passing day.

And he was terrified. Afraid that the child would die, either during the nine months or—worse—at birth. How would he ever comfort Grace if she should lose this second child, coming as it was so long after the first? After the beloved son who had died? He could survive the pain. The only person he really needed was Grace, though he did of course ache with longing to hold this child of theirs. But Grace? Would she be destroyed by the loss of her baby?

And he was terrified that Grace would die. Would he be as fearful if she were ten years younger? he wondered. Was it natural to fear for the life of the woman one had impregnated? He would not want to go on living without Grace. He would have done so, of course, had she decided to go with Sandersford. He would do it doubtless if she died in childbed or from any other cause. But he would not want to. And if it was the bearing of his child that killed her, he did not think he would ever be able to talk himself back to life again. Unknown to Grace, he had had a private talk with Doctor Hanson, and he knew full well that the dangers that faced both her and the child were only enhanced by her age.

He was aware of her restlessness, though he did not understand its causes. He knew that it irked her to sit indoors and allow him to coddle her, to watch the gardeners do every task in her beloved garden while all she could do was walk sedately through it, her fingers itching to get down among the flowers to perform their miracles. He knew that when they walked, she fretted at his slow pace and willed him to take just a few more steps before turning to go back home again. He knew that she longed to do more visiting and more entertaining.

And he gave in, against his better judgment, when Amberley's betrothed arrived and various social entertainments were planned in her honor. He took Grace to the Courtneys' informal dance, the Carringtons' picnic, Amberley's garden party, among other things.

But he ended up feeling uneasy. She could do nothing strenuous, of course. She could not dance or walk any great distance. And he found himself watching her almost constantly, though she had begged him not to feel obliged to keep her company at every moment of every entertainment. He was proud of her, proud that their friends and neighbors would see that she carried his child. And he ached with love for her, observing her converse with Miss Purnell and others with her usual quiet charm.

And he wondered if she was happy. There was no reason in the world why she should not be. She had freely chosen to stay with him—or had she? She had been pregnant before that infernal letter from Sandersford had arrived. And she had told him that bearing a son was what she wanted to do—she very rarely admitted the possibility that it might be a daughter. And she seemed perfectly contented with his company by day and his lovemaking by night. Indeed, it could no longer be said that he made love *to* her almost nightly. To his wonder, he had found since their reconciliation that he made love *with* her.

There was no reason to believe her unhappy. But he found himself, quite against his will, watching her with ladies of almost her age, ladies with grown children, and he wondered if she perhaps found it humiliating to have a younger husband who had forced her into beginning a new family.

And always, returning to haunt him against all reason, was that knowledge that when she had made her decision regarding Sandersford, she had not after all been free to make a free choice. He had begotten his child in her perhaps a week before that letter came.

It was absurd. He had every reason to be happy. He *was* happy. But he watched his wife with unwilling unease. Did she love him? She had never said she did. And it did not matter if she did or not. Love was only a word. She showed him love, or respect and loyalty and affection anyway. They were enough. Quite enough.

But did she love him? Absurdly, totally absurdly, he was afraid to ask. And afraid to say the words himself for fear they would be unwelcome and embarrass or even distress her.

GRACE ATTENDED THE wedding of the Earl of Amberley and Miss Alexandra Purnell in the village church during September, and the wedding breakfast afterward at Amberley Court. There were only two weeks remaining until her expected confinement, and she was feeling quite huge, but she assured Peregrine that she was quite well and that riding in the carriage could not do her the harm that it might have done a few months before.

But she did not have to plead. He was quite as eager as she for her not to miss such a rare and glorious event as the marriage of the Earl of Amberley. And he reassured her when she mentioned her size that they were not in London, where perhaps the presence of a very pregnant lady in public might be frowned upon. In the country, people were far more tolerant and willing to accept life for what it was.

"The only thing you must absolutely promise me," he said with a grin, "is that you will not begin your pains in the middle of the church service or the wedding breakfast. Not only would you divert everyone's attention from the bride, but I might give in to the hysterics or a fit of the vapors."

"I promise," she said, and spread her hand over her swollen abdomen. "Oh, Perry, this son of yours is going to be a boxer, I swear. I sometimes wish he did not have to practice on me."

"Your daughter is going to be a dancer, is she?" he said, lifting her hand away and setting his own in its place.

Grace liked the earl's bride very well and had been pleased to find her a regular visitor during the past couple of months when she was confined more and more to her home. They would be friends, Grace liked to think until she remembered that there must be a fifteen- or sixteen-year gap in their ages. And yet their husbands had been childhood friends and the earl was, in fact, two years older than Perry. It was a little awkward, but it was an awkwardness that she was going to have to accustom herself to. And not before time. She had been married to Perry for two and a half years.

Were all marriages as hard to adjust to as hers was proving to be? she wondered. Even if husband and wife seemed suited in every way, were there still inevitable problems of adapting to each other once the nuptials were over?

She watched the earl and his bride as they stood and kneeled together at the front of the church. They were a beautiful couple and seemed very well-suited in character. Would they live happily ever after from this day on? If rumor was at all true, their association had certainly not had an auspicious beginning. But at this particular moment they were very deeply in love with each other. That seemed very obvious to Grace.

And gracious, she thought later as she watched the earl and his new countess move among their guests after the wedding breakfast, those two had known physical love already. And she flushed in shock at her own improper intuition and glanced self-consciously at Peregrine, half-expecting that he would have read her thoughts.

"Are you feeling quite the thing, Grace?" he asked, leaning forward and covering her hand briefly with his.

"Yes, thank you," she said, "I am quite well. Your son must be sleeping. Will they be happy, Perry? I do hope so. I like them both excessively."

"I could never quite picture Edmund married," he said. "He is a handsome devil, of course. I used to be envious of his good looks. But he is a very private person too. They seem fond of each other, though, don't they? I suppose if they want a happy marriage, they will have it. It all depends on how much they want it, doesn't it?"

They were interrupted at that moment by Lady Madeline and Lord Eden, the latter looking extremely dashing in the green uniform of an officer of a rifle regiment. Madeline was clinging to his arm. A few months before at the age of two-and-twenty, rather late in life, he had finally defied his family's reluctance and fulfilled a lifetime ambition to buy himself a commission in the army. He was off to Spain the following week to join the British troops there.

"It all depends on how much they want it." The words echoed in Grace's mind for the rest of the day and the days to come. Marriage was not quite so simple, though, was it? Both she and Perry doubtless wanted a happy marriage, and had from the start. And they had that now, did they not? But it had not come easily and it had not come merely from the wanting. They had both had to work hard and give a great deal to achieve the measure of harmony and contentment they now knew.

And she could still not say that they were perfectly happy. Happily-ever-after happy. There were always the niggling doubts. Perhaps such happiness was impossible to achieve in real life. Perhaps because a married couple must always be made up of two distinct people, perfect harmony, perfect togetherness was an impossible illusion, the stuff of dreams and romance. Perhaps she and Perry were as happy as a married pair could ever hope to be.

And perhaps people never reached a pinnacle of happiness, even an imperfect one. Perhaps one could never say that now one was as happy as could be, and that was the way things would always remain. She and Perry would always have to work on their marriage, fight to retain the contentment they had won. That was true of any marriage, she supposed. For theirs perhaps it was more so than usual. The age gap would always create awkwardnesses and doubts and feelings of inadequacy in both of them. But the problems would never be insurmountable unless they chose to make them so.

When she was eighty and he seventy, the age difference would be almost unnoticeable, she thought with a smile of amusement.

"Not allowed, Grace," Peregrine said, taking her by the elbow. "I absolutely forbid you to enjoy a joke that I cannot share. Out with it."

"I was thinking that when I am eighty and you seventy, no one will notice the age difference," she said.

He grinned before looking at her a little more seriously. "Do you think they notice now?" he asked. "Do I look so much younger than you, Grace? I do not see it when I look in the mirror and when I look at you. And I doubt that our friends do. We are just Perry and Grace to them. I don't plan to still be crawling about among flower beds when I am seventy, by the way. Your eighty-year-old knees will have to take you alone then, I'm afraid. I will not be able to keep up with you."

She laughed.

"I think we might just be able to get close to Edmund and his bride now," he said.

The new Countess of Amberley held out both hands to Grace as they approached, and smiled warmly. "I am so honored that you came, Grace," she said. "Are you very uncomfortable? You should not be standing so much, should you?"

Grace took her hands. "You look very beautiful, Alexandra," she said. "And of course I cried at the church, just like every other lady present. Except you, that is. And I am quite well, thank you."

The countess looked up, bright-eyed, at her new husband, who was talking with Peregrine. "Perry has promised Edmund that he will send word as soon as your time comes," she said, "so that Edmund may go and pace the floor with him. I will not come. I don't believe that you will feel like making social conversation at that time." She laughed and squeezed Grace's hands. "But I will come and visit afterward as soon as I may and duly admire your child. You must be very excited. And frightened?"

Grace smiled. "Yes, both," she said. "I am glad the weather has been kind to you today. And I am glad that you decided after all that the wedding would be here. The Misses Stanhope were ready to hold a wake, I believe, if you had removed to London or Yorkshire."

"Papa favored St. George's in London," Lady Amberley said. "And I am not at all in the habit of defying Papa. But Edmund and I decided this together. This is where we belong, where we love to be even though I came here for the first time only a few months ago. It made sense that we also marry here. Oh, and today I am so glad. I have all my friends around me and I have never had friends before. You must know what I mean, Grace. Do you know?"

"Yes," Grace said. "This is a special part of the world.

We are fortunate, you and I, that our husbands live here."

"Our husbands," the girl said with a breathless laugh. "How strange that sounds, and how very lovely." She looked wonderingly at the earl again, and he smiled and moved to her side.

"Lady Lampman," he said, "I must tell you how grateful I am that you have come to our wedding. It would not be quite right to be without my oldest friend on such a day, and one who got me into so many scrapes as a boy, I might add. Yet I am sure he would not have come and left you at home alone. If you will pardon me for noticing your, ah, condition, I must say that I think it heroic of you to have traveled all these miles."

"You don't know Grace," Peregrine said with a grin. "I have had to have new locks put on all the garden sheds so that she does not sally forth into the garden at the dead of night to create new flower beds. And I have to tie her arm to my side when we are out walking so that she does not break into a gallop. You are looking at a man who is almost worn out from the exertions of chasing after a, ah, pregnant wife, Edmund."

"Perry," Grace said, and all four of them laughed.

"We are pleased to have you here anyway, Lady Lampman," the earl said, extending a hand to her, "aren't we, Alex? And if you wish to take Perry to sit down before he collapses, ma'am, please feel free to do so."

Peregrine took Grace's arm and smiled down at her as bride and groom turned away to greet another group of well-wishers. Her eyes were bright, her cheeks flushed with color, sure signs of fatigue. "I am going to order the carriage to be brought around," he said. "And you may not argue with me, Grace. You are tired and I am in the mood to play tyrant. Besides, that daughter of mine is going to wake soon and want her dancing lesson again. Or has she started already?"

"I think he is stirring," she said. "And I am in the mood to play obedient wife, Perry. I am tired, I must confess. But do you mind leaving early? I am afraid I am spoiling your enjoyment."

"I am expecting a child too within the next two weeks, you know," he said. "Has no one told you? I feel excitement too, and emotional turmoil, and anxiety, and fatigue. And, no, you need not look at me with suspicion. I am not teasing you. I have never been more serious."

16

IT WAS AWKWARD TO HOLD GRACE IN THE CARRIAGE on the way home, Peregrine found. He could not just cuddle her against him as he could remember doing during the same journey late on Christmas Day. But by sitting sideways himself, he did manage to cradle her head on his shoulder and take some of her weight against himself. She was very tired. She held both hands over the bulk of her pregnancy. Perhaps he should not have allowed her to attend the wedding, after all.

"I am glad we came, Perry," she said, as if she had read his thoughts. "Was it not all very splendid?"

"Very," he said. "Are you comfortable, Grace?"

"Mmm," she said. "I think they are going to be happy."

"Do you?" he said, and wriggled her head into the warm hollow between his neck and his shoulder. He held her while she relaxed more against him and while her breathing became deeper and more even.

He was thinking of his own wedding, in the same church more than two years before. He had been a married man for more than two years! It seemed impossible. And yet that wedding and the weeks that had preceded it could be something from another lifetime altogether. As he held his sleeping, very pregnant wife against him, it was hard to believe that she was the same woman as the quiet, dignified sister of his friend the rector, whom he had married to save from the humiliation of having to seek employment.

He had cared for her then. He had thought he cared. And he had thought it such a simple thing, to marry her and to comfort her for the rest of his life. Even after she had told him her history, he had thought that it would be easy. And yet marriage had proved the most difficult undertaking of his life. It was impossible, he believed now, to be married and not become totally involved in the relationship. At least, it was impossible for him.

Grace was now more dear to him than anything or anyone else in his whole life. She was a person now, a complex, dearly beloved person, not just the figure of respect and, yes, pity that she had been at the start. But even love brought its own complications, its own doubts and fears and dissatisfactions.

Somehow, through two and a half difficult years, they had reached a plateau of harmony and contentment. Even love, perhaps. Certainly love on his part. But he could not be certain that this state of affairs would remain for the rest of their lives. Or even that he wished it to do so. Marriage was a living, dynamic relationship that must keep growing if it was to survive. They would have to want to be happy if they were to be so. That was what he had said to Grace earlier about Edmund and his bride. But the same applied to himself and Grace and to any married couple.

They must want to be happy. He did. He wanted it badly enough to be prepared to work at his marriage for the rest of his days. Did Grace? He could only have faith that she did. There were no certainties when one was married. Because, however close one became to another person, one never became that person. That person was always a different being. It was a risky and a trouble-some business, marriage.

Would he do anything as rash as marrying Grace if he

had it all to do again, knowing what he now knew? Would he choose to live if he could go back beyond his mother's womb and have the choice? Foolish question! Life was worth living despite all its problems and dark times. And his marriage was more precious to him than anything else in his life had been, despite the uncertainties and the heartache. And the continued uncertainty and his constant terror for Grace's life and that of their child.

The carriage jolted to a stop before their front door.

"Oh," Grace said before he could kiss her awake, "I have been sleeping. And, Perry, I have been leaning on you and you have nothing against your back. You must be in agony."

"Worn to the bone. A mere shadow of my former self," he said cheerfully, "as I was telling Edmund a little while ago. I will be very glad when this daughter of yours finally puts in an appearance, Grace. Perhaps I will be able to drag myself around again afterward."

"Silly," she said. "Your son will take his own sweet time in arriving, I am sure. Why should he hurry when he has a father who will hold him and his mother so comfortably?"

"Do you want me to throw you both from the carriage?" he asked.

"No thank you," she said. "The servants might think we have quarreled. Get down from here, Perry, if you please, and offer me your hand like the gentleman you pretend to be."

Peregrine laughed and vaulted out onto the cobbled driveway. He had noticed only recently that he could joke with his wife and she could hold her own with ease.

ONE REMEMBERED THAT it was painful, Grace thought, lying on her side relaxing, waiting for the next onslaught of pain. One remembered that it was worse than any other pain one could imagine. And one knew that as time went on the pains became so frequent and so intense that one hung onto one's sanity by the merest thread.

And yet one did not remember. Not until it happened again. As soon as it did start again, one thought, *Oh, oh, here* it *comes.* Yes, this is what it was like. And one knew exactly why it was that nature, or God, arranged matters that women did not really remember.

She did not know what time it was—late afternoon, perhaps? There was still daylight outside. It had been well before daylight when she had finally woken Perry, sure at last that this was no false alarm. She did not know where he was now. He had sat with her, holding her hand and looking as white as a ghost, until Doctor Hanson had arrived. Then both the doctor and the housekeeper had urged him to leave, and he had done so after Grace had smiled at him and told him that she would feel better without having him to worry about. He had not even grinned in response.

Would it never be over? The pains had been crashing through her world at two-minute intervals for several hours, yet Doctor Hanson still said that she was not fully dilated, that the child's head was not moving down. He was standing quietly at the window, looking out. The housekeeper sat in the chair beside her bed, bathing her face with a cool cloth every few minutes, chiding her gently every time she bit her lip, advising her to scream instead.

She could not scream. If she did not hold on to the little control she had left, she would become demented. Soon now she would see her son. She must think of that. Soon she would hold him in her arms. Soon Perry would be able to come back. Was anyone downstairs with him? Had Lord Amberley come, as promised? Was Perry calm?

Would it never be over?

She concentrated every power of her mind on not giving in to panic as she felt the familiar tightening of muscles and descended into another wave of pain.

"THIS IS RIDICULOUS! Damned ridiculous!" Peregrine slammed down his billiard cue onto the table. "There are some concerns that just cannot be drowned out by other activities, Edmund. It's very kind of you to have spent a whole day desperately trying to entertain me. I appreciate it. But it can't be done, you know. I am going out of my mind."

The Earl of Amberley sighed and laid his cue down beside the other. "I don't know what else to do, Perry," he said. "I have no experience at this sort of thing, you know. What do you want to do?"

"I want to go up there to her," Peregrine said. "Dammit, Edmund, this is as much my child as it is Grace's. It's not fair that she should be going through all this alone while I am downstairs playing billiards, for the love of God."

"And enjoying yourself enormously," his friend said ironically.

"I'm going up," Peregrine said. "There must be something I can do."

"It's not allowed," Lord Amberley said. "It's not done."

"Dammit," Perry said. "Would you stay away if it were the countess, Edmund? Grace has been going through this since five o'clock this morning. And that was only when she told me. It must have started long before that. Would you stay away?"

"If it were Alex?" his friend said quietly. "No. No, Perry, I would not be able to stay away. Do you love Lady Lampman, then? I have often wondered since that nasty occasion when you dealt me a bloody nose. Not that it is any of my business to know, of course."

"You have doubtless earned my confidence after spending a whole day with me here," Peregrine said with the ghost of a smile, "when you have a bride of no more than a week waiting at home. Yes, of course I love her, Edmund. More than my own soul, I sometimes think. What if she dies? God, what if she dies?"

Lord Amberley gripped his shoulder. "She won't die," he said. "She's not going to die, Perry. What can we do to take your mind off things? We never lacked for things to do when we were boys, did we?"

"I don't think climbing forbidden cliffs would help at the moment," Peregrine said. "I'm going up there, Edmund."

But even as he said the words, the butler arrived to announce that dinner was served. And Peregrine went to the dining room and even succeeded somehow in swallowing a few mouthfuls of food out of deference to his guest, who ate as little as he did if he had only been alert enough to notice.

SHE HAD TO push. The need, the purely physical need, was quite irresistible. And a voice was telling her to push. Quite unnecessarily. Her mind was no longer functioning. Only her body. She was pain, racking pain, the only instinct left in her the instinct of survival, the need to rid herself of the pain, rid herself of her burden. She could no longer feel the cool cloth against her face and neck or her husband's hands gripping her own wet ones.

And then finally, mercifully, the pain burst from her and she was free. Free to sink into oblivion, into a pain-free nothingness. She let go of the final instinct to live.

"Grace!" A voice would not let her go. "Grace!" Not that it was a loud voice or a demanding voice. It was quiet and gentle. But it would not let her go. It was a voice that meant something to her, a voice she could not take with her if she went.

"Grace," it said, "we have a daughter. It is a girl. Can you hear me? No, you must not die. I won't let you die. Please!"

There was a baby crying somewhere. It was a sound she could not escape. It would not let her go. And there was a face in her line of vision. She must have her eyes open, then. She did not know who it was. But it was a familiar face. It was a beloved face. She wanted to see it more clearly.

"Perry?" she heard a high, thin voice say a long time later. She closed her eyes with the effort.

"We have a daughter," he said. Her hands were coming back to her. Someone was clasping them. "We have a daughter, Grace. Can you not hear her? She is squawking enough to waken the servants." He grinned.

It was Perry, she thought. He was Perry. "A daughter?" she said, not sure quite where her mouth was or how she formed the words. "She is alive?"

"Very much so," he said. "I don't think she likes being washed, Grace."

Her body was coming back to her. There was another involuntary contraction of muscles and a wave of pain and the soothing voice of the doctor telling her, or telling someone, that it was all over now, that very soon now she would be able to rest.

"Look at her, Grace. Oh, look at her."

But she could not look away from him for the moment. Why was he crying? Was the baby dead? Was she dead?

And then a little bundle of linen was being laid in the arms that did not yet belong to her, and she saw her child, quiet now, red and wrinkled, its face and head distorted from the recent passage of birth. Beautiful.

Oh, beautiful beyond description. She could not go. She could not go and leave this child behind. Or that other beloved person. Where was he?

"Perry?"

He was there still beside her, white-faced, smiling, crying.

"A daughter," she said. "She is alive. She is alive, Perry."

"Yes," he said.

It was not him laughing, she realized, but herself. Or was she crying? She could not see him.

"Perry," she said, "hold her. I want to see you hold her."

She could see him enough to know that the smile had disappeared. "I don't think I dare," he said. He reached out and touched one tiny curled hand with his index finger.

"Hold your daughter," she said. "Papa."

The little bundle was gone from her arms. Someone was murmuring gentle endearments. Someone with a familiar, much-loved voice. The baby had stopped crying. She could let herself go. Grace slid down the seductive slope toward an unknown destination that seemed far more desirable at the moment than any of those things or people who had made her laugh and cry and come back to herself a moment ago.

"I AM SORRY, Alex." The Earl of Amberley lay beneath his wife, her body cradled comfortably on his own, her head nestled on his shoulder, the single blanket, his greatcoat, and her cloak covering her. "I have failed you already and we have been married only a week."

"You have not failed me," she said, turning her head and kissing his chin. "You have just been used all your life to retreating into yourself whenever there is a problem. You cannot easily change the habit of a lifetime just because you have a wife. You told me before we were married that you would have difficulty not excluding me from your life at times. And I told you, once I knew that you loved me, that I would not let you do so. So I followed you here. I was not even sure you would be here. I thought perhaps you were still at Reardon Park."

They were lying in a small stone hermit's hut a mile or more from Amberley Court, long a hideaway of the earl's. It was more than an hour past dawn.

"It was terrible," he said, one hand playing with his wife's long dark hair, the other over his eyes. "All day yesterday and then all night after Perry had gone to her. I could not drag myself away."

"Is she really likely to die?" the countess asked hesitantly.

"She was bleeding a lot," he said. "I am sure Perry's housekeeper would not have said so much if she had not been so tired and so worried. And the child was a long time coming. She is exhausted. And of course she is not a young woman."

"But nothing is sure?" she asked. "You did not talk to the doctor or Perry?"

"No," he said. "Neither of them would leave her. Alex. Alex, it is a cruel life for women." He hugged her to him.

"I think it is rather sure," she said after a pause. "Will you mind, Edmund? Will you be very embarrassed?"

He groaned against her hair. "Embarrassed?" he said. "Oh, Alex, my love."

"But a child after fewer than eight months, Edmund," she said.

"So," he said, "the world will know that we were lovers before our nuptials. Shameful indeed! I just wish you had not raised the subject at this particular time. I'm afraid for you, Alex."

Later that same morning the rector's wife met the Misses Stanhope at the church door with the news that the rector had been called to Reardon Hall.

"The child?" Miss Letitia asked.

"A girl, and doing well," the rector's wife said.

"Lady Lampman." Miss Stanhope's voice broke a silence that none of the three seemed wishful to fill. Her words were a statement rather than a question.

"She had a hard time, poor lady," the rector's wife said.

Miss Letitia fumbled for her handkerchief only when a tear dripped from her chin onto the frilled ribbons of her cap. "Poor dear Sir Perry," she said. "He is fond of her."

"She was married from our house," Miss Stanhope said.

The Misses Stanhope paid a call on their friend Mrs. Morton and she on Mrs. Courtney and Mrs. Cartwright and Mrs. Carrington. But they were mournful visits. There was no joy in the afternoon's gossip. Though, as with most gossip, it greatly exaggerated the negative.

Mr. Carrington found his wife in tears.

"Why, Viola?" he said. "What is this? I have not pinched you in a week, is that it? It is just that having passed my fiftieth birthday, I thought perhaps it was time to grow a more dignified image, dear. There was no implied insult to your charms. Dry your eyes now and come and be kissed."

"Don't tease, William," she said without any of her usual outrage. "It is Lady Lampman."

"Oh," he said. "Lost the child?"

"No-o," she wailed. "The child is well. But she is dying, William, or passed on already. The doctor has been at Reardon Park since yesterday morning, and the rector was called there this morning. Oh, the poor dear lady. She has been good for Perry, has she not? Oh, don't just stand there, William. Hold me. Please hold me. Poor dear Lady Lampman."

IT WAS A cold, gray, blustery November day with almost nothing to recommend it to the senses. Two warmly clad figures made their way slowly along the lane leading from Reardon Park, the lady leaning quite heavily on the man.

"It feels so good to be outside again, Perry," Grace said, lifting her face to the cold wind.

"We must turn back soon," he said. "You must not overdo it and exhaust yourself or catch a chill, you know."

"It is so wonderful just to be alive," she said. "Is it not, Perry? Do you not feel it?"

"It is very wonderful to have you alive," he said. "I almost lost you, Grace." He covered her gloved hand with his own.

"No, you didn't," she said. "You kept me alive, Perry. It would have been so much easier at one point to die than to fight back to life. But you would not let me go."

He squeezed her hand.

"Perry," she asked hesitantly, "are you at all disappointed that I did not give you an heir?"

"What?" he said, drawing them to a stop and staring down at her, incredulous. "How could you possibly ask such a thing, Grace? And be without Rose? I would not exchange Rose for a score of sons."

"If I were fifteen years younger," she said, "or ten even, I could give you more children, Perry, and it would not matter that the first was a girl. But I am afraid that perhaps I can give you only this one. I was almost two years married before conceiving her."

"How strange you are sometimes," he said. "You worry a great deal, don't you, Grace? About being ten years older than I. How many times have I told you that it does not matter to me? I would not have you one day younger even if I could. Because I would thereby alter you, and I would not do that for worlds. I love you as you are. Just as you are. And the gift of a daughter that you have given me has filled me so very full of happiness that I am afraid I would have no room in my heart for half a dozen sons. Or even one. I don't want you to have more children, Grace. I cannot take the risk again of losing you."

"Are you happy?" she asked, looking up at him wistfully. "Truly happy, Perry? And do you love me?"

He touched her wind-reddened cheek with his gloved fingers. "I have never said it, have I?" he said. "Why are they the hardest words in the language to say? Yes, I love you, Grace. Oh, of course I do. I love you. Do you believe me, or will you be doubting again tomorrow?"

Her eyes were bright with tears. "I have done so much wrong in my life," she said. "I do not deserve such happiness, Perry. I don't deserve you."

"You have no regrets?" he asked. "You were expecting Rose when . . . " He smiled lamely. "You were expecting Rose."

"Oh, Perry," she said, "I had a great and fortunate escape when I was young. I might have married him. I would be married to him now. And as unhappy with him as I am happy with you. I was dazzled by him, overpowered by his charm as a girl. And frightened by him after you and I were married. I was afraid for a while that I deserved no better and that you deserved a great deal better than me. I thought you deserved a young and beautiful and vibrant girl, Perry."

"Absurd," he said.

"I do love you," she said. "Oh, I do love you, Perry. And together we have made Rose. Life is so very miraculous."

"She knows me already," he said.

"Of course. All women know you," she said. "You have only to smile and they all capitulate. Why should our daughter be any different? I have to confess that she never fails to stop crying when you pick her up."

"She knows that I have a weakness for the female gender," he said. He bent and kissed her lips before turning with her to walk back to the house again. "Especially her mother."

She laid her head against his shoulder. "Everyone has been so kind," she said, "visiting me and sending their good wishes. Did you know that Alexandra is increasing, Perry?"

"No," he said. "So I am to return the favor and pace floors with Edmund, am I?" He shivered. "Ugh! November! What an ugly day. Turn your poet's eye onto this scene, Grace, and make beauty out of it. Quite a challenge even for you, I think."

"Oh, not at all," she said. "Just look around you, Perry, and imagine all the seeds of spring buried and awaiting their chance. They cannot be held back forever, you know. And look at the sky. Those dark and lowering clouds. Why is it daylight nevertheless? Because there is blue sky and sunshine just beyond those clouds, and even the clouds cannot keep out all the warmth or all the light of the sun. And the wind? It is chilly. And it is life. It is not the chill of the grave but the invigorating breath of life. Look. It has made your cheeks and your nose rosy. And mine too, doubtless. It is a beautiful day, Perry. A new day. A new tomorrow."

"You are right," he said with a laugh, hunching his shoulders against the cold. "Whatever would I do without you, Grace? I would still be looking about me in the greatest gloom, counting the months to spring. And since it is such a lovely day, my girl, and you have just proved it to me, you can stand here with me outside our door to be kissed instead of waiting for the greater warmth of your sitting room. Hold your face up to me."

"You expect me to grumble now and beg to be taken indoors for my kiss, don't you?" she said, smiling up into his eyes and putting her arms up around his neck. "I want a good long kiss before you take me inside, sir. And I don't care if the servants see us, either."

The chill of the November wind did not abate as they stood locked in a close embrace on their doorstep. Nor did the clouds part to allow one glimpse of the blue sky and sun Grace had spoken of. But they did not notice and would not have cared if they had. For in each other's arms they found all the warmth and brightness the sunniest day could have brought.

In each other they found the eternal promise of spring.

*Get ready to fall in love
with a brand-new series from Mary Balogh. . . .*

WELCOME TO THE SURVIVORS' CLUB.

*The members are six gentlemen and one lady,
all of whom carry wounds
from the Napoleonic Wars—some visible
and some not. These tight-knit friends have helped
one another survive through thick and thin.
Now, they all need the perfect companions
to teach them how to love again.
Learn how it begins in:*

The Proposal

Featuring the beloved Lady Gwendoline Muir from
One Night for Love and *A Summer to Remember.*

Available from Delacorte in hardcover.

Turn the page for a sneak peek inside.

1

GWENDOLINE GRAYSON, LADY MUIR, HUNCHED HER shoulders and drew her cloak more snugly about her. It was a brisk, blustery March day, made chillier by the fact that she was standing down at the fishing harbor below the village where she was staying. It was low tide, and a number of fishing boats lay half keeled over on the wet sand, waiting for the water to return and float them upright again.

She should go back to the house. She had been out for longer than an hour, and part of her longed for the warmth of a fire and the comfort of a steaming cup of tea. Unfortunately, though, Vera Parkinson's home was not hers, only the house where she was staying for a month. And she and Vera had just quarreled—or at least, Vera had quarreled with *her* and upset her. She was not ready to go back yet. She would rather endure the elements.

She could not walk to her left. A jutting headland barred her way. To the right, though, a pebbled beach beneath high cliffs stretched into the distance. It would be several hours yet before the tide came up high enough to cover it.

Gwen usually avoided walking down by the water, even though she lived close to the sea herself at the dower house of Newbury Abbey in Dorsetshire. She found beaches too vast, cliffs too threatening, the sea too elemental. She preferred a smaller, more ordered world, over which she could exert some semblance of control—a carefully cultivated flower garden, for example.

But today she needed to be away from Vera for a while longer, and from the village and country lanes where she might run into Vera's neighbors and feel obliged to engage in cheerful conversation. She needed to be alone, and the pebbled beach was deserted for as far into the distance as she could see before it curved inland. She stepped down onto it.

She realized after a very short distance, however, why no one else was walking here. For though most of the pebbles were ancient and had been worn smooth and rounded by thousands of tides, a significant number of them were of more recent date, and they were larger, rougher, more jagged. Walking across them was not easy and would not have been even if she had had two sound legs. As it was, her right leg had never healed properly from a break eight years ago, when she had been thrown from her horse. She walked with a habitual limp even on level ground.

She did not turn back, though. She trudged stubbornly onward, careful where she set her feet. She was not in any great hurry to get anywhere, after all.

This had really been the most horrid day of a horrid fortnight. She had come for a month-long visit, entirely from impulse, when Vera had written to inform her of the sad passing a couple of months earlier of her husband, who had been ailing for several years. Vera had added the complaint that no one in either Mr. Parkinson's family or her own was paying any attention whatsoever to her suffering despite the fact that she was almost prostrate with grief and exhaustion after nursing him for so long. She was missing him dreadfully. Would Gwen care to come?

They had been friends of a sort for a brief few months during the whirlwind of their come-out Season in London, and had exchanged infrequent letters after Vera's marriage to Mr. Parkinson, a younger brother of Sir Roger Parkinson, and Gwen's to Viscount Muir. Vera had written a long letter of sympathy after Vernon's death, and had invited Gwen to come and stay with her and Mr. Parkinson for as long as she wished since Vera was neglected by almost everyone, including Mr. Parkinson himself, and would welcome her company. Gwen had declined the invitation then, but she had responded to Vera's plea on this occasion despite a few misgivings. She knew what grief and exhaustion and loneliness after the death of a spouse felt like.

It was a decision she had regretted almost from the first day. Vera, as her letters had suggested, was a moaner and a whiner, and while Gwen tried to make allowances for the fact that she had tended a sick husband for a few years and had just lost him, she soon came to the conclusion that the years since their come-out had soured Vera and made her permanently disagreeable. Most of her neighbors avoided her whenever possible. Her only friends were a group of ladies who much resembled her in character. Sitting and listening to their conversation felt very like being sucked into a black hole and deprived of enough air to breathe, Gwen had been finding. They knew how to see only what was wrong in their lives and in the world and never what was right.

And that was precisely what *she* was doing now when thinking of them, Gwen realized with a mental shake of the head. Negativity could be frighteningly contagious.

Even before this morning she had been wishing that she had not committed herself to such a long visit. Two weeks would have been quite sufficient—she would actually be going home by now. But she had agreed to a month, and a month it would have to be. This morning, however, her stoicism had been put to the test.

She had received a letter from her mother, who lived at the dower house with her, and in it her mother had recounted a few amusing anecdotes involving Sylvie and Leo, Neville and Lily's elder children—Neville, Earl of Kilbourne, was Gwen's brother, and lived at Newbury Abbey itself. Gwen read that part of the letter aloud to Vera at the breakfast table in the hope of coaxing a smile or a chuckle from her. Instead, she had found herself at the receiving end of a petulant tirade, the basic thrust of which was that it was very easy for Gwen to laugh at and make light of her suffering when Gwen's husband had died years ago and left her very comfortably well off, and when she had had a brother and mother both willing and eager to receive her back into the family fold, and when her sensibilities did not run very deep anyway. It was easy to be callous and cruel when she had married for money and status instead of love. Everyone had *known* that truth about her during the spring of their come-out, just as everyone had known that Vera had married beneath her because she and Mr. Parkinson had loved each other to distraction and nothing else had mattered.

Gwen had stared mutely back at her friend when she finally fell silent apart from some wrenching sobs into her handkerchief. She dared not open her mouth. She might have given the tirade right back and thereby have reduced herself to the level of Vera's own spitefulness. She would not be drawn into an unseemly scrap. But she almost vibrated with anger. And she was deeply hurt.

"I am going out for a walk, Vera," she had said at last, getting to her feet and pushing back her chair with the backs of her knees. "When I return, you may inform me whether you wish me to remain here for another two weeks, as planned, or whether you would prefer that I return to Newbury without further delay."

She would have to go by post or the public stagecoach. It would take the best part of a week for Neville's carriage to come for her if she wrote to inform him that she needed it earlier than planned.

Vera had wept harder and begged her not to be cruel, but Gwen had come out anyway.

She would be perfectly happy, she thought now, if she *never* returned to Vera's house. What a dreadful mistake it had been to come, and for a whole month, on the strength of a very brief and long-ago acquaintance.

Eventually she rounded the headland she had seen from the harbor and discovered that the beach, wider here, stretched onward, seemingly to infinity, and that in the near distance the stones gave way to sand, which would be far easier to walk along. However, she must not go *too* far. Although the tide was still out, she could see that it was definitely on the way in, and in some very flat places it could rush in far faster than one anticipated. She had lived close to the sea long enough to know that. Besides, she could not stay away from Vera's forever, though she wished she could. She must return soon.

Close by there was a gap in the cliffs, and it looked possible to get up onto the headland high above, if one was willing to climb a steep slope of pebbles and then a slightly more gradual slope of scrubby grass. If she could just get up there, she would be able to walk back to the village along the top instead of having to pick her way back across these very tricky stones.

Her weak leg was aching a bit, she realized. She had been foolish to come so far.

She stood still for a moment and looked out to the still-distant line of the incoming tide. And she was hit suddenly and quite unexpectedly, not by a wave of water, but by a tidal wave of loneliness, one that washed over her and deprived her of both breath and the will to resist.

Loneliness?

She never thought of herself as lonely. She had lived through a tumultuous marriage but, once the rawness of her grief over Vernon's death had receded, she had settled to a life of peace and contentment with her family. She had never felt any urge to remarry, though she was not a cynic about marriage. Her brother was happily married. So was Lauren, her cousin by marriage who felt really more like a sister, since they had grown up together at Newbury Abbey. Gwen, however, was perfectly contented to remain a widow and to define herself as a daughter, a sister, a sister-in-law, a cousin, an aunt. She had numerous other relatives too, and friends. She was comfortable at the dower house, which was just a short walk from the abbey, where she was always welcome. She paid frequent visits to Lauren and Kit in Hampshire, and occasional ones to other relatives. She usually spent a month or two of the spring in London to enjoy part of the Season.

She had always considered that she lived a blessed life.

So where had this sudden loneliness come from? And such a tidal wave of it that her knees felt weak and it seemed as though she had been robbed of breath. Why could she feel the rawness of tears in her throat?

Loneliness?

She was not lonely, only depressed at being stuck here with Vera. And hurt at what Vera had said about her and her lack of sensibilities. She was feeling sorry for herself, that was all. She *never* felt sorry for herself. Well, almost never. And when she did, then she quickly did something about it. Life was too short to be moped away. There was always much over which to rejoice.

But *loneliness*. How long had it been lying in wait for her, just waiting to pounce? Was her life really as empty as it seemed at this moment of almost frightening insight? As empty as this vast, bleak beach?

Ah, she *hated* beaches.

Gwen gave her head another mental shake and looked, first back the way she had come, and then up the beach to the steep path between the cliffs. Which should she take? She hesitated for a few moments and then decided upon the climb. It did not look quite steep enough to be dangerous, and once up it, she would surely be able to find an easy route back to the village.

The stones on the slope were no easier underfoot than those on the beach had been; in fact, they were more treacherous, for they shifted and slid beneath her feet as she climbed higher. By the time she was halfway up, she wished she had stayed on the beach, but it would be as difficult now to go back down as it was to continue upward. And she could see the grassy part of the slope not too far distant. She climbed doggedly onward.

And then disaster struck.

Her right foot pressed downward upon a sturdy looking stone, but it was loosely packed against those below it and her foot slid sharply downward until she landed rather painfully on her knee, while her hands spread to steady herself against the slope. For the fraction of a moment she felt only relief that she had saved herself from tumbling to the beach below. And then she felt the sharp, stabbing pain in her ankle.

Gingerly she raised herself to her left foot and tried to set the right foot down beside it. But she was engulfed in pain as soon as she tried to put some weight upon it—and even when she did not, for that matter. She exhaled a loud "Ohh!" of distress and turned carefully about so that she could sit on the stones, facing downward toward the beach. The slope looked far steeper from up here. Oh, she had been very foolish to try the climb.

She raised her knees, planted her left foot as firmly as she could, and grasped her right ankle in both hands. She tried rotating the foot slowly, her forehead coming to rest on her raised knee as she did so. It was a momentary sprain, she told herself, and would be fine in a moment. There was no need to panic.

But even without setting the foot down again, she knew she was deceiving herself. It was a bad sprain. Perhaps worse. She could not possibly walk.

And so panic came despite her effort to remain calm. However was she going to get back to the village? And no one knew where she was. The beach below her and the headland above were both deserted.

She drew a few steadying breaths. There was no point whatsoever in going to pieces. She would manage. Of course she would. She had no choice, did she?

It was at that moment that a voice spoke—a male voice from close by. It was not even raised.

"In my considered opinion," the voice said, "that ankle is either badly sprained or actually broken. Either way, it would be very unwise to try putting any weight on it."

Gwen's head jerked up, and she looked about to locate the source of the voice. To her right, a man rose into sight partway up the steep cliff face beside the slope. He climbed down onto the pebbles and strode across them toward her as if there were no danger whatsoever of slipping.

He was a great giant of a man with broad shoulders and chest and powerful thighs. His five-caped greatcoat gave the impression of even greater bulk. He looked quite menacingly large, in fact. He wore no hat. His brown hair was cropped close to his head. His features were strong and harsh, his eyes dark and fierce, his mouth a straight, severe line, his jaw hard set. And his expression did nothing to soften his looks. He was frowning—or scowling, perhaps.

His gloveless hands were huge.

Terror engulfed Gwen and made her almost forget her pain for a moment.

He must be the Duke of Stanbrook. She must have

strayed onto his land, even though Vera had warned her to give both him and his estate a wide berth. According to Vera, he was a cruel monster, who had pushed his wife to her death over a high cliff on his estate a number of years ago and then claimed that she had jumped. What kind of woman would *jump* to her death in such a horrifying way, Vera had asked rhetorically. Especially when she was a *duchess* and had everything in the world she could possibly need.

The kind of woman, Gwen had thought at the time, though she had not said so aloud, *who had just lost her only child to a bullet in Portugal,* for that was precisely what had happened a short while before the duchess's demise. But Vera, along with the neighborhood ladies with whom she consorted, chose to believe the more titillating murder theory despite the fact that none of them, when pressed, could offer up any evidence whatsoever to corroborate it.

But though Gwen had been skeptical about the story when she heard it, she was not so sure now. He *looked* like a man who could be both ruthless and cruel. Even murderous.

And she had trespassed on his land. His very *deserted* land.

She was also helpless to run away.